Rescue Mission

ALPHA TACTICAL OPS BOOK THREE

KENDALL TALBOT

Copyright

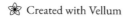

About the Author

Romantic Book of the Year author, Kendall Talbot, writes action-packed romantic suspense loaded with sizzling heat and intriguing mysteries set in exotic locations. She hates cheating, loves a good happily ever after, and thrives on exciting adventures with kick-ass heroines and heroes with rippling abs and broken hearts.

Kendall has sought thrills in all 44 countries she's visited. She's rappelled down freezing waterfalls, catapulted out of a white-water raft, jumped off a mountain with a man who spoke little English, and got way too close to a sixteen-foot shark.

She lives in Brisbane, Australia with her very own hero and a fluffy little dog who specializes in hijacking her writing time. When she isn't writing or reading, she's enjoying wine and cheese with her crazy friends and planning her next international escape.

She loves to hear from her readers!

Find her books and chat with her via any of the contacts below:

www.kendalltalbot.com
Email: kendall@universe.com.au

Or you can find her on any of the following channels:

Amazon
Bookbub
Goodreads

Books by Kendall Talbot

Alpha Tactical Ops Series

Escape Mission

Hostile Mission

Rescue Mission

Stealth Mission

Shadow Mission

Rogue Mission

Treasure Hunter Series:

Treasured Secrets

Treasured Lies

Treasured Dreams

Treasured Whispers

Treasured Hopes

Treasured Tears

Waves of Fate Series

First Fate

Feral Fate

Final Fate

Maximum Exposure Series:

Extreme Limit

Deadly Twist (Finalist: Wilbur Smith Adventure Writing Prize 2021)

Zero Escape

<u>Stand-Alone books:</u>

Lost in Kakadu (Winner: Romantic Book of the year 2014)

Jagged Edge

Double Take

If you sign up to my newsletter you can help with fun things like naming characters and giving characters quirky traits and interesting jobs. You'll also receive my book, Treasured Kisses which is exclusive to my newsletter followers only, for free.

Here's my newsletter signup link if you're interested:

http://www.kendalltalbot.com.au/newsletter.html

Chapter One

MAYA

I would have rather done a midnight raid in hostile territory than continue down Thunder River rapids with the bunch of fat bankers in my rubber raft. But that wasn't an option. These guys had paid me a lot of money, or rather their employer had, to take them white water rafting for the day.

My job was to show them how to work as a team. However, these four selfish bastards had zero comprehension of what it meant to work together.

Clutching the tree branch I was using to hold the raft against the shore, I stood at the rear of the boat with my shoulders back. Their eyes bounced to my breasts as if they were magnets and the four of them were just fat lumps of metal.

"Listen up, guys. The rapids we just did are nothing compared to what's downriver. If you don't work together and follow my instructions, then you're going to end up in the water, and you'll have to swim all the way to the ocean. Do you want that?"

They all lowered their gaze, and not one of them answered.

"Well, do you?"

I glared at each of them, but they couldn't even look me in the eye.

Not even Peter, and I'd pegged him as the man with the most potential in the group.

But that was why they had come to me. I was the team bonding champion. *Apparently.*

"Grab your paddles. When I let go of this branch, the river will take us. At first, it's going to be nice and cruisy. So, kick back and enjoy this amazing scenery. Then there will be a few more rocks for us to bounce over, and then the river gets narrower. What happens when a team gets narrower, Adam?"

"It gets more powerful."

"That's right. When you have a lot of people, the pressure is defused. When a team gets narrower, each person holds more power. Think of the river like that. She's a powerful bitch, and she's about to show you just how much."

I slapped my paddle into the water, giving them a little splash. By their ghastly expressions, you'd think I'd poured acid over them.

"When I tell you to paddle backward, you paddle backward. When I tell you to dig in and paddle, what are you going to do? Peter?"

"I'll paddle." Peter said it like he was ordering cupcakes.

"Not I'll paddle." I mimicked his response. "You will fucking dig that paddle in and scoop the water like it's a nasty little employee you've been trying to get rid of. Got it?"

He nodded.

"So, Peter, what are you going to do when I say paddle?"

"I'm gonna drive my paddle into the water and scoop that fucking bitch out."

I grinned at him.

He grinned at me.

I turned to Joe. "What are you going to do, Joe?"

"I'm gonna fucking dig that bitch."

"Good," I said. "And you, Hurun?"

"I'm gonna fucking paddle!"

They were finally getting it. The test would come when we hit Devil's Dive. The five-foot waterfall that was coming up was always a surprise package, and if they didn't listen, one of them, or maybe even all of us, would get thrown into the water.

"Are we ready to do this?" I asked with all the motivational joy I could muster.

"Yes," Peter and Hurun said together. The other two just nodded.

"I said, are we ready to do this? Say hell yeah!" I yelled like my sergeant, Blade, had done in the army.

"Hell yeah!" they yelled in unison.

It was the first thing they'd done as a team. *Progress.*

Thunder River could be deceiving with the way the sun glistened off the surface, and lush trees leaned over from the riverbank, creating beautiful reflections in the mirrored water. It gave the impression that we were out for a nice, easy paddle.

But that would be wrong.

I have taken white water rafting groups down Thunder River nearly every week since I started my adventure business Executive Rush two years ago. I'd had everything from backpackers to the executive bastards that were in my boat today. And I hadn't lost a person yet.

But my time in the army had taught me many things. Working together was king. Trusting your mates was queen. Putting your body on the line was the whole goddamned chessboard. And that life was no fucking game.

Life was short, and you had to live in every moment.

My sister died when she was nineteen, and every day since then, I wished I'd had more moments with her. Not a day went by when I didn't think of her or the asshole who murdered her.

I let go of the branch, and at first the raft hugged the left-hand side of the river. Using the paddle, I pushed us away from any jagged branches sticking out from the shore.

"Okay, who's on my left?" I asked.

Adam and Peter raised their paddles.

"Good. That means you two are on my right." I pointed at Hurun and Joe.

"Paddle backward."

The four of them dug in like a bunch of six-year-olds.

"Together!" I yelled. "One. Two. One. Two. That's it. Now you got it. Now you're working as a team. Look at you go. On my left, paddle."

Adam and Peter dug in.

"Stop. Okay, we are in the middle of the river, drifting at about five miles an hour. Around the next bend, our speed will quadruple and about six hundred yards beyond that, it's going to get narrow and nasty."

They all chuckled. Their expressions confirmed they underestimated just how nasty this was going to get.

"Okay, men. You've paid me a lot of money to get bitch slapped."

They burst into laughter, but Joe was as jittery as a patient at a vasectomy clinic.

"Let's see if we can get you all working together. Everyone dig those paddles in and pull. And again. Dig and pull. One. Two. Three. Yes! You're doing it. You're working as a team. I'm impressed."

Adam grinned at me like I was his favorite schoolteacher.

I grinned back. I'd learned a long time ago that flirting with men could be useful. Some of those bastards had been too busy checking me out to notice the weapon I'd used to kill them.

My military service in the army had been some of the most honest days of my life.

Protecting my country.

Eliminating bad guys.

Working with a team of men and women who I knew would take a bullet for me.

I'd thought I would be an army sniper and medic until my pension kicked in. I never envisaged being booted out of the only career I ever wanted.

Forcing my brain to be in the moment, I used my paddle to point ahead. "See those tiny rapids? They're created by submerged rocks. We're going to cruise over them nice and easy. You can stop paddling and enjoy the ride. It'll be fun."

Again, Adam flashed his grin at me. He was the only one amongst them who didn't have a double chin. He was handsome, with maybe a couple of mixed cultures in his breeding. A lineage that gave him olive skin and dark eyes. Spanish, perhaps?

Maybe he was thinking he could hook up with me later.

That was never going to happen. It wasn't that I was against having sex. I just wasn't into having sex with a guy like him who had more

4

money than he could spend in a lifetime and thought that wealth defined who he was.

"Pull your paddles in with the handles down, just like I showed you, and grip onto that rope."

They were a little clumsy but they got it. The front of the raft dipped, then bulged upward. The rocks thumped underneath their feet and disappeared out the back.

We cruised around the bend in the river, where the rapids began their real show. White water tumbled over dozens of obstacles, squirting out at random intervals to reveal rocks that were impossible to see otherwise.

"On my right. One paddle."

The men did as they were told.

"Paddles up."

"Oh, Jesus!" Joe blurted.

If he was worried about what he was seeing now, he was the man I needed to watch once we hit the real rapids.

"On my left. Two strokes, please. One. Two. Paddle up."

Their four paddles stuck out the raft like a pair of cheering arms as we hit the rapids in the middle of the river.

The rubber raft bumped and glided over the submerged rocks like it was designed to do.

A pair of giant boulders loomed ahead of us. I always wondered if those two had once been one massive rock that the water had carved through over the millennia. The five-foot drop on the other side of them was like a massive liquid tongue, sucking us in and then spitting us out like we were poison in its throat.

"Okay, men, listen up. Now we're getting serious. Up ahead is Devil's Dive. It's a tiny waterfall—"

"How tiny?" Joe's eyes bulged.

"It's just a four-foot drop on the other side," I lied. The size of the drop didn't matter.

If they did their jobs right, that is.

"And the boat may fold in half as we crash down on the other side. But don't worry, it will right itself within a second."

Joe made a noise like he was about to vomit.

5

"On my right. Paddle. Get into it. Quick, Joe! Get your paddle in there. Joe, dig deeper. Work together. Do it. Together, you two. This is it. Paddles in! Wedge your feet and hang on!"

I sat and wedged my foot into the base of the raft, securing me in position.

The men looked like they were going to piss their pants, and it took all my might not to burst out laughing. We reached Devil's Dive doing about thirty miles an hour. The front of the raft aimed between the rocks. Joe squealed as we punched through the gap. We were airborne for the count of two. Then, the front of the raft speared into the water, curling a wave over the top of all of us and drenching us to the core.

The boat righted.

I cheered. "Woo hoo! Look at you guys go. You did Devil's Dive. Give yourselves a high-five."

The four of them high-fived each other, and Adam flashed his perfect white teeth at me. But the rapids were far from over. They were just beginning.

"Get your paddles ready, boys. Now we're getting into the fun stuff."

Joe glared at me like I was a tomahawk missile about to hit. The whites of his eyes bulged, and his lips were drawn to a thin line. He had behaved like a macho dickhead when I'd done the debrief that morning.

He wasn't so macho looking now.

"We are coming up to Witch's Cauldron. It's a whirlpool. If we don't do this right, we'll be sucked into that bitch and will be spun around like we're in a washing machine with no off switch."

Joe moaned and the blood drained from his face.

"Our goal is to stay away from that big rock. The one that's shaped like a V-dub on steroids." I pointed. "See it?"

Joe's eyes got even bigger.

"On my right, dig in. Paddle. One. Two. Stop."

"Remember, if you fall in, hang onto your life jacket and put your feet downriver. Keep your head above the water and don't struggle. We will come and get you."

Joe's mouth fell open like one of those creepy clowns at the penny arcade.

"You'll be okay, Joe," I said.

He was the biggest man amongst them, both in height and weight, but fear was written all over his face.

"Let's do this. On my right, dig in again. Go. One. Two. Come on, put some muscles into it. Go. One. Two. Dig in. Joe, dig in! Do it. Christ! Dig in."

Joe froze with his hands strangling his paddle.

"Son of a bitch. We're too close. And we're too late. Everybody, hang on!"

The torrent grabbed us like a giant fist. We were no match for its power and were sucked into the rock's vortex. Joe's paddle snagged on the rock, scooped under his belly, and flipped him out of the boat like he weighed barely ten pounds.

"Hang on," I yelled at everybody else.

The raft curled around the giant rock and bounced off the edge. I pushed with all my might with the paddle, forcing us away. The ass end of the raft was sucked into the current, pulling us from the rock and spinning us around backward.

"On my right, paddle, paddle, paddle."

Adam and Peter put everything they had into each stroke.

We spun around and I stood, scanning the river ahead. "Anybody see Joe?"

Unless his feet got wedged under a rock, he would pop up to the surface.

The lifejacket will save him—I hope.

Chapter Two

NEON

An explosion ripped through the silence. Peeling paint dislodged from the ceiling above me, falling onto my head and shoulders like confetti. Beyond the resort pool where the water was infested with algae, four Balinese-style huts sat with crumbling thatch roofs that would be full of bugs and critters I didn't even want to think of.

"Action," Linda Goodwin, the movie director, yelled from the scaffolding above me.

Flames licked into the air behind the huts, and a second explosion rattled the buckled floorboards beneath my feet. I clenched my fists, hoping Matthew Jones, the stuntman who was hired because he had a similar physique to me, completed the zip-lining stunt this time.

Clutching onto what was designed to look like a leather belt, he flew across the front of the huts, with his feet barely ten inches off the swampy water. This was his third attempt at this scene.

He'd better complete the stunt this time, or Linda was going to lose her shit.

Matthew splashed into the pool that was covered in green slime so thick it was a wonder he didn't bounce on the surface.

He disappeared beneath the disgusting moss, and I shuddered.

"Cut!" Linda threw her clipboard over the scaffold railing, and it clattered to the decrepit timber veranda below her. "Jesus Christ! How hard is it to get someone to do their goddammed job?"

She glared down at me, and I raised my eyebrows, silently portraying an, *I told you so*. We'd already had the discussion about me doing this stunt. She knew I could do it. My big break into Hollywood was as a stuntman. But once I started taking lead roles in blockbuster movies, producers were too scared to let me perform my own stunts.

Becoming famous had become my double-edged sword.

On one hand, it was incredible to be at the top of my game. On the other, it was bullshit not to be performing the action scenes I loved.

As Matthew dragged himself from the water, Linda climbed down her ladder, marched to her clipboard, and snapped it up from the buckling floorboards.

I waved to get her attention. "I'm taking a time out."

"Yeah, you and me both."

She and I went separate ways.

I walked along the veranda heading for the temporary demountable that would be my home for at least the next three months. I had a bucket load of money in the bank, and yet every year I spent months living in a cabin that was smaller than my bathroom in my Beverly Hills mansion.

As I walked past dilapidated buildings that had been rotting away for twenty years, I wished I was alone. But I wasn't. My bodyguards were my constant shadow.

I'd had two attempted kidnappings in the last five years, and with the amount of money riding on this film, the producers and moneymen behind *The Last Resort* would pay any ransom.

My parents would too.

They'd already done it once.

But that was the problem. Now the whole world knew I was a commodity that could be traded for a lot of cash.

It seemed everyone was out to get a piece of me.

Before I'd arrived on this abandoned island, the structural engineers had spent weeks safety testing the dilapidated buildings and adding reinforcing to those that looked ready to crumble. The engineers assured us that the bridge spanning from the main island to a much smaller island was so safe it would probably remain standing for another fifty years.

Didn't look like it to me. Half the railings were missing, and several planks beneath my feet wobbled as I strode across it. Below the bridge was a narrow strip of water, and nine derelict row boats were lined up along the shore like a weird art installation.

"Hey, Neon? Can I ask you something?" Shane's squeaky voice behind me didn't match his bulky physique. Steroid abuse had done that. He was a big bastard, broad, tall and bulky, but he sounded like a nine-year-old kid.

Pausing on the bridge, I turned to him. "Yeah, what?" I didn't mean to sound so angry.

Shane jerked back, raising his hands in a peace gesture. "Don't worry."

"What is it?"

"I said don't worry."

"You've got my attention now, so tell me what's up." I softened my tone.

Shane had been my bodyguard for eight years. Each year he got fatter and slower, and I was getting tired of his constant whining. But he'd saved my life once. He was a man I could trust. In my line of business, that was hard to come by.

Shane cleared his throat. "I, um, I was just wondering if you thought there was gonna be a delay?"

"Yeah, I'd say so. Now that the stuntman can't get himself across the pool." I shook my head. If it was me doing that stunt, I'd do absolutely everything not to fall into that disgusting water.

Shane groaned.

"Have you got somewhere you'd rather be?"

"No." Shane stepped back. "Not just yet, but I was hoping to go home for Christmas."

I waved my hand. "Well, you can kiss that idea goodbye."

Shane clamped his jaw.

I didn't know what his problem was. I paid him a ton of money to be my bodyguard. And Derek, my second bodyguard, who was always two paces behind Shane.

Shane drove his fat fingers over his buzz cut.

"What's your problem, Shane?"

"I told you. I was hoping to get home for Christmas." He raised his voice. He never did that.

"And I told you, you can kiss that idea goodbye."

"It's just . . . my baby sister is pregnant, and for the first time I'm gonna have a niece or a nephew at Christmas. It was gonna be like, special and everything."

I shrugged. "Jesus, Shane, then why did you sign on for this contract?"

He cocked his head. "You didn't give me a choice."

"That's a lie." I knew for a fact that Shane had agreed.

Marcus, my manager always ensured my bodyguards could stay for the term of the movie contract before he signed them on. Last thing we needed was trying to find security when we were in the middle of nowhere.

Derek inched closer. His shifty eyes cruised toward the buildings behind me. I could never decide if that big bastard was looking out for me or had it in for me. He'd been my bodyguard for four months, but he was yet to prove his worth.

That was the problem with hiring new bodyguards. The only way to truly know if I was getting what I paid for was when I was in trouble. By then, it was too late.

"Neon, I've been working for you for eight years, and I've never asked for much," Shane said.

"Except with every new film location, you ask for more money."

Shane squinted at me, and I could almost hear the cogs churning in his brain.

"You're free to go whenever you want." I turned to walk away.

Blazing sunshine shimmered off the inlet water below the bridge like the blinking eyes of a thousand people engrossed in our discussion.

"Really? After eight years, you'd just ditch me like that." Shane's whiny voice elevated in pitch.

I spun back to him. "And this is what you don't seem to understand. You are my employee, Shane. We are not friends."

"You don't have any friends, you obnoxious bastard!"

Glaring at him, I stepped a pace closer.

He stepped back.

Shane was a foot taller than me and at least a foot wider, but his bulky middle made him slow.

"Shane, without me, you're just a tired old bodyguard looking for work."

"Don't you dare." Rage simmered in Shane's eyes.

I cocked my head, making him finish his sentence.

He aimed a fat finger at my chest. "If you fire me, I'll sue you for wrongful dismissal."

I took a step closer, clenching my fists. "That's the Shane I know . . . always looking for a way to get more money out of me. I have given you every single pay increase you've asked for. You are paid well above your worth. You'd never win a case against me."

Over Shane's shoulder, Derek had an expression like a stonefish. If he was listening to our discussion, he showed no signs.

I took another step toward Shane. He didn't back away this time.

He puffed out his chest and clenched his jaw.

I glared up at him. "You are free to leave—"

Shane swung his fist.

I ducked his arm and punched his flabby belly.

He grunted, swung again, and his punch connected with my shoulder, driving me backward two paces.

"You fucking idiot." Clenching my fists, I lowered my shoulder and charged him. I grabbed his waist, putting everything I had into taking him down.

We burst through the bridge railing.

Shane screamed in my ear as we plunged into the water below.

We landed on one of the abandoned row boats along the shore.

The timber siding shattered as Shane's back slammed into it and a large wooden splinter pierced through his shoulder. He screamed in pure agony.

I scrambled off him, and with my heart in my throat, I clawed out the water as fast as I could, and leaped onto the sandy shore.

The boat was half in, half out of the water and healthy weeds grew in the upper section of the boat.

Shane wrapped his hands around the spike and whimpered. Tears flooded his eyes. Blood oozed through his fingers.

On the bridge above, Derek looked down at us with an expression of sheer indifference.

"Shane, are you okay?" I asked.

"No, I'm not okay. You fucking moron."

His legs dangled in three feet of water and a school of fish swimming around his ankles glinted in the morning sun.

I glared at Derek. "Don't just stand there, you idiot. Get help."

Derek's boots thundered on the bridge as he sprinted back toward the crumbling resort.

The narrow stretch of water between the two islands was shallow enough that fish and rocks were visible. It was vastly different from the swampy resort pool, and the smaller lagoon-style pool that was even more of a cesspool.

Still, I couldn't force my legs to step into the water again.

Shane glanced at me over his bloody shoulder. His face twisted with pain. "I'm going to sue your fucking ass for millions."

Ignoring his comment, I wanted to go to his side to reassure him that everything would be okay.

But I couldn't. My mouth went dry. A chill snaked up my spine.

Fear of water had been shackling me since I was nine years old.

And with it came shame. The twin emotions were like clashing tornados, twisting together, growing in intensity. Destroying my sanity all over again.

Chapter Three

MAYA

A bright yellow streak appeared on the river surface about fifty yards ahead.

"There," Adam yelled, pointing forward.

I bounded across the raft and sat where Joe had been seated. "Everyone, paddle. Dig in. Let's go. Work together. Dig and pull. Dig and pull. Dig. Pull."

Joe was face up, with one arm across his life vest and his feet aimed downstream, exactly as I had instructed. His face was contorted with distress.

"Get right up next to him," I said.

The right-hand side of the raft wedged next to Joe, and I grabbed his lifejacket. If he wasn't as big as a fridge, I would have hauled his ass onto the boat.

"Adam, help me," I said.

Gripping the shoulders of Joe's life jacket, Adam and I dragged him into the raft.

With a howl, Joe flopped into the bottom, between the legs of the remaining men.

He had a graze on his left cheek.

"I've broken my fucking arm." He reached for his left elbow.

"Everyone, grab your paddle. On my left, paddle. We're aiming for that side of the river. Let's go. One. Two."

As we eased into shore, I grabbed a branch and used it to swing us into a small eddy next to the embankment. "Adam, hold us here."

I squatted over Joe's right leg to examine his arm. A lump had swelled above his elbow. The funny thing about elbows was that they damn well hurt when you banged them hard enough. I cupped his hand and straightened out his arm.

Clenching his teeth, he sucked in air, wincing in pain.

I felt around the joint and ligaments.

"What the hell are you doing?" he hissed.

"I'm assessing your injury."

"You're fucking hurting me."

"You don't have any broken bones. A nasty bruise. That's all."

"What the fuck would you know?"

"I'm a qualified army medic. And I've seen just about every brutal injury known to man." I looked into his bloodshot eyes, and keeping my tone calm, I said, "And I'm telling you, this is nothing."

I pushed back from him and sat on the inflated side. "Okay, men, we have a wounded soldier here. This is where our teamwork will be tested. Adam, switch over to the right-hand side. Joe, you're over there in Adam's spot."

His eyes popped. His jaw dropped. "I can't paddle. Look at me. I'm injured. I want my fucking money back."

I shrugged.

"You can have your money back. I don't have a problem with that. But that doesn't change the fact that I need you . . ." I swept my hand at the other three men. "We need you. Or none of us are getting downstream."

It wasn't true. We could handle the raft and upcoming rapids with the four of us, but I wasn't going to let him off that easily.

Joe shot his gaze from one man to the next.

"White water rafting isn't about the boat or the water," I said. "It's about you proving to yourself that you can do more than what your body thinks you can do. It's about the freedom to do anything you want. It's about your power. Raw mental power."

16

I nodded at the men, gearing up for the speech I'd told many times over. "This is about proving that you are more than just a man who sits in a boardroom, making decisions with the flick of a pen. This is about proving that you get things done, no matter what obstacles are thrown at you."

I swept my hand to nature's beauty. "Look around. These rocks have been here for millions of years. Look at the men in the raft with you. You guys only have eighty years on this earth. A hundred if you're lucky. It's what you do with those years that count. What is your legacy? What do you want to teach your children?"

I lowered my gaze to Joe who was still hugging his arm and whimpering. "Do you have kids, Joe?"

He nodded. "Four."

I winked at him. "Hey, you big stud. Do you want your kids knowing that you let down your team because of a bruised arm?"

Shaking his head, he lowered his gaze.

"Hell no. You want them to know that you had one hell of a bruise, but that didn't stop you. You did your job. You beat the river. And you worked with your team to save us."

I could almost hear the rage burning in his brain.

I'd seen the look before. Women didn't talk to men like him that way. These guys were used to casting women aside like snotty tissues.

It amazed me how often men underestimated what I could do. My body always caught their attention, but it was my mind that got results. And my weapons.

I clutched Joe's paddle. "What's it going to be, Joe? Are you finishing this trip? Or is this the end for the whole team?"

"Come on, Joe." Adam grinned at his teammate, then me.

Joe groaned and sat up. "Okay. I can do this."

"Of course, you can. Now sit where Adam was. Peter, that means you have to work harder to help Joe out. You good with that?"

"Absolutely." He pumped his fist.

"The rest of the river will test your teamwork, but I know you can do it. We can do it. Do I hear a hell yeah?"

"Hell yeah!" they all said together.

"Hell yeah," I cheered louder than the lot of them.

I pushed off from the bank, and the river sucked us back into its control.

We tackled the next set of rapids without incident, and the remainder of our trip was uneventful, except Joe made sure we knew how much pain he was in.

But they worked together. It was like a switch had been flicked. They watched out for Joe. They encouraged each other, and they followed my instructions like perfect soldiers.

By the time we pulled into shore, Joe's elbow was the color of a storm cloud, and he had a lump the size of an egg over the bone. Despite that, Joe wore that injury with pride.

Like I'd seen hundreds of soldiers do on the battlefield, Joe had pushed through the pain to get a job done.

If only all the injuries I'd treated were as superficial as Joe's was.

"Pull the boat onto the sand, guys. I'll be back in a sec."

The small beach lined the parking area for the McKinnon Pass hiking trail, and usually by the time I returned to my car after rafting downstream, there would be at least one other car there. Not today though.

I sprinted to my Rav4 and removed my fully stocked first aid kit and an ice pack I kept in an icebox for times like this. Bruising and white water rafting often went hand in hand.

When I returned to the men, they had the boat on dry ground and had removed their lifejackets. As they sat on the side of the raft, their expressions were a mixture of utter exhaustion and exhilaration.

That was what missions were like in the army. Exhilarating. Exhausting. But many times, they were also fucking scary.

After a second triage of Joe's injury, I assured him it was just bruising and put his arm in a sling. "Hold this icepack on that bruise. It will reduce the swelling."

As the jokes started flying, I chose Peter to come with me to grab my car and trailer on the other side of Pioneer Mountain, where we'd started our trip. Peter was like a junkie on a high, chatting non-stop about the rafting like I hadn't been there.

On our return trip, he drove my Rav4, and I took my Jeep with the trailer, leading the way back to the remaining men.

Working together, we secured the raft onto the trailer. It was always a good way to end the day.

With nobody dying.

I wish I could say that about my last mission in the army.

By the time I drove the men back to our starting point at Firefly Café, Joe was acting like he was a national hero. When we said our good-byes, he shook my hand and made no mention of the refund he'd asked for.

Once they were gone, I strolled into the café and up to the barstool at the front counter that had become my favorite seat.

"Hey, Maya, how was the trip?" Zena wiped her hands on her checkered apron as she approached the counter from the other side.

I shrugged. "Just a few bumps and bruises, and one pathetic bastard. Nothing I couldn't handle."

Zena giggled. "There's nothing you can't handle."

I laughed with her. "Not yet anyway."

"You coming over to Blade's soon? I have an Osso Bucco that I've been cooking all day."

"Hell yes to that. What time?"

"I'll be there about four thirty."

"Perfect. See you then."

Back outside, I jumped in my Rav4 and wound the windows down to cruise through town. Risky Shores had been my home for only two years, and yet it was more of a home to me than the place I'd grown up in.

My little bungalow was a small Queenslander, painted so white it hurt my eyes to look at without my sunnies on. I parked in the carport, climbed the six stairs, and crossed the veranda that ran around the entire house.

Locking the front door behind me, I tossed my car keys into a giant clam bowl on a side table. As I walked the length of the hallway that stretched from the front door to the back, I stripped out of my damp clothes.

Showering after white water rafting was one of my favorite pastimes. It was long, hot, and therapeutic enough to wash away the tiny threads of anger I had over Joe's reaction in the boat today.

It amazed me how often a man as big as him could crumble when they sustained such a minor injury. He'd been ready to give up.

It was bullshit.

Now he was going to gloat about how brave he was forever.

He wasn't brave. I'd seen bravery on the battlefield many times over.

Brave was having your leg shot to shit and still completing your mission.

Brave was not giving up when a soldier was dying in your arms.

Brave was owning up to decisions that ruined lives.

Trying, but failing, to force down my fury, I stepped from the shower and toweled off. I tugged on shorts and a t-shirt, and at the kitchen table I turned on my laptop.

As I ate a bowl of cold leftover chicken and asparagus risotto from Zena's café, I googled John Grayson. There were hundreds of John Grayson's on social media. Even more on Google. But there was only one I was searching for: my father.

He was the reason I'd joined the army.

I wanted to learn how to shoot to kill. And when I found that bastard, he was going to know exactly how good I was with a sniper rifle.

After forty minutes of searching, which turned up nothing, I shut down my computer, grabbed a bottle of wine from the refrigerator, and returned to my vehicle.

The 1996 Rav4 was a fun car and was great for advertising too. A lot of my business came from the phone number plastered over the car doors and the trailer that was hooked up to my other car . . . an old Jeep.

At Blade's place, I pulled the Rav into the curb, grabbed my wine, and strode to the new security panel he'd had installed next to his giant roller door.

I pressed the call button. "Heya, anyone home?"

"Come on in," Zena responded, and the small door, built into the giant roller door, popped open. That too was another addition. Since our last mission at Alpha Tactical Ops had gone pear-shaped, Blade had upped security around his place tenfold.

I shut the door behind me and as I inhaled delicious aromas of beef stew, Charlie raced across the concrete floor toward me. I scooped her up, and she licked my cheek.

"Hey, girl." Ruffling her ears, I aimed for the kitchen.

It was a typical Saturday afternoon at Blade's warehouse apartment. Zena and Blade were on the cooking side of the massive kitchen counter. Levi and Billie were on the other side, watching Zena whip up something delicious. Viper and Cobra were thrashing things out at the pool table.

"Hey, guys." I waved to Viper and Cobra.

"Maya, 'bout time you got here," Cobra called out.

Viper grunted and nodded at me. That was about the extent of his 'happy to see you' welcome.

I handed my wine to Zena. She put it in the fridge and topped a glass with wine from an open bottle.

After shuffling into my designated seat beside Billie, I nestled Charlie on my lap and ran my hand over her smooth hair.

"Hey, Billie, Levi, how are you guys doing?" I asked.

They had become inseparable since they'd hooked up three months ago, and Levi had never looked happier. Wish I could say the same about Viper. Nothing seemed to make him smile.

As I took a sip of my wine, Cobra cheered. "Ha! Told you, you were in trouble."

He slapped Viper on the back. Viper cracked his knuckles and swigged the last of his beer.

"That's not good. Cobra's beaten Viper three times already. Viper's going to be pissed." Levi's grin could light up a city.

Despite his grumpy ass demeanor, Viper was a good man. We'd all been trying to snap that bullshit out of him for years. So far, no such luck.

Shaking my head, I turned back to Billie. "Any luck with the job hunting?"

"No." Billie lowered her gaze to her full wine glass. Since that disaster in Antarctica, the poor woman had been booted out of the climate change profession she loved, but her qualifications meant she was too skilled for half the jobs she'd applied for. But because she'd worked at the university for twelve years without a holiday, she'd received a large severance pay. From what she'd told me, she'd saved a bucket load of money in the last decade, so at least she wasn't stressed about her finances.

I patted her arm. "You'll find something. I know you will."

"I hope so. I'm getting sick of searching." Her eyes lit up. "But at least my spare time gives me a chance to scour for information on that submarine. I may have found something."

"Hang on, wait for me." Cobra bounded over on his bionic leg. "What did you find?"

Billie removed a sheet of paper from her pocket and spread it out on the counter. At the top, she'd hand-drawn the image she'd found underneath the ice in Antarctica. "As you know, this is what I found on the surface of the submarine."

She pointed at the drawing. Inside a circle, she'd drawn three rivets on one side, and an E with two dots above it.

Everyone gathered around the kitchen counter nodded.

"I want to pre-empt this by saying that my research has been limited to only google, so this list is by no means exhaustive."

We all nodded. Viper cracked his knuckles, and the diamond in the chunky ring on his little finger sparkled in the lights.

"As we know, the E with the dots is from the Russian language and based on my research, Russia had two hundred and eighteen submarines active during World War Two."

"Ha, I thought it would be more," Cobra said.

"I thought less," Viper added.

"Of those submarines, eighty-seven had the letter E in the name. Of those eighty-seven, all but six are still accounted for."

"Six?" Blade cocked his head.

Billie pointed at the names she'd written on the paper. "Yes *Losharek, Nelsha, Kashalet, Rostev-on-don, Kanyen,* and *Mezokami,* are the submarines that I haven't been able to find any information on since they were launched prior to or during the war."

I tapped the paper. "But how does a submarine go missing?"

Billie shrugged. "Some sink."

"But surely a disaster like that would make world news?" I asked.

"Yes, unless that submarine was somewhere it shouldn't be." Cobra grinned like he'd unlocked a top-secret computer code.

I shuffled off my barstool, lowered Charlie down, and strode to our wall of clues. We had three distinct sections. The far-right had all our info on our disastrous mission in Kyrgyzstan. The middle was dedicated to the mess that had happened at Arrow Dynamics. And the last section contained the material on Billie's discovery in Antarctica.

Somehow, the whole lot was linked.

A lot of people had died because of this hot mess.

We were yet to figure out what the hell it all meant.

At the base of the wall, I plucked a Nikko pen from the bucket, and above the hand-drawn picture of the submarine, I wrote '6 missing Russian submarines.'

It wasn't really a surprise that the sub in the ice was Russian, given that it was the Russians who had massacred everyone at Station Eleven in Antarctica. But it was good to know it was a fact.

Billie came over with her list, and we taped her data of missing subs to the wall.

All seven of us stepped back, admiring the wall of clues that made no sense.

I put my hands on my hips. "So now we have a Russian sub connected to the gold that was found in Antarctica and Arrow Dynamics. There are too many coincidences amongst all these clues."

"Yeah, and we can't figure any of it out." Blade drank the last of his beer.

A phone behind us rang.

"Hey, that's the Alpha Tactical Ops phone." Zena jogged to the kitchen.

"It's probably Hawk," Levi said.

"Welcome to Alpha Tactical Ops. How may I help you?" Zena sounded like a receptionist in a lawyer's firm.

I returned to the kitchen barstool and rubbed a bruise I had above my knee from fishing that asshole out of the rapids today. Stupid shit could've killed himself.

Zena looked at me as she spoke into the phone. "Yes, we have a female bodyguard."

I scowled and shook my head.

"Of course, she's available." Zena cupped the phone. "Maya, are you available tomorrow?"

No, I mouthed, even though I was available.

"On Kangaroo Island. Yes, I know the one. It has the abandoned resort."

I shook my head harder, but Zena ignored me. We had all made an agreement that Alpha Tactical Ops came first over everything, especially while we were trying to get the business up and running with legitimate jobs. Preferably ones that didn't end up with people in body bags.

"How long will you require our bodyguard?" Zena continued on the phone. "Three days. Yes, and when would you like her to start?"

Zena blinked at me, listening. "Perfect. I can make that happen. And where shall I send the invoice?"

She grabbed a pen and jotted down the information.

Groaning, I topped up my wineglass and glanced at my red finger-nails. "Damn it. I was going to get my nails done."

Zena hung up the phone, grinning like a weirdo. "Oh, my god! You won't believe who you will be a bodyguard to."

She did some kind of squee noise.

I shrugged. "Elvis."

"Neon Bloom." Her eyes bulged like golf balls.

"Great." I groaned.

"Who?" Billie asked.

"You're kidding, right? Neon Bloom! Hottest bachelor in Hollywood."

Zena grabbed her other phone and jabbed the keys.

"Here, check him out. Holy smokes, he's hot." She held a photo toward Billie, then me. It was a close-up of a man on a beach. "Neon Bloom. You lucky bitch."

As I studied the photo of the handsome man with hair that was somehow both perfectly styled and perfectly ruffled, with his glowing white teeth and flawless tan, I didn't feel so lucky. His expression was that of a man who thought the world owed him.

I'd had my share of obnoxious bastards to look after in my Executive Rush business.

Last thing I needed was a cocky playboy to babysit.

I'm going to hate every minute of this.

Chapter Four

NEON

After yesterday's nightmare with Shane's brutal injury, and the grilling my manager, Marc, gave me last night, all I wanted to do was get off this damn island and say *screw you* to the lot of them. But in my line of business, taking key roles when they were available was the only way to succeed. I was just twenty-nine, and I was not going to be another washed-up actor in LA wishing I'd done something different.

Although, I already did wish I'd done something different. I wished I'd simply given Shane the boot and walked away. It would've been the smart thing to do. Once he recovered from surgery to remove the stake through his shoulder, I expected to get a call from his lawyer.

He would probably sue me for millions.

I didn't care about the money. I had already earned more money than I could spend in my lifetime. And one day, I would inherit my parents' multibillion-dollar fortune.

It was more the stigma that went with my attack on Shane that pissed me off.

He would say it was an unprovoked attack and the paparazzi would lap up every word like starving hyenas.

I should have been the better man and walked away.

Too late, though. Now I would have a lawsuit against me.

After Shane had been helicoptered off the island, Marc had somehow managed to find Shane's replacement. I'd argued with Marc over that too. I did not want another fucking ogre like Derek shadowing me.

When Marc suggested he find a female bodyguard, I had figured that would be an impossible task. So, I'd agreed. After all, we were on an island, forty miles off Australia's east coast. What were the chances of finding a woman bodyguard at such short notice?

But he'd fucking found one. Marc was a miracle worker like that. It was why he'd been my manager since he'd secured my first movie deal.

I expected the woman bodyguard to be the size of Derek and just as ugly, but she was neither. Maya Grayson was stunning, and she had a woman's physique that would make my co-star Camilla Carmichael hate her on sight.

Now that was a catfight I'd pay good money for.

Maybe Camilla would give Linda a reason to put filming of *Last Resort* on hold. That would be perfect. It would take the focus off me for a change and switch the blame on her.

I could take a break for a while. I'd done back-to-back movies since I'd had my big break with *Crystal Bay* eight years ago. Since then, I hadn't had a holiday that lasted more than a week.

I could cruise the Greek Islands. Or climb Machu Picchu in Peru. I'd always wanted to do that.

The only good news was that while I'd been sorting out the chaos with Shane, Matthew Jones had finally completed the stunt that had delayed production by two days.

Today's shoot was in the lobby area of the crippled resort. The scene was a snooze fest. I could do it with my eyes closed. No stuntmen required. Instead, it was all about the lighting and the crumbling walls around us. And Camilla Carmichael.

Because the scene required her to flash a bit of boob, at her request, the crew was down to the bare minimum.

Linda's hair was scrambled all over the place this morning, making her look like a scientist on speed rather than one of the top-grossing movie producers of the century. She was another reason why I had to get this movie done. It was my first time working with her, and if I fucked things up, I would be lining up for acting gigs in B-Grade horror movies instead.

Maya and Derek were in the shadows, yet I could see the sexy pocket-rocket well enough. She looked relaxed, however her steely expression and alert gaze said otherwise. I didn't know what credentials she came with, but Marc assured me she had the goods to do her job.

She was probably on edge because the action scene we'd just wrapped up involved men chasing Camilla and me with weapons that looked real. Camilla's screams had sounded legitimate, and the flames had been real, but the gunfire had been fake.

On top of that, there had been about a hundred people in the decrepit resort lobby, all doing stuff to make the chase scene look genuine.

Anyone new to being on set probably had no idea what the fuck was going on.

As that scene finished and the crew prepared for the next, Camilla and I sat in canvas chairs at the side of the room to avoid the organized chaos. The makeup artists and costume designers fussed over us. Food and drinks were offered by the catering staff. Linda ran through her vision of the next scene. Camilla and I rehearsed our lines.

My attention kept drifting to Maya who leaned against one of four giant marble pillars centered in the lobby. Beside her was Derek and he dwarfed her by at least a foot. Yet somehow, she was the one commanding attention.

Whatever Derek was talking to her about had her looking as bored as a gigolo in a nunnery.

She sure did provide some decent eye candy. Her blonde hair was in a thick braid that curled over her shoulder. Her skin was flawless. And her eyes . . .. A few years ago, I did a movie where my character had a wolf for a pet. My wolf's eyes were an intense blue that were simply mesmerizing. Maya's eyes were like that, impossibly blue, incredibly fascinating.

I'd lived a lifetime surrounded by women with fake hair, fake lashes, fake lips, fake boobs, and even fake asses.

Although I'd only seen Maya up close when she shook my hand

27

early this morning, she looked like the genuine article. That made her a rare commodity.

She was fucking hot. And fucking confident. That too was rare. Many women I associated with were bad-asses on the screen, but get them alone and they were often pathetic, either whining about something or bitching about it.

"Neon, are you ready?" Linda was positioned on the second-floor balcony above us. Her squeaky voice projected through her megaphone and bounced off the slate floor like a ping pong.

"I'm ready."

I'd been ready for hours. My makeup had been completed since before the sun came up at five o'clock, and I'd been waiting for everyone else to get their shit together ever since.

Waiting around was the other annoying thing about my line of work. I spent a lot of time doing nothing. And when my mind started to wander, that was dangerous. I had some serious shit in my past that liked to creep up on me when I least expected it. It was the reason I started acting. I never envisaged it would take me to the top of Hollywood's elite though.

"Camilla. What about you? Ready?" Linda asked.

"Yes." Camilla adjusted the ripped shoulder of her expertly stained shirt and nodded at me. Camilla may only be twenty-three, but she'd been acting all her life. She was good at it too. I admired her professionalism. Unlike the stuntman yesterday, I could count on her to know her lines and nail this scene first go.

I clutched Camilla's hand. It was cold. Her hands were always cold —like her heart.

We paused in the rear of the grand lobby, and silence fell around us.

As if she was a magnet, my attention was attracted to Maya. She'd slipped into the shadows of the hallway that led toward the accommodation wing of the resort.

Our eyes met, and she gave me a slight nod.

For some reason, sparks fired through me that had my groin throbbing. What was it about her?

Camilla squeezed my hand, dragging my attention back to her. Her almost black eyes drilled into me. She'd caught me looking at Maya. *Was she jealous?* It wouldn't surprise me. Camilla was jealous of anyone more beautiful than her.

A hush fell on the large reception area. The red indicator light on the camera aimed at us blinked. The crewman holding the clapperboard snapped it shut, and Camilla glossed her bottom lip with her tongue.

"And . . . action." Linda lowered her megaphone and as a machine rained millions of particles of paper, designed to look like the aftermath of an explosion, over us, we sprinted over the rubble-strewn tiles into the center of the lobby.

"What the hell was that?" Camilla swept her gaze up to me. She already had her tears on the go.

I shot my gaze left and right, then back to her. "Fucking hell, they have shoulder rocket launchers."

"Jesus! They're never going to stop chasing me, are they?" A tear spilled from her left eye and trickled down her grubby cheek.

"Listen to me. They're not getting you that easy." I cupped her cold cheek. "I made a promise, Tia, and I will keep it. Nobody will ever hurt you again. Nobody."

She leaned into my hand, and her shirt slipped sideways, revealing just enough of the bulge in her cleavage to confirm she wore nothing underneath.

Screams erupted from outside.

I tried to recall seeing that in my script but couldn't.

Camilla ran her tongue over her lip again and as I eased closer to her, the cameraman glided toward us. Camilla's eyelids fluttered closed.

The screams grew louder. I paused, and when Camilla opened her eyes and frowned, I knew she was as confused as I was.

Derek strode across the lobby, aiming right for me.

"Cut!" Linda yelled. "What the hell is going on?"

Derek came in behind me and pressed a gun to my temple. "Do as I say!"

"Shit! Derek!" I stepped back. "What the fuck are you doing?"

His arm snapped around my neck. "Shut up."

The confusion in Camilla's eyes morphed into terror.

Three men stormed into the area. People screamed and fled for the exits.

Camilla sprinted away, but a man with a gun jumped in front of her.

He aimed the gun at her head. "Don't move. On your knees."

Camilla shot her hands up and fell to her knees.

A bullet slammed into the side of the gunman's head, and he tumbled to Camilla's feet like a sack of potatoes.

Behind him, Maya shifted her weapon from the dead guy toward Derek.

"Let him go," she yelled across the lobby.

Bullets slammed into the tiles in front of Maya. She aimed her weapon to the upper balcony and without flinching fired. One. Two.

A man tumbled over the railing and slammed onto the slate next to Camilla with a sickening crunch.

Camilla jumped to her feet and raced away screaming.

Maya aimed her weapon at Derek again. "Let him go."

Derek flicked his gun toward Maya. She dove out of sight. Derek fired three shots. One pierced Camilla's back. She careened forward and crashed into the ancient reception desk, splintering the front panel in two.

"Fuck!" My jaw dropped. My heart thundered. "You killed her, Derek. You fucking killed her."

Derek dragged me into a hallway. As people ran across the lobby screaming, Maya sprinted across the slate tiles with her gun drawn, chasing after me.

I clawed at the arm around my neck. It was like scratching steel. "I can't breathe."

"Shut the fuck up." Derek dug the barrel of the gun deeper into my temple.

A gunshot exploded from the lobby. Several more followed. One. Two. Ten. These sounded every bit real. As did the screams.

My feet stumbled over something as Derek dragged me further into the hallway.

More gunfire erupted, and a man shrieked in agony. Then he stopped.

"Put the gun down." Maya's voice boomed from nowhere.

Derek yanked me backward and aimed the gun toward her voice.

"He's got a gun." I tried to yell, but my voice was like I'd swallowed sand.

"Shut up, you stupid fuck." Derek whacked the gun into my temple.

Stars danced across my eyes, and I had to grip his arm to keep upright.

He'd dragged me into the accommodation wing of the hotel. When we'd arrived on the island, our first scene had been filmed in this section. For eleven years, this building had been three floors of deluxe hotel rooms with furnishings from all over the world. But since the resort had been abandoned twenty years ago, plants and animals had moved in, making the walls, carpet, and what was left of the crumbling furniture their home.

Shouts from the lobby grew louder, as did the screams. I had only seen three gunmen, and Maya had shot two of them. It sounded like a dozen more had stormed into the lobby.

Once they figured out where Derek had taken me, they were going to come after us. I had to stop him.

I punched over my shoulder, connecting with his face.

Derek grunted and squeezed tighter around my neck.

"Where are you taking me?" I scratched my nails along his arm.

He didn't flinch.

Gasping, I clawed at his fingers, but he was a beast.

He shoved through the door to the stairwell. The curved stairs were once a grand feature, but the carpet was green with moss, the wallpaper was peeling, and a vine snaked up the wall like a cancerous vein.

"Let him go, Derek." Maya's voice filled the stairwell.

"Fuck off." Derek aimed over the curved balustrade and fired two rounds to the level below.

Silence filled the void.

Jesus! Did he kill her?

Questions whizzed through my mind.

How many bullets does he have?

What does he want with me?

I strained to listen, but all I heard was Derek's ragged breathing.

At the next level, he pulled me onto the second landing. Many doors

31

were wedged ajar with vines as thick as my wrist crawling across the peeling plaster. The patterned carpet was water damaged and rotting away, and the windows were either covered in decades of sea salt, broken, or missing altogether.

This wing of the hotel was designed so every room had a view of the pool and the ocean in the distance, and a long narrow hallway at the back connected them all. But without an operating lift, the only access to the upper levels were the stairs situated at opposite ends. It was dark and disgusting.

I searched for something I could grab onto, but the corridor was empty, and the rooms I managed to peek into had nothing except crappy old furniture.

Derek adjusted his arm around my neck, and I wedged my fingers between his forearm and my throat, trying to pull him away.

"You're suffocating me." I could barely breathe. I could barely think.

"Let him go!" Maya's voice drifted to me.

Derek aimed over my shoulder and fired. The gun blasted in my right ear.

His bullets slammed into the wall and took out a lightshade that shattered into a million pieces.

"You've got nowhere to go." Maya's voice was calm, in control.

"Move," Derek hissed, dragging me backward.

I clawed at his arm and stumbled back with him. A high-pitched squeal rang in my right ear. Stars danced over my eyes.

"I'll give you one more chance. Let him go, or you're dead." Maya's voice came from nowhere.

I couldn't see where she was. The corridor was long and narrow. If she was near, I would see her.

Derek fired again. His bullets slammed into a wall. A doorframe. The ceiling.

I tried to punch him again, but my aim was off, and my arms were weak. I needed air.

Gunfire boomed in the distance.

Jesus! How many gunmen are there?

Derek's breathing was loud and ragged.

"Derek, please, what are you doing? Let's talk about this." My voice was a brittle croak.

"Shut up." He squeezed tighter. Blackness seeped into my vision. My mind tumbled back twenty years to another time when I'd pleaded for my life.

I'd thought I was going to die then.

It was a miracle I hadn't.

I needed another miracle now.

Chapter Five

MAYA

I dove into a room as a bullet slammed into the doorframe at my feet, taking out a chunk of timber. The peeling wallpaper was equal parts pink and moth-eaten. I didn't even want to know what kind of spider left the giant web connecting the phone cable on the wall above me to the crumbling lampshade on the credenza.

I clicked my gun magazine out and checked my rounds. Seven bullets left. Based on the number of shouts I'd heard in the distance, I was going to need every one of them. Or steal a weapon from one of those assholes.

I had no bloody idea what was going on, but this was no simple babysitting job. When I got my hands on Neon fucking Bloom, I was going to strangle him myself. And his manager Marc. And Zena for putting me in this goddammed mess.

I should have known something was off when Marc took my cell phone. He said it was the movie producer's strict policy. No phones on set so I couldn't receive a call that could potentially ruin a scene, nor could I take photos.

My ass. Marc knew this was coming.

Now I had no comms, and no damned backup.

Grunts down the hallway drifted to me. Derek had his arm around

Bloom's neck, and if he didn't know what he was doing, the stupid bastard could suffocate him.

Huh. Maybe that would be a good thing.

One thing was certain. They, whoever *they* were, wanted Neon Bloom alive.

Lucky for me, Derek was the only man with Neon, and the way he shot his gun, he was no expert. Based on the conversations I'd had with him in the last four hours, he was as dumb as dog shit.

"Move." Derek's voice echoed down the corridor.

With my gun drawn, I peeked around the doorframe into the hallway. Derek and Bloom were silhouetted against the window at the opposite end of the hallway making my view of them a scramble of arms and legs that made it impossible to work out whose was whose.

They didn't seem to be moving.

Shit! He was waiting for his pals.

As soon as they arrived, I would lose my advantage.

I needed to get around behind Derek, but the second I stepped into the hallway, I would become target practice.

I strode through the hotel room to the glass doors that were smothered in so much sea salt the view was nonexistent.

Gripping the handle, I yanked it down. It didn't move. Twenty years of rust had cemented it in place.

At the window, I yanked at the pane. It slid open so fast, it slammed to the other side and disintegrated into a million tiny shards.

I jumped back to the wall and gripping my weapon, I aimed at the door, ready to extinguish every bastard that came running at me.

It didn't happen.

"Move," a man yelled.

A woman shrieked.

I peered out the window. Through the tropical jungle below, a group of civilians was being marched along a path with their hands in the air. I counted six gunmen who were herding the hostages alongside the swampy pool.

Below the window was a veranda that had once been decorated in colorful blue tiles in an intricate mosaic pattern depicting jumping dolphins. Now there were as many tiles missing as there was gecko poo.

Leaning out the window, I scanned the outside of the building. Each of the twenty hotel rooms had their own veranda. I could get behind Derek this way.

More shouts rang out below and I ducked back into the shadows.

"Don't worry, we'll get him," a man said.

He sprinted with another man along the path, heading back to the lobby.

Shit! They're coming.

The veranda option would take too long. Ditching that idea, I ran to the door. Derek and Bloom were still a tangle of silhouetted limbs at the end of the corridor.

With my stomach clenched as tight as a spring, I gripped my gun and shot out the door. Sprinting away from Bloom, I pictured Derek swinging his weapon toward me. I clenched my fists and forced my legs to run like the wind. A bullet shattered a wall light as I dove through the doorway into the stairwell.

"Derek, where the fuck are you?" a deep voice boomed from the floor below.

I jumped to my feet and sprinted up the curved stairwell.

Without pausing at the top, I ran along the corridor that was a near replica of the second level I'd left. Every step was a battle between trying to run quietly and racing as fast as I could to the opposite end of the corridor.

Ahead, the window had no glass, offering a view over swaying palms and a thatched roof that had seen better days. At the stairwell, I launched down the stairs, and with my gun ready, I peeked over the balustrading in case Derek had taken cover in the stairwell.

"Derek! Answer me, you bastard." The booming voice at the opposite end of the corridor had an American twang to it that was so out of place with my hometown of Risky Shores.

"I'm on the second floor. And hurry up. That bitch is around here somewhere."

That's right, asshole. I'm coming to get you.

At the landing to the second level, one of the double doors was barely hanging on by a hinge, but its angle provided enough room for me to dive through it without risking squeaking hinges.

By my guess, Derek would be about fifteen feet along the corridor. I also guessed he would be facing away from me, toward his asshole friends.

Time to move.

With my finger on the trigger, I hunched over and slipped through the gap in the door.

The floorboards beneath me creaked. *Shit.*

My feet slipped. I half fell, half dove across the hallway.

Derek was right there. He spun around. His grip around Neon's neck was brutal.

"Neon, duck." I raised my arm.

Derek raised his gun at me. Neon's eyes popped. His jaw dropped.

I pulled the trigger.

My bullet slammed into Derek's arm. His gun went flying.

I launched to my feet.

Derek cried out as he stumbled backward and his bloody hand sprayed blood up the wall.

I raced forward. "Neon, move!"

Neon blinked like crazy. Stupid bastard looked like he was on another planet.

Thundering footsteps sounded from the other end of the hallway.

I grabbed Neon's wrist and yanked him toward me. "Run."

Derek scrambled to his feet and went for his gun.

I kicked open the door and it shattered into four chunks. "Move."

I shoved Neon ahead of me.

The temptation to stay and fight was huge, but I only had six bullets, and I had no idea how many men were charging our way.

On top of that, if they were smart, they would spread out and approach Derek from all available angles. Neon and I would be sitting ducks in that hallway.

Neon clutched the railing as he ran down the stairs. Either his balance was off, or he had a gallon of adrenalin gushing through him that was making him wobbly. Probably both.

"Where is he?" the American voice boomed.

"They went that way," Derek answered.

"Fuck. Neon, run!" I scrambled around in front of him, grabbed his wrist, and dragged him down the last couple of steps.

Leading with my gun, I steered Neon into the ground floor corridor. I shot my gaze left and right. All clear.

"Let's get out of here." Dragging Neon behind me, I raced to the rear exit of the building.

I shoulder charged through the exit door and it disintegrated like it was made of papier-mâché. A path led away from the building. It was covered in moss and disappeared into a forest of shrubs and trees.

"You with me, Neon?"

He made a noise like his tongue was an angry animal. "Yeah."

"Good. Keep up with me."

We ducked under low branches, and I swiped palm fronds out of our way as we kept up our pace. "Any idea where this goes?"

"No." His voice was a brutal croak.

Derek sure had done a number on his throat.

"We need to get off this path and hide."

"Okay." At least he was keeping pace with me.

"Is your head okay?"

He frowned.

"The cut on your forehead." I pointed at the nasty gash near his hairline.

He touched the wound. "Oh, that's just makeup."

Bloody hell. I shook my head and picked up my pace.

"Sorry." He didn't sound sorry.

We sprinted past a tram car with four carriages and a miniature train that had once been the engine. The red and yellow paintwork had long ago faded, and a tree had managed to enter one side of the train driver's window and continue growing out the other. In another decade, that train was probably going to be halfway up that tree.

A toppled sign beside the path offered two choices, the marina or the kids' playground. Making a snap decision, I chose the marina, hoping that the sign was actually pointing the right way.

"Where are we going?" Neon's voice was improving.

"The marina. With a bit of luck, there may be some boats around."

"I doubt it."

"Yeah, why's that?"

"There's a no-go zone around the island."

"A what?" I shot my gaze over my shoulder to him.

"It's to stop assholes with powerful cameras taking photos of the movie action from a distance."

"Well, that's just great."

The dense jungle disappeared around us and we stepped onto graying timber that had once been a trendy boardwalk for visitors who came to the island via their fancy yachts.

A couple of thatch huts had been reduced to mangled timber and straw, and of the pontoons that had formed the marina, half were underwater, and half were gone altogether. Only the main middle pontoon remained and even that looked like it was on its last legs.

"Where is he?" The American voice carved through the vegetation behind us like a machete.

I spun toward the voice. The path we'd come along vanished into the scrub. Any second now, one of those assholes was going to come storming along that path. Or fifty of them. I had no fucking idea. Until I did, our only option was to hide.

The crippled huts provided zero cover. Over the edge of the board-walk, a rusty ladder fed into the water.

I grabbed Neon's wrist. "Get in the water."

His eyes popped and sheer terror carved up his handsome features. "No."

"Let's go." I yanked him to the edge of the boardwalk. "Get on that fucking ladder or I'll shoot you myself."

"Split up." The voice boomed authority. "You four take the marina. We'll go this way."

"Neon." I slapped his cheek.

His jaw dropped.

"Get on the ladder now!" I dug my fingers into his arm and hauled him toward the ladder.

Spinning toward the path with my gun raised, I prayed the bastards took their time.

"Get in the water, Neon," I hissed through clenched teeth.

This was cutting it fine.

Neon spun with this back to the ocean, gripped the railing, and climbed onto the first ladder rung.

What the hell was his problem?

I glared into his wide eyes and spoke through clenched teeth. "Move! Or we both die."

He shuddered like a volcano about to erupt.

Returning my attention to the path, I dropped to one knee and inhaled deeply. I rested my finger on my gun trigger and as I studied the pathway, I let my breath out slowly.

A small splash confirmed Neon hit the water.

I jumped onto the ladder and scrambled down. Lowering into the warm water to my waist, I stepped onto sand, clutched Neon's arm, and shuffled beneath the boardwalk so our backs were against a block retaining wall. Like a couple of kids playing hide and seek, I turned to Neon and indicated shush with my finger over my lips.

Only this was a game where people got killed.

Neon looked like he was going to piss his pants. His wide, darting eyes flicked from the water to me and back again.

Jesus! He's about to lose his shit.

I clutched his shoulder and leaned into his ear. "Hey, it's okay. They won't find us."

His gaze met mine, and I was struck by the fear driven into his eyes. I'd seen men crazy with fear many times before, but that was on a battlefield where bullets and bombs had been raining all around us. Neon's fear was equal to that.

That convinced me Neon knew exactly who owned that American accent and what the bastard wanted.

I had every intention of finding out once we were out of this mess.

If we got out of this mess.

Footsteps thundered onto the boardwalk above us. Clutching Neon's wrist, I pressed a finger to my lips again.

Through the slats in the timber above us, I could just make out the shape of three men. Or was it four?

"Where the fuck are they?" The accent was American, but it was a different accent from the booming one I'd heard earlier.

"They can't get too far. It's an island." That was Derek. That bastard's high-pitched voice was in my head now. He was going to regret he ever met me.

Neon shuddered, but his gaze wasn't upward. He was glaring at the water.

Son of a bitch! Jellyfish.

Four jellyfish with large, translucent domes and tentacles as long as my body, drifted back and forward with the waves that crashed into the block wall holding up the boardwalk.

I gripped Neon's arm and shook my head, trying to convey that no matter what, he had to keep quiet.

One man above us made a disgusting noise and spat into the water. The fat, yellow glob landed barely three feet from us and as a jellyfish carved through it, the man's shadow appeared in the water.

He's admiring his spit.

"Jesus, look at the size of those jellyfish." I didn't recognize this new voice above us.

Three more shadows joined the first.

A piercing sting ripped across my left ankle. Fire blazed up my shin and calf muscle as a tentacle draped across the exposed flesh above my sock.

Fuck. Fuck. Fuck.

Clenching my fists, I squeezed my mouth shut, forcing down a scream burning in my throat.

Using my other shoe, I kicked at the jellyfish, praying the rest of its tentacles wouldn't get me. Or worse, Neon.

Neon's terrified gaze increased as I scraped the jellyfish off my leg with my boot, confirming he would not cope with that horror.

The shadows shifted above us, and another man spat into the water.

Blinding pain zipped up to my groin. I sucked air through my teeth, fighting it.

The jellyfish drifted back and forward.

The men took turns spitting into the water.

Neon's eyes grew even wider. He looked about ready to have a complete meltdown. If he did, we would be killed.

I did something I hadn't done since the night my sister died.

I prayed.

Chapter Six

NEON

The assholes above us were so close, I heard them breathing. But it was the water surrounding me that had fear barging through me.

It's just water. It's just fucking water.

My childhood horror was a demon, forcing its way into my mind, bringing with it the terror that had changed my life.

Nothing could eradicate my fear of water. Although I knew it was stupid, I couldn't help my throat going dry, my heart thundering in my ears, and my brain setting to explode.

Maya clutched my arm, drawing my attention to her.

She shook her head, silently trying to convey something.

Maybe I'd made a noise. If I did, I hadn't noticed. Staring into the tiny waves crashing into my thighs, I clenched my fists and forced my mind away from my childhood nightmare to my current one.

My bodyguard, Derek, and his asshole buddies wanted to kidnap me. They'd already made that known.

It would be about money. It always was.

The shadows shifted back from the water, and I dragged my gaze upward. Four men stood directly overhead. If they looked down through the slats, it was likely they would see us. My only visual of them was the underside of their boots. I couldn't make out their faces or even what they were wearing.

"Maybe the others found him and that bitch?" The voice was Derek's.

When I got my hands on him, that bastard was a dead man.

I couldn't believe he was the mastermind behind this kidnapping attempt. The disorganized asshole could barely stitch two sentences together.

No. Someone had used him to get to me.

How long had he been planning this? In the weeks since we arrived on this island? In the four months since he started working for me? Maybe he'd been working on this kidnapping for years, just waiting for Marc to hire him as my bodyguard?

If that was the case, another question came into play. Was Marc involved?

That question was terrifying. I'd known Marc for ten years. I trusted him. I'd confided in him. If he was involved, then that was going to be some rotten shit I'd have trouble dealing with.

Maya had her gun ready. After what I'd seen back in the hotel, she could easily kill all four men above us. The fact that she didn't proved she was thinking this through.

That jellyfish sting would be brutal, and yet she stayed in control. I didn't know a single woman who would be so brave. Or man, for that matter.

That put Maya at the top of my most interesting person list.

As did her gun skills. I'd done some shooting practice over the years, but I was not as good as I'd like to be. And putting a bullet into someone took it to another level.

Yet when she'd saved me from Derek, she hadn't flinched.

"I hope we don't need to spend the night here. This place is a dump," a man said above us as they shifted away.

"Shut up, and keep your eye on the prize."

"Yeah." It sounded like someone had their back slapped. "We've started this now. We have to do whatever it takes to finish it."

The boots turned and vanished from above us.

"Yeah, I still don't want to . . ." The voice drifted away.

Maya's lips were in a straight line, and I had the impression she was still fighting off that jellyfish sting. She tilted her head toward me, sweeping those blue eyes of hers my way.

She nodded, and I understood that to mean we were going to be okay.

I nodded back.

The voices were gone for some time before we shifted from our hiding place. Maya climbed the ladder, and when she paused at the top rung to peer over the boardwalk, I studied her sexy butt and well-toned legs below her calf-length pants.

The raised, red welt on her ankle looked angry and fucking painful.

She raced up the top ladder rungs and I followed her onto the boardwalk. At the top, I crossed the timber to where she sat on the grass. She'd removed her shoe and sock. The jellyfish sting was a brutal stripe around her lower leg like she'd wrestled herself out of ankle cuffs.

"Neon, you need to piss on the welts."

I jerked back. "What?"

"Just do it." She pulled her cargo pants up over her knee.

My jaw dropped and it took everything I had not to burst out laughing. "Shit, you're serious."

"Yes, I'm serious." Her gaze drilled into me.

Even cranky, she's damn hot.

"Okay. Okay." I pulled down my zipper. "You going to watch?"

"No." She rolled onto her hands and knees, revealing the back of her calf where the welts were even worse.

She peered toward the path where I assumed Derek and the other three bastards had gone. "Don't piss on my pants."

"Is this some kind of survivalist technique?"

Her calf muscle was perfectly defined. *Hot damn, she's fit.*

"According to my friend Levi, it is. Quick, we've got to move." Her sexy ass was directed right at me.

"I'm trying. This is a first for me."

"First for me too," she mumbled.

"Could have fooled me."

"Vinegar is the best option, but I'm fresh out. Now hurry up."

"Shhh. I'm trying." I needed to piss so bad the pressure in my bladder was painful, but this was too weird.

"Neon!"

I peed on her ankle.

She winced and jerked away.

"Keep still." I chuckled.

"It fucking stings."

"You asked me—"

"Shut the fuck up and get it done already." She rolled her ankle side to side.

I finished peeing, tucked myself away, and zipped up. "Well, that was a first."

She sat up, investigating the red welt. "Goddammit."

"What?"

"It stings *and* stinks. Did you eat asparagus?"

"What?"

She jumped to her feet.

"Joking." She thumped my shoulder. "Stay there."

She sprinted back to the ladder, climbed down, and disappeared from view.

I waited for her to reappear, unable to wipe the smile off my face.

Maya climbed up the ladder like an Olympic gymnast. As she strode back to me, her blonde hair glistened in the sunshine, and her flushed cheeks added another dimension to her stunning looks.

She sat on the grass and twisted the water out of her sock. "So, what was that shit about?"

I frowned. "What? You asked me to piss on your leg."

"No." She yanked on her wet sock. "When we were in the water. You were scared out of your mind."

It would be easy to say no, and defend myself. But she'd already proved she was a smart one.

"Oh, and you weren't?"

She tugged on her gym shoe. "Yeah, I'll admit that was close. But you need to fill me in on what's going on."

"What do you mean?"

46

"Derek and those assholes. Why do they want you?" She did up her laces with so much angst it was a wonder they didn't snap.

I huffed. "Money."

She removed her other shoe and sock and twisted the water out of that sock too. "Is that all? Money?"

"What else would it be?" I sat on the grass and following her lead, I squeezed out my socks.

"A crazy girlfriend."

I cocked an eyebrow. "Yeah, right."

Maya yanked her laces together like she was tying a prisoner. "Look, if I'm going to save your ass, it's best if you tell me everything."

I pulled on my shoes and tied the laces. "You know as much as I do."

She stood and rubbed her hands on her pants. "Tell me about Derek."

I eased to her side. She was about a foot shorter than me, but she had a presence about her that made her so much taller.

"Marc hired Derek as my bodyguard about six months ago."

"What happened to the bodyguard before him?"

"Allan? He quit."

She leveled her gaze at me like I was roadkill. "After something you did?"

"No, I have no idea why he quit. Is that okay with you?"

"It's a bit convenient that Derek got the job, and now he's out for you." Maya clicked out the magazine on her weapon and with her jaw clamped and her gaze intense, she checked the bullets.

Her hands were tiny, and her movements were concise.

"Whatever." She rammed her weapon into the holster on her hip. "Let's go."

She sprinted off.

Maya was the real deal. And smoking hot.

She reached the intersection where the path entered the scrub before she turned to check if I was following.

I caught up with her. "Where are we going?"

She pointed to her right. Slotting in side by side, we ran along the path together.

"I need to find a phone," she said. "Where's yours?"

"In my trailer."

"Right, then that's where we're headed."

My trailer was on a second island, connected to the main island by the bridge that Shane had crashed through.

"You do know that's literally at the opposite side of this island, right?"

"No, I don't. I arrived on this island this morning. I'm relying on you to get us where we need to go."

"That's going to be a problem. I've only been in the main hotel area, the pool area, and the temporary containers they choppered in for our accommodation for the next six months."

"How long have you been filming here?"

"Three weeks."

"Huh." Maya crouched behind a shrub that had taken over three-quarters of the pathway.

"What are you looking for?" I eased in beside her. She smelled amazing, subtle scents of vanilla and flowers.

She cocked her head at me. "Bad guys."

"Yeah, funny."

"Shush."

Stifling a chuckle, I shut my mouth and stared at the path ahead. Other than the rustling palm fronds above us, there was no sound.

In the last three weeks, one sound had been constant: the waves. But in the middle of this jungle, I couldn't hear the ocean. The silence was eerie. I didn't have a lot of that in my life. My days were filled with interactions. With directors and actors. With fans. With women. Silence did not play a part in my life.

And yet, here with Maya, it was somehow perfect.

"Let's go." She darted around the shrub, and I admired her sexy ass as she sprinted ahead of me. If the sting on her leg was giving her any grief, she didn't show it.

At the intersection where we'd originally left the main pathway to head to the marina, we paused again.

"We have two choices." Maya used two fingers to point along the path. "Back toward the main hotel area, or that way."

She pointed in the opposite direction, which the sign indicated was toward the playground.

"The bad guys are probably in both directions." I shrugged.

"That's the assumption." She nodded. "And we don't know how many tangos we're dealing with."

"Tangos?"

"Bad guys."

"I know what tangos are. Are you ex-army or something?"

She glared at me. "Yeah, or something. You have a problem with that?"

Her jump to defensive was as surprising as it was brutal. I raised my hands in a peace gesture. "Calm down, just asking."

She rolled her eyes. "We're going this way."

She dashed off, using the bushes leaning in from the left-hand side of the path for cover.

I had to sprint to keep up with her. Damn, she was fast.

Her admission about the army was surprising. I imagined she was too short to be in the military, and I never pictured anyone so pretty in army uniform. Then again, what would I know? Hollywood was my life. Maya and I couldn't be any further apart in career choices.

Maya squatted down, and I eased in beside her. Ahead, three kangaroos were on the path, looking at us.

"They're small kangaroos," I said.

"That's because they're rock wallabies."

"Same thing, right?"

"Wrong. Different species. Whoever named this island got it wrong. There have never been kangaroos here, only rock wallabies."

The animals darted away like they were spooked. Maya plucked her gun from her holster and snapped it left and right. Silence smothered my ears like they were filled with cotton wool. It was weird.

Maya flicked her long braid over her shoulder. "We need to get off this path. You good?"

I shrugged. "Yes."

With her leading with her gun at the ready, we sprinted along the path. We dodged around shrubs working on overtaking the path and under tree branches as thick as my thigh. Moss on the concrete was so thick in some sections it was slippery, forcing us to slow down.

The path led us to the children's playground where plants had reclaimed the play area. We ducked under the slippery slide that had tiny mounds of bird shit dotted all over it. I searched the tree above and spied at least six birds' nests.

Vines had grown through the swing chains locking them in place, and the merry-go-round had a massive palm growing through the middle of it. The result was like a weird artistic sculpture that would suit many Hollywood homes I'd visited over the years.

This place was fucking creepy. But if Maya was sensing any of the weird vibes I was, she didn't show it.

A golden spear of light carved through the vegetation and glinted off the saddle on a carousel horse that was missing its head.

Maya followed the beam of light and groaned. "The sun's setting."

I looked at my wrist but had forgotten I'd taken off my watch. "What time is it?"

"Must be about five-thirty. In half an hour, the sun will set and give us a new range of problems."

Despite her comment, Maya didn't look perturbed. If anything, she was the opposite. Like she lived for the challenge that complete darkness would bring.

She ran her tongue over her lip. "I hate to say it, but I think we're in for one hell of a night."

"What? Out here?"

She pulled her lips to a thin line. "Not exactly. We better—"

She stopped talking and crouched down, yanking me down with her.

"What's wrong?"

Her blue eyes flared at me, and she shook her head.

A whistling noise drifted to us, getting louder. Whoever it was, they were not trying to be discreet.

Maya leaned into my ear. "Keep quiet."

She stood, unclipped her gun holster from her thigh, and handed it to me. "Hold this. Don't touch my gun."

She spoke to me like I was a naughty child.

Holding the gun belt I stood at her side, and Maya pulled her weapon from her second gun belt around her narrow waist and clipped out the magazine, checking for bullets.

I searched the path for who was whistling, but he still wasn't visible.

Maybe it's a trap?

I eased toward Maya to voice my concern, but she shushed me with a finger to her lips.

Maya removed her gun belt from her waist and handed that belt to me too. She slotted her handgun into the back of her pants and pulled her navy shirt from her pants and undid the top two buttons.

She rolled her eyes at me, and I tried to process what that meant. With the bulge of her cleavage showing as she leaned toward me, I could barely think at all.

"Stay here. I'll be back." Her hot breath whispered off my ear.

I adjusted my position to watch her walk toward the whistling. She tugged her hair out of her braid and tousled her long hair down her back.

A man appeared on the path about thirty yards ahead of her.

He stopped whistling and raised his hand. I couldn't see him properly, but his stance confirmed he was armed.

Maya raised her hands. "Please, don't hurt me. I . . . I was lost."

"Get down on your knees." The man charged forward.

Maya lowered to her knees with her arms up. "Please, don't hurt me."

"Who are you?" The man hovered over her, aiming the gun in her face.

Maya launched to her feet, wrapping her hands over his gun hand, rammed her body underneath him, and flipped him onto his back.

Holy shit.

She aimed the bastard's own gun at his eyeball. "Don't move!"

Clutching both her gun holsters, I raced toward her.

She shot me a glare that was pure rage. "I told you to stay."

"But—"

She shook her head. "Shut up, and get—"

The asshole grabbed the gun and pulled the weapon over his shoulder, yanking Maya off her feet. She lurched forward but twisted sideways and rammed her elbow into his neck.

The man's head jerked forward as he bucked beneath her, but neither of them let go of the gun.

"Drop it, bitch!" The gunman snapped his head forward, trying to headbutt Maya. He connected with her chin instead.

Maya released a furious growl and yanked his arm upward. Somehow, she scrambled to her feet and dropped knee-first into her attacker's groin.

He shrieked like his testicles had exploded.

She pulled back on the gun.

He released a demonic cry and clutched her hands in his. "You're gonna die, bitch!"

I kicked the bastard's knee.

Maya wrestled with the gun. He did too. Her strength was incredible.

I kicked his knee again and howling, he yanked Maya sideways.

A flock of cockatoos screeched as they took flight around us.

The gun exploded.

Chapter Seven

MAYA

I jumped off the attacker and stood. He was dead.

"Jesus Christ!" The bullet had gone through his chin and a bloody mess covered the path behind him.

I spun to Neon. "I told you to stay where you were."

His bulging eyes shifted from the dead guy to me. "I was helping you."

I marched to him and shoved his chest. "I wanted him alive, dickhead."

Neon stumbled back, tripped over a moss-covered branch, and fell on his ass. He blinked at me like I was a freak.

It was the same look I received from many men. They always underestimated me.

"I helped you," he hissed through clamped teeth.

"I didn't need your fucking help."

"Looked to me like you did."

I glared at him, then shaking my head, I strode back to the dead guy. "God damn it! I wanted him alive so we could find out what the hell's going on. Do you know him?"

"What?" Neon stood, and dusting his hands on his jeans, he returned to the path.

"Do you know this guy?" I spoke to him like English was his second language.

"No. I don't know him."

Squatting down, I rifled through the dead guy's pockets. They were empty. No wallet, or keys, or phone. Not even a scrap of paper. A new level of worry shot through me.

These bastards were organized. Whoever was running the show made sure they had no ID on them. And that meant they were prepared to fight to the death.

Tucking my shirt back in, I strode to Neon.

"Give me that." I snatched my gun belt off him. "What kind of trouble are you in, Neon?"

He leveled his gaze at me. "What're you talking about?"

I was struck by the interesting mix of green and blue in his irises. Maybe they were fake.

Yanking my belt tight around my waist, I did it up and returned my gun to the holster. "These guys are pros."

He handed over my thigh holster. "I know as much as you do. I can't even believe Derek was involved. He was a useless idiot."

I strapped the holster tight around my leg. Tugging my hair into a braid, I met Neon's gaze. His twisted expression told me he was genuinely confused.

A level of sadness lingered in his eyes as well.

I secured my hair with a band and flicked my braid over my shoulder. "Yeah, well, that useless idiot was bloody organized. And that means we're in trouble."

I turned back to the body. If there wasn't blood splattered all over the path, I would drag his body into the bushes. But it was pointless.

"That gunshot will have the rest of those assholes heading this way." I tucked the attacker's weapon into the back of my cargo pants.

"Want me to take that?" Neon held out his hand.

I cocked my head at him. "You know how to use a handgun?"

He graced me with those interesting eyes of his. "Point and shoot."

"Yes, but have you ever shot a man before?"

His twitchy reaction told me all I needed to know.

"Have you? I mean other than him." He nodded at the dead guy.

"Yes." There was no need to elaborate. Civilian men couldn't comprehend my military career. I wasn't about to explain my sniper skills to a man who made a career out of pretending to be a hero.

I showed him where the safety was on the gun and how to switch it, then handed him the weapon. "Don't go shooting your toe off."

He scrunched his face like he smelled dog shit. "I won't."

"But, Neon, if you do fire that gun, don't waste the bullet. Aim to kill."

"Got it." As he tucked the gun into the back of his jeans and pulled his shirt out, a swift breeze had the palm fronds and leafy trees swaying around us. Through a patch in the dense canopy above, the clouds were mottled shades of orange and yellow.

The sun was setting. We were about to be in pitch darkness.

A flock of lorikeets took to the air together as if making the most of the last rays of sunshine. I squatted to adjust the wet laces on my left boot.

Neon studied the bloody body, and something crossed over his expression. Relief. Confusion. Rage. Or maybe it was recognition. I couldn't tell.

"So, you really have killed other people?"

"We better move." I dodged his question and stood. Civilians also couldn't understand the complexities of war.

He sighed, like he half expected me not to respond, and swept his hand toward the path. "Lead the way."

I sprinted along the track, around the playground, and onto the next path that led away from the play area and disappeared into the vegetation. The bushes were so dense on the meandering path it made seeing ahead impossible.

Birds chirped. The golden hues in the sky above morphed to pink. Neon's pounding boots kept pace beside me.

I glared at him. "You sound like a damn horse."

He rolled his eyes. "Costume boots. They make them heavier for sound effects."

"Great."

His tight-fitting shirt was in a shiny material that resembled plastic, showing off the contours of his chest and revealing muscles beneath that material that I hoped were not fake.

I snapped my gaze away, pissed off that I was even considering what he had beneath that costume.

"Where are we going?" His croaky voice was gone.

"This way."

"Very funny."

"Well, how the fuck should I know, Neon? I landed on the island this morning, so I haven't had the luxury of scoping it out. And so far, you've been as useless as tits on a bull."

"Hey! I told you I was trying to help."

"So you said. You could help by telling me what's on the island."

"I only know the disgusting pool and the main hotel, but just the lobby and that accommodation section Derek dragged me into. And the other island with the demountable crew huts where I met you this morning."

I'd arrived at the island by boat that had been driven right up onto the secluded beach in a horseshoe-shaped bay. From there, I'd been escorted by Neon's manager, Marc, who had listed the dos and don'ts of being a bodyguard to a Hollywood movie star.

Do stay with him at all times.

Don't talk to him unless absolutely necessary.

Do not under any circumstances ask for a photo or autograph.

I remembered thinking that Zena was going to be pissed about that. Taking a photo of me with Neon Bloom had been her one and only request.

From that beach, Marc had led me over grass that looked like it had been trampled by a herd of elephants and onto a cracked pathway. That path had led to the crumbling bridge to the temporary accommodation sheds that had been set up on the narrow strip of land.

Once I'd put my bag into the room that I would be sharing with four other women, Marc took my phone off me and walked me to meet the man I was in charge of protecting. Neon Bloom had the last accommodation hut in the row. His was twice the size of mine, and yet he was the only person using it.

Marc had knocked on Neon's door. When the cocky playboy had opened it, he'd barely glanced in my direction.

He was looking at me now. Killing a man to save his life would have done that.

Men did not expect a woman like me to take lives.

During my tours of duty, by underestimating me, I'd been able to eliminate eight enemy targets in very close proximity, and five of them even saw me coming.

The path curved ahead of us, limiting our view even more. I hugged the left-hand side, utilizing the cover of the vegetation as much as possible. But if a bunch of gun-wielding men came running around the corner, we were screwed.

"What do these guys want, Neon?"

"Probably to kidnap me for a ransom." He spoke way too loudly.

"Lower your goddammed voice."

He grunted.

"Why did Marc take my phone off me?"

"It's Linda's instructions. She always takes the phones from everyone."

"Why?"

"She's paranoid about scenes being leaked before the movie is released."

A clearing appeared up ahead.

"Is it possible Marc's behind this?"

"I fucking hope not." The venom in his tone had me studying his handsome features.

Neon was movie star material. Straight nose. Cinnamon-colored lips that were perfectly contoured. Skin that was impossibly flawless. It was easy to see why he was Hollywood's most eligible bachelor.

Around the bend in the path, a building appeared. I raised my fist, indicating for Neon to stop. We eased into the side of the path behind a shrub that may have once formed part of a hedge.

The large building had a covered portico entrance and a side wall that only had one window at the very end. A mural that had once covered the entire wall was just about gone, but there was enough to recognize people laughing, colorful party balloons, and a wine bottle and wine glasses.

The building was dark and from our vantage point there was only one entry.

Shouts rang through the bushes behind us.

"Sounds like they found the body," I said.

Neon glanced at the path we'd run along and turned back to me with an odd smile. "They don't sound happy."

"Nope. Not at all. Dead comrades will do that." I grinned with him. "Let's go."

Leading the way, I headed for the front of the building. The entrance was wide open and the glass doors that had once been in position were now a mass of glass shards over the front portico.

We sprinted over the shattered glass and into a carpeted foyer covered in leaves, twigs, and other rubbish. One side of the foyer had a canteen offering food and drink, but the shelving was ruined and both doors on the glass fridge were cracked and dislodged.

A glass cabinet positioned on top of the front counter had popcorn printed across the lightbox. Inside, the popcorn that had rotted away over the years was now a disgusting green mess covered in mice shit.

On the other side of the room was another counter. Shoe and ball hire details were written on the sign above.

Beyond the entrance was a bowling alley with eight lanes, and at the front of each lane were circular seating areas. A couple of alleys looked like they'd stopped in the middle of a game. Bowling balls with dust all over them were lined up like cannon armory on a rack. A row of shoes suggested that six adults had been the last to use that lane.

The fabric on the custom-built seats was equal parts red material and green mold. Toppled wine glasses, beer bottles, and popcorn containers littered a glass table centered in the seating.

"We need to hide." I studied each of the side reception areas.

"Where?"

The front two areas were too small and too obvious to hide behind.

"Follow me." I sprinted along the front of the circular seating areas and at the last alley, I ran onto the timber bowling lane. Dust and paint flakes that had dislodged from the ceiling over the last couple of decades covered the smooth surface, making it even more slippery. Holding my hands out for balance, I ran toward the four bowling pins still standing at the end. I was halfway along when I realized my mistake. We were leaving a trail of footprints.

Too late.

At the end of the lane, I ducked under the scoreboard that had a crack through the glass and dodged around the bowling pins, careful not to knock them over. Neon slipped in behind me, and I was impressed with his flexibility.

"In here," a voice boomed behind us.

I grabbed Neon's wrist and yanked him into the dim area. A broken window in the distance provided just enough light to see mechanical arms, circular conveyor belts, and toppled bowling pins. It also created enough shadows to make us slow right down.

"Where'd they go?" The American man's voice reached us. It was a different tone from the two I'd heard earlier.

I led Neon around crates and slabs of plasterboard that had been eaten away by time and mice, or rats, that had left poop everywhere.

"Here. Down this way." It was another voice. That made at least three assholes.

"Come out, Neon. We have you surrounded." That was Derek.

A gun blast ricocheted off the dusty timber floors and shouts bounced around the place making it impossible to work out where the gunmen were.

If it was me and my team, we would spread out and converge on this rear area of the bowling alley together. Picturing that this was exactly what they were doing, I yanked Neon's wrist and dragged him deeper into the darkness.

Another window was in the distance but between it, and the one behind us, we had very little visibility. But this could play to our advantage.

At the end of each bowling lane was the mechanism to catch the bowling pins and turn them around, ready to use again. Underneath each of these devices was a crawl space of about two feet. I pointed at the gap and shoved Neon forward, indicating he climb in first.

To his credit, he didn't argue.

Once he was hidden from view, I pulled my gun from my holster and crawled in beside him until the warmth of his body was pressed against mine. Pulling my arms forward, I rested on my elbows with my gun ready. It wasn't an ideal stance for perfect aim, but I had no choice.

Neon's breathing was short and sharp, and his clamped teeth had the muscles along his jawline bulging. I wanted to tell him not to panic but couldn't risk talking, so I pressed my fingers to my lips.

Nodding, he made a gun symbol with his hands.

I shook my head. Last thing I needed was him setting off a gunfight with us wedged in like sardines.

My heart thundered in my ears and the dampness of my wet pants became cold on the floor.

Competing odors of dust and concrete invaded my senses. And I could smell Neon's divine cologne: pine and ocean scents mingled together. A fresh aroma that represented the wilderness somehow. It even smelled expensive.

Neon stiffened, and movement to my left snagged my attention. Silhouetted against the window in the distance, the stalker was just a shadow. It wasn't Derek. This guy was shorter than Neon's bodyguard and stockier, and he was either bald or had a baseball cap on backward. Crouching over, he held his weapon with both hands and walked with precision.

This guy was no dumb thug. He was a skilled operator.

If I was going to take him out, I'd have one chance. If I missed, all hell would break loose.

But without knowing where his accomplices were, it was a chance I was not willing to risk unless I was forced to.

"You see them?" Derek shouted from the end where Neon and I had come from. Unlike his friends, Derek was not demonstrating the same level of professionalism.

That made him the least of my concern.

But where was the third guy?

Another movement caught my eye. It zipped across the floor and stopped.

A spider. *No. No. No!*

It crawled toward us like it was drawn to our warmth. It was as big as my hand, and its body was the size of a fucking mouse.

"Roy, you got anything?" Derek's booming voice made both Neon and I jump.

"Will you fucking shut up, you moron?" Roy was barely ten feet away.

The spider shot forward again and then stopped. My heart thundered in my ears as I glared at it.

I clutched my gun.

I searched the darkness for the missing man.

I willed that spider to stay right where it was.

Beside me, Neon's leg jittered.

That spider was big, and I sure as hell did not want that thing crawling over me.

Especially when armed men were closing in on us.

The spider shot forward. I flinched.

Neon swiped it with his hand, sending the spider flying.

Roy swung his weapon toward us. I put a bullet through his brain. He flew backward, crashed through a jumble of equipment, and fell like a sack of potatoes. A bunch of bowling pins fell with him, clattering onto the concrete.

"Stay here," I hissed at Neon. I rolled out of my hiding place and crouched down.

Bullets pinged off metal and punched into the wall. Glass exploded.

The aim was so bad, I assumed it was Derek.

Where the hell was the third man? Clamping my jaw, I forced calm into my brain. I crouched behind a stack of milk crates filled with bowling pins, waiting for the missing man to appear or until I was forced to kill Derek.

My preference was to keep Derek alive. I needed his intel.

Bullets slammed into a wall and pierced a sheet of metal siding on the next bowling pin machine.

That's it, keep firing those damn bullets, you stupid shit.

A few more shots rang out. Then the gun clicked. He was out of ammunition.

I jumped out of my hiding place and aimed at Derek. He was also silhouetted against the minuscule sunlight from the window behind him.

Derek reached down his leg.

"Don't do it!" I yelled.

I had no idea if he was going for another gun, but I wasn't willing to risk it.

"Put your hands up, Derek."

His hands stayed at his side.

"Derek! Don't make me kill you."

He lowered his arm to his thigh. "You fucking bitch. Where's Neon?"

"Don't do anything stupid, Derek. It's not worth it." I shifted my aim from his head to his chest. The bigger target was more of a certainty in this light.

Derek froze.

I tensed.

"Maya!" Neon's cry was loaded with panic.

I spun around. As I dove sideways, I aimed at a man silhouetted in the distance and pulled the trigger. He dove away, firing his gun.

I crashed into the tower of milk crates, scattering the bowling pins in a thundering mess.

Scrambling for balance, I jumped to my feet. I hid behind a large gas tank and crouching down, I scanned the darkness for Derek, expecting him to be running my way. But he wasn't. It took a few beats to find him. He was flat on his back on the floor. Dead still.

Shit. The third man must've shot him. I wanted Derek alive.

At least I only had one asshole to deal with.

I peered around the tank and a bullet pinged off the gas cylinder, three inches from my hair. *Son of a bitch.* He had me cornered.

I strained to listen. Silence was so loud it screamed in my ears.

He waited for me to move. I waited for him. A Mexican standoff with deadly consequences.

But the bastard had no idea who he was dealing with. My aim was impeccable and my speed was excellent.

I planned my next move: dive out from my position, take aim, and shoot. It would be over before the bastard even blinked.

A shuffling noise added to the silence.

Is that Neon? He better stay where he is, or I'll shoot him myself.

"I'm here, you bastard." Neon's voice was loaded with cocky bravado.

Christ almighty. Does he have a death wish?

"I'm coming out. Don't shoot." Neon's voice bounced around the equipment.

God damn it! If he crawls out of that hiding spot, he'll be between me and the third man.

And that put me in a position I did not want to be in.

Chapter Eight

NEON

On my stomach, with barely any room to move, I dragged my body over dust-covered concrete.

The silence was incredible.

Where the hell was Maya?

Is she okay?

Two guns had been aimed at her. All because of me. It was my fault she was in danger. She was putting her life on the line for me, and she didn't even know me.

I had to stop this. I had to save Maya.

"I'm coming out. Don't shoot."

Where's the gunman? And Derek. Where's he?

Rage coursed through my veins like hot lava as I clawed sideways another two inches. I was so sick of being targeted by ruthless bastards. Sometimes I wondered if things would've been different if my parents hadn't paid that ransom when I was a kid. But if they hadn't, I wouldn't have survived another night in that hellhole.

Money had been the motivation for that kidnapping back then. It would be the same now.

But to get the cash ransom, they needed me alive.

I just hoped this gunman got that memo.

Once I was free of the hiding space, I crouched down and fished the gun from the back of my jeans. I'd held many fake weapons in my life. They didn't feel like this. This was heavy and cold.

I readied to put myself in the firing line. "Don't shoot. I'm coming out."

"Come out with your hands up." The American's voice boomed about the room.

I couldn't see him. I couldn't see Maya either.

Oh, God! She'd better be okay.

Clenching the gun, I hoped like hell I was making the right decision.

I rose to standing and peered over the top of the equipment toward where I thought the man was.

"Hands up," he hollered.

A gun exploded. The gunman flew backward and hit the concrete in a full body slam, spewing dust into the air. I spun around. Maya sprinted past me, stopped at the gunman, and aimed her weapon at his chest.

He didn't move.

She nudged him with her foot, then shaking her head, she turned to me. "Do you want to fucking die?"

"What the hell? I thought *you* were dead."

With her expression twisted into a scowl, she raced past me again and stopped at another body.

I studied the man on the ground. "Is that Derek?"

"Yep. His mate shot him."

"Really?"

"Caught in the crossfire, the stupid bastard. But now we still don't have anyone to interrogate. And we don't know how many of these assholes there are."

She strode back to me, holstered her gun, and put her hands on her hips, thrusting her magnificent tits toward me. "You have a real problem with following orders."

"Give me a break! I thought you were dead."

"If *I* was dead, they would have yanked you out of that hiding spot."

"I didn't know. Okay!"

She shook her head, and it pissed me off way more than it should have. I didn't know her, and she sure as hell didn't know me.

"How hard is it to keep one of these assholes alive?" She strode back to Derek and checked his pockets, but came up empty.

"These guys are pros, Neon. We're in some serious shit."

"Pros? In what way?"

She strode to the last man she'd shot. "They've emptied their pockets."

Frowning, I tried to understand the implications of that.

"It makes their bodies harder to identify," she clarified.

"Shit."

"Yeah. Shit, all right. These guys are prepared to die for this." She hit me with her blue eyes that were only just visible in the light. "Whatever *this* is."

She grabbed the weapon that had skidded across the floor when the gunman went flying. After tucking it into the back of her pants, she adjusted her shirt, again bulging her cleavage in a way that caught my attention way more than it should have. "Let's get out of here before their mates come looking for them."

With her leading the way, we exited the bowling alley by striding along the bowling lane at the opposite end to the one we'd arrived on.

At the shattered front doors, we paused to peer outside. The sun had slipped away and darkness had settled over the island. Stars dotted the blackness above, providing some light, but the moon was yet to make an appearance.

I tried to remember last night's moon, but I had zero recall. After the incident with Shane, I'd downed a bottle of Barossa Shiraz, which was a surprisingly good Aussie wine, and then I'd gone to bed alone wishing I was anywhere but this fucking abandoned island.

As I sprinted along another path with Maya at my side, I had a strange feeling we were destined to meet. It was weird. I'd never felt like that with a woman before. I'd never really had the chance. Many women threw themselves at me. They were pathetic.

Maya, however, was different. She looked at me like she'd rather spit on me than sleep with me. And that made her fascinating.

Another building materialized in the darkness ahead. Maya and I eased into the side of the path to study the layout. Again, it had no lights. This one was a different shape from the bowling alley. Two sides were visible, revealing a wide veranda with a timber railing along the length of it.

Unlike the last building, there were several entry points.

"What do you think? Is it safe?" I asked.

Maya blinked at me like she was surprised I sought her opinion. It surprised the heck out of me too.

"Only one way to find out." She pulled her gun from her holster. "Stick with me and stay frosty."

"Stay frosty?"

Was she kidding?

"Yes, keep cool and stay alert."

She wasn't kidding.

Leading the way, she aimed for the four timber steps to the side veranda. She bounded up them like a gymnast. I stomped onto the first step, and my foot went right through the timber. Pain ripped up my shin.

I cried out. "Shit."

Barbs of ancient timber clawed at my flesh, pinning my leg like a snared animal.

With her gun raised, Maya peered through what was left of the windows.

Excruciating pain speared in two directions, up my leg and to my toes. Warm liquid oozed down my ankle. Blood.

"Jesus, Bloom." Maya squatted on the veranda. "You sure like to do things the hard way."

"Give me a break." I hoped it was dark enough that she couldn't see the agony on my face.

She shifted to the next step down and rested her hand on my knee. "Can you pull it out?"

I tried to lift my leg but winced. The downward angle of the splinters dug deeper into the wound. "Damn it. It's stuck."

"Okay, don't panic."

"I'm not panicking," I hissed.

"Your tone proves you are."

Christ! I clamped my jaw, but rather than fire the retort on my tongue, I channeled the bravery she showed when she was stung by that jellyfish.

She shifted closer, and I breathed in the apple scent of her hair. It was like a refreshing tonic after the dust from the bowling alley.

"Hold still." She clutched my leg below my knee for support, and using the butt of her gun, she bashed the jagged splinters downward.

Clenching my jaw, I fought the torture by imagining what Maya had beneath that navy shirt. Firm breasts. Toned stomach—

"Shit," I hissed.

"Sorry." She didn't sound sorry. "Try now."

I raised my leg slowly, twisting it slightly as I lifted. Once the top of my boot appeared, I pulled the rest of the way out.

"Good stuff. Let's get inside and take a look." She curled her arm around my waist to support me, and I was struck by her tenderness. Maya had been all army precision so far. This nurturing side was new.

And fucking sexy.

I hobbled through the doorway and into a bar that looked like it was made for a 1960s Western movie. Tiny, mirrored squares that must have been on the disco ball dangling above covered the central dance floor.

A massive bar stretched the full length of the left-hand side of the building. The mirror along the back wall was miraculously still intact and enough light penetrated from outside to see our reflections.

From the dance floor, I hobbled to a carpeted area that was sticky under my boots. There was probably twenty years of animal piss on that carpet, *and* whatever had been spilled on it prior to the resort being abandoned.

With her arm around my waist, we dodged around toppled bar stools and settled at a table with four dining chairs that were thankfully made of metal and looked sturdy enough to hold my weight.

"Sit here," she ordered. She strode away, possibly to scout the area.

I sat and pulled the leg of my jeans above the wounds.

Although I could barely see the damage, it looked like I'd been attacked by a tiger. Striped gashes ran from halfway down my shin to the top of my boot. I touched the jagged flesh and winced. I hoped to Christ

I didn't need stitches because that was not going to happen any time soon.

I searched for Maya but couldn't see her. Maybe she was checking the perimeter? Her professionalism was impressive. A thousand times better than any bodyguard I'd had over the years, including Shane who'd been with me for a long time.

His sudden departure was probably a stroke of luck because he would never have fended off those attackers like Maya had.

Where is she?

I searched the nightclub, but I was all alone. Usually that was my preference, but not when a sexy bodyguard was my alternative. Maya had already proved she was so much more than hired protection, though. Her skills went beyond anything I'd ever seen.

I bet her story was much more fascinating than any woman I'd met.

Over the top of the bar, copper piping threaded like some kind of ancient heating system. Rows and rows of glasses still hung upside down over the bar counter.

To my right was an old jukebox that would probably be worth a lot of money, despite its decrepit state. For many years, I collected old twelve-inch LP vinyl records. Then collectors clued onto my passion and became greedy with their attempts to sell me rare albums. It was like everything I showed an interest in. Just when I thought I knew a person enough to trust them, they would do something that ruined that illusion.

Maya appeared out of the dimness, hooking her gun away as she strode toward me. "We're safe at the moment."

She squatted at my leg and gently lifted it onto the other seat. "Jesus, Neon. You've made a mess of yourself."

"Thanks."

She rolled my leg to check the back of my calf. "You need stitches."

"You think so?"

"I know so."

"Oh." Random questions rushed through me at once. How was she so certain? How could she be so calm? Why did she smell so damn good?

70

"I was a medic in the army," she said. Maybe she'd sensed my confusion.

"Oh." For someone who had to use dialogue for a living, I was struggling with mine. Maya was messing with me in ways that had eluded me for a long time.

Maybe forever.

She tilted my leg the other way, shaking her head. "I need to find water to clean this wound."

"I'm okay."

She placed her hand on my shoulder. "No, you're not. Last thing you want is infection to set in. Trust me on that."

"You must have seen some horrific injuries in the army."

She tilted her head. "Yeah. You could say that."

I wanted to touch her. Her cheek. Her hair. Her boobs. I nearly chuckled at that. Maya would tackle me to the ground like she'd done to that man on the path.

Then again, maybe I'd like that.

She stood, bringing her perky breasts to eye level.

It was a few beats before I dragged my eyes away, but when I glanced up, her cocky expression said she'd caught me checking her out.

I couldn't decide if that was a good or bad thing.

"Keep your leg elevated and try to calm your breathing."

"I'm calm."

"Hmm."

"Hmm, what?" I frowned at her.

"Just making sure you're not acting."

"No. I'm calm."

"Okay, let me see if I can find anything behind the bar to help." She strode away, and I was treated to a couple of seconds of her sexy ass before I couldn't see her at all.

My wounds stung and throbbed in waves that went up and down my leg at the same time. I had been a stuntman for many years and had suffered my share of injuries. Gashes on my left hip and shoulder blade that had to be stitched back together. A broken toe that hurt like a bitch. Dozens of scrapes and bruises.

But nothing as serious as this.

I was lucky to have Maya with me. She'd said she was an army medic, but her fighting skills convinced me she was much more than a medic.

She returned carrying a large metal bowl.

"Did you find water?" I asked.

"Amazingly the taps did run, but the water smelled rusty, so we can't risk it. I could barely see in there. But I did find some food."

"You're joking, right?"

She held something up in both hands. "Canned food."

"Ummm."

"They're canned. So, they'll be fine."

"You know this place has been abandoned for twenty years, right?"

"Yes. But I'm starving. Desperate times . . ." She plonked the cans on the table.

"I'll pass, thanks."

"Your loss. I'll open them in a minute. What are you wearing under that shirt?"

Frowning, I tried to recall what I'd put on before the sun rose this morning. I shook my head. "Nothing."

"That'd be right." She undid the buttons on her shirt.

"Hello. This is taking nurse Maya to another level."

"In your dreams, buddy." She peeled open her shirt, and as I peered in the darkness, desperately wishing I had more light, she draped her shirt over the back of a second chair.

"Close your eyes, Neon."

"I can't see anyth—"

"Close your eyes," she ordered.

"All right, bossy boots."

She giggled, and the sound was delightful.

I wanted to peek, but it was pointless. We were in near darkness anyway. "Can I look yet?"

"Wait."

A zipper sounded, and I pictured her stepping out of her cargo pants. What was she doing?

"Okay, you can look now."

Maya was on her knees, next to my leg. It looked like she had her navy shirt back on.

"Help me out here." She handed me a warm, white cloth. She must've been wearing this beneath her shirt. It took all my might not to sniff it.

"Hold my shirt out like this." With gentle but firm hands, she folded my fingers over the fabric and tugged my hands apart. "Hold it tight."

I pulled the shirt tight, and she sliced her knife down the middle of the white fabric.

"What're you doing?"

"Making a bandage. Hold this section now." She carved the shirt again. Repeating the process, she made two large sections and two narrow strips.

"Sorry you had to wreck your shirt."

"I'll live. It's touch and go for you though."

I chuckled.

"I'm serious, Neon. You put yourself in danger back there."

"Fucking hell, Maya. Why can't you understand why I did that? I couldn't hear you and I sure as hell couldn't see you. I didn't know if you were alive or dead. You took off like a maniac. Seems to me like you're the one with a death wish."

She draped the cloth around my leg, added the second strip, and pulled tight.

I winced and shuddered at the pain. "Shit. Careful."

"Sorry. Did that hurt?"

"What do you think? You're the medic."

"Sorry." She genuinely sounded sorry that time.

She draped her warm hand over my leg and squeezed. "From now on, unless you confirm I'm dead, I want you to believe I'm alive. Okay? No more negative thoughts."

"Man, you're stubborn."

"Men have trouble listening to me, so I need to be."

"You don't even know me, Maya, so don't lump me in with every other asshole you know."

"I'm not. I'm basing my opinion on the four times you've gone against my instructions already."

"Four times? You were counting?"

After draping the second section of fabric around my leg, she tugged it in position with the second strip of bandage. She was much gentler that time. "That's the best I can do for now. But Neon, this wound is pretty bad. You need to get these stitched ASAP."

"The crew always has first aid supplies, but they are probably in one of the accommodation sheds."

"That's around the opposite side of the island. It's pitch-black outside, and after what happened to your leg, it's too dangerous to walk around out there in the dark."

"What are we going to do?"

Maya cruised her hand over my shoulder, and my heart thumped like I'd done a hundred-yard dash. "We'll settle here for a while and hope the moon comes up. Was it up last night?"

I shook my head, but then realizing she couldn't see, I said, "I can't remember."

She reached for the canned food. "Let's see if these are edible?"

"What's in them?"

"I think the label said tomato soup, so we'll see."

"Ah, you go first."

"Thanks," she said, all chirpy as she stabbed her knife into the top of the can. The tin squeaked as she worked her blade around the rim. She raised the jagged lid and sniffed the contents.

"And . . .?"

"Smells like tomato soup. You smell." Her fingers brushed mine as she passed the can toward me. "Watch the lid. It's sharp."

I sniffed the contents. "Huh. It does smell like tomatoes. Doesn't mean it's edible."

A metallic sound indicated she was fishing around in the metal bowl again.

"You're not seriously going to eat that?"

"Of course. You've probably never been starving in your life, have you?"

I hated her question and the way she asked it, like she knew everything about me. She didn't. I knew exactly what it was like to be starving, but that was a time in my life that I'd been trying to forget forever. I sure didn't want to share it with Maya.

A sipping noise confirmed she really was eating from the ancient can.

"How is it?"

"Tastes like tomato soup. Here, try." She shoved the can across the table toward me.

I collected the spoon she'd put near my hand and as I rubbed it on my shirt to clean it, I heaved a breath.

She huffed and set about opening a second can. "If you're not going to eat it, I will."

"Man, you're bossy."

Maya giggled and it was the sweetest, most genuine laugh I'd heard in a long time. Maybe ever. In my industry, fake laughter came with the territory. Everyone liked to pretend they were having a good time.

"You haven't even seen me get pushy, Neon." She peeled open the top of the second can.

I chuckled with her, and damn it felt good.

I dipped the spoon into the can, sniffed again, then took a tiny slurp onto my tongue. "Huh. You're right. It does taste okay."

"Yep. Now eat up. We have no idea where our next meal is coming from."

I shifted my wounded leg to the floor to adjust my seat closer to the table.

"Neon. Did you just lower your leg?"

"Yeah."

"I told you to keep it elevated. What is your problem with following instructions?"

I couldn't tell if she was serious or joking, but I raised my leg onto the chair anyway.

"I bet you were a naughty boy as a kid," Maya said.

I resisted answering. My childhood was split by one defining moment. Before that, I was just a young kid oblivious to the dangers in the world. After that, though, I knew more than any nine-year-old boy should ever know.

Only a handful of people knew what happened, and I had no intentions of sharing it with a woman who seemed to have a low opinion of me.

Shifting my focus off my childhood nightmare, I forced every spoonful of that soup into my mouth. I forgot about it being a twenty-year-old can of food and finished the entire contents. "I didn't realize how hungry I was."

"Adrenalin does that." She put her can into the bowl and returned her knife to the sheath on her waist.

"I guess so."

"I know so."

My last meal was before sunrise. During today's scenes, I could have eaten a mountain of food, all prepared by a professional five-star chef. It had been one of Camilla's demands. She was so damn fussy, and calorie counted everything she put in her mouth.

Camilla! Oh my god, she was shot. "Maya, do you think Camilla is dead?"

"Camilla?"

"My co-star, the woman I was with when Derek took me. He shot her."

Maya placed her hand over my wrist. "I don't know. I'm sorry. I was only watching you."

I nodded, not that she would have noticed. "I'm grateful you were. If it had been Shane protecting me, I'd be screwed."

"Who's Shane?"

"The guy you replaced."

A low hum thrummed from her throat.

"What?" I asked.

"Is there a possibility Shane is behind this?"

I huffed. "I doubt it."

I told Maya about what happened on the bridge. That already felt like days ago.

"Okay, you're right, it sounds like a pure coincidence that he was taken off the island the night before the attack. What about Derek? What's his story?"

"About six months ago, when Allan resigned, Marc hired Derek."

"What's his history?"

"I don't know. Marc handles all of that. You know, now that I think of it, Allan's departure was strange."

"In what way?"

"Allan told me many times how much he needed the job and how much he loved it. Yet one day he just didn't turn up for work and sent his resignation via a text message."

"Sounds like he's someone you should have a chat with once we get through this."

"If we get through this."

"There you go with the negative vibes, Neon."

"Come on, Maya. We're outnumbered. And we have no idea how many more gunmen are out there."

"No, we don't. But they never factored me into their plans." She pushed back on her chair. "Stay here and keep that leg up."

"Where are you going?"

"Just checking things out."

"Yeah, well, don't go making me save your ass again."

"Ha!" She giggled. "Is that what you call it?"

I could only just make out her shape as she headed toward the front entrance of the bar. Once she disappeared, a weird silence settled over the room like a dense fog. I hated silence because my mind would plunge into the extreme silence that had smothered me when I had been held captive all those years ago.

Instead, my mind did something nice for a change and provided lovely images of Maya. Her rosy cheeks. Her incredible eyes framed with long black lashes. Her throwing that man, who was nearly twice her size, over her shoulder.

Maya was a real woman, and after this was over, I wanted to get to know a whole lot more about her.

A deep growl filled the silence.

I shot my gaze about the darkness. *What the hell was that?*

"Maya, are you there?"

Another animal growled outside, deeper and longer.

Is that a dog?

It didn't sound like any dog I'd ever heard.

Was it a bear? *Do they have bears in Australia?*

Two growls, deep and ferocious, carved through the silence.

Shit! Are they dingoes?

During our briefing about the island, we were informed about the rock wallabies, iguanas, and the abundant species of birds, and as a side note they mentioned the wild dingoes. *Do not feed them. And whatever you do, do not try to touch them.*

Another menacing growl was paired with one more. The hairs on my neck stood to attention. I searched the table for a weapon and had a choice between the large metal bowl and the empty soup cans.

"Maya! Where are you?" I yelled.

"Jesus, Neon. Are you trying to tell those assholes where we are?" She appeared as a shadow next to my shoulder. "What's wrong?"

"We've got some dingoes for company."

As if on cue, a dingo released a long mournful howl like it had lost a lifelong partner. A few more of them, still out of sight, growled and snarled. It grew louder and more ferocious. They sounded like there was a large pack of them right outside the window.

"Shit. Okay, we need to get our backs against a wall. Can you walk?"

"Yes, I'm fine. Can I put my leg down?"

She slapped my shoulder.

"Wise ass." She grabbed my hand. "Let's go into the kitchen behind the bar."

I was surprised by how much pain coursed up my leg with each step. Hopefully I didn't need to do any running, or I was screwed.

I hobbled behind Maya as she wove into the bar area. We entered through an open doorway to another room that was even darker than the room we'd exited.

"There might be some knives or other things in here we can use to fend them off," Maya said.

"Or you could shoot them."

Maya gasped. "Three things. Dingoes are a protected species. And I would never kill an animal."

"Not even to save me?"

"No. Animal first, you next."

"Right. It's good to know where I sit in the pecking order. And what's the third thing?"

"I don't need to draw any attention to where we are."

"Right. Good thinking."

"At least one of us is. Now shush and see what you can find to throw at those dogs if they come in here."

As I felt along the counter, my fingers skipped over inch-thick dust and piles of lumps that were probably animal shit. The area smelled dirty and moldy, just like the disgusting lagoon pool that was as green as a swamp. It was likely food had rotted to dust in this kitchen.

From what I'd seen of the resort, only the bare minimum had been salvaged after the resort was abandoned. It was like they just closed the doors and walked away.

But even then, many doors were open.

"I found a couple of salt shakers and some huge pepper grinders," Maya said.

I moved faster, trying to find something useful. As I explored higher, my hand clipped a row of pots dangling below a shelf. They clanged together like a church bell that needed some serious tuning. "How about some pots?"

"That will work. Put them on the counter so we can grab them easily."

A dingo's angry snarl shredded the silence.

"Shit!" I stiffened. "Where is it?"

"I can't see a damn thing."

A second growl joined the first. Then another. Three became six. A dozen.

They were in the building.

Maya pulled me toward her, and I hobbled on my injured ankle.

"Fuck! Do you think they can smell my bloody wound?"

She clutched my arm. "That's absolutely what they can smell. So, keep quiet or we're in deep shit."

Chapter Nine

MAYA

The urge to use my gun to scare off the dogs was huge. But if they had the scent of Neon's blood, we were already in trouble. I pulled out my knife. I would kill a dingo, but only if absolutely necessary.

The growling grew louder. As my heart pounded in my ears, I pictured a pack of wild beasts creeping behind the bar, right outside the kitchen doorway.

In the blackness, I rummaged for something else to use as a weapon. I brushed a cylindrical item and thought it was another salt shaker. But it had a softer feel. Wax. A candle. I found another, and several more.

Maybe there are matches.

Neon would've left a trail of blood all over the carpet out there. That was what had the wild dogs in a frenzy. Thank God I'd covered Neon's leg before we came into the kitchen.

I'd thought Neon would freak out once I told him the dingoes could smell his blood. But he was quiet. His wounds were nasty, and they would sting like crazy. The cuts were deep and needed urgent treatment, or the consequences could be deadly.

Just like the pack of dingoes. And the assholes trying to kidnap him.

You're going to love this gig, Zena had said. *It'll be a walk in the park compared to your other missions.*

She couldn't have been further from the truth.

A dog yelped like it had been bitten, and I pictured it scampering away from the leader of the pack.

All my previous missions had been done as part of a team. This solo bullshit was not for me. I loved knowing someone had my back.

Feeling across the counter, I found a small heavy block. It was made of metal and fit into the palm of my hand. The top flipped up. "Hey, I found a lighter."

"Great."

I tried to ignite the flame a few times, but nothing happened. "Shit. It's out of gas."

"Let me try."

I held the lighter forward, searching for Neon's hand. Our fingers brushed, and I was surprised by the warmth of his palm as he grasped the lighter from me.

A low growl invaded our space.

A dingo was in the kitchen with us.

Dread zipped up my spine.

I reached for Neon, and we nudged backward together.

I fumbled along the counter for a large pepper grinder and gripped it like a baton.

Neon stepped in front of me, maybe trying to protect me. His breathing was short and sharp.

A fierce growl erupted from right in front of us. A dog snarled, as did another. Teeth gnashed together. Their growls were ferocious. Deadly. They smelled of rotten meat and dog shit.

"Jesus, how many are there?" Neon hissed.

"I don't know." It sounded like twenty.

Neon cried out. He fell to the floor, slamming into my knees. "It's got my leg!"

"Shit!" I threw the pepper shaker, grabbed a heavy saucepan, and climbed over Neon. "Neon! Duck!"

I had no idea if he followed my instructions this time, but I swung that saucepan back and forward like a tennis racket. It slammed into something.

A dingo yelped and seemed to cry as it scampered away.

I hit another. It howled and whimpered as it ran off. I kept swinging, over and over, each time stepping forward. I stopped at the doorway, and a dingo howled in the distance as if calling his pack to give up the fight.

When the dingo stopped howling, silence fell over the derelict bar again.

I raced into the kitchen. "Neon. Are you okay?"

I reached for him.

He clutched my hand as I tugged him upright. "Are they gone?"

"For now. Yes." I put the saucepan on the counter.

"Jesus! That was close."

"Did it bite you?"

"No, worse. It tore my jeans."

"What?" I giggled.

"I'm serious. I love these jeans."

I slapped his chest. "Well, now, you can keep them as a souvenir of the fourth time I saved your life."

"Four. I don't think so."

"Yep, sure is. I'm asking for a pay raise."

He chuckled, and it was natural and fun.

I curled my hand around his back. "Come on, let's get out of here before those dingoes come back for another go."

Neon flicked the lighter, making tiny sparks color the darkness. He did it again and a flame glowed from the top. "It works."

"Quick, light one of these candles." I snatched a candle off the counter, and he lit the wick.

A warm glow filled the room. We lit another two candles. He clicked the lid on the lighter and slotted it into his pocket in a slick practiced move.

"What?" He caught me watching him.

"Did they teach you that move in Hollywood?"

"What move?"

"That sexy lighter maneuver."

"Oh, you thought that was sexy."

"No, I'm just saying that move with the lighter . . .. It was kind of corny, don't you think?"

"But you said sexy." His grin took my breath away.

"Yes, and now I'm saying corny."

He bumped his hip to mine. "It's okay, you can call me sexy."

"Pfft. In your dreams, hotshot." I blew out one candle and shoved it into my pocket for later use.

"Hotshot now."

I rolled my eyes. "Jeez, maybe I won't save your ass next time."

"You will. You can't help yourself."

"Actually, you have that right. Now grab a weapon. Let's go." I plucked a frying pan off the counter, grabbed a lit candle, and marched toward the door.

At the bar, I peered over the top, searching for movement outside, but the glow from my candle stopped me from seeing any further than about two feet.

Neon gasped behind me, and I spun to him. Pain drilled across his expression.

"Hey, are you okay?" I asked.

"Yeah. I'm good."

"You don't look good."

"Gee, thanks." His shoulders sagged.

"I mean the leg."

"Oh, so the rest of me looks good." He winked.

I jerked back. "Wow, are you always this cocky?"

"Never."

"That's not what I heard."

"Really, what did you hear?" He drove his hand through his thick hair.

"Will you just be quiet? I'm trying to save your ass here." I hooked my arm around his waist. "Lean on me for support."

"Yes, boss."

"That's better. And don't you forget it."

Side by side, we hobbled out of the bar, holding our candles in front of us.

At the entrance, I removed my arm. "Stay here."

I blew out his candle.

"Hey, what did you do that for?"

"With that flame you might as well have a giant target painted on your chest."

"What about yours?" He nodded at my candle.

"I'm quicker than you. Now stay here, keep quiet, and try not to get eaten. Or shot."

"Yeah, well, no promises on either of those." He rolled his eyes like another attack was a foregone conclusion.

I was perplexed over how calm he was. I didn't know too many civilians who would handle this mess like he was. I certainly didn't expect a Hollywood movie star to downplay the attacks, and his wounds.

If anything, I thought he'd be the opposite.

Cupping the candle flame, I strode along the side veranda that I'd already ventured across a couple of times. In its heyday, this bar would've had magnificent views over the lush gardens that were now so overgrown it was impossible to make out the individual trees.

The back of the building had another veranda that was longer and wider than the side ones, and its view was over the ocean. When we'd first arrived at the bar and I'd done my rounds, the setting sun had provided enough light to orientate myself. The direction the sun had set was where Risky Shores was—a good forty miles away.

That was where most of my team was too. But they might as well have been in Sydney because without my phone, I had no way to contact them.

Zena had booked me with Neon's manager for three days. So, she wouldn't think anything was suspicious if I didn't call her until my contract was over.

That meant either Neon and I had to wait out the three days until Zena started to question my absence, or we had to take control of the situation before it took control of us.

I returned to Neon. "Hey, you're still alive."

He chuckled. "Yeah, it's a goddamned miracle."

"Do you think you can walk?" I lit his candle with my flame.

"Yep. I'm good. Lead the way."

Rather than risk the steps Neon had crashed through earlier, I shielded my flame with my hand and led him along the veranda to the side exit. "Watch the steps. Stay on the edge."

Neon hopped down the stairs and we stepped onto a path that was nearly consumed with overgrown plants.

Neon eased in beside me. "Where are we going?"

I pointed ahead. "I think this path will lead us back to the resort. And if we don't run into any bad guys, hopefully we can find something to stitch your wounds."

He sucked air through his teeth.

I glanced at him over my shoulder. "You okay?"

"Yes. Except for the part where you stitch me up."

"Don't be such a pussy."

He glared at me. "I'm not a pussy."

"Don't worry, it won't hurt any more than when you did it."

"Well, that hurt a lot."

"Exactly." I flashed him a grin.

He rolled his eyes. "You're crazy."

"You only just figured that out?"

Another narrower path peeled away from the main one but disappeared into the darkness.

"Where does that go?" Neon asked.

I cocked my head. "Let me polish my crystal ball, shall I?"

"Huh." He studied me like he had something profound to say.

"Huh, what?"

"Nothing." In the candlelight, the intensity in his gaze had my stupid heart fluttering. That never happened. "Don't go trying to analyze me, Neon. That will get you nowhere."

"Only if you give me the same luxury." The corners of his mouth lifted into a slight smile, and it was so damn cute I imagined he'd practiced it in the mirror dozens of times.

"Done," I said. "No analyzing Neon Bloom. Noted."

"You're a funny one, Maya."

"Likewise, Neon."

We ducked beneath a thick branch that crossed over the path. On the other side was a large mound of gray fur. Whatever the creature had been, it must have died some time ago. We gave that a wide berth and carried on, heading into absolute darkness.

"I'm guessing the moon didn't come up last night," he said.

"Never know, we may still get lucky."

Another smaller pathway led off our main one, but Neon didn't ask about this one.

Voices carved through the darkness. I blew out our candles and shoved Neon onto the smaller path. Clutching his hand, I dragged him into a bush that had spikes stabbing my back. I pulled the gun from my waist holster and strained to listen to where the voices were coming from.

The voices got louder. Two men at least.

"—getting sick of searching this island."

"Stop your bitching."

"I'm serious. I thought we would have found him by now."

"He'll turn up. It's not like he can go anywhere."

"But without him, the plan is fucked."

"Quit your fucking worrying. We've factored in delays."

Their voices became muffled, and I closed my eyes, concentrating on sound only.

"—work out who that bitch is?"

They were talking about me.

"Supposed to be a bodyguard, but I don't know—"

"How did he find her so quickly?"

"Risky Shores, but it seems weird to me."

I snapped my eyes open. Shit. They knew where I was from. That could put my whole team in danger.

A beam flared through the bushes. A flashlight.

We needed that flashlight.

I squeezed Neon's arm, hoping he understood I wanted him to stay right where he was.

With my gun in one hand and the frying pan in the other, I inched back along the route toward the main pathway that seemed to circum-navigate the island. Although I didn't know where we were in relation to the central resort, I had the impression we were close. If I fired my weapon, we'd have the whole army of kidnappers storming toward us.

"Bloom will come when he's starving."

"Yeah, fucking bastard was always getting his meals served to him on a platter. I'm going to kick his teeth out when he comes begging for food."

They know Neon personally.

Maybe the whole damn film crew was in on this kidnapping.

That meant I couldn't trust anyone but Neon.

The circle of light from their flashlight revealed where they were. I frowned. If they were trying to find Neon, they were making it damn easy for me to both hear and see them coming.

Either they were as dumb as dog shit, or they were only pretending to do their job.

Or this was a trap.

I needed to keep these bastards alive so I could find out what the hell was going on.

With my heart pounding in my chest, I holstered my gun, but left the clip undone, and clutched the frying pan in my right hand. One man lit a cigarette, and the orange glow pinpointed exactly where his head was. If I had my sniper rifle, he'd be dead by now.

"I'm already sick of this place." The tip of the cigarette flared.

"Just shut up, will ya? Sloan knows what he's doing. Stick to the plan and we'll be rich."

Sloan! At least we now had the name of the man in charge.

If I could get hold of my team, Cobra could track known criminals with that name. By the size of this operation, I was guessing these guys had some history.

Slinking into the shadows, I made myself as small as possible as the men strode past the intersection of our two pathways.

I counted to three. Then, I jumped out and smashed the frying pan over the head of the smoker. The cigarette went flying as he tumbled into the bushes. The second man spun to me and snatched the pan from my hands.

I rammed my foot into his groin, and he buckled over with a howl.

I aimed my gun at his temple. "Don't move."

The asshole grabbed my wrist, pushing the gun upward. I drove my knee into his balls again. Crying out, he jerked forward, and his head smashed into my forehead.

Stars danced across my eyes and my feet wobbled beneath me.

An arm thrust around my neck.

My gun was gone. I clawed at the arm strangling me as the man lifted my feet off the ground.

Punching over my shoulder, I aimed for his head and connected with something. He barely flinched. His grip on my neck tightened.

I couldn't breathe.

Without any traction on my legs, my counterattack was pathetic.

I jabbed my fingers over my head, hoping to take out his eyeball with my fingernail.

He squeezed tighter.

Changing plans, I reached down, raised my leg, and unhooked the clip on my thigh holster.

He yanked me sideways, maybe knowing I was going for my second gun.

I kicked and clawed. I rammed my elbows backward.

The man was a beast. My fight grew weak. I gasped for air.

Oh, God. I'm in trouble.

"Neon!" My voice was barely a whisper.

I scratched at the arm around my neck. "Neon. Help!"

A massive clang reverberated about the bushes. The man holding me crumbled like a sack of potatoes. We hit the concrete as a tangle of arms and legs.

I sucked precious air into my lungs.

Neon stood over the attacker. Pointing with the frying pan, he said, "You shouldn't hurt women."

He pulled his shoulders back and smiled at me like he was playing out a scene in a movie.

I shook my head, holding back a chuckle. "Thank you."

He helped me to my feet. "Are you okay?"

"I am now." I rubbed my neck.

"You needed my help that time. Right?"

"Yes. You did okay. And we didn't kill anyone."

"Okay? That was better than okay."

"You want a medal?"

"No."

I plucked the flashlight out of the bushes, found my weapon and holstered it, then shone the light into the face of the smoker guy I'd hit first. He didn't even flinch. "Do you know him?"

Neon came in beside me. "He looks familiar, but I'm not sure."

"By what he was saying, he seemed to know you."

A frown crinkled Neon's forehead. "We have hundreds of crew with every movie, so who knows? Maybe I've worked with him in the past."

I shone the flashlight on the second guy, and again Neon shook his head.

The two men were out cold, yet neither of them had any blood. My victim, though, had a massive lump over his cheekbone that could mean a broken bone. I felt no remorse.

I checked for a pulse on both men. "They're alive, but they're going to have nasty headaches when they wake up."

"Good." Neon smirked, and I had the impression he was enjoying himself. Maybe he thought it was like one of his movies.

"Help me drag them off this pathway." I grabbed the arm that had been around my neck. If Neon hadn't whacked him when he did, I would have passed out. So maybe I did have someone covering my back after all.

We dragged the guy who had nearly strangled me along the narrower pathway, then repeated the move with the second guy and dumped his body beside the first.

I handed Neon the flashlight and squatted down to fish through their pockets. Easing back, I shook my head. Nothing other than their weapons. The flashlight, though, was a good score.

I kicked the knee of one man, but he still didn't move. "We need to find something to tie them up before they wake."

Neon shone the light along the path that disappeared into vegetation. "Must be something at the end of this path."

"Lead the way then."

Neon hobbled ahead of me.

"How's your leg?"

"Fine. How's your neck?"

"I'll live."

The end of the path was barely twenty feet away and it met with a little bungalow that had become host to a vine that was doing its best to conceal the timber building.

Three little steps met with a veranda that ran the length of the front of the building. The front door was shut and locked.

"Stand back." I kicked the door and it split into about sixteen pieces.

"Jeez, I hope I never get on your cranky side."

I flashed him a smile. "Got you worried?"

"Yep."

"Good. Give me that." I snatched the flashlight from him and stepped over the shattered doorway.

The bungalow was decorated with plush furnishings and colorful patterns that were so eclectic that they somehow went together. But it was like stepping back in time. Unlike the buildings we'd seen so far, this one seemed to have remained intact. No water damage was visible, and the vegetation that was trying to take over the building on the outside had failed to penetrate the interior.

I played the flashlight around the room and my heart skipped a beat. The wallpaper was exactly the same as the wallpaper that was in the room where my sister had died.

Memories crashed through me like a tsunami. My feet froze to the floor.

Neon's voice drifted to me but it was like I was stuck in a cloud.

Emotions swelled through me, and my heart just about cracked in two as the last words my sister ever said to me echoed through my brain.

They're all liars, Maya. All of them.

"Maya. Maya. Are you okay?"

Neon draped his hand over my arm, yanking me back from visions of Lily's bloodshot eyes.

"Hey." Neon squeezed my hand. "What's wrong?"

I shook my head, trying to cast the horror free. "I'm okay."

"You don't look it. Did that guy hurt you?"

"No. No." I cleared my throat. "Did you find something to tie them up?"

Neon indicated toward velvet rope that was used to loop the curtains in place.

"Perfect. But so is this place. Let's drag them in here and tie them up. When they wake, we'll get some answers out of them."

Working together, Neon and I pulled the two men into the little bungalow. Forcing my gaze away from that wallpaper, we tied both men facing away from each other, with their hands behind their backs and their feet bound together.

Those two were not going anywhere.

Now we just had to wait until they woke.

"Let's check out the rest of this place," I said.

Using the flashlight, we went along a hallway to a bedroom with a double bed draped in pretty floral linen. It looked like housekeeping had prepared the room that morning.

A wave of exhaustion crashed through me.

"I'm okay to watch those two if you want to take a rest." Neon studied me and I felt like he was trying to read my mind.

I hoped not. I wasn't in a good headspace at this moment.

"I'm serious," Neon said. "If anything happens, I'll wake you."

It was tempting, but after seeing that wallpaper, if I went to sleep, I'd probably dream about Lily. I already had enough problems without adding my guilt over my sister's death to the mix.

"Let's check out what else is here." I strode from the bedroom.

We entered a bathroom with a spa bath big enough for six adults. Candles, fake flowers, and little shampoo bottles were lined up on the window ledge.

We left the bathroom and after a quick check on our captives, who were still unconscious, we walked to a lounge area. Sofas had been positioned to look outside large glass doors. Before the vegetation went wild, I imagined it would have had a spectacular view over the ocean.

A chunky television rested on a cabinet, a record player stood in the corner, and there were also cushions and a rug and a coffee table. All in pristine condition.

The kitchen was bigger than the one I had at home.

Neon and I gravitated toward the fridge, and we chuckled as we both reached for the handle simultaneously.

Neon stepped back. "Ladies first."

Grinning at him, I tugged open the door. It looked like the fridge had been stocked the day the island had been deserted. It had cans of baked beans and jars of jam and vegemite and a plastic tub of margarine. On the bottom shelf were trays topped with green and black blobs that were growing their own fur. The top shelf had barbecue sauce, a mustard jar, and honey that was rock solid.

In the door was beer and wine.

I reached for the XXXX beer. "Thirsty?"

"I'm willing if you are."

In the kitchen drawers, we found a bottle top opener and cracked open the lids on both the beers. As if choreographed, Neon and I sniffed the liquid first.

"Still smells like beer," I said.

Neon raised his perfectly trimmed eyebrows. "These could be worth money. Maybe they're a vintage collection."

I took a sip and it somehow tasted both bitter and sweet.

Neon sipped too and scrunched up his nose. He was probably used to drinking hundred-dollar bottles of wine. Or even five-hundred-dollar bottles.

"Is it okay?" he asked.

"It's better than nothing."

Neon eased his back against the counter and the expression on his face told me he was about to ask something that I did not want to answer. "What happened back there, Maya?"

"You mean when that guy tried to strangle me to death?"

"No," he said in a singsong manner. "I'm talking about in that lounge room. You were staring at the wall like you could see a ghost."

Huh. He nearly had that right.

"Just a blast from the past, that's all."

"Looked like more than that to me."

"It was nothing. Okay?" I glared at him, and when he jerked back, I felt like an asshole. After all, he'd just saved my life.

I flicked my hair over my shoulder. "I'm going to use the bathroom. You okay here for a bit?"

He shrugged. "Sure."

I took one of the candles and the lighter, leaving Neon with the flashlight.

I made my way to the bathroom, shut the door, and lit the candle.

My reflection in the mirror over the basin wasn't pretty. My hair looked like I'd wrestled with a raccoon. I had a scrape on my chin that I couldn't recall getting, and another cut above my eyebrow already had a bruise swelling around it.

Yanking out my braid, I gave my hair a good tousle.

I turned on the tap and it shuddered like it was coughing up a furball. A trickle of rust-stained water splashed into the white bowl, and it looked like blood.

My mind tumbled back fourteen years.

Gripping the basin, I tried to force away images of Lily lying on those blood-stained sheets with that hideous wallpaper as her backdrop and my mother praying to God to save my sister. The blood between Lily's legs was terrifying enough but it was the blankness in her bloodshot eyes that had scared the hell out of me.

Lily had been four years older than me and was just over nineteen when she'd died. I'd looked up to her. I was proud of her. I wanted to be her.

She was so much fun and was always going to one party or another. But in the weeks before she'd died, she'd slipped into a downward spiral and nothing I said could stop her from crying. She seemed to shrivel into herself.

Tears pooled in my eyes, and I flicked them away, angry that they were even there.

It had been fourteen years since I'd held Lily's hand as she slipped away, and yet it felt like yesterday.

Forcing back the tears burning in my eyes, I pushed away from the sink and tugged my hair back into a braid. I shoved Lily from my mind. I had enough to worry about without adding my anger over her death to the mix.

Unable to ignore the burning in my bladder anymore, I undid my cargo pants and hovered over the toilet to pee. There was even a fresh roll of toilet paper on the wall. I curled a few layers away, checking that there were no creepy crawlies inside before I used the paper. One thing I learned in the army was that if an opportunity arose to go to the toilet, I should go. And that toilet paper was a luxury not to be missed, no matter how old it was.

I stood, and as I went to pull up my pants, I noticed the red welts snaking up from my ankle. The jellyfish sting. I peeled out of my cargo pants, hung them on a hook, and used the candle to check out the damage. It looked like someone had attacked me with a bullwhip that had gone right around my leg. The welts were huge and red. Thankfully there was no more pain.

A knock sounded on the door. "Maya, are you okay in there?"

"Yeah, I'm just checking out my jellyfish stings."

"Oh, show me."

"I'm fine."

"Come on, I want to see. Please?"

"Okay. Okay. Jeez." I didn't bother putting on my cargo pants. That was another thing I learned in the army: how to be confident in my underwear in front of men.

Grumbling under my breath, I opened the door.

Neon's gaze bounced from my face to my bare legs, and he winced. "Jeez, that looks so painful. Does it hurt?"

I stepped back from him and propped my right leg up on the bathtub. He shone the flashlight onto the red welts, giving us both a better look.

"I've had worse. Thanks to your magic potion, it's stopped stinging."

Neon flashed his sexy grin. "My magic potion."

"Apparently. Okay, your turn. Get your pants off and sit down. I want to check out the cuts on your leg." I grabbed the flashlight off him, and while he zipped out of his jeans, I searched through the bathroom cupboards.

There were more rolls of toilet paper and little bottles of shampoo and creams and soap.

"Hey, hey look." I held up a tiny sewing kit.

"Oh jeez, I don't know, Maya. Can't we wait a little bit longer?"

"Sure." I placed the sewing kit next to the sink. "But don't blame me if your leg drops off."

Neon sat on the edge of the bath and his long, tanned legs showed defined muscles. I followed the contours of his chest that were clearly visible beneath that tight-fitting costume top. His smirk indicated he'd seen me checking him out.

He waggled his head. "I usually wait until the second date before I get down to my underwear."

"That's not what I heard, Mr. Hollywood bachelor of the year."

"So, you did Google me."

"I didn't, but my friend did. She's a little infatuated with you."

He tilted his head and the flames reflecting in his eyes made his expression soften and his sexiness elevate.

I need to get away from him before I do something I might regret.

I tugged on my cargo pants and clutched the flashlight. "I'm going to check the rest of those kitchen cupboards, see if there's anything we can use in there. Stay here."

As I walked past our captives, I shone the light their way. They were still zonked out. If we'd hit them hard enough, they could be out for days. We couldn't wait that long to interrogate them. Neon and I needed to find more food and fresh water well before that, or we would die of dehydration.

In the kitchen, I searched through the cupboard underneath the sink and found a little plastic box with a red cross on the lid.

A flickering candle preceded Neon's arrival in the kitchen.

"I told you to stay in the bathroom. You really do have a problem with following orders."

"I thought we'd have more room out here." Neon sat on one sofa and propped his wounded leg onto the coffee table. He put the candle down beside his ankle.

I popped open the lid on the first aid kit. "Must be your lucky day, Neon."

"Really? If it was my lucky day, I wouldn't have nearly been murdered several times."

"See, that's what's lucky about it. You're still here."

He rolled his eyes.

"Look. Bandages." I held up two rolls, still sealed in plastic. A little brown bottle was also in the tub, but when I shook it, the bottle seemed to be empty. I removed the lid and whiffed. Iodine. Unfortunately, it had evaporated to nothing. The kit also contained tweezers, scissors, bandage tape, gloves, and gauze.

I held up the tweezers. "Aha. Now we're talking. We'll get those splinters out, then I can stitch you up."

"Look, Maya, it's not that I don't trust you, but I think we can hold off on stitching my leg for a little while."

I shrugged. "Sure. Like I said, it's your leg. But I am going to wrap the wounds in these bandages."

He leaned back on the sofa and placed his hands behind his head like he was about to watch a show on television. "I'm all yours."

I unwrapped the T-shirt from around his leg and gradually peeled open the fabric. I'd lost track of time since Neon had obtained this injury, but it was still bleeding, and that could mean two things. Either there hadn't been enough time to activate the full blood clotting mechanism, or he had foreign objects in the wound that his body was trying to eradicate.

I shone the flashlight into the bloody gashes. Splinters were embedded all through his jagged flesh. Every movement would be agony.

Shaking my head, I met his gaze.

Neon's expression morphed from mild amusement to alarm. "What?"

I snapped the tweezers together. "I need to remove the splinters, and that's not optional."

"Oh, is that all? By the look on your face, I thought you were going to chop my leg off."

"I haven't ruled that out yet."

"You have a terrible bedside manner."

"If we were in bed, I'd let you have that opinion." I offered him a smile.

He returned a smile that reached his eyes in a way that was sassy and sexy as all hell. "Does that mean I'm going to get you into bed?"

A heat wave curled up my neck and I fought it with a little laugh. "In your dreams, buddy."

I pulled on the gloves and snapped them into position, surprised they'd survived the decades concealed in plastic. "They certainly don't make these like they used to."

I held up my gloved hands.

"Go gentle, doc."

I slapped his knee. "Just shine the flashlight here and keep still."

The angle of the light revealed just how brutal the wound was. Using the tweezers, I pulled at the end of a splinter and Neon stiffened. The splinter was much longer than I expected and when I placed it onto the lid of the first aid kit, Neon winced.

"Keep still, Neon."

"Tell me why you joined the army."

"What?"

"I need a distraction. Why did you join the army?"

"I wanted to learn how to shoot."

He chuckled.

I glared at him.

"Oh, you're serious. But couldn't you just join a shooting club or something?"

Not with what I had planned.

"It's not the same."

"So, how long did you serve?"

"Nine years."

"Why did you leave?"

I yanked out a splinter.

Neon winced.

Shit, that was a bit rough. Feeling terrible about not being gentler, I asked, "How long have you been acting for?"

"Ahh, answering the question with one of your own. Why didn't you just say you don't want to talk about it?"

"I don't want to talk about it."

"I can tell."

I plucked out another splinter that was much longer than the last. Flinching, Neon sucked air through his teeth.

"Sorry. That was a big one."

"I can see that. Are there many more?"

"Heaps. So, keep still."

"I am." He spoke through clenched teeth.

As I put the sharp fragment onto the plastic lid next to the others, blood oozed from the hole I'd removed a splinter from.

I touched his knee. "Stay there."

Grabbing the flashlight, I strode toward the bathroom. Our captives were still in the loungeroom. Still unmoving.

In the bathroom, I grabbed a fresh toilet roll from beneath the sink. It was wrapped in waxy paper. Toilet paper wasn't ideal to wipe away blood, but it would have to do.

I returned to Neon, and for once he'd followed my instruction. Maybe it was because of the blood dribbling down the sides of his calf. Or maybe it was because he finally understood how serious his wounds were.

"Here. Remove the wrapping, please." I handed him the toilet roll and sat on the coffee table again.

"Shine the flashlight over here, and if you can, dab away the blood so I can see the wounds properly."

The next splinter I worked on was as thick as a pencil, but fortunately it didn't go too deep. I pulled it out and Neon dabbed at the bloody gash.

He peeled away the paper, but the wound still oozed blood.

I put my hand over his to press back down on the wound. "Keep applying pressure."

His expression was unreadable as if he was numb.

Fearing he was about to pass out, I said, "You didn't answer my question, Neon."

"And you didn't answer mine."

"Okay, you go first, and then I'll answer your question."

"You first."

I stared at him. "Neon, I'm trying to concentrate here. And you need a distraction. So, tell me, how long have you been acting?"

"I started when I was nine."

"Nine. Wow, you were young. What made you start?"

"That's another question."

"Just answer the question."

"Wow. Were you also a terrorist interrogator in the army?"

I giggled.

"I have ways to make you talk." I attempted a Russian accent.

He wiggled his brows. "Sounds like fun."

"Not the way I do it. Come on, tell me. What makes a nine-year-old boy take up acting?"

A haunted expression crossed his eyes, and I felt terrible for pressing him to answer. But as much as I wanted to tell him he didn't need to respond, my curiosity overpowered that urge.

He made a weird face like he was fighting nausea.

I lowered my eyes, and a heavy silence fell upon us.

Neon cleared his throat. "When I was nine, I was kidnapped."

Chapter Ten

NEON

Maya gasped and leaned toward me, placing her hand on my bare thigh. "Oh, Neon, I'm so sorry. What happened?"

I couldn't believe I was about to tell Maya about my kidnapping all those years ago. I'd been trying to forget it forever, but the reality was, I never would. It had changed my life.

"Was it someone you knew who kidnapped you?"

"Yes, our butler. Joseph."

"You had a butler?"

Oh, crap. My fame, and the fortune I'd accumulated from it, were self-made and on public record for the world to see. But I never told anybody about the wealth I was born into. People tended to get weird when money was involved.

But I was beginning to like Maya. For some crazy fucked-up reason, I wanted her to like me too.

She squeezed my thigh, and I was drawn into those stunning eyes of hers like they were magnets. "You don't have to tell me if you don't want to."

"I'll share . . . if you tell me your dark secrets."

"Who says I have dark secrets?"

"Me."

She curled her lip into her mouth and the desire to pull those lips to mine was incredible. Her gaze drifted from my eyes to my mouth.

Does she want to kiss me too?

Her lips parted like she was about to reveal an incredible truth. I reached forward, curled my hand around her neck, and pulled her to me. Our lips met, barely touching, and our kiss was tender and sweet and fucking amazing.

I couldn't remember a kiss like that. It was like she wanted me, but was trying damn hard to hold back. Women never acted like that with me. Women often threw themselves at me. This was hotter than anything I'd ever experienced.

Maya eased back and her expression was equal parts a grin and a frown. She playfully slapped my thigh. "You'll do anything to get out of telling this story, won't you?"

"Are you complaining?"

"If you do that again, I will be." She grabbed the tweezers, snapped them together with a scowl on her face, then leaned toward my mangled leg again.

As I let the silence hang between us, I tried to comprehend my feelings for this woman who I barely knew. Maya was firing sparks inside me like I'd never felt before.

She cleared her throat. "So, this butler who kidnapped you, was he caught?"

When she glanced at me, I nodded.

She pulled another splinter and slotted it on the plastic lid next to the dozen she'd already removed. "How long was he your butler?"

"He worked for my parents for twelve years. His son and I were best friends."

A noise thrummed in her throat. "Twelve years is long enough to know someone."

"You never know someone. Not properly." I'd had too many experiences that proved that fact.

She cocked her head at me like she was trying to read my mind. That would be impossible. Acting had taught me how to shut off my emotions.

"Did he hurt you?" She pierced me with her blue eyes.

"Physically, not really."

We stared at each other, and it was like she could feel how deep my emotional wounds went.

That scared the hell out of me.

Finally, she nodded. "The trauma must have been horrific. You were only nine. I hope you received therapy?"

"Acting. That was my therapy."

Frowning, she tugged another splinter, and I clenched my jaw against the sting. The splinter popped free, and I dabbed away a dribble of blood. Her tenderness was a dramatic contrast to the woman I'd witnessed fighting men twice her size.

"So, they caught the butler. Was he charged?"

"Yes. He was convicted and committed to twelve years in jail."

Her chest deflated. "It's never enough, is it? They should have castrated him and let him bleed to death."

The venom in her tone was palpable. Whatever happened to Maya was much worse than my childhood hell.

The two of us were so different, and yet we both had a fierce tragedy in our past that linked us together. I just hoped Maya trusted me enough to share her heartbreak with me.

I cleared my throat. "So, there you go. That's why I took up acting. Your turn. Tell me why you joined the army."

"I already told you, I wanted to learn how to shoot." There was so much angst in her response that my chest ached for her.

"Hmm. I get the impression it was more than that. Were you running away from someone?"

She blinked at me. "Why do you think that?"

I groaned; she wasn't going to like my answer. "Because I did a movie . . . Fire Island. Did you see it?"

"No. I must've been killing bad guys in Kyrgyzstan when that came out."

"Sorry." I lowered my gaze to the gashes on my leg.

Maya and I were worlds apart. While she'd been dodging bullets, I'd been shooting blank ones.

"I'm sorry. That was uncalled for." She rattled a breath through her lips. "So, what does that movie have to do with me joining the army?"

"The hero, Maximus Kane, ran off to the army after a woman broke his heart. I played Maximus."

"Huh. That's Blade's story."

"Who's Blade?"

"My friend. He was also my team leader in the army."

"Cool name."

"Codename."

"Ahh, do you have a codename too?"

She scooped a loose hair from her forehead and shrugged one shoulder. "Ghost."

I cocked my head. "Why Ghost?"

She put the tweezers down, grabbed the toilet roll off me, and as she dabbed the bloody gashes, I had the impression she was stalling her response.

I waited. She kept dabbing.

She opened one of the bandages and peeled off the end. "Are you sure you don't want me to stitch these wounds?"

"I'm sure."

Her wolf eyes looked set to devour me. "For the record, I disagree with that decision."

"Duly noted."

She scrunched her nose. "Were you a lawyer in one of your movies?"

I huffed. "Yes. In *Tipping the Scales*. Did you see that one?"

Starting at my ankle, she rolled the bandage over my wounds. "I don't get to the movies very often."

"Well, Ghost, maybe I could take you to an opening night with me?"

"No, thanks."

That was unexpected. She was the first woman to pass on that offer. "Why not?"

"It's not my scene."

"What is your scene?"

She finished with the first bandage and opened the packet for the next one. "Jeez, you're nosy."

"And you still haven't answered why your codename is Ghost."

When she finished with the second dressing, she cut the end of the bandage down the middle and used the two parts to tie it into position.

She tapped my thigh. "All done."

As Maya got busy shoving the bloody paper into the plastic box, I kept silent.

She snapped the lid shut and reached for the flashlight.

"Is Ghost because you're scary?" I grinned at her.

A smile crawled on her lips, but she looked to be fighting it. "Yeah, that's it."

"No, it's not. Come on, tell me."

"You don't want to know, Neon."

"I do. I want to know everything about you."

She glared at me like I was a stalker. "No, you don't."

"How do you know what I want?"

"Have you seen *A Few Good Men*?" she asked.

"The movie? Yes. Why?"

"Because there was one line in that movie that was so true. You, as in civilians, can't handle the truth."

A groan came from the other room.

Maya jumped to her feet. Aiming the flashlight ahead of her, she marched to the two assholes who'd attacked her. I chased after her, wincing at my stinging wounds and hobbling like an old man.

The men were back-to-back, tied to chairs, so they couldn't see each other.

Maya shone the light into the face of the smaller man with a scraggly goatee. "About time you woke up, asshole."

He squinted against the glare, inhaled a disgusting-sounding breath, and spat toward Maya.

She simultaneously dodged his spit and whacked the man over the head with the flashlight. "Do that again, and I'll kick you in the nuts."

The man sucked air through his teeth. "What do you want?"

Maya grabbed another dining chair, positioned it in front of him, and sat, meeting him at eye level. She put the flashlight on the ground so it lit up his body.

I stayed back in the shadows, keen to watch her work.

She pulled a gun from her holster and aimed the weapon at the guy's knee. "What's your name?"

"Fuck off."

"Okay, Fuck Off. Why are you after Neon?"

"Why do you think?"

She jolted to her feet and punched the man's groin.

He jerked forward, howling.

Her speed and commitment to that move were equally impressive and terrifying. I was so glad she was on my side.

She sat on the chair again and sighed like she was bored out of her brain. "I can do this all night, Fuck Off. But I'm guessing your balls won't be able to handle it."

His evil glare was better than any acting I'd ever seen. "What do you want?"

"Answers." Her voice was as sweet as honey.

Fuck Off wriggled on his seat, maybe trying to direct blood back to his testicles.

"Your leader is Sloan. Am I right?"

I frowned at Maya. *How the hell did she know that?*

The man nodded.

"What's his first name?"

His face twisted into a frown. "I don't know. We just call him Sloan."

"How many men are with you?"

He shook his head and his gaze found me in the shadows. "You're a dead man, Bloom."

Maya punched his balls again.

"Fuck. Fuck. Fuck." He spat at her, but the bloody blob fell on his jeans.

"You talk to me, and only me. You hear?"

"You're dead too." He squirmed on his seat, and it looked like he was trying to cross his legs, but the ties around his ankles made it impossible.

Maya held her hand forward like she was studying the quality of her red nail polish. "Funny, I don't feel dead."

"You can't hide on this island."

She shrugged one shoulder. "And yet here we are. Hiding. And we've captured you two assholes."

"You've pissed off the wrong man, bitch. He's going to tear you apart piece by piece."

"Yeah. Yeah. Now answer me. How many men does Sloan have?"

"I don't know. Ten. Twelve."

"What's his plan?"

"I don't know." He spat the words at her.

Maya balled her fist and stood.

"I don't know, okay? It was supposed to be easy. Grab that bastard and hold him and the hostages until we get our money."

"Who's paying the ransom?"

"His parents. Who do you think?"

Maya turned to me with a frown that darkened her eyes.

I never did get around to explaining just how rich my family was. I wouldn't be able to contain that secret now.

She turned back to Fuck Off. "How are you getting off the island?"

He scrunched his lips. "By boat."

His response wasn't that confident, and I had the impression he didn't really know.

"When?"

"Once we get our money."

"And when is that?"

He snarled at me, and Maya kicked his shin. "When?"

Fuck Off snapped his gaze to her. "They won't pay until we prove Bloom is alive."

Maya smiled a truly beautiful grin. "Well, isn't that a bitch."

"You're the bitch."

"I don't disagree. What do you know about me?"

"That you're a dead woman."

"We've already been through that. What else?"

He waggled his head. "I don't know. That you're his bodyguard. That you started yesterday, and you've killed three of our men."

"Actually, it's six."

They obviously haven't found the men in the bowling alley.

His eyes flared.

Maya shrugged. "But they were all assholes."

"You're lying!"

"Derek was one of them. Stupid bastard should have stuck to body-guard duties rather than kidnapping."

Fuck Off slumped in his seat and seemed to melt. Maybe he was wondering if Maya would kill him too.

I was wondering the same thing.

Killing an asshole who was attacking us was one thing. But killing one who was tied to a chair . . . that was next level.

"Where are they keeping the hostages?"

His defeatist expression confirmed he'd given up the fight. Maybe he'd accepted his fate. "In the gym building, next to the pool."

She looked at me.

I nodded. "I know where it is."

Maya stood. "I'm guessing Fuck Off isn't your real name. So, what is it?"

"Bruce."

"And your friend?"

"He's my brother. Rob."

"Well, Bruce, it's your lucky day."

"Yeah, well, it don't feel like it."

"I'm not going to shoot you."

The tension jamming my stomach washed away with her declaration.

Bruce crumbled even further into the seat.

Maya pulled her chair away from him. "But there won't be a second time. Understand?"

"Yes. Yes."

She kicked his knee, but there wasn't any malice in it. "Say thank you."

"Thank you."

Maya strode to the bedroom and grabbed a pillow.

Oh shit. Is she going to smother him?

My heart thundered in my chest as I darted my gaze from Maya to Bruce. I should stop her, but I couldn't make my body move.

Besides, I doubted I could stop Maya from doing anything.

She pulled the pillow from the case. "Now, Bruce, there is a pack of wild dingoes around here. We've already run into them once."

She tugged the pillowcase over his head.

"Hey! What the fuck?"

She gave his cheek two quick slaps. "Bruce. Bruce. Are you listening?"

"What're you doing?"

"Dingoes are attracted to movement. So, you and your brother need to keep very still, and if I was you, I'd keep quiet. Especially with that blood you spat onto your leg. Dingoes can smell blood a mile away."

He released a wild groan. "Fucking hell."

"Shush. And don't forget, if I catch you again, you're going to have more than bruised balls to worry about."

Maya slotted her gun into her holster and grabbed the flashlight from the floor.

She waved at me to follow her.

We strode outside, and using the flashlight to guide the way, she led me onto the path.

Maya's professionalism impressed the heck out of me as did everything else about her. "That was amazing."

She spun to me, and with a scowl twisting her beautiful features, she shoved me into the bushes.

Chapter Eleven

NEON

I dragged my body free of the prickling branches. "Jesus, Maya, what the fuck was that for?"

She put her hands on her hips. Fury flared in her eyes. "What aren't you telling me, Neon?"

"What are you talking about? I've told you everything."

She turned off the flashlight. "What have your parents got to do with this?"

I reached for her, brushing my fingers over her arm.

She snapped her arm away. "Neon, I need to know everything if I'm going to help you."

This was not how I wanted to do this.

I sighed. "Have you heard of the Beverly Hillbillies?"

She punched my stomach.

I doubled over, more from shock than pain.

"What the fuck, Maya?"

She could punch much harder than that. I'd seen her do it several times.

"Stop mucking around."

"I wasn't." I shuddered. "My dad bought a block of land in Texas fifty years ago. Four years after buying the land, Dad tapped into one of the biggest oil reserves Texas had ever seen. He averages one billion dollars a year in profit. And that's just the income he has on the books."

Maya was silent, and I hated that she couldn't see me so she could see I was telling the truth.

"My parents were multibillionaires by the time I was born."

Maya released a sound, and I wished I knew what she was thinking. "Well, at least that explains the butler."

"Not really. He was one of our trusted employees. I'll never understand why he did that to me."

"I mean *why* you had a butler."

"We had about twelve staff back then. A driver. Gardeners. Chefs. Mom has her own personal physician and physiotherapist and yoga instructor. You name it, they had it. They have even more now."

"Lucky for some," Maya said.

"No, Maya. You're wrong. I hate the wealth. Because of my family money, I can never have a normal life. I can't even walk along the beach without bodyguards. My parents have six armed security guards on their property at all times. They are prisoners in their own home."

"So, how come this info didn't show up when I googled you?"

I clenched my fists, pissed off by the suspicion in her voice.

"Because when I changed my name to Neon Bloom, I tried to walk away from my family name. Then my acting career took off and I made my own money and people are still trying to kidnap me. Which is why I need to have fucking bodyguards."

"And even them you can't trust." Maya's tone softened.

Maybe she was understanding that my life wasn't as great as everyone assumed.

She turned the flashlight back on and shielded it with her hand. "Come on. We have to keep moving and find a phone. I need to contact my team. We need help with these assholes."

I grabbed her hand, spinning her toward me. "Maya, you have to believe me. I have no idea what's going on."

She tilted her face toward me, and my breath hitched at her beauty. In my line of work, I was surrounded by beautiful women every single day. Maya was breathtaking and it took all my resolve not to kiss her again.

Her gaze lingered on me, and I wondered if she wanted me to do exactly that.

"I believe you, Neon. But if it's your parents' wealth these assholes are trying to tap into and they're expecting a big payday, that means we're not dealing with a couple of dumb kidnappers. The logistics behind this attack was extensive and well planned. They had to infiltrate your crew, get these men on this island unnoticed. Have an escape plan. I bet they've been planning it for months. So, getting the jump on them is not going to be easy."

"What do we do then?"

She stepped back from me and glanced skyward. "It doesn't look like the moon is going to be our savior tonight and we can't risk walking around with this flashlight. I don't know about you, but I need to rest."

I huffed. "I'm so glad you said that. I feel like I've been awake for three days."

"Adrenaline does that. Let's see if there are any more of those bungalows along this path." She placed her hand over the flashlight, shielding it somewhat, and led the way.

"That was pretty clever back there, with the dingo thing."

"Thanks. I thought so myself."

"I certainly wouldn't have thought of it. For a moment there, I thought you were going to smother him."

"I thought about it." She shot a glance at me over her shoulder.

I hoped it was a joke. From what I'd seen so far, Maya was lethal. And that meant I was with the best person in the world to get me through this mess.

We came to another intersection with a path that went in the opposite direction to where I expected more bungalows would be. Without discussion, Maya strode onto the new path. Several yards along, she squatted at a sign that had toppled over and become the host for a vine that had long ago died. She peeled the dead creeper away.

"This path takes us to the theater. I assume that's back at the main resort." She stood, flicked her thick braid over her shoulder, and met my gaze like she expected me to know the answer.

"I don't know."

"Let's go find out."

"Really?"

"Yep. So far, the men we've bumped into were all searching for us away from the resort. My guess is they've searched the main hotel already. They will never expect us to double back toward them."

I shrugged. "You're the expert. Lead the way."

She turned off the flashlight, plunging us into darkness.

That was another thing I rarely had in my life. The catchphrase: lights, camera, action was how I liked to live my life. I always had something on the go. It was my defense mechanism to stop my mind from slamming back to my nine-year-old self. I'd been running from that forever.

As my eyes adjusted to the blackness, the stars appeared through the dense canopy above as tiny pinpricks of light, and shapes and shadows materialized around me.

We arrived at a pair of grand double doors that looked to be made from one giant slab of timber. The left-hand door had dislodged from a couple of hinges and fallen forward, offering an opening to the inside.

Maya lowered to her hands and knees and poked her head through the gap, giving me an incredible view of her butt. I wished I had more light to fully appreciate that spectacular view.

She reversed out the gap and stood.

"All clear." She handed me the flashlight and pulled her gun from her holster. "Keep that light off unless I say, and do exactly as I tell you."

"Okay. Should I have my gun ready?"

"Hell no. You'll probably shoot me in the back."

"Thanks for the vote of confidence."

"Just stay behind me and don't do anything stupid."

"Well, don't go getting your sexy ass in trouble again."

"You been checking out my ass?"

I've been checking out everything.

I cocked my head. "You stripped down to your underwear in front of me. You wanted me to check out your butt."

"No, I didn't."

I blinked at her. "Yeah, you did."

She slapped my chest. "No, I didn't. You just took the liberty."

"Well, don't go wiggling your sexy ass in front of me." I grinned.

She grumbled and placed her hand on my chest. "Neon, if we run into anyone, let me handle it. Okay?"

"But what if—"

"Hey." She tapped my cheek with her palm. "I'd take a bullet for you. But if you keep pissing me off, I may change my mind."

She can't be serious. "But—"

"Let's roll."

She lowered to her hands and knees and crawled through the gap in the door.

Clutching the flashlight like a baton, I chased after her. On the other side of the door, dirt and rubble crunched beneath my hands and knees like we were on a gravel road. It didn't make sense.

No light penetrated the area, but I had a sense that we'd entered a large room.

Maya fumbled for my hand. "Give me the light."

I handed it to her, and she turned it on, shielding it with her palm. Rows of theater seats stretched to our left, but they were covered in rubble and crap.

"What happened here?"

Maya shone the flashlight to the roof. The ceiling of the grand theater had been decorated in stunning artwork, but a large section had caved in. The seats and everything else had suffered under the elements for decades.

"Come on, let's see if there's somewhere to hide down there." She used the light beam to highlight the curtains across the stage.

She led the way down steps to the left of the seats, heading toward the stage at the bottom. As we had entered the theater at ground level, the stage must've been built below ground. We climbed down the steps onto the stage which was also covered in rubble.

"Careful, I don't need you falling through any more timber."

"Me neither." My leg still stung, but it was much better with the splinters removed.

Heavy velvet curtains hung from the ceiling. Maya pulled one aside and waved her flashlight around backstage.

She shone the light on a door. "Let's see what's in there."

Behind the curtain, she crossed a stage that had half a pirate ship filling most of the area.

"Maybe they were performing Pirates of the Caribbean."

She clicked her fingers. "That was the Johnny Depp one, right."

"Yeah, have you seen that movie?"

She tilted her head at me. "I have actually. Have you met him?"

"Johnny Depp?"

"No. Santa Clause."

Wise ass. "Yes, I've met Johnny a few times."

"Huh."

She didn't elaborate her thoughts, and I couldn't tell if she was impressed or not.

With the flashlight off, we were once again plunged into absolute darkness. After a few beats, where I assumed she was listening for voices, she tugged open the door. The hinges creaked so loud I froze.

When armed men didn't come charging at us, she opened the creaking door the rest of the way and turned on the flashlight again.

Beyond the door was a set of steps. She led the way, and at the bottom we entered a narrow hallway. The first door had a large gold star attached to the front.

"Found your office," she said.

"Very funny."

She opened the door, waved her light around the room, then backed out again. "Let's see where this hallway leads."

She continued along the corridor, and the next room was also set up for a lead star in a show. The following room was full of costumes, and hair and makeup areas. At the end of the hallway was another door but it didn't have a sign indicating what was beyond.

Again, she turned off the light to listen. Nothing but complete silence.

She opened the door which thankfully didn't creak like the last one, and we entered yet another long corridor.

"We're still underground," I said.

"Shh," Maya hissed at me.

We walked along the corridor to a set of stairs leading up to our right. A sign next to them indicated that the stairs led to Back of House, Management, and Medical Clinic.

Maya tapped her red fingernail on Medical Clinic and looked at me.

I shook my head. "I'm fine."

She nodded once, then carried on along the corridor to another set of stairs that led to reception and lobby, but she didn't pause there. An open doorway appeared on our left and we stepped into a large industrial kitchen. The place looked like it had been ransacked. Every door was open, and pots and pans and equipment were scattered everywhere.

Maybe the assholes had been looking for us in there and got pissed off when they didn't find us.

A doorway on the right led to a large industrial laundry.

Maya backed out of the rooms, and we returned to the corridor. A little further along, the passage ended at an elevator that didn't have any signs on it.

"We must be beneath the hotel. This would be for housekeeping and room service," I whispered.

Maya nodded. "Let's go back to the theater."

We retraced our steps and entered through the door to the theater passage. She strode to the costume room, and I followed.

"See if you can find something that would make noise," she said.

"What for?"

She picked up a joker's hat and gave it a shake. The little bells on the end of the joker's four soft horns rattled. "I want something to make a noise that will give us a head start if someone comes through that doorway."

I rifled through the costumes that were of a decent quality and in very good condition. "Some of these would fetch a fair price."

"No unnecessary talk, please."

I pulled a face at her and kept looking.

"How about a bell?" I raised the copper bell and it clanged. "Sorry."

Hitting me with a foul glare, she snatched it from me with her hand around the bell's tongue. "Perfect. Now grab one of those costumes."

"Which one?"

"A big one."

117

Frowning, I grabbed a pink ball gown and followed Maya back to the door we'd come through. She carefully put the bell down and grabbed the gown. She shoved the fabric under the door, and then stacked the rest up on itself. On top of the fabric pile, she carefully placed the bell.

She stood. "Perfect. Now they can't see our light under the door and if they do barge through, we'll hear them coming."

I nodded. "Clever."

Maya's sassy grin seemed to light up the hallway. "Thanks. Now, let's get some rest."

She led the way back to the room with the large gold star on the door. Leaving the door open, she propped the flashlight onto the makeup table so the light reflected in the mirror and bounced onto the ceiling.

Along one wall was a purple sofa with maroon cushions. She plucked one of the cushions and bashed the shit out of it, dispersing a cloud of dust about the room.

I fanned it away. "You right there?"

"Just checking there are no spiders in my pillow." She placed it on the carpet.

I cocked my head. "Maya, you can have the sofa."

"I'm fine on the floor."

"Maya. Please, I can't let you sleep on the floor."

"Why not? Trust me, I've had way worse."

"Will you stop being so stubborn?"

Her jaw dropped. "Just being practical."

I snatched the pillow from the carpet and sat on the sofa with the pillow on my lap. I patted the cushion. "Here, now lie down."

She huffed. "You just want my head in your lap."

"Exactly."

She curled her lips into her mouth, yet she didn't move toward me.

"I'm not going to bite you."

"Aren't you worried about bugs in that sofa?" she asked.

"No. Like you, I've had worse."

"Huh. Not like I have."

"Is everything a competition with you?"

She nodded. "Pretty much."

"For God's sake, Maya, will you just lie down?"

Maya dragged a chair next to the sofa. She removed her gun and placed it on the chair within easy reach. She unclipped the gun holster from her waist and placed it next to her gun.

Turning to me, she frowned. "You need to sit at the other end of the sofa."

Rolling my eyes, I did as she instructed.

Her expression indicated she'd thought I would argue with her.

I was over arguing. I just wanted to rest.

She grabbed the flashlight, and with her thigh holster still attached to her right leg, she lay on her side on the couch and lowered her head to the cushion on my lap. Her position meant she could grab two weapons in the blink of an eye.

I didn't think I'd ever felt so safe in my life.

She turned off the light and both darkness and silence filled the room.

"You comfortable?" I asked.

"Yep. Goodnight, Jethro." She giggled.

"Ha, so you do know the Beverly Hillbillies."

"I think so. Jethro was the dumb one, right?"

I slapped her shoulder. "You're mean."

"You don't know mean."

I rested my hand on her shoulder. "Maya."

"Hmmm."

"Were you serious when you said you'd take a bullet for me?"

"Of course. That's what you hired me to do."

"But . . . but you don't even know me."

"I wasn't hired to know you, Neon. I was hired to protect you."

"I can't believe you'd do that for me." I cruised my hand up her arm, feeling her silky flesh.

"Yeah, well, let's hope I don't have to prove it."

I closed my eyes and listened to her breathe. "Maya?"

"You're not going to let me sleep, are you?"

"Sorry. But can you tell me why your call sign is Ghost?"

Moaning, she wriggled on the sofa. "I wish I never told you that."

"I don't. I want to know everything about you."

She inhaled a sharp breath. "You may change your mind after I tell you."

"Try me."

"Okay, I'm called Ghost because I can sneak up to an enemy target and kill them before they even see me. Stealth mode is my secret power."

"Wow. Will you marry me?"

She slapped my knee. "Why'd you have to ruin a perfect moment?"

I huffed. "You think hiding in a dusty room so we don't get killed is perfect."

"I've had worse," she said, matter of fact.

"So you keep saying."

"Because it's true. Now shush, or we'll never get any rest."

"Yes, boss," I said.

"Ha. I like the sound of that." She curled her hand over my leg, and it was the most glorious sensation I'd had in years.

I just hoped I'd have the pleasure of experiencing much more of that, and much more of Maya, once we were out of this mess.

If we get out of it.

Chapter Twelve

MAYA

A loud screeching noise pierced the darkness. I jolted upright.

"What the hell was that?" Neon asked.

"Shh." I grabbed my gun and the flashlight and jumped to my feet.

The darkness was so complete and silent, I believed our little hiding space hadn't been compromised. I placed my hand over the flashlight and risked turning it on. Squinting against the glare, I got my bearing, strode to the door to our room, and peered into the corridor. It was completely dark, and confident we were safe, I turned back to Neon. "All clear."

"Neon Bloom." A voice boomed from invisible speakers.

Neon and I met each other's gaze.

"I know you and your bitch can hear me. You have one hour to come to the main lobby or I will shoot a hostage. That's one hour, Bloom. The clock is ticking."

"Fuck!" Fear filled Neon's eyes.

The confident, handsome man I was with yesterday crumbled away.

"What are we going to do?" His hand hovered near his mouth like he was holding back a scream.

I pulled on my gun holster and clipped it in place. "For starters, we are going to see if we can get a visual on that asshole."

Neon drove his hand through his hair, revealing a vein that zigzagged across his temple. There was so much turmoil in his expression, I was equally torn between wrapping my arms around him and telling him everything would be okay, and slapping his cheek to make him pull his shit together.

I did neither. "Neon. We've got this, okay?"

"Okay. What should I do?"

I adjusted my gun belt on my hip. "You stay right behind me and do exactly as I say."

He nodded. Every ounce of his cockiness was gone.

"Time to move." I checked the corridor was empty. "Let's roll."

I led him back toward the stage where we climbed the steps and peered around the drapes. Sunlight streamed in from the massive hole in the roof and I relished the golden glow.

The room we'd spent the night in had been so dark we'd missed sunrise. I tucked the flashlight into my pocket. "You ready?"

Fear darkened his eyes and although fear was a powerful motivator, it also made people do crazy things.

"Neon, look at me."

He lowered his eyes to mine and the distress in his hazel irises was genuine.

"Are you with me?"

He heaved a loaded breath. "I couldn't live with myself if he killed people because of me."

His turmoil commanded me to edge closer to him, and I pressed my hand to his chest, right over his heart. "It's not because of you. It's because of him. You haven't done anything wrong. These assholes have their own agenda, and you and the hostages are just unfortunate collateral damage."

He stared at me as if he couldn't process my comment, then shook his head. "I still can't live with that, Maya."

"Look, for all we know he could be bluffing."

His shoulders sagged. "And he could mean every word he said."

Neon clamped his jaw like he was in control, but his eyes said otherwise. I needed him to stay frosty, and the best way to do that was to keep moving.

"We need a visual on these guys so I can get a handle on their operation." I tapped his chest. "Stay with me, okay? Don't do anything crazy."

I squeezed his hand once and released. Turning back to the curtain, I pulled it aside. There was no movement amongst the rows of theater seats.

"All clear. Let's go."

I strode toward the end of the stage and down the steps. The chairs were in rows that gradually became higher as we walked away from the stage. Toward the back, every seat was covered in rubble from the roof collapse. Years of exposure to the elements had turned the fabric black with moss but the fabric on the chairs that had escaped nature had somehow retained their lush red color.

At the top of the theater, we exited out the double doors we'd come in through the night before.

As I scanned the path and bushes surrounding us, I breathed in the crisp air, trying to eradicate the dust from my throat.

With Neon just behind me, I hustled along the path leading away from the theater. Neon's lopsided steps were a reminder of his wounds.

"How's your leg?"

"Fine."

I squinted at him over my shoulder. "Tell me the truth. How's your leg?"

He huffed. "It stings, but it's not killing me."

"Okay. Don't go dying on me from an infection to those wounds."

"Never. How's your leg?"

"Great. Your magical pee helped. Hey, that sounds like a great movie title for you . . . Neon and his Magical Pee."

He chuckled, and it showed me a side to him that I'd love to see more of.

Damn it. What am I thinking?

Neon and I ran in different circles. Once this was over, I would probably never see him again.

Jogging side-by-side, we followed the path back to the intersection we turned off last night. Around us, the shrubs were densely overgrown and above us, a massive flock of lorikeets screeched their morning welcome as they flew from tree to tree.

Neon's limp was significant, confirming that his declaration that his leg was fine was false.

We turned onto the wider path that circumnavigated the island.

"Do you think those men you tied up in the bungalow are still there?" he asked.

"I hope so. They'd have no chance of getting out of the knots I used on the ropes."

"They could break the chairs."

"You mean, like they do in the movies?"

He frowned at me. "Yeah, I guess."

"Have you ever tried it? A metal chair doesn't break that easily. Especially when you don't have the help of your arms."

"Sounds like you're talking from experience."

"I am."

He did a double take. "Can you tell me about it?"

"Nope."

"Aw, come on. Tell me."

"If I told you, I'd have to kill you."

His eyes bulged, and I fought the smirk crossing my lips.

"Hey." He playfully slapped my shoulder. "I can't tell when you're joking."

I gave him my dagger eyes. "I'm not joking."

Sunlight pierced through gaps in the canopy like laser beams, and I welcomed both the warmth and the light they provided. We reached a bush covered in thorns as long as my fingernails that had taken over the entire path and there was no way to climb over it.

"Do we have to go back?" Neon asked.

"See if we can get around it first."

We backtracked a little and entered the bushes, shoving branches heavy with the morning dew out of our way. Angling away from the path, we pushed through shrubs and ducked under branches. We startled a small rock wallaby and as it darted away, three more joined the first and the foursome disappeared in the camouflage of the vegetation.

In the distance, waves crashing into the shore penetrated the bushes adding to the pleasant vibes.

"You hear that?" Neon asked.

"Yes, we must be close to the cliff edge. Be careful. I don't want to have to save your ass again."

"But you're so good at it."

"Don't test me."

When I thought we'd gone far enough, we aimed back toward the path.

Once we'd returned to the crumbling concrete, we continued in an eastern direction. Every ten yards or so, a smaller and narrower path darted off to the right. Based on their positioning, I assumed there would be little bungalows that overlooked the ocean at the end of each path.

We arrived at another intersection and this one had a sign that was still in position. Unlike all the other signs we'd seen so far, this one was devoid of strangler vines and decades of decay.

The sign had arrows showing the directions for the main lobby, the pool, reception, and bungalows twenty-four to thirty located in the opposite direction to all the rest.

I pointed at Neon's chest. "Stay here. I'm going to check—"

"Hell no. I'm sticking with you, Maya."

"Not this time. I need to stay agile, and I can't be worrying about you."

"Whilst I'm flattered, you don't need to worry about me."

I slapped his chest. "This isn't a fucking movie."

"I know that."

"Keep your voice down."

He clamped his jaw and glared at me.

"I'm trying to save your ass."

"And the best way is with me at your side. I am not staying here, and you can't make me."

I cocked my head. "I have ways to make you do exactly that."

"Sounds sexy. Bring it on."

A giggle released from my lips. Annoyed with myself, I shook my head. "Okay, but don't go blaming me if you get dead."

"Well, that would kinda be impossible."

I stepped back from him to meet his gaze. "If I say run, you fucking run, okay?"

He nodded and raised his hand. "I solemnly swear to run like the wind. Hey, can I use a gun this time?"

"Nope."

"Party pooper."

I gave an exaggerated eye roll. "Now shush and keep right on my tail."

He saluted me. "Yes, boss."

Twigs and leaves crunched under our feet. Branches caught in the ocean breezes swayed overhead. The sun provided plenty of light, possibly too much.

We dodged around the biggest hibiscus bush I've ever seen; its lush red flowers were as big as Neon's hands. I ducked at rustling bush sounds and through a field of baby palm fronds, dozens of wallabies darted away like we'd caught them having a party.

The outline of a roof appeared through the vegetation, and the end of the path met with a crumbling building. All the doors and windows were missing yet there was no glass around.

Maybe Neon's film crew had removed it all?

At the back of the building, we stepped onto the concrete portico that was mottled with moss and dead leaves and stood with our backs against the brick wall. Neon's breaths were steady, and he wasn't showing any of the apprehension I had charging through me.

I raised a finger to my lips.

He nodded back.

With my gun locked and loaded, I crept along the back wall and peeked around the side. The portico stretched to the next corner. Overgrown jungle filled the distance, but thankfully, despite the pool being more like a swamp, the sun still glinted off the water, allowing me to get my bearings.

On the other side of that pool was the gymnasium and day spa where the gunmen and hostages would be.

I crept along the side, ducked into an open doorway, and entered the remains of a crumbling cafe. Chairs and tables were toppled over, and the glass cake stand at the coffee counter had imploded inward.

Hugging a sagging bookcase loaded with dusty books, I ducked down below the front windows which were also missing glass.

Neon came to my side, and we eased up on our knees to peer through the windows.

Across the other side of the pool, the building that contained both the gym and day spa had a thatched roof and a large timber veranda that overlooked the pool. Two men with machine guns across their chests smoked cigarettes at the far-right corner of the building.

Through two large open doors, the hostages sat on the floor in two rows with their backs against the wall. Their legs were positioned in front of them, and it looked like they had their hands tied behind their backs.

"Jesus, Neon. There are at least twenty hostages in there."

He nodded. "I see them."

The hostages became restless, and they all turned their heads toward a man who marched through the middle of the room. Everything about him screamed authority.

He stopped at the feet of one hostage.

She shook her head, and with her face contorted with fear, spoke to him. From our distance, I couldn't hear what she said.

The asshole stepped forward, gripped her hair, and dragged her to her feet.

Her terrified shrieks bounced across the water to us.

"Shit! Maya. That's Linda, the producer."

I clutched Neon's wrist. "Look away."

He snapped his wrist free. "If anything happens to her, it's because of me. I need to see this."

Shaking my head, I squeezed his wrist again. "No, Neon. You—"

"Neon Bloom."

The kidnapper gripped Linda's hair and spoke into a microphone that projected his voice across loudspeakers that miraculously still worked around the complex.

"You have one minute, Neon, or Linda is dead." He fired his weapon into the air.

Shrieks of terror from Linda crashed into me like a sonic boom.

If I had my sniper's rifle, I'd take that bastard out. But I could only see three gunmen. I had no fucking idea how many more there were.

"Thirty seconds, Bloom. Tick, tick, tick."

Neon shifted beside me, and I clutched his wrist, pulling him downward. "Don't you dare move."

"I need to stop this."

"They're going to kill the hostages anyway, Neon."

"You don't know that."

"Yes, I do. They're not wearing masks. That means all those hostages have seen their faces. They won't let anyone live after that, including you and me."

Neon clutched his chest and his face twisted with horror. "Fuck!"

"I hate to say this, but the hostages are the only thing keeping you and I and the remainder of them alive. Without them, he's got no bargaining chips."

"Ten. Nine. Eight."

Linda screamed.

I grabbed Neon's shirt and pulled him down.

"Four. Three."

I dove on top of him.

"One!"

Linda screamed. The gun exploded.

Everything went silent.

Chapter Thirteen

NEON

Terror clawed through me. "Fuck! He killed her. Oh my god."

Maya clamped her hand over my mouth. Hovering over me, she shook her head. "Shh."

My heart thundered in my chest. Acid burned in my stomach.

Maya's wide eyes showed she was as horrified as I was over Linda's brutal murder.

"Bloom!" The voice boomed from the speakers. "Linda's death is on you."

I shook my head, trying to free myself from Maya's grip, but she wouldn't release me.

"In one hour, I will kill another hostage. Tick. Tick. Tick."

Cries from the other hostages reached us from over the pool.

"I'm going to let you free, but don't do anything stupid, okay?" Maya glared at me.

I nodded.

Maya slowly removed her palm from my mouth. After studying me, she climbed off my chest and eased up to peer through the window.

I sat with my back to the wall and as I stared at my torn jeans, I tried to comprehend what the fuck just happened. Linda was dead . . . because of me. I clamped my eyes shut and visions of Linda flashed across my mind. Her smile when a scene went to plan. Her scowl when it didn't. Her energy and excitement when—

"Hey." Maya shook my shoulder, and I snapped my eyes open. "Let's get out of here."

She peered through the window again, and I joined her. Linda's body was slumped on the decking. Her head was turned toward me, but her blonde hair covered her face. Five gunmen stood over her like they were admiring their slaughter.

Maya turned to me. "I'm going to kill every one of those bastards."

"Good."

The throbbing beat of a helicopter carved through the silence.

Maya peered out the window, searching the sky.

Five gunmen near Linda aimed their rifles skyward. The five gunmen became ten. Ten became fifteen.

Jesus, how many are there?

The man who'd shot Linda barked orders at them, but I couldn't understand what he was saying.

All of them remained under the cover of the veranda to the gym, hiding from the helicopter. But they held their weapons, ready to attack. Whoever was in that chopper wasn't one of theirs.

The helicopter flew over the pool area in a blaze of red and yellow.

"Holy shit. That's Levi." Maya grabbed my wrist. "Let's go."

Crouching over, with me following her, we dashed past bookshelves. At the door, she peered outside, aiming her gun left and right, then she took off at a sprint.

Chasing after her, I whispered, "What are you doing?"

She bolted for the rear of the crippled cafe. As the helicopter's thumping rotors dissolved into the distance, Maya sprinted along the path with such speed I struggled to keep up with her.

"What's going on?" I called toward her. She didn't answer or stop, and with each pace she got a little further ahead of me.

At the intersection in the path, I anticipated her going right, back in the direction we'd come from. But she went the opposite.

"Maya. Maya, will you just hold up?"

She scowled at me over her shoulder. "Just keep up with me, Neon. This is important."

Hobbling as best as I could, I chased after her. We dodged around shrubs, jumped over logs, and scared the shit out of a flock of lorikeets that had been eating a patch of grass nearby.

A narrow path appeared on our right, and the sign detailed that bungalow number thirty was at the end of that path.

Maya didn't stop. She ran harder. The gap between us grew bigger as she sprinted away from me.

What the hell is going on?

In the distance, Maya halted and waved me forward, then she disappeared into the bushes.

Shit! Pumping my arms, I clenched my teeth, forcing through the pain in my leg.

The path she disappeared along was for bungalow number thirty, the last one along this section of the island. I ran along the moss-covered concrete, and at the end, I avoided another disaster by jumping over the steps, onto the veranda, and through the open door.

Maya had stripped a sheet off the bed and had it spread out on the floor. She handed me a cup. "Find some water."

"What?"

"Get water in the goddamn cup, Neon." She sprinted away.

Fucking hell. I turned on the kitchen tap, and it hammered a few times before rusty water spewed from the faucet.

Maya rummaged around in the kitchen and produced a bowl and large spoon. But she barely glanced in my direction as she raced past me and out the front door.

"What the fuck's going on, Maya?"

She didn't answer.

I strode to the living room and Maya returned, tipped the water into a bowl that was full of dirt, and swirled the muddy concoction around with the spoon.

"Um, Maya, what the fuck?"

"We need to paint a sign. You start at the top right. We need a large HELP." She dipped her finger into the muddy paste, and at the bottom right-hand corner she did a large M.

Following her lead, I pushed my finger into the warm mud. "What's this for?"

"The pilot in that helicopter is my friend Levi. He's with air/sea rescue. If we're lucky, that chopper will come right back this way once he's rescued someone."

"How's this?" I pointed at my writing.

"Good. Now write, fifteen tangos have hostages."

I put more mud on my finger.

"Work fast, Neon. We don't know how long we have." The distress in her eyes radiated urgency.

"What do we do once we're done?"

"Find a place high enough for Levi to see it, and somehow draw his attention."

Her creativity was brilliant.

When we finished, the sign read:

HELP! 15 Tangos have hostages.
 Stealth meet at island marina after sunset.
 Need first aid + food.
GHOST/NEON

With the sign done, she scooped the sheet off the floor and folded it so the wet writing was on the outside. She nodded at me. "Let's go."

She sprinted away.

I chased after her. "Where are we going?"

"To find some high ground."

"What about the lighthouse?"

She flashed a grin over her shoulder. "Brilliant. Let's go."

"But they might see us."

"It's a risk we need to take. Now keep up." She left the path and barged through the shrubs like she knew exactly where she was going. Maybe she did.

Her level-headedness was like nothing I'd ever experienced before. If I'd been with any of the women I usually socialized with, or even my previous bodyguards, I'd be dead by now.

Squinting against the sunshine, I searched through the trees for the lighthouse and caught a flash of red in the distance. "There."

"Got it," Maya replied, all professional.

She slammed through bushes like a machine and flicked branches back at me that whipped my chest.

With each bush I charged through, my leg stung more. *Maybe I should've let Maya stitch my wounds.*

The ocean came into view, and then the beach. We stumbled onto an area with small yellow-leaved bushes that may have once formed a hedge. Above them, massive palm trees swayed in the breeze.

Maya ducked behind a bush, and I joined her. Whilst I panted with exhaustion, she gave me the impression she could run around the island three times and not even break a sweat.

Shielding the sun with my hand, I searched the beach. It was the horseshoe-shaped cove where I had first stepped foot on the island. "I know where we are."

"Me too." Maya peered across the ocean, probably looking for the helicopter.

The ocean had steady waves that were perfect for surfing, and there were barely any clouds in the sky. I rarely took the time to admire scenery but for some reason, today's setting captured me. Maybe it was because Maya was in the view.

Or maybe it was because this could be the last time I would ever see a setting like this.

"Let's go." Maya flopped the bed sheet over her shoulder and took off through the bushes that skirted the beach.

The lighthouse was positioned on a rocky outcrop that stuck out from the land like a fat thumb. To get to it, we had to go right around to the other side of the cove.

Halfway along, Maya squatted down and squinted through the bushes toward where the main resort would be. But the vegetation was so dense we couldn't even see the rooftops. Hopefully that meant they also couldn't see us.

Maya dashed away again, and I chased after her. Once we'd reached the area where the sand met with the rocks, she turned to me. "Stay here."

I glared at her. "Hell no."

Squeezing her eyes shut, she clamped her jaw and heaved a breath. She snapped her eyes open. "Once we get into the lighthouse, we'll be trapped."

"Exactly, that's why I need to be with you."

"Neon, you're already puffing. You won't be able to run up or down the stairs quickly enough."

"Yes, I will."

"You won't be able to fight off any tangos."

"I've got my gun."

"You've also got a death wish."

"Look, Maya, people have been trying to capture me my whole life. For the first time ever, I feel the safest I ever have. And that's because of you. The best place for me is with you."

"Jesus Christ, you're a stubborn bastard."

"So are you."

"I'm trying to save you, Neon."

"You have saved me. In more ways than you'll ever know."

A frown wrinkled her forehead.

I clutched her cheeks and planted my lips on hers. But my kiss was brief, way too brief.

She pulled back, shaking her head. "Jesus. Okay, let's go. But, Neon, don't get dead."

"I won't."

We scrambled up the rocks and at the top, she ducked down to scan the area and as I admired her sexy butt, I waited for her signal.

After waving me forward, she folded the sheet into a bundle and handed it to me. "Don't lose that."

"I won't."

As she stared up to the circular railing at the top of the lighthouse, she unclipped the clasp on her thigh holster and undid a second clip on her knife sheath.

She leaned into my ear. "It's imperative that we do this silently. Any noise, and the whole damn lot of them will be on top of us."

"Okay, got it."

"Keep on my tail." She put her finger to her lips, then scanned the bushes around us, out to the ocean, and up to the top of the lighthouse. Then, she took off.

Clutching the sheet under my right arm like a football, I crouched over and raced after her.

She darted around bushes, sprinted to the rear of the lighthouse, and stopped with her back against the wall facing the ocean. I joined her side, and she nodded at me. The woman was a machine. She wasn't even puffing, and she still looked as stunning as she had yesterday morning.

That already felt like a week ago.

She snapped her gaze to the ocean and shielded the sun with her hand. "Shit."

She snatched the sheet off me and sprinted around the lighthouse. I raced after her.

Without hesitation, she ran through the doorway, and I followed.

Inside the lighthouse, she dashed up the curved stairs. I tried to keep right on her ass by taking them two at a time. My heart thundered in my chest. My jaw hurt from clamping my teeth, and my leg stung like a bitch.

I put everything I had into keeping up with her, but she still got away.

Dragging myself upward by pulling on the railing, I could barely breathe by the time I stumbled through the doorway at the top. The blazing sunshine blinded me, and it was a couple of beats before I saw Maya. She waved her hands frantically trying to catch the attention of the chopper pilot.

I joined her, clamping my jaw so I didn't accidentally holler for help.

She billowed out the sheet and tugging at a top corner each, we held it tight and continued waving to the chopper.

It came at us at a hundred miles an hour and zoomed right overhead.

I blinked at Maya. She blinked at me.

"Did he see it?" I asked.

Her eyes darkened. "I don't know."

The chopper noise petered out in the distance. Then it changed and seemed to grow louder. Maya leaned over the railing, searching the sky in the direction the helicopter went.

Gasping, she pulled her head back. "He's coming around."

We spread the sheet out again, and the helicopter came in from the side of the island. The chopper came so close I saw the pilot.

"Lift it up," Maya hissed at me.

We raised the sheet, then Maya dropped her end, crossed her arms over in an X above her head, then flicked her hand and mouthed, Go!

The chopper roared overhead, and the thumping rotor noise returned to silence.

"It worked." Her eyes lit up.

I tugged her to my chest like she was the most vulnerable creature in the entire world. But she wasn't. Maya was the most capable, talented, incredible woman I'd ever met.

She wrapped her arms around me, and I welcomed the embrace by kissing the top of her head.

"I can't believe that worked," she said with a relieved huff.

I squeezed her harder. "I can. You're amazing."

"Thanks." She pulled back, and the sassy grin on her lips took her stunning looks to extraordinary.

My hand lingered on her shoulder. "I mean it, Maya. I've never met anyone like you."

"That's because there is no one like me." She winked and swooped her long blonde braid over her shoulder.

Fresh ocean air drifted up to us, yet I was so mesmerized by Maya I could hardly breathe.

Her breathtaking beauty commanded me to inch closer. I focused on her full lips, wondering how they could still be the color of pink cotton candy.

Maya tilted her head, capturing me with her wolf-blue eyes.

We were both silent. Words were pointless anyway. Nothing could describe the desire flowing through me.

I curled my hand over her cheek and closing her eyes, she leaned into my palm. Taking that as a sign, I kissed her.

She parted her lips, allowing me access, and arousal stirred in my groin as I tasted her. Our tongues danced in a delicious quest to savor each other. Maya whimpered into my mouth, and my cock throbbed as I deepened our kiss.

I slipped my fingers around her neck, roving over her warm skin as our breaths mingled. Clutching her tighter, I crushed her lips to mine and our hips moved as one.

Maya pressed her hand to my chest, and as a moan tumbled from her throat, she pushed back.

A breath escaped her lips and drifted away in the ocean breeze. "Well, that was a surprise, Mr. Hollywood Bachelor."

Her voice was barely a whisper.

I tilted my head, annoyed that she'd lowered our incredible kiss to that moniker, yet a little laugh escaped me. "A good surprise, I hope?"

She glided her tongue over her lips, and it took every ounce of my control not to taste her sweetness again. "An interesting one."

Voices drifted up to us. Maya ducked below the railing, yanking me down with her.

She crept to the side and peered over the railing.

Ducking back down, horror twisted her features. "Two tangos just entered the lighthouse."

"Jesus! We're trapped." A chill raced up my spine. "What do we do?"

Chapter Fourteen

MAYA

I grabbed Neon's shirt, pulling him to my face. "Get down, and don't move."

I shoved him into the corner.

He did as I instructed.

I pulled my knife from my sheath. I'd prefer a gun but couldn't risk the noise alerting the rest of these assholes to our location. I had a few things in my favor. There were only two hostiles, and they didn't run to the lighthouse like they were on the attack. I had the impression they were sent to investigate what the helicopter had hovered for but didn't suspect a thing.

At least, that was what I was hoping.

I eased to the side of the doorway, listening for them. They were easy enough to hear; the pair were chatting like they were out for a Sunday stroll.

I braced for my attack.

Their voices grew louder and echoed as the men climbed the circular stairwell inside the lighthouse. They were discussing a football game where the Texans were beaten by the Broncos, and they seemed mighty pissed about it.

Good, bring that distraction right to me, dickheads.

Clenching the knife, I inhaled deeply and let my breath out in a long slow stream. My insides were as tense as steel. I was ready.

One of the men made a disgusting noise and spat. "Do you think we'll be home in time to see the 49ers game?"

"I hope so. Those tickets were expensive."

"Yeah. But hey, once this shit is over, we won't have to worry about money again."

"Ain't that the truth."

The sun crept out from behind a cloud, piercing a beam right where we were, on the ocean side of the lighthouse. It was another tick in my favor as it would momentarily blind the men once they stepped onto the top outlook.

"What do you reckon about this Bloom guy? Sloan seems real pissed that he—"

A man stepped through the door. I froze, holding my attack until the second man appeared.

Squinting at the glare, the first man raised his hand. The second man revealed himself, and I punched his throat. He tumbled backward.

I kicked the side of the first man's knee. He toppled sideways with a howl, and I punched his temple. He slumped to the floor like a dead man.

The second man launched himself at me.

I ducked under his swinging arm and jumped behind him.

"Don't move." I jabbed my knife into his back. Not deep enough to kill him, but enough to let him know that I could.

The asshole rammed his fist backward, connecting with my stomach.

It knocked the wind out of me. The knife tumbled from my hand as I buckled over.

He spun around with his fists clenched and a weird grin on his ugly face.

Gritting my teeth, I charged at him, putting everything I had into tackling him to the ground. I connected with his stomach, drove him into the wall, and rammed my knee into his balls.

Crying out, he punched my back.

I grabbed his gun, pulled it from his hip holster, jumped away, and aimed it at his head.

He slapped the gun, knocking it from my hand, and it sailed over the railing. He punched my shoulder, spinning me away.

My hip slammed into the railing. I pulled my gun.

The other man on the floor wobbled to his feet. I ducked under his punch, yanked his arm over my shoulder, and snapped his elbow apart. As I flipped his body over mine, his feet connected with the other guy's jaw, and two of his teeth went flying.

Both men cried out in pain.

I rammed my fist into the larynx of the guy on the floor, cutting his cry in an instant.

"Don't move, bitch." A gun was rammed into my back.

A fierce growl erupted from the corner. In a blur of movement, Neon drove up from his position and charged at the gunman.

In a flurry of arms and legs, Neon picked him up and hurled him over the railing.

The gunman screamed all the way down.

"Fuck! Neon, run!" I grabbed the sheet from the floor and my knife and shot through the doorway. I sprinted down the stairs as fast as I could. "Christ! What did you do that for? The whole fucking lot of them would've heard that scream."

"I saved you."

"Yeah, well, you may have also killed us both. Now, run."

Around and around we raced down the stairs. Each time I had a visual of the ground floor entrance, I expected armed men to storm the lighthouse.

By some miracle, we reached the bottom. I paused at the door, ready to shoot any fucker who got in my way.

"Follow me." I raced out the door and sprinted to the rocks that led down to the beach. But rather than cross the sand, where our footsteps would track our departure, I raced into the bushes, hoping the vegetation would provide cover.

If the men reached the top of the tower before we hid, they would see us plain as day.

At a bush with leaves the size of skateboards, I ducked down and pulled Neon into the cover with me. "Shh."

With us pressed together, our breathing combined as the repetitive waves crashed into the shore behind us.

Shouts drifted our way.

"Find that fucking bitch!"

Neon leaned into my ear. "I don't think they like you."

I scowled at him. "Shush."

Neon seemed way too calm considering the mess we'd just dodged. Maybe he thought he was in a movie. Or maybe he thought he was invincible. Either way, his calm demeanor was a surprise. Any other civilian I knew would be out of their mind with fear.

Shouts echoed through the bushes around us, and I made Neon lower his face to the ground. "Stay completely still."

My hope was the gunmen would expect us to run away rather than stay put.

Lucky for us, the overgrown vegetation provided the perfect cover and gave them plenty of areas to search. Shouts rang out everywhere, and several times it sounded like a herd of elephants were crashing through the bushes.

It wasn't until the bruises I sustained in that attack started to throb that I prepared to move. I leaned into Neon's ear. "Time to roll. Stay right with me, okay?"

He nodded.

Crouching, I scanned the bushes. All clear.

With Neon behind me, I crept through the shrubs that skirted the beach. Keeping distance from the lighthouse, I headed toward the bridge that led to the second island where the demountable buildings had been brought in for accommodation.

If I were them, that was exactly where I'd expect a person on the run to go, and I would post an armed soldier there for that exact scenario.

We needed to head inland. Turning away from the bridge before it even came into view, I angled away from the ocean. The further we went, the denser and quieter the bushes became, and every step on the leaves and twigs were like cracks of thunder.

We stumbled onto a path, and I grabbed Neon's wrist and dragged him back into the vegetation.

We crouched behind a massive log that was so thick with moss that barely any bark was visible. Birds chirped overhead and a crow released a solemn cry somewhere in the bushes around us. Other than that, we seemed to be all alone.

"Neon Bloom." A voice blared from the distance.

"Oh no. No. No!" Neon's eyes flared.

"That stunt has cost the life of another hostage."

"Fuck!"

I clutched my hand over his mouth. "Shh."

"Tell him your name," the voice boomed.

Neon's wide eyes drilled into me.

"Tell him your name!"

A quivering voice came over the loudspeaker: "Tammy Holden."

"You hear that, Neon? Tammy Holden is going to die because of you."

Neon wrestled beneath me and moaned through my hand.

"Don't move." I pressed harder.

A gunshot boomed through the speakers, followed by screams from the rest of the hostages.

"Bloom. Her death is on you. You have twenty minutes to come out, or I will kill another one."

Neon wriggled.

I shook my head.

"No," I whispered. "He's going to kill the hostages anyway. By not answering his demands, you are keeping some of them alive."

Neon's eyes pooled, and it carved a chunk off my heart.

"Twenty minutes, Bloom. You fucking asshole."

Silence washed over us. Even the birds had stopped chirping.

I released my grip over Neon's mouth, rolled to his side, and gripped his hand.

"How do you know?" His Adam's apple bobbed up and down.

"What?"

"How can you be so sure he'll kill the hostages anyway?"

"They won't leave any witnesses behind."

143

Neon crumbled. "Jesus. We're fucked."

"No, we're not. We need to get to the marina. My team and I will take out these bastards. I promise you, Neon."

His chin quivered, and for the first time since I met him, he looked truly vulnerable.

"How's your leg?"

"I'll live."

"I know you will. Are you ready to keep going?"

He inhaled a shaky breath and then nodded.

"Good, just stay with me and keep quiet."

I rose to a crouch, and with my gun ready, we climbed over the log and crossed the path to the other side. When we entered the bushes again, a weird silence engulfed us. It was like the beautiful tropical island was mourning the horror it just witnessed.

On one hand, the gunmen seemed like amateurs.

Their leader, Sloan, however, was controlled and ruthless.

I had a feeling he was either ex-military or he'd been killing people his entire life. It wasn't easy putting a bullet through someone's brain. I would know. I had killed fourteen men that way, but every one of them was a known terrorist or vicious murderer. To kill an innocent woman demonstrated absolute brutality.

My first kill was still etched in my mind like I'd pulled the trigger that morning.

Mahmoud Shah Al Aziz was a terrorist who was in the middle of raping a woman when I'd killed him. Pulling that trigger, even though he deserved to die, had been the hardest thing I'd done in my life. With each kill, I had to force myself to think of the people I'd save by killing that monster.

Yet on this island, I may have a few more innocent deaths on my hands before we could save those hostages. For that, Sloan was going to know it was me who put a bullet in his brain.

The vegetation thinned a fraction and a couple of yards later, we reached what had once been a lagoon-style swimming pool shaped like a large kidney bean. The water was the color of pea soup, and the fake island in the middle with two palm trees had crumbled inward, making the palm trees cross over like a large X.

Voices drifted to us through the vegetation. I ducked down, and Neon crouched with me.

I couldn't work out where they were coming from.

The voices grew louder, and I snapped my gaze left and right.

I snatched the sheet off Neon, scrunched it to as small as possible, and rammed it under a thick bush to conceal it.

Someone coughed in the distance.

Shit, they're getting closer.

I leaned into Neon's ear. "Let's get in the water."

Neon jerked back, shaking his head.

I grabbed his arm. "Get into the water."

"No." He shuddered, and his eyes bulged with more fear than I'd seen on him so far.

The voices continued to grow louder. I searched the bushes, but I couldn't find their origin.

I dug my nails into his arm. "If we go back into the bushes, we could run right into them. The water is our only option."

"I'm not doing it, Maya." He spoke through clenched teeth.

His rigid stature convinced me he wouldn't.

"Do you want to die?"

He shook his head. "I'm not—"

I pinched a pressure point in his hand and when Neon crumbled under my vice, I yanked him forward. "Come with me."

Neon was like a zombie as I pulled him toward the edge of the pool. His erratic breathing punched in and out.

What the hell is wrong with him?

I dragged him to the railing at the top of a ladder that disappeared into the swamp. "Get in."

He trembled. "I can't."

"I'll be right with you. We'll do it together," I whispered in his ear, trying to stay calm despite my heart thundering in my ear.

"I can't."

I clutched his cheeks, drawing his gaze to mine. "Yes, you can. Now follow me."

The voices bounced everywhere like they were surrounding us, ready to attack. Their casual tones suggested otherwise though.

I turned and entered the pool backward. "Come on, Neon. You've got this."

I slinked into the warm water, scooping a layer of moss away. Reaching up, I grabbed his ankle and he jumped.

What the hell?

"Neon," I begged. "Get in here now, or we both die."

Neon clamped his jaw and squeezed his eyes shut. I yanked on his jeans, trying to pull him in with me.

He snapped his eyes open and the sheer terror in his expression was brutal. He reached for the ladder railing and lowered his uninjured right leg into the water.

"That's it. You've got this."

Inch by inch, he slipped into the water, but he was so slow I was tempted to knock him out and manhandle him into the swamp with me.

When he was waist deep, I grabbed his shoulder and dragged him in.

He gasped.

"Shh."

His chin trembled and his bulging eyes revealed his terror.

Christ! He really is scared of the water.

The voices became louder.

If I didn't get him to that island, we were both dead.

Chapter Fifteen

NEON

Swampy water sucked at my sanity, dragging me back twenty years to that rotten well I'd been trapped in for days. I could smell that foul stench. Darkness crept into my vision, threatening to engulf me. My breaths burned in my throat.

Maya clutched my arm. "Swim."

I couldn't let go of the ladder.

She scooped away green scum, released her grip on the ladder, and swam off. The moss moved back into position as if removing her existence.

That was how I'd felt in the well. Like I didn't exist. Only my kidnapper had known where I was. For days and nights, I'd stood in that ankle-deep water, waiting.

Waiting to be rescued. Waiting for food. Waiting for the sun to rise.

Waiting to drown.

"Neon." Maya appeared in front of me like an angel. She peeled my fingers off the ladder. "We have to move. Hang onto my shoulder."

I squeezed her shoulder so hard I'd make bruises, but I couldn't help it.

We left the safety of the edge, and she forced me across the swamp, heading to what was left of the island in the middle.

Men's voices seemed to bounce off the water and I couldn't tell if it was two people or ten.

Something slithered over my ankle and gasping, I let go of Maya's shoulder.

She grabbed my hand and spun around so she swam backward. Kicking underwater, she maintained her gaze on me, and as I stared into her eyes, we crossed the swamp to the island in the middle.

The roots on the palm trees in the fake island had split the island in half, making a watery gap big enough for us to squeeze into. Maya shoved me into the space first, and I clung to a root as thick as my arm. Beneath the water, I found a ledge to stand on and I fought the urge to use it to launch myself from the swamp.

Maya must've read my mind because she pressed on my shoulders, making me sink down to my neck. She ducked her head back and covered her hair and face with moss. Then she turned with her back to me and pressed her body to mine, shielding me from whatever horror was to come next.

Alternating my gaze between the slime in Maya's hair and the bushes around the pool, I tried to drag my mind from the water around me.

My ragged breaths gushed out of me in short sharp gasps.

The voices grew louder.

Maya shifted around to face me and pressed her finger to my lips, motioning me to shush.

She rubbed more slime onto her lovely skin, making my beautiful bodyguard look like a creature from the swamp.

Adjusting her position, she angled so she would be able to see the opposite edge of the pool, and I could see the left side of her face.

I stiffened as a man appeared through the bushes, and I lowered into the water to my chin.

A second man followed the first, and they strolled to the edge of the pool and lit cigarettes. Both men were clearly visible, which meant if they peered hard enough our way, they'd see us.

My heart thundered in my chest and ears. Fear inched up my spine.

Maya lowered further until the water was over her mouth and chin. Only her eyelids moved.

The men silently sucked on their cigarettes and leaned their heads back to blow the smoke skyward. Both had a rifle across their chest.

Their silence was weird. Maybe they were as horrified by those brutal murders as I was.

If Maya was right, and they didn't intend to keep any hostages alive, then these men were just as guilty as that bastard who'd pulled the trigger.

I searched their faces but didn't recognize either of them. If they had been part of the movie crew, then I hadn't noticed them. Then again, I never paid too much attention to the crew. I wished I did.

I wished a lot of things.

Like being able to save Linda, Camilla, and Tammy.

Like putting an end to this horror.

Like being able to have a normal life.

"You think he's gonna give himself in?" the taller of the two gunmen said.

"Fuck no. He's an asshole. He doesn't care who dies."

I stiffened, and Maya reached back and squeezed my arm.

"Then what're we going to do?"

"We have to find him. And that bitch."

"I wouldn't mind having a piece of her. From what Hank said, she sounds fucking hot."

The shorter guy backhanded his friend's chest. "Let's go. I've gotta eat something."

"You're always hungry." They flicked their cigarette butts into the pool, turned, and entered the scrub.

"That lunch wasn't enough. I tell you what—"

Their voices absorbed into the bushes.

Maya's rigid body remained stiff beside me. She shushed me again by pressing her finger to her lips, and we waited.

And waited.

It was way too long before she finally shifted and waved for me to follow her. Gripping my hand, she dragged me back across the pool and we climbed the ladder. We ran into the vegetation, leaving wet footprints in our wake. She grabbed the sheet she'd hidden under a bush and continued running.

It was several yards before she ducked down, hiding behind a massive bush covered in small black berries. I squatted with her.

"Are you okay?" she whispered.

"Define okay." I rolled my eyes.

She placed her hand on my forearm. "That was close. If you didn't get into that water . . ."

She didn't finish her sentence. She didn't need to.

I lowered my gaze. Being afraid of water was embarrassing. Before now, my parents were the only people who knew that about me. Somehow, I'd managed to get through my adult life without anyone learning of my weakness.

Now Maya knew. I felt like a stupid fool.

I'd never had treatment for my phobia. I barely admitted it to myself.

And yet it was always there, like a giant elephant sitting squarely on my chest.

"Hey." Maya brushed her hand up my arm. "It's okay. What you did was very brave."

I huffed.

"Why didn't you tell me you were scared of water?"

I bulged my eyes. "I don't know. Maybe because I barely know you."

She scooped slime off her cheek and flicked it away. "Do you have any other phobias I need to know about?"

"No," I snapped.

She squeezed slime from her braid. "Don't worry. Your secret is safe with me."

Her tone was loaded with frustration.

I groaned. Pissed off at myself for both having the stupid fear, and for talking to Maya like that, I said, "I'm sorry."

"No need to be. Let's keep moving."

She took off through the bushes, running at a cracking pace, jumping over shrubs and ducking beneath low-hanging palm fronds. Her blonde hair was green from the swamp. I feared if she got too far ahead, I'd lose her altogether.

I had no idea where we were going, but Maya maintained a course that seemed evident to her. Every so often she glanced skyward.

Is she using the sun to orientate herself? That wouldn't surprise me; Maya was the perfect soldier.

Blazing sunshine appeared through a clearing ahead. Before she reached the area, Maya squatted in bushes, and I slotted in at her side.

We'd reached the playground again, which meant we'd gone right around the island.

"Clear." Maya bolted away.

She hadn't even waited for me to catch my breath.

Was she pissed at me? I fucking hoped not. I was doing enough of that for both of us.

Chasing after her, I raced toward the slippery slide near the swings that were barely visible beneath a thriving vine.

I hobbled around the merry-go-round, wincing at the pain in my leg. It was getting worse. My wet jeans were strangling my calf and the rubbing made the wounds sting like hell.

Her gaze darted from my wounded leg to my eyes. She shook her head like she was absconding a naughty child.

"It's the wet jeans," I said as I eased in beside her beneath the slippery slide.

"And the open wounds."

I didn't reply.

She frowned at me. "You okay to keep moving?"

"Lead the way." I swept my hand forward.

Maya handed the rolled-up sheet to me. "Hang onto this."

"Why are we keeping it?" I grabbed it off her.

"Because we don't want those assholes finding it. We have no way to convey a change of rendezvous point to my team."

"Huh."

"Huh, what?"

"You think of everything."

"Just trying to keep one step ahead of those bastards."

"It's more than that, Maya. I'm really lucky you're here."

She swept a green lump off her cheek. "Thanks, but we're not out of the woods yet."

"Literally," I said as I followed her into the bushes.

"Let's keep the chatter down. I need to be able to hear them."

"Yes, captain."

She snapped her gaze to me over her shoulder with an expression that was equal parts sassy and sexy. My heart skipped a beat. Today was one of the worst days of my life, and Maya was stirring up sensations in me that added to the chaos.

It was yin and yang. Mars and Venus. Agonizingly wonderful.

I'd had dozens of women. I'd had two steady relationships that both lasted just on twelve months. But I'd never had the kind of desire I was feeling toward Maya.

Maybe it was because she wasn't throwing herself at me. She seemed uninterested.

Except for when we'd kissed. That had felt real.

Hopefully I'd have a chance to explore more of that before this was over.

And after.

Would she want to see me after all this bullshit?

Maya pushed through a palm frond that was the size of her and held it back for me to pass.

"I like what you've done with your hair." I wriggled my brows. "That green tinge suits you."

"Very funny. At least it doesn't stink like some of the shit I've crawled through."

And here I was thinking that it stunk a lot. Or maybe my senses were being tricked into smelling that well again. That happened more often than I wanted. It could be simple things like rain falling in a muddy puddle or a dead animal on the side of the road. I couldn't even sniff milk that was past its use-by date.

As if she was following some invisible path, Maya shifted direction and headed left.

"How do you know where you're going?"

"A hunch. Now shush."

Slipping in behind her again, I was treated to a fine view of her sexy ass as she climbed over a log. Maya didn't have an ounce of fat on her. Her muscles were well defined, yet not too big to put her out of proportion. I'd seen many stunt women who went so far with their muscle toning that sometimes they doubled as male characters.

Maya retained her femininity, yet she was still badass. And fucking awesome.

Sounds of waves crashing into shore drifted to me, and within a short distance, we stepped onto the boardwalk that skirted the edge of the marina.

Maya slapped my chest. "My hunch was right."

Smiling, I nodded. I didn't think there was a thing Maya couldn't do.

Darting her gaze from the bushes we'd come from to the crippled hut at the end of the main pier, Maya strode away.

I followed her, inhaling the cleansing scent of the ocean.

She took the sheet off me and placed it onto the timber decking. She pulled the gun from her thigh holster and rested it on the sheet, then she did the same with the weapon in her hip holster and removed a third from the back of her cargo pants. She pulled the knife from the sheath and placed it next to her guns.

"You're channeling Lara Croft."

"Ha. Not quite. I do my own stunts." She tilted her head my way and grinned. Her smile was so spectacular a breath hitched in my throat.

She peeled out of her boots and poured out swamp water.

"What are we doing now?" I asked.

"I'm going for a swim." She placed her boots upside down on the decking.

"What?"

"I found a leech on my arm earlier. So, I want to make sure I don't have any more of those bloodsuckers on me. Salt water will do the trick."

"Fucking hell, can this get any worse?" I scanned my arms and shuddered.

She undid the buttons on her navy shirt and peeled it open to reveal a plain black bra and a finely toned body beneath. If Maya was shy about undressing in front of me, she didn't show it.

With repeated glances toward the bushes, she stepped out of her cargo pants.

"You get a good look?" She cocked her eyebrow.

"Sorry." I snapped my gaze away, yet I didn't miss the smirk on her face.

Did she like me watching her?

She grabbed her gun. "You coming in with me?"

Shit. I looked at the water. Compared to the swamp we'd been in, this was pristine. But I couldn't do it. I shook my head.

"Your loss. Keep an eye out, Neon. If you hear anyone coming, whistle. Okay?"

"Can I have a gun?"

"No."

"How come you get to have all the fun?" I pulled a sad face.

"Because that's what you paid me to do."

"You're mean."

Grumbling, she handed a gun to me. "Here. But *if* you need to shoot . . . shoot to kill. Got it?"

I saluted her. "Got it."

She grabbed her knife and gun and slinked away like a cat. At the ladder, she put the gun onto the edge of the boardwalk, clamped the knife between her teeth, and climbed down until she disappeared below the edge.

I pulled off my shoes, dumped out the water, and rested them upside down like Maya had done with her boots. I removed my socks and quickly searched my feet and between my toes for blood-sucking worms.

Thankfully, I didn't need to deal with that horror.

I unzipped out of the costume shirt I'd been wearing for a day and a half and scanned my arms and legs. The fresh air on my skin felt like a soothing tonic.

I squeezed the water out of my socks and the swampy odor invaded my nostrils. Shuddering at the damn stench, I turned to search for Maya but couldn't see her.

Waves crashed into the shore with therapeutic repetition, but other than that, there was no other noise. Beyond the pier, the ocean stretched as far as I could see, and in the distance, olive green hills of the mainland were just visible.

Is Maya's team really coming?

She seemed certain they were. Who was her team? And why didn't she ask for the police instead?

They were good questions. Ones I hoped she would answer.

Maya popped her head above the ladder.

"Hey." She waved me over.

I hobbled her way.

"Take these."

I gasped. "You found oysters."

"And there's plenty more where they came from."

I grabbed the oysters from her, and she slipped back into the ocean. Like a mermaid, she glided beneath the water, treating me to a truly magnificent show as she duck-dived and swam underwater toward the stumps on the pier.

I carried her haul to the sheet, and by the time I returned to the ladder, she had another batch.

Maya repeated the move twice more, providing enough oysters for a feast. "That should do it for now."

She rolled her head back, fanning her long hair out in the water, then climbed the ladder. "The water is beautiful. Are you sure you don't want a swim?"

I shook my head. "I'm fine."

"Okay, but you still need to get your pants off."

I grinned at her. "Are you always this romantic?"

She gave me an in-your-dreams look. "You won't be thinking I'm so romantic if you find a leech on your balls."

"Shit." I raced to the sheet, dumped the load of oysters from my arms, and unzipped my jeans. The wet denim was a struggle to pull down and with my jeans around my knees, I checked inside my jocks.

Maya clamped her jaw like she was holding back a laugh.

"Yep. I'm fine." I yanked off my wet jeans and turned my back to her. "Are there any on my back?"

"Shit, Neon. Hold still."

"Oh God, what is it?"

She rested her hand on my shoulder blade. "You had a wet leaf."

She handed it to me, grinning like a lunatic.

"Not funny, Maya."

Giggling, she slapped my arm. "Come on, that was funny."

"No, it wasn't." I tossed my wet jeans onto the boardwalk with a soggy plop.

She grabbed a handful of her hair and squeezed out water. "Sorry. That was a bit mean of me."

"A lot mean."

"Okay. You're right. I'm sorry." She offered her hand. "Friends."

Friends? I'd like to be a whole lot more than just friends.

I shook her hand. Her grip was firm, and yet somehow also gentle.

As she squeezed more water from her thick hair, I picked up an oyster. "So how do we get into these things? I'm starving."

"I'll handle the oysters. But, Neon, as your doctor, I'm insisting that you bathe your wound in the salt water. And not just that. Leeches love blood. They could be beneath that bandage."

"Fuck." I raised my leg. The bandages Maya had applied yesterday were covered in blood and green slime.

I sat down, undid the knot keeping the bandage in place, and peeled it away.

"I wish you'd let me stitch those wounds." She groaned. "Damn it. I left that sewing kit in the bungalow."

"I'll be fine."

Maya shook her head. "That swamp was a Petri dish of germs. Bacteria is probably already working its way into your system. You need to get into the ocean and give those wounds a good scrub. It's going to hurt like hell, but it's better than the alternative."

The last section of bandage stuck to the jagged, bloody flesh, and I winced as I peeled it away. The smell made me gag.

"Christ!" She offered her hand. "Get up, Neon. We need to clean that wound."

I gripped her hand, and Maya helped me stand.

Every step toward the ocean was like walking through wet concrete, but I had to do this. The thought of getting into that water terrified me. The stench of my bloody wound scared me more.

Maya put her gun next to the ladder and climbed down to the water first. With my heart thundering, I forced my legs to follow her down.

The water was warmer than it looked, and I winced as the salty ocean stung my jagged flesh like a thousand needles.

"Hang onto the ladder," she said.

I gripped the ladder like it was a safety harness, and Maya lifted my leg to the surface. As gentle as an angel, she bathed my wound, scooping water over the jagged cuts and swirling red clouds in the water. The sting was brutal, and my heart thumped to a pounding beat.

But my attention was captivated by Maya. Her professionalism. Her tenderness. Her concern.

Her everything.

She released my leg. "There you go. That's the best we can do for now."

Standing on the sand, with the water up to my waist, I reached for her and pulled her toward me.

She floated my way and our lips met as she wrapped her legs around my waist.

I glided my hand over her back, feeling her silky wet skin. She parted her lips and our tongues danced in an eager quest to taste each other.

I flicked the clip on her bra, and Maya moaned as I cupped her breast, squeezing her delightful flesh in my palm. Her legs tightened around my waist as she pressed herself tighter to me.

Her breasts were perfect.

She moaned again, and I did too as our kiss deepened.

She glided her fingers up my back and along my neck, driving delightful shivers over my scalp.

Her nipple hardened beneath my caress, and I pinched her delicate bud.

Gasping, Maya pulled back. Her eyes shifted from me to the ocean around us, and her expression changed from being lost in a world of lust to aware of where we were.

She unhooked her legs and slipped off me, clearing her throat. "Well, it looks like we found a way to cure your fear of water."

I smiled. "Hmm, I'm not sure. I think we need to try some more."

Giggling, she flicked her gaze between my eyes and my mouth, and my cock throbbed at the intensity in her expression.

I reached for her and she eased away, repositioning her bra and clipping it up. "Neon, have you forgotten about the assholes trying to kill us?"

My shoulders slumped as Maya turned away and climbed the ladder. Her bare back was everything dreams are made of: sexy, silky, and stunning.

I followed her out of the water and back to our stash. She put her gun down next to the others and over to the side, she squeezed water from her long hair and tousled it.

It took all my might to tear my gaze from her. All my life, I'd been surrounded by women who'd do anything to get naked in front of me. But Maya was the first woman I'd met who I truly wished would do it.

We gave our clothes a quick wash in the ocean and laid them out to dry in the sun. She also gave the bloody bandages a wash and spread them along the boardwalk too.

Back at the hut, she turned the sheet over so the muddy writing faced downward, and we sat on the sheet with our backs against the weathered timber.

Using her knife, she cracked open an oyster and handed it to me.

I waved it away. "Ladies first."

Maya scooped her knife beneath the oyster and tipped it into her mouth.

How did she make everything look so damn sexy?

"Oh my god. That tastes so good." She moaned.

She closed her eyes and as she inhaled, her chest rose and fell, drawing my attention to the swell of her breasts. It was like watching flames in a cozy fire. That was what she was doing to me, lighting fires inside me. But these I did not want to put out.

Did she feel the same?

She cracked a second oyster apart and handed it to me. "I hope you like seafood."

"I do." I gulped the oyster down. "Oh wow, that's the best I've ever tasted."

"And probably the freshest."

"That's for sure."

As we feasted on the oysters and warmed our bodies in the hot sun, it was tempting to believe Maya and I were merely on a picnic, rather than hiding from ruthless killers.

After we'd eaten, we tossed the empty oyster shells into the ocean, and Maya washed our sheet, removing all evidence of our written request to her friends.

We spread the sheet out in the sun too. Then with our backs against the remains of the thatched hut, and Maya's weapons within reach, we sat peering over the ocean.

We were both silent. I had no idea what Maya was thinking, but I wondered how I could get a repeat of the amazing kiss, without getting back into the water.

"Hey, Neon, how long have you been scared of water?"

I groaned. That wasn't the conversation starter I was hoping for.

She placed her hand on my knee. "I've never met anyone with that phobia. Did you nearly drown? Is that how it started?"

Squeezing my eyes shut, I leaned my head back against the timber. Images of my kidnapping flooded my mind, and I snapped my gaze to the ocean.

Maya glided her hand up my thigh. "Tell me, Neon."

A knot of panic burned in my chest. Revealing my childhood horror was not something I'd planned on telling Maya, and yet at the same time, I wanted to. I wanted her to know everything about me. The real me. The man who was so far hidden from the world, I forgot who he was half the time.

My connection to Maya was as powerful as the ocean in front of us. Maybe sharing my painful past would draw her closer.

She squeezed my leg, coaxing me to release my nightmare.

I heaved a long breath. It was time. "You know how I told you about being kidnapped when I was nine?"

"Yes."

"Well, he held me captive in a disused well."

"A well? As in a water well?"

"Yes. For two days, I stood ankle deep in water that stunk of shit and dead animals."

She caressed my leg and her haunting eyes found mine. "Oh, Neon, that would have been terrifying."

159

"When I couldn't stand anymore, I had to sit in that disgusting water, and the only light I had was the circle of sunshine that was visible for only a short amount of time. The night was the worst. It was so dark."

"Bloody hell, Neon. Now I understand why you're scared of water. Your fear makes perfect sense."

"For a long time, my parents couldn't even get me to shower, and I still can't get in a bath, let alone that." I waved my hand toward the ocean.

Maya crawled over my lap, straddling my legs to face me. "But you did get in."

I sighed. "You helped."

She placed her hands on my bare chest. "No, Neon. I didn't knock you out and throw you in. Though I admit I thought about it. You forced through the fear to get in."

I nodded. "I did, didn't I?"

"And now that you told me this, what you did in that swamp was incredible."

Huffing, I curled my fingers over her thighs, wishing she would kiss me again. My cock throbbed to life as my eyes captured the half-naked woman in my lap. Her long lashes. Her cotton-candy lips. The tiny droplets of water that glistened off her bare shoulder like diamonds.

Her lips parted. Her tongue slicked her lips, and she leaned forward.

Hoping I read her signals correctly, I met her halfway.

Our kiss was tender at first with our lips barely brushing together. Then, she leaned forward more, crushing her lips to mine. I roved my hands over her glorious curves, savoring every inch of her flesh.

I unclipped her bra, and she whipped the lingerie off in a flash. She wriggled forward and my groin throbbed beneath her movement. Maybe she felt the bulge in my jocks because she glided her hips back and forth, captured my lips with hers, and pressed her tongue into my mouth.

I clutched her breasts, caressing and squeezing her glorious mounds.

She curled her hand around my neck, pulling me closer.

Eager for more, I slipped my hand into her panties, and Maya eased up from my lap, giving me room to explore.

I plunged my finger inside her and as she gasped, her warmth wrapped around my finger. I was torn between watching this incredible woman lose herself to my touch and closing my eyes to savor the feel of her hot body.

She squeezed her thighs, trapping me in her clutches, and I thrust my finger, harder and faster. She rolled her head forward and sucked on my neck.

My cock throbbed to a painful beat as I drove my finger inside her over and over.

A cry left her throat and a glorious warmth spilled onto my hand.

I kept up my momentum, drawing out Maya's orgasm until she flopped onto my chest.

As she planted delicate kisses on my neck, I slid my hands over her warm back.

A sigh tumbled from her lips. "Wow, that was—"

A crackling noise erupted behind us, and we both jumped. Maya scrambled off my legs and grabbed her gun.

The crackling grew louder.

"There's a speaker under here." She pointed at the mangled thatch hut.

As we pulled away pieces of timber, the crackling became squealing. We couldn't understand a single word.

But we didn't need to.

That fucking asshole was killing another hostage.

Chapter Sixteen

MAYA

We couldn't understand Sloan's voice on the crackling speaker, and I was equal parts fucking pissed off and grateful. Neon didn't need to hear what was going on.

He already knew. The sadness in his eyes washed a darkness over him like a locust plague.

There wasn't a damn thing he could do to help them.

The squealing pitch from the speaker somewhere beneath the crumbled hut switched to crackling again.

A huge bang erupted from beneath the rubble.

"Fuck!" Neon kicked a piece of timber, hurling it so far it skidded off the boardwalk into the tumbling waves.

"Hey." I wrapped him in a bear hug. "Hey, shh."

"That fucker he, he . . ." Neon didn't finish his sentence.

I squeezed my breasts to his bare chest, wishing I could take away his pain, but he was as stiff as a surfboard.

He inhaled a shaky breath. "Who did he kill?"

I shook my head.

"Who?" A sob caught in his throat.

I tried to pull away to look up at him, but he gripped me tighter in his arms.

"Here I am, hoping to get laid," he said, his words a strangled croak, "while someone else is getting their brains blown out half a mile away because of me."

"Don't do that to yourself, Neon. It's not your fault."

"It fucking is, Maya." He jerked out of my clutches and stormed off.

"Shit." I snatched my bra, shirt, and gun from the ground and chased after him.

He was fast but still limping.

As I tugged on my bra, I searched the bushes. The sun had passed overhead since we'd arrived, and its golden rays speared along the access route to the marina, giving me a visual of about fifty yards along the pathway before it vanished into bushes.

But the distance wasn't enough. If gunmen came running along that path, Neon and I were screwed.

Neon reached the end of the boardwalk and with his back to me, he looked out to the ocean. His body was rigid as he stood with his arms folded over his chest. When he reached up to his face, I imagined he wiped away tears.

I paused about ten feet from him, giving him time to himself, and pulled on my shirt that was nearly dry and did up the buttons. I spun to a rustling noise in the bushes and aimed my gun toward a shrub that was the size of a baby elephant.

A rock wallaby bounced out of the scrub and darted onto the boardwalk. Three more smaller ones appeared, and they played follow the leader, jumping along the weathered timber and disappearing into the bushes at the other end.

I lowered my gun and turned back to Neon.

He was watching me, but his expression was twisted and heartbroken.

"Are you okay?"

"No, Maya, I'm not fucking okay."

"Sorry. Stupid question."

He huffed and rolled his eyes skyward. I followed his gaze to a pair of seagulls that swooped and dipped with the ocean breeze.

My attention drifted back to Neon. "Hey, will you come back to our gear, please? It's hard for me to protect you out in the open like this."

"You can't protect me, Maya. Nobody can."

"Excuse me, but I have been doing exactly that."

"Yes. This time. But what about next time? Or the one after that? They will never stop."

"Who? Who won't stop?"

"Them." He swung his arm open, indicating to the other side of the island. "And when it's not them, it will be some other fucker. It's never going to end. And now it's not just me who's in danger. It's the people I'm with. It's . . . it's." He choked on the final word.

I strode to him and wrapped my arms around his bare chest.

He squeezed me to his body and his thumping heart pounded in my ear.

I glided my hand up his back, feeling the dip and grooves of his muscles. "I'm sorry, Neon. I'm so sorry this is happening to you."

He curled his hand over my hair. "But it's not just me anymore."

"No, it's not. And I'm sorry for that too."

"Nobody will come near me again. I'm toxic. Deadly."

"I will." I eased away so I could look at him. The sadness in his eyes carved a chunk from my heart.

He softened his stance. "Thanks."

"Now, will you please come back to the hut? We're sitting ducks out here."

He released his grip, and I reached for his hand. Walking with our palms squeezed together, we returned to our measly belongings.

I picked up my cargo pants. "Damn, they're still wet."

"I prefer them on the floor anyway."

I chuckled. "Really?"

"Really." Neon wore only a pair of Dolce & Gabbana black briefs, yet he didn't make a move toward his jeans. I'd seen many military men in their underwear; none of them looked as sexy as Neon.

He was lean, muscular, and incredible. His muscles were well-toned, probably from custom-designed workouts. He had olive skin, broad shoulders, and stunning looks that would stand out in any crowd. Even in Hollywood.

It was a pity we went in different circles because I'd like to get to know more about him.

If we get out of this fucking mess, that is.

Dragging my eyes away, I returned my pants to the ground, flipping them over so the other side could dry in the sun.

I folded over the sheet and laid it out next to the remaining wall of the hut. We sat side by side. Ahead of us, the sun reflected off the water like a disco ball on steroids. A slight breeze brought with it scents of the ocean that I loved. I could never live anywhere that didn't give me that simple luxury every day.

I rubbed my hand over my thigh where a bruise was forming over my quad muscle.

"Nice bruise," Neon said.

"Thanks. I can't believe I let that guy get the jump on me at the lighthouse."

"It was two against one. You did amazing."

"I got lucky. If he'd pulled a weapon, I'd be dead."

"You're still amazing."

I huffed. "Thanks."

He pointed at the lily flower tattooed on my middle finger. "That's cute."

"Thanks."

He leaned forward, trying to look me in the eye. He wanted to ask me something, and whatever it was, I wasn't going to like it.

"Hey, Maya?"

Here we go.

"Yeah?"

He nudged his shoulder to mine. "Why do you have angel wings tattooed on the back of your neck?"

I groaned. That was a conversation I didn't want to have. But given that Neon had opened himself to me and shown me his vulnerable side, I wanted to tell him. I was tempted to even share more about myself.

And that never happened.

Men never wanted to know the real Maya, and I'd made it my mission to guard myself against such inquisitions. Yet here I was, preparing to tell a story that even Blade and my team didn't know.

"It's hard, isn't it?" He heaved a sigh.

"What?" I cocked my head at him and our eyes met, deepening our connection.

"Opening up. Sharing secrets."

"Oh. That."

Neon picked at a chipped fingernail. He probably had his nails done every week.

I hated that my mind went there. Neon may be a Hollywood superstar with all the money in the world, but I'd seen a side to him that I never thought possible. He deserved to see a side to me that nobody had either.

I ran my hand over the back of my neck. Even though I rarely saw that tattoo, I'd never forget it was there. "Both my tattoos are for my sister, Lily."

"Oh Jeez, Maya. She died young."

I blinked at him, frowning.

He shrugged. "The dates below the angel wings. She was only nineteen when she died."

"Huh, you really did look at my tattoo."

He shrugged again. "You're good to look at."

I cocked my head. "Does that work for you?"

"What?"

"That direct approach. My clothes are better on the floor. I'm good to look at. Who says stuff like that?"

"Me. Obviously. And yes, it does work."

"Oh, I bet it does." Not that Neon would need to try hard. He ticked so many boxes on the Hot Hollywood Hunk spectrum that he would just need to look at some women and they would peel out of their clothing.

"You're changing the subject," he said.

"What subject?"

"Your angel wing tattoo."

"I told you it was for my sister."

He twisted his position to look at me better. "We're a good pair, aren't we?"

"What do you mean?"

"We're both guarded, pretending to be something we're not."

"Who says I'm pretending?"

"Me."

"I wasn't pretending when I killed those assholes."

"I'm not talking about that, Maya. I'm talking about pretending everything is hunky dory with your life, when clearly, it's not."

"I never said my life was hunky dory as you put it. You assumed that."

"Okay, you're right. I'm sorry." He rested his hand over mine and squeezed. "So, what happened to your sister?"

I tugged my hand from his and pressed my palms over my eyes until bright spots danced behind my eyelids.

Can I really tell a relative stranger a story that I haven't even told my best friends?

After what we'd been through and what he'd shared with me, it seemed right. Neon seemed right. And that admission scared the hell out of me.

I removed my hands and squinted at the glistening water. "My sister and I shared a bedroom, and I came home from school to find her on her bed covered in vomit and blood. She was conscious, just, but she wouldn't talk to me."

"Shit. How old were you?"

"Fifteen."

His gaze softened at me. "Oh, Maya, I'm so sorry."

A wave of anger reared inside me and I forced it down. "I was holding Lily's hand when she died."

"Jesus! So, she was still alive when you found her? Was an ambulance called?"

"Yes, she was alive, barely. And no, no ambulance was called." I clenched my jaw, forcing away the images of my mother praying to God to save Lily.

Why didn't I call an ambulance? Why?

"Maya, please?" He curled his hand over my shoulder and squeezed me to him. "I can see you're hurting. Tell me what happened."

I moaned. "It's a long story."

Neon swept his hand to our view. "And we have nothing to do until your friends get here."

I wriggled out of his embrace and strode to my cargo pants. Confirming they were dry, I tugged them on, and my shoes and socks. I also strapped my gun holsters in position.

Neon watched me dress, and I refused to look him in the eyes. A wave of sadness washed through me along with a tornado of other emotions. Anger, but that always came when I thought of my sister, and guilt. There was also embarrassment . . . I'd been so brainwashed by my parents and their trust in faith, that I had believed God would save Lily.

But there was something else crashing through me, and it was so unprecedented it dominated nearly everything: desire.

Desire for Neon.

Maybe it was because Neon had opened up so completely to me. Men never did that. They were always guarded. Macho. I'd seen it in all my team—Blade, Levi, Cobra, and especially Viper; he had some shit going on that was deep.

I swept my gaze to Neon, and he looked at me so completely that another crazy thought steamrolled over all my others: we were destined to meet.

That was totally messed up. Neon and I lived in different worlds, and it took a crazy bunch of circumstances to put us together. After this, we'd go back to our own lives and never see each other again.

I needed to stop my craziness before my emotions took over too much and put me in another mess I'd have trouble climbing out of.

"Maya, it's okay, you don't have to tell me." Disappointment marred his expression, and my heart clenched.

I have to tell him about Lily.

After his revelation, it was the right thing to do.

He needed to get dressed first before my body did things that I wouldn't be able to stop.

"You better put your jeans on, just in case we, um . . ."

"Sure." He stood and when he put his wounded leg down, he stumbled.

"Hey, let me check your wounds first." I squatted at his feet and examined the cuts down his shin. I shook my head. "Neon, these are still bleeding. You need stitches."

"I'm fine."

169

"No. You are in danger of getting an infection, and that could cost you your leg."

He bulged his eyes at me. "A bit dramatic, don't you think?"

"No, it's not."

He grumbled.

I strode to where I'd laid out the bandages in the sun. They were still covered in blood and slime stains, but at least they were dry. As I rolled them up, a crackling noise erupted from the speaker hidden in the thatch.

"Shit." I dropped the bandage, and with rage blazing through me, I yanked away bits of timber and metal, searching for the source of the horror. A squeal blared from a thicket of crumbling thatch roof. I pulled it apart, found the rusted speaker, and yanked out the cords.

The squeal was replaced with the sounds of crashing waves from the ocean behind us.

I tossed the wires away. Clamping my jaw, I dusted my hand on my pants and returned to Neon. His sorrow was so palpable he looked like he'd implode.

No words could explain what was cascading through my mind.

He would be the same.

I wanted to wrap my arms around him and share our pain. But for my own sanity, I had to walk away.

"I'm going to wash my hands, then I'll redress your wound. It's not ideal with those used bandages, but it's all we have." I marched to the edge of the boardwalk.

Hooking my leg around the ladder railing, I leaned into the water to scrub my hands. The lack of antiseptic was an issue, but at least I had salt water. I'd saved men in much worse conditions than this.

But most of them were soldiers I didn't know. Neon was different. He was a part of me now, forever forged into my brain. If anything happened to him, especially when I could have done something to stop his bleeding, that would crush me.

Air drying my hands, I returned to Neon. He'd tugged on his shirt and had his jeans in his hands, ready to pull on.

"Hey, keep your pants off."

"Now who's being direct?" He attempted a joke, but his humor didn't reach his eyes.

"Sit there." I nodded at the sheet.

He did as I requested, and I picked up the bandage I'd tossed away and rolled it up. Kneeling at Neon's feet, I applied the dressing. Silence mushroomed between us like a storm cloud.

Maybe he was questioning what the hell was going on between us too.

I finished with the second bandage. "Done. I hope that's enough to get you through until you get proper treatment."

"I'll be okay. Besides, this will all be over once your friends get here."

I glanced at the horizon. It was at least two more hours until sunset. It couldn't come soon enough.

"Right. Until then, rest that leg."

"Yes, boss." He winked at me.

He pulled on his jeans, and I couldn't drag my eyes from the bulge and flex of his sexy ass. His grin confirmed he'd caught me peeking, but thankfully he didn't say anything.

Nor did he say anything when we sat side by side on the folded sheet again.

The seagulls squawked overhead like they were yelling at us for invading their space.

The waves continued to crash into the blocks beneath the boardwalk. The sun continued its slide into the distance. The longer the silence stretched between us, the less I wanted to share the story of my sister's death. I was certain to cry. And if he comforted me like he'd done a few times already, I wouldn't be able to hold back.

"Hey, Maya?" He said my name with a pleading lilt.

I braced for the Lily question again. "Yeah."

"Do you think I could see you again after all this?"

"Oh." Wow. I wasn't expecting that.

"Is that a yes?"

Anxiety curled inside me. "Um, I don't know, Neon. It's just—"

"Just what?"

I cleared my throat, stalling to formulate my answer. "You and I . . . we're different people."

"But I thought we'd established we have a lot in common?"

"I'm not the Hollywood type."

His eyes lit up. "Actually, you'd fit in perfectly."

I scrunched my nose at him. "I don't think so."

"I do. You're stunning. You have an amazing body. You're confident."

"There you go again with that brutal honesty."

"I mean it. Hollywood isn't ready for a woman like you."

"All the same. No, thanks. I have my own business."

"As a bodyguard?"

"No, actually, I own Executive Rush. It's an adventure activity business, where people with heaps of money and no clue how to save themselves pay me to take them white water rafting, or rappelling, or canyoning, or some other activity like that. Usually it's for team building."

He nodded. "Huh. I could see you doing that. I bet you whip their asses."

"You got that right."

He released a massive sigh and shook his head.

I blinked up at him. "What?"

"I was a stuntman before I became an actor. I miss all that action stuff. They won't let me do it now because they're worried I'll hurt myself. And delays in filming cost money."

"Well, maybe I could throw you off a mountain one day?"

He burst into laughter. It was manly and lovely, yet it was laced with something else. A touch of sadness maybe.

It seemed that the pair of us both had regrets.

I just hoped I didn't regret meeting Neon.

Chapter Seventeen

NEON

Maya's negative response to my request to see her again after this mess was a surprise. And another first. I'd never had a woman turn me down before.

The sun had long ago disappeared, and the golden glow on the horizon had gradually morphed to black. The sounds around us seemed to get louder.

Just like when I was trapped in that well. At night, I'd heard the frogs, and the owls, and indecipherable sounds that had scared the shit out of me.

Except now the sounds that dominated were the crashing waves, and Maya's soft breaths. I pictured her lips and her glorious breasts. My fixation on her was growing by the hour, and I couldn't decide if that was good or bad.

Maybe she was right. We lived in different circles. When my work wasn't in LA, it was at a film location somewhere around the world. I could spend eight months of each year away from my multi-million-dollar home in Beverly Hills.

It was the reason why my two longest relationships had crashed and burned. I was never around, and when I was, the last thing I needed was a woman telling me what social engagement I had to attend.

I wasn't ready to settle down anyway.

I may never be. Not when I was constantly worried about getting kidnapped and putting those around me in danger.

Maya stiffened beside me. "Shh."

She stood up from our folded sheet, and I joined her.

"Here they come." Her hot breath whispered in my ear.

Searching the ocean, I tried to find something to confirm she was right. I couldn't see anything other than the dark water that reflected a scattering of stars above.

Maya left my side and using the glow from the night sky, I followed her.

We stood at the ladder, staring off toward the ocean. A dark shape came toward us.

Damn, she's good.

A rubber boat pulled in alongside the ladder.

"Maya, thank Christ you're okay. What the fuck's going on?" A tall blond man climbed the ladder and wrapped her in a bear hug.

"It's a long story, Wasp, but I'm so glad to see you guys."

Two more men followed Wasp onto the boardwalk, and the final guy handed two bulky bags up to them. As if they'd been planning this mission for weeks, they worked together like a fight scene choreographed to perfection.

The final man climbed the ladder and offered his hand to me. "You must be, Neon. I'm Blade."

"Blade, thank you for coming."

Blade released his grip. "So, Ghost, what the hell's going on?"

Ghost? I'd forgotten that was her code name.

Maya introduced me to Cobra and Viper. As she informed her team of the situation, they opened the bags and strapped on enough weapons to support a small army. Maya's team didn't waste any time on small talk, and within minutes of their arrival, they were ready to move again.

Maya gripped my arm. "We'll be back for you—"

"What? No, Maya. I'm coming with you."

"Jesus, not this bullshit again." She slapped my arm.

I stepped back. "I told you. The safest place for me is with you. I'm coming."

"Don't make me tie you up, Neon."

I clenched my fists. "I'll scream my head off."

"Then I'll gag you."

I groaned. "You need my help with the hostages."

"Have you two lovers finished arguing?" Grinning, Wasp cocked his head at Maya.

She scowled at him. "Tell Neon he has to stay."

"I won't get in your way. I promise," I said.

Maya grumbled, "Oh, like the last two times."

"This is different. Now that you have your team, you won't need me to save your ass."

Cobra chuckled, and when he stepped back like he thought Maya would thump him, I noticed he had a prosthetic right leg.

"Listen up," Blade called. "We'll stick together. It's Neon they're after, so as long as he's with us, we'll know he's safe."

"Thank you." I nodded at Blade.

"Don't thank me yet. We have no idea how many tangos we're dealing with. But we do know they're well-armed, and from what Maya said, they're willing to die for this cause. That makes them fucking deadly."

"I'm still thanking you. Maya saved me several times already. But if you can save the rest of those hostages, I can't thank you enough."

Viper popped the magazine out of his handgun and snapped it back into position with a deadly scowl. "You finished fucking around? Let's roll."

Blade nodded at me. "Stay behind us and do as we say."

Maya slapped my chest. "Try not to get yourself shot."

We formed pairs with Maya and Blade trotting in the lead. Wasp and Cobra followed behind them and Viper slotted next to me at the rear.

Maya led them along the path heading away from the marina. At the intersection of the marina path and the main pathway that circumnavigated the island, she headed toward the bowling alley.

It seemed like a week ago since we'd had the shootout in there.

"There are three dead tangos at the rear of the bowling alley," Maya said. "But I only killed two of them. The other was shot by friendly fire."

"He was my bodyguard, Derek," I added.

"Huh." Viper grunted at me. "Was he the mastermind behind this bullshit?"

"I don't think so." I shook my head.

"We think the asshole who's shooting the hostages is named Sloan," Maya said.

As we ran past the bar, Maya explained how I hurt my leg and how I refused to let her stitch me up.

"That was a stupid move." Viper snarled at me.

Unsure whether he was referring to me crashing through the timber or my decision not to get stitched up by Maya, I kept my mouth shut.

We jogged past several paths that led to the bungalows, and Maya explained how we'd left two tangos tied to chairs in one of them. All the pathways looked the same, and I couldn't decide which one would lead to the two brothers. If they were still there.

In front of me, Wasp and Cobra jogged side by side. If I hadn't seen Cobra's fake leg, I wouldn't have realized he had one. Wasp was a big guy, at least four inches taller and broader than me. The way he'd wrapped Maya in a bear hug suggested they knew each other well.

Does she have a partner? We'd never discussed anything like that.

That would suck.

Christ! What the hell am I thinking?

Maya had made it clear she wasn't interested in seeing me again. Like she'd said, we lived in different worlds.

At another intersection, Maya led us along the path that met with the crumbled theater.

One by one, we crawled through the hole in the doorway and paused on the inside.

The silence engulfed us like we were in outer space. Blade turned on his flashlight. Maya looked at me, and a smile danced on my lips at her attention.

"Neon Bloom," a voice boomed around us.

"Shit. He's killing another hostage." Maya's expression morphed to horror.

"You have three minutes to come out, or I'll put a bullet through Monique Dempsey's brain."

I clutched my chest. "Oh my god. She's my makeup artist."

"Let's roll." Maya sprinted down the steps alongside the rows of theater chairs.

At the stage, she bounded up the stairs with her team right on her tail. Fighting against the pain in my leg, I struggled to keep up with them.

Maya sprinted across the stage, past the velvet curtain, and aimed for the door on the other side. She paused for me to catch up, then with her gun ready, she yanked open the door.

We entered the corridor and sprinted to the exit where we'd shoved the ball gown at the base of the door. It hadn't moved. Maya pulled away the bell that we'd positioned there and the crumpled dress.

"Two minutes, Bloom."

"Shit. Please, don't let her die." Dread scurried up my spine like fire ants.

Blade clutched my arm. "Just keep your cool, Neon."

"Turn off the light," Maya said.

Blade switched off his flashlight, plunging us into absolute darkness. A slight breeze confirmed Maya had opened the door.

A faint glow filtered into the tunnel. Maya raced toward the light, which would be the stairwell that led up to the reception area. She paused at the base of the light, and again waited until I caught up.

Maya leaned in and whispered, "Up these stairs are the reception and lobby areas of the resort. The front of the building overlooks the main pool." She looked at me. "From there, we should be able to see the gym and spa building on the left where the hostages are being held."

"One minute, Bloom. Tick. Tick. Tick."

I jolted at the sadistic voice. "Shit. Shit."

My heart thundered in my ears.

Blade got in my face. "Keep your cool."

I nodded. "Okay, but please don't let anyone else die."

"Unless it's bad guys," Wasp said.

"Okay, listen up," Blade said. "Spread out, watch your six, and shoot to kill."

"Roger that," Maya and her team all said in unison.

"You three, go right." Blade pointed at Wasp, Cobra, and Viper.

"We'll go left." He nodded at Maya and me. "Let's roll."

With their guns drawn, Wasp, Cobra, and Viper ran up the stairs, paused at the top, and disappeared. We were right on their tail, and at the top, I stayed behind Maya as she sprinted to the reception counter. Light streamed in through the front doorway, suggesting the attackers had massive floodlights set up.

I gasped at a body wedged in the splintered reception desk. Camilla! A bloody stain covered the back of her shirt and a pool of blood had dried beneath her.

A wave of nausea raced up my throat. I gagged.

Maya spun to me, clutched my arm, and dragged me into the area behind the reception desk.

"Stay down," she hissed in my ear.

"Ten seconds, Bloom." Sloan's voice ricocheted around us.

Maya put her finger to her lips.

"Stay here." She jabbed my chest.

Blade shot out from behind the reception desk and ran toward the side of the front entry.

"Eight seconds."

Maya raced after him.

The rest of Maya's team flanked the other side of the entrance.

"Five. Four."

They're too late. Monique is going to die.

"Three."

Oh my god! I have to save her.

"Two."

"I'm here!" I screamed at the top of my lungs. I leaped to my feet and ran to the open doorway. "Don't shoot. I'm here."

With my hands raised and terror piercing my brain, I stepped into a field of light.

A gun exploded.

Chapter Eighteen

MAYA

I jolted at the gunshot. With my heart slamming into my chest, I expected Neon to go flying backward in a bloody mess.

But he didn't. A breath escaped me, and my legs nearly buckled beneath me.

"Son of a bitch!" I hissed under my breath. "He killed the hostage."

Blade clutched my arm, maybe to stop me from chasing after Bloom. I wouldn't. One good thing we had in our favor was those bastards needed Neon alive to get the ransom. The rest of the hostages though . . ..

"Why did you kill her?" The horror in Neon's voice broke my heart.

"Come here, Bloom. Where's that bitch of yours?"

"She's dead, okay? That bastard stabbed her on the lighthouse, and now she's dead."

Blade glared at me.

I nodded and whispered, "At least Neon's thinking straight."

"Why did you kill Monique? I told you I was here."

"Get over here, Bloom!" Sloan's voice crackled with rage.

"Why did you kill her? Why?"

From my cover behind the entrance, I couldn't see Neon. I wished I could, to make sure he was okay. But he wouldn't be okay. Seeing someone murdered like that . . . in cold blood . . . changed people forever.

Footsteps thundered outside, but we couldn't see them to work out how many men were charging at Neon. But across from us, Wasp, Cobra, and Viper hid behind a desk that had *Tours* written across the front. From their angle, they should be able to see everything I couldn't.

"Let go of me," Neon yelled.

Stomping feet and grunts and groans gave me the impression Neon was putting up a fight. He would have pure anger raging through his veins.

The noise died down and across from us, Wasp raised five fingers.

"Five tangos," I relayed to Blade. "But that's not all of them."

"Let's go over there." Blade pointed to the other side of the lobby where the rest of our team was.

Following his lead, we retraced our path to the rear of the lobby and dodged around toppled chairs, debris, and two bodies to reach the other side.

I slotted between Cobra and Viper. From my new vantage point, I could see between the two massive marble pillars on the front portico of the lobby area. Neon kicked and jerked, trying to break free of the two men who dragged him across the paved area surrounding the resort pool.

The rectangular swamp reflected the powerful floodlights that were positioned on both front corners of the gym building.

The trouble with those lights though, was they gave the kidnappers the edge. They had a perfect visual of the surrounding area; however, the glare blinded us.

Neon vanished from view.

I turned with my back to the counter and slumped to the floor. "Shit! I can't believe he did that."

Cobra eased back to look at me. "He's fucking brave. I'll give him that."

"Fucking stupid, you mean?" I snapped.

"No, I don't. He tried to save that woman. You and I would do the same."

I nodded. Cobra was right. I'd put my body on the line to save many civilians.

"I still can't believe he did it." I looked at Blade. "What do we do now?"

"They need him alive to get the ransom money, right?" Blade asked.

I nodded. "That's what I heard."

"Okay. We know he's safe for now. It's the hostages I'm worried about." Blade squinted into the floodlights and shook his head.

"Me too. He's going to kill them all. Then, once he has the cash, he'll kill Neon too."

"And probably all his team. He's one ruthless bastard," Viper added.

"I agree," I said.

"What's at the back of that gym building?" Cobra asked.

I shook my head. "No idea."

"Let's find out. Lead the way, Ghost." Blade pulled me up from the floor.

Crouching down, I led my team to the back of the lobby. From there, I crossed into the accommodation section of the building, where I'd saved Neon the first time. That already seemed like a week ago.

Assuming the kidnappers were preoccupied, I took a gamble and remained on the ground floor. If gunmen came in from both ends, we'd be trapped, but it was the quickest way to exit the area.

We made it through unscathed and stepped onto a path that fed into the overgrown vegetation. A sliver of moon had popped into the sky, providing enough light to make out shapes and allow us to move without the aid of a flashlight.

We were well trained in running in stealth mode, and even though I had four burly men in my wake, I couldn't hear any of them.

Silence had returned to the island. Not even the crickets made a noise.

I tried to picture Neon, and rather than see his handsome face, all I saw was a gun aimed at his temple.

If I don't save him, this will ruin me.

Leading my team along the path, I didn't stop until we reached the intersection with the larger path that circled the island. Pausing there, I risked turning on my flashlight and used the beam to point to my left.

"If we go that way, we'll end up back at the marina. This other way goes toward the second island and the lighthouse where there should be pathways that take us inland back to the resort."

"There's a second island?" Wasp cocked his head.

"Yes. It's much smaller than this main one and connected by a bridge. That's where they put the accommodation trailers for the film cast and crew."

"Okay." Blade nodded at me, taking over. "We stick together, but if we get separated, we'll meet at those accommodation trailers."

"Roger that." It was a good plan. From the second island, we could fend off any attack by picking them off as they crossed the bridge.

"With a bit of luck," Blade said, "they believed Neon's story about Maya being dead. If not, they could still be out looking for her. So, keep lively. Any sign of movement, dive into the bushes. We don't want to start a firefight, or they'll know they're not alone. At the moment, surprise is our advantage."

Blade nodded at me. I nodded back. It was good to have him in charge.

"Maya and I will take the lead."

I turned off the flashlight and falling in beside Blade, I trotted along the path. On our left, we passed three smaller paths that led to bungalows ten, eleven, and twelve.

A shape on the path materialized out of the darkness. Blade raised his arm. We halted in position, and after a couple of beats that confirmed we were still alone, we strode to the form.

It was another tram car. I turned on the flashlight, shielding it with my hand. This train was in better shape than the first one Neon and I had found. Even the paintwork looked decent. It would probably fetch a decent price at an antique auction.

We sprinted around the engine and four carriages behind the train, and past another three paths to more bungalows. Another shape appeared over the treetops ahead.

I pointed toward it. "The lighthouse."

Blade nodded at me. "Which way are the hostages?"

I aimed my arm at a forty-five-degree angle, pointing inland. "Straight through there."

Blade pulled us in together. "We can't risk staying on this path any further. Time to go bush."

"Great," Viper grumbled.

I slapped his chest. "When did you get so grumpy, Viper?"

"You know when." He grunted at me.

I squinted at Viper. He was referring to the bullshit that ruined our team in Kyrgyzstan, but he was a grumpy bastard well before that.

"Maya," Blade said, drawing my attention, "do you know the way?"

"I've been through this bush once already. The resort is that way, and the gym building is in front of that. There's a lagoon pool in the middle of that bush too."

"You take the lead. I'll take the rear. Let's keep this tight and stay frosty."

I turned off my flashlight, pitching us into near darkness. After waiting a couple of beats for my eyes to adjust to the dimness, I left the path and climbed over a fallen log.

I shoved aside a giant palm frond.

A piercing scream carved through the silence.

I ducked down. "What the hell?"

Gunfire exploded.

"Fuck. They're killing the hostages," I hissed.

"Go. Go. Go," Blade said.

Barging forward, I shoved away branches and leaves.

More terrified screams added to the first, followed by another single gunshot.

Christ!

"They're picking them off one by one," I said.

"Move," Blade said. "Those screams give us cover."

Viper charged in front of me, carving a path through the bushes like a bulldozer.

Much quicker than I expected, we reached the lagoon pool. The open air was minor relief but also had us exposed. I pointed the direction for Viper, and he took off.

A woman's shriek of terror tore through the silence. A gunshot cut the scream off.

"Bastards." My chest squeezed.

I'd seen senseless killing before, but that'd been in war zones where people's lives were traded like coconuts at the market. This was Australia. About fifty miles from my home. This was brutal. Barbaric.

A wide building appeared through the vegetation, and we crouched beneath a large jacaranda tree.

"This looks like the rear of the gym building," I said to Blade. "The main resort is that way and the lighthouse is that way."

A glow over the rooftop of the building in front supported my theory, as that would be from the floodlights they'd set up.

"Maya, you stay here and shoot any bastard that tries to escape," Blade said.

I nodded. "Roger that."

"Viper, you and Levi take that side. Cobra, you're with me. Let's kill these fuckers."

They took off at a sprint, skirting around the sides of the building and disappearing from my view.

I retreated from the back door of the building and found a position that kept me hidden in the bushes, yet also gave me a perfect visual of the exit. If any of those murderers came through that door, they'd get barely two paces before I put a bullet in them.

Inhaling a deep breath, I let it out slowly, calming the thumping ache in my heart.

My mind swung between Neon and hoping he was okay, to those poor hostages and the terror they would be suffering at the hands of those ruthless bastards.

Their gutless actions had me wondering who the hell this Sloan asshole was. It took some effort to find a group of like-minded assholes who were capable of killing innocent people or allowing someone else to do it.

They would not get away with this.

It's now my personal mission. They will wish they never put Neon Bloom in their sights.

"Hands up!" a voice boomed from the other side of the building.

Gunfire exploded inside. People screamed.

Shouts rang out. From my team. From the bastards. And from the hostages.

Guns blasted. Ten rounds. Twenty.

I tried to picture the chaos, wishing I was in there with them.

The back door burst open, and a man sprinted onto the dark veranda carrying a rifle across his chest. He was on the top step when I gunned him down. He fell face-first onto the steps and slumped to the bottom.

Flashes of light blazed through the open doorway. Gunfire exploded. Shouts continued.

"Don't move, asshole!" Blade's voice thundered from somewhere inside.

A man appeared in the doorway. I readied to fire.

Neon!

A thick arm was around his neck, forcing him out the doorway.

My breath trapped in my throat as I squeezed my weapon, ready to put a bullet in the brain of the big bastard behind him.

Neon was marched onto the veranda. The man behind Neon was bigger than him by about two inches. Sloan.

He used Neon as a shield, and I couldn't get a clear shot.

The screams inside grew louder as the gunfire continued. Lights flashed inside like a fucking disco.

"Keep moving, asshole," Sloan barked in Neon's ear.

Neon moved toward the steps. I readied to take my shot once he dipped lower than Sloan.

"Shit!" Sloan ducked down.

Damn it! He must've seen the body on the stairs.

"I have a gun in Neon's back," Sloan yelled.

Neon clawed at the arm around his neck.

"Move," Sloan ordered Neon.

Neon shifted right to get around the body. I kept absolutely still, waiting for the perfect moment.

I was one of the best marksmen the Australian Army had ever seen. I'd even contemplated entering the Olympics. But shooting a target was easy. Shooting an asshole, when someone I cared about was in my line of sight, was another thing.

At the bottom of the stairs, Sloan nudged Neon forward. "Move. Keep it slow."

Neon gripped the arm and opened his mouth like he was fighting for air.

I couldn't tell if Sloan had seen me, but the bastard could have angled Neon any way, yet he picked the one angle that stole my advantage.

I couldn't get a clean shot.

Sloan and Neon shifted away, increasing the distance from me. Each step made my shot harder. Each step added another risk to Neon's life.

Sloan shifted his angle again, so he walked backward, dragging Neon with him.

The bastard must have some kind of sixth sense.

As the gunfire continued inside, Sloan dragged Neon into the bushes.

Shit! I waited until they vanished altogether before I eased up from my cover and slinked after them.

My heart thundered in my chest as I crawled through bushes, ducking under branches and giant leaves. With each step, I expected a gunshot to take me out, but I couldn't back down.

I had to save Neon.

They headed toward the lagoon. An idea blazed through my brain. I would swing around the back and take him from behind.

Casting caution to the wind, I changed direction and ran straight toward the lighthouse.

Gunfire from the gym changed to a couple of shots here and there. It was nearly over. I prayed my team was all still standing.

I stumbled onto the path much quicker than I anticipated and just about face-planted onto the moss-covered concrete.

I ducked down and listened for Sloan.

Come on, Neon, give me a sign.

The moon had shifted to above the island, and its glow was both a blessing and a curse. While it improved my visibility, it also hampered my attempts to remain hidden.

"Let go of me!" Neon's strained voice drifted through the vegetation.

Heading toward his voice, I made myself as small as possible and pushed through the bushes.

"Who are you?" Neon asked. "What do you want from me?"

I slipped over a log and lay flat on the dry leaves, waiting for their voices to point the way again.

"You still haven't figured it out, have you? You stupid bastard." Sloan's voice was thick with hatred.

"Figured what out?"

"Who I am."

"Tell me." Neon's voice was a brittle croak.

"Shut up and move!"

Inching from my position, I aimed my gun forward and crept toward the voices.

My foot stomped on a twig, and the sound of it snapping was like gunfire.

A bullet slammed into a tree to my left, splintering a branch in two.

I ducked.

Shit! My cover is blown.

"I'm gonna kill him," Sloan called. "You hear me? Neon is a dead man."

But Sloan could have done that already. Figuring he still needed Neon alive, I dashed left and hid behind a bush covered in a mass of orange flowers.

Squinting through the shrubs, I caught movement.

Sloan swung Neon around like he was a rag doll, twisting his body left and right and making it impossible to take him out.

Dashing forward, I ducked behind the next bush. A bullet slammed into the ground three feet from me.

Fuck! That was close.

Running as fast as I could, I aimed for a massive gum tree. Bullets slammed into vegetation around me.

I dove behind the tree trunk and a bullet punched into the bark.

Fuck, he knows where I am.

"No!" Neon cried out.

I peered around the tree. Neon kicked backward and punched over his shoulder, trying to connect with Sloan.

Breaking cover, I raced to the next tree. I crouched down, aimed my gun toward the men, and yelled, "Neon! Duck."

Sloan spun Neon around, his gun over Neon's shoulder. His grip was still around Neon's neck.

Neon blocked my way.

I fired to their right, and the bullet pinged off the pool ladder.

Sloan dragged Neon backward.

I fired again, hitting the ground two feet to their left.

"Let him go," I yelled. "I have you surrounded."

"You fucking bitch!" Sloan fired my way.

Bullets slammed into trees, shrubs, and ground.

That's it, you bastard. Use up those bullets.

"I'm going to fucking kill you!" Sloan fired at me. Then he shoved Neon forward.

Neon stumbled sideways. Sloan aimed at Neon and the gun exploded.

A spray of blood flew through the air.

"No!" I screamed.

Sloan bolted into the bushes and disappeared.

Neon's shriek of agony cut off as he fell face-first into the lagoon.

Chapter Nineteen

NEON

Clawing at the water, I gulped the disgusting swamp into my throat. I gagged. I spat. I fought for air.

Pain blazed through my body.

My eyes were open, but I saw nothing but green.

Agony tore through me and I screamed again, sucking putrid filth into my lungs.

My mind tumbled back twenty years, pitching me into that well. I smelled the stench that had fogged my brain for decades. Cold leached up my spine.

Maya drifted into my focus. Her beautiful face. Her stunning eyes. Her kissable lips.

But I had no energy to crawl toward her. Her hair wafted around her like an angel's halo. That was what Maya was . . . an angel.

Firm hands gripped my waist. Water surged around me.

I popped to the surface and inhaled a massive breath.

"That's it, Neon. I've got you." Maya's voice was a sweet melody, luring me back from a dangerous abyss.

Somehow, I glided over the water. My mind was a dense fog.

"Get him out, quick," Maya yelled to someone.

Rough hands wedged under my armpits, dragging me from the swamp. My eyes were open but all I saw were green shapes.

"Get that bastard, Blade. He went that way." Maya's voice was thick with fury.

I blinked back the green haze. Shapes materialized. "Maya?"

A hand pressed on my thigh. A scream burst from my throat as blood squirted into the air.

"Neon, you stay with me, babe. You hear me?"

"Babe?"

"Yes. That's it, Neon. I'm here. It's Maya. You stay with me."

Blood squirted onto her chest.

"Christ! There's damage to his femoral artery," she said. "Viper, hold his leg. I have to stop this bleeding."

Viper pressed down on me with the weight of a fridge, and I howled at the agony.

"That's it. You fight it, Neon," she said. "Levi, get me a chopper. Now!"

"I'm on it." Levi pulled his phone from his pants.

I blinked back the green, and Maya's beauty emerged through the fog. "Am I going to die?"

"No, you're not. We've been through way too much to end like this."

"Chelsea, this is Levi. We need the chopper at Kangaroo Island ASAP." Levi's voice carved through the thumping headache behind my eyes. "We have a male victim with a gunshot wound to his leg."

"Son of a bitch!" Maya pulled a knife from her belt.

"What are you doing?" I asked. Her beautiful image wobbled in and out of my vision.

"I need to cut your leg and stem that flow from your artery."

"No." A wave of nausea blazed up my throat. "No!"

"Cobra, hold his leg." Two clamps pressed my leg to the pavers.

Maya's blade sliced into my flesh.

I bucked at the inferno blazing up my leg and into my groin.

I wanted to scream but couldn't. I wanted to kick and punch and fight off whatever was causing the agony, but my arms wouldn't move.

A dark fog seeped across my eyes.

Voices drifted to me, men and a woman who shouted orders.

A concrete blanket pinned me down.

A tear escaped my eye, and Maya came into my vision. Blood covered the front of her shirt, and her beautiful face twisted into terror.

I wanted to wrap my arms around her, to tell her my feelings. But I could barely breathe. I couldn't think either.

"What's happening?" I couldn't decide if the words left my tongue.

Levi leaned into my face. "Hang in there, Neon. The chopper's on its way. You hear me?"

I wanted to say yes, but my brain wouldn't reach my lips.

Blackness oozed into my eyes, and I floated upward like I was in a hot air balloon. My body trembled as trees drifted overhead. The moon was a great big light, blinding me.

Fire crawled over my body, and I moaned at the agony.

"Hey, Neon, I'm right with you. I'm right with you."

"Maya?" I smacked my lips together, trying to produce moisture.

"Yes, I'm here. We're taking you to the chopper. We'll have you at the hospital in no time."

Fog shackled my brain, smothering my thoughts. "What happened?"

"Nothing. You'll be fine."

A tremendous roar erupted around me. I opened my eyes and the room swirled. I saw men in bright red vests, cables dangling everywhere, and a curved room.

I saw blood.

And I saw Maya. She cupped my cheek. "You hang in there, babe. I still have a story to share. Remember?"

She smiled, and it was the sweetest thing I'd ever seen.

I closed my eyes, and as the roar grew louder, I focused on a bright light.

"He's crashing!"

The bright light faded. Everything went black.

Chapter Twenty

NEON

I blinked my eyes open and groaned. A pounding behind my eyes was like someone was using a jackhammer to escape my brain.

"Hello, sleepyhead. You're awake."

Peering through one eye, I squinted against the glare, searching for the source of the voice. "Where am I?"

A big-breasted woman in a white nurse's uniform placed her hand on my forearm.

"You're in Rosebud Hospital." She checked the tube stretching from a hook next to my bed to the back of my arm. "You gave us quite a scare."

I tried to clear my throat, but my tongue was like leather.

The nurse pierced the top of a sealed water cup with a straw and fed the tube into my mouth. As I sucked the liquid gold, I tried to piece together how I got there, but I had nothing.

She removed the straw.

"What happened?"

"You're lucky to be alive, that's what. If it wasn't for that army medic, you wouldn't be here."

"Maya?"

The nurse clicked her fingers.

"Oh, you remember her, do you?" She winked at me. "I'm not surprised. She had a few doctors drooling over her. And nurses, if you know what I mean."

She tapped her nose like we were sharing a naughty secret.

"Is she here? Can I see her?" I tried to sit.

The nurse pressed her hands to my shoulders. "Hold your horses there, cowboy. You've been through major trauma and your body is still trying to piece you together."

"How long have I been here?"

"Three days."

My jaw dropped. "Three days."

"You've created quite a stir. We've had to bump up security because people have been trying to sneak in to see you."

"Damn paparazzi. They're like vultures," I mumbled.

"The crazy fans are worse." She patted her hair. "I wouldn't have your life for anything. I'd have the damn photographers catching me with a hole in my pants or a coffee stain on my shirt."

She shuddered like she was fending off a ghost. "No, thank you. Once I head home each day, it's the quiet life for me."

I had no idea what a quiet life was, but it sounded perfect.

I blinked at the blank television screen on the wall at the end of my bed. "What happened on the island? To the hostages? Did they save them?"

"Okay, this chit chat isn't helping you. Let me get some—"

I clutched her arm. "Please, tell me. How many hostages did they kill?"

She patted the back of my hand. "Too many. Let me get someone who can tell you."

I slumped back. She was right. Even one murdered hostage was one too many.

"Can you put the television on, please?"

She reached for a remote in a pocket behind my bed and after flicking a few buttons, she settled on a channel and handed me the remote. "The four o'clock news will be on in ten minutes. The story about what happened on Kangaroo Island has been headlining for days."

A groan tumbled from my throat as I clutched the remote. "You didn't answer my question. Is Maya here?"

She frowned. "You know, she did hang around for a while, but I can't say I've seen her today. There is a man who has been though."

"Who?"

She scrunched her nose. "Mark somebody."

"Marc Harkness?"

"Yes, that's his name."

"Please . . . can you send him in?"

She heaved a sigh. "I'll check with the doctor first."

"Thank you."

A tiny smile crawled across her lips. "You know, you hear stories about superstars being all pretentious and demanding and stuff. It's nice to know they're not all like that."

I huffed, and as she walked away, I dialed up the volume on the television.

The doctor arrived as the news began and my attention was split between answering his questions and watching the screen. By the time he finished and walked out the door, I still had no idea what was going on.

Marc was escorted to the door by a security guard who was the size of a gorilla. Marc's eyes were wide, and his hair was all over the place making him look like he hadn't slept for a week. He probably hadn't.

"Jesus Christ, Neon." He marched to my bed and shook my hand. "You scared the crap out of me."

He dragged a chair over the floor and sat beside my bed.

"Tell me what happened, Marc? How many hostages were killed?"

He moaned. "Six."

"Oh, Jesus." My chin wobbled, but I fought it. I would save my tears for later. "I saw him murder Linda and Monique. And I heard him kill Tammy. Who else?"

Marc's bloodshot eyes bulged. "Erica, Bronte, and Helena."

"All women? What the fuck? Why?"

"Everyone is still trying to piece it together."

"Did they catch him? Sloan?"

"You know his name?" Marc cocked his head, and a wave of what looked like suspicion crossed his expression.

"Yes. Maya interrogated one of the killers for information."

"Yes. Maya, your temporary bodyguard. She's quite the hero."

I frowned at him. "Why do you say it like that?"

"Like what?"

"Like you're pissed with her."

Marc did his exaggerated eye roll that he'd practiced to perfection. "She's a stubborn one. She's refusing to take interviews, so the reporters are hounding me for details about her."

"What kind of details?"

"Did you know she saved your life by cutting your leg open to pinch your femoral artery so you didn't bleed out?"

A wave of nausea curled in my stomach. "No. Wow!"

"Exactly. Now you know why they want to interview her. She saved the hero in a real-life action movie."

"I'm not a hero, Marc. She is."

"But you are, Neon. Everyone is talking about how you sacrificed yourself to save a hostage."

"What?" I frowned. "But I didn't. I didn't save any of them. I tried to save Monique, but that bastard still killed her."

"Yes, but you tried. You could have been killed yourself."

"I wish I was." I squeezed my eyes shut, trying to force that brutal image of Monique being shot in the head from my mind. But it was there. Forever.

Marc wrapped his clammy hand over my arm. "Don't be like that. This wasn't your fault."

I glared at him. "This was every bit my fault. It all happened because of me."

"No. It was because of that gunman."

"He shot six women because of me. What happened in there, Marc? In that gym? How did he choose the hostages?"

Marc shook his head. "Don't try to analyze it, Neon. It will mess you up."

"I'm already messed up. *You* don't seem to be though."

He jerked back. "What does that mean?"

"It means you're looking mighty calm for someone who just survived a hostage situation."

"That's exactly the reason I'm calm . . . I survived."

"And you witnessed six brutal murders."

He shook his head. "I didn't see them."

I blinked at him. When Maya and I had been on the other side of the pool, watching that bastard murder my movie producer, we'd seen the hostages on the floor, lined up so they could see everything.

I forced my brain to go back there, to recall if I'd seen Marc.

The machine at my side began beeping.

Marc pushed back on his chair. "I better let you rest. We have a lot of work to do when you get out of here."

"Work? What do you mean?"

"We have to jump on this publicity wagon while we have a—"

"What?" My jaw dropped. I leveled my gaze at him, and if I could have slammed my fist into his nose, I would have. "Get the fuck out of here."

"Neon, calm down. You don't—"

I pointed at the door. "Get out."

He raised his hands. "Neon, you're just—"

"Get out! Get out!" I screamed so loud my throat burned.

As Marc scurried out the door, two nurses and the security guard ran into the room. "Get him out. I never want to see you again, you fucking bastard!"

The security guard clutched Marc's arm and marched him away.

The nurses flanked me on either side, and the one with the massive breasts pressed on my shoulders. "Hey, calm down. Your blood pressure is spiking."

Fucking bastard! I can't believe he's worried about fucking publicity when all those women died.

Rage raced through me like cannonballs. I clenched my fists until my nails dug into my flesh.

"Do you want a drink?" The second nurse offered the straw.

"No. I want Maya. The woman who saved me."

"Okay, we'll see what we—"

"No! I need to see her." I clenched my fists so hard my arms shook. "I need to see her. I need Maya."

"Okay. Okay." They both patted my arms like I was a puppy.

"First, you need to calm down," the big-breasted nurse said.

"I can't until I talk to Maya." I banged my fists on the bed.

"Calm down, Mr. Bloom."

"No. No." I thumped the mattress. "No!"

The skinny nurse slammed a big red button beside the bed. Two more nurses and a doctor ran into the room.

"Bring me Maya. I want to see her."

They pressed down on my arms. I wrestled against them. "No. Help me."

The doctor injected something into the tube attached to my arm.

"What are you doing?" I hissed at him.

"We're calming you down, Mr. Bloom."

"I don't want to calm down. I want Maya."

"Okay, we'll work on that. But you need to get your blood pressure down. Take a few deep breaths." He placed his hand on my chest. "That's it. Take it easy."

The people around me wobbled in and out. The walls did too.

Warmth washed through me like molten chocolate. I inhaled a deep breath and exhaled by rattling through my lips.

"That's it. Close your eyes."

I did, and the room still spun in lazy loops.

"Who is Maya?" The doctor's voice drifted to me.

Maya is the most beautiful, brave, and funniest woman I've ever met.

I couldn't make my lips form the response in my mind.

She was the woman who had saved me. And not just medically.

As blackness seeped into my mind, Maya's stunning blue eyes came into view. A wonderful calming aura wrapped around me, and I imagined I had her in my arms.

But as darkness overtook me, Maya drifted from my vision, and I had a terrible feeling I would never see her again.

Chapter Twenty-One

MAYA

I reached the door to Neon's hospital room, and a breath escaped me over how feeble he looked. The vibrant, commanding Hollywood hunk I'd met on Kangaroo Island seemed to have shrunk into himself.

His eyes were closed, and his deep breathing and a machine beeping were the only sounds. I didn't want to wake him, but I'd been told he was making such a scene over needing to see me that they had to sedate him to calm down.

I knocked on the glass panel beside the door.

"Go away," Neon croaked.

"Hey, Neon, it's me—"

His eyes lit up and a grin swept across his lips. "Maya. You came."

I strolled to the chair beside his bed.

He reached for my hand. "It's so good to see you."

"Well, you certainly don't make it easy. This place is guarded better than Fort Knox. I had to get Viper to help me get in through the morgue in the basement."

"Really?"

"Yeah, Viper knows an undertaker who helped us get in. Otherwise,

I would have had to go through a massive crowd *and* some serious security."

He rolled his eyes. "Sorry about that. The paparazzi are sneaky bastards."

"Tell me about it. Thanks to you, our phones have been ringing off the hook at Alpha Tactical Ops."

"What? Why?"

"Your manager, Marc, did a press conference a few days ago, and the stupid bastard released Alpha Tactical Ops' name to the world. Zena has jobs lined up for the next six months."

Neon huffed and squeezed my hand. "You and your team deserve all the accolades. I can't believe what you did to save me."

"You didn't make it easy, that's for sure."

"Sorry about that."

I chuckled. "No need to be. We got lucky, that's all."

"Thank you for saving the hostages."

I lowered my gaze to my lily tattoo on my finger. "I wish we'd saved everyone."

"I do too. Has there been any sign of Sloan?" Neon asked.

I shook my head. "Unfortunately, not. And we don't have a clue who he is. Captain Baker of the Risky Shores police department has been grilling us non-stop about how he got away. Nobody has any idea. We don't even think Sloan is his real name."

Neon frowned. "Why do you think that?"

"He's a ghost. Cobra has been running what little we know about him through the databases and so far, we've come up with zip."

"Shit. Did any gunmen survive?"

"One lived for a day, but he died before we had a chance to interrogate him."

Fear washed over Neon's expression that was so dark it crushed my heart.

I turned my hand over and squeezed his palm to mine. "We'll get him, Neon."

"If anyone can, it's your team. You guys are incredible." He pulled my hand closer to him and squeezed. "You're incredible."

I looked into his troubled eyes and my heart skipped a beat. I had no idea what was going on between us, but it was dangerous, and I needed to stop it. "Neon—"

"Maya, will you have dinner with me when I get out of here?"

I tilted my head. "Neon, I'm sorry, but I can't."

"You can't have dinner with me?"

"You know it's more than dinner."

"We can start with dinner."

"No, we can't." I sighed. "I can't risk it."

"Risk what?"

"Neon, I'm twenty-nine years old and I—"

"You're twenty-nine! Wow. That's so old."

I chuckled. "Exactly. I don't have time to mess around with a relationship that's doomed to fail."

"Wow, you're always so dramatic. What do you mean doomed to fail? How can you be so certain?"

"We already went over this. You and I run in different circles."

"So are you limiting your relationships to men who live in Risky Shores? Is that what you're telling me?"

"It's not about where I live. I can do my job just about anywhere in the world. It's not that, Neon. You're a Hollywood superstar. I can't live in that world. It's not for me."

"But how do you know?"

"I know I can't live with paparazzi following me all day hoping to get a snapshot of me at my worst."

"I've seen you at your worst, Maya, and you're the most beautiful swamp monster from the deep I've ever seen."

I giggled. "Swamp monster?"

He fluttered his ridiculously long lashes. "Yes, even with all that green slime over your face, you still looked beautiful."

I shook my head. "There you go again with the brutal honesty."

He reached for the handle over his head and winced as he pulled himself higher on the pillows. "It's better than bullshitting, isn't it?"

"It is, and that's why I'm giving you my brutal honesty now. I could never live the Hollywood lifestyle you do."

"Something happened on that island, and you know it."

"I know that we were in a crazy situation, and our emotions were all over the place."

"It was more than that."

I stood and leaned forward to kiss his forehead, but he shifted so our lips met.

My chest squeezed as I kissed the first man I'd let into my heart.

But I couldn't do this. Not when it was destined to fail. That would ruin me.

I had to walk away.

I pulled back. "I'll check out one of your movies one day."

"Maya. Don't go. Please. Don't do this."

"I'm sorry. I have to before it's too late."

"Maya. Please." A deep sadness washed over his expression.

"Goodbye, Neon."

With my heart fighting to beat in my chest, I turned and walked out of his room and past his security guards. By the time I hit the corridor, tears flooded my eyes. I flicked them away, angry that they were there. A lump formed in my throat that was so big I could barely breathe.

Resisting the urge to run full tilt out of that disinfectant-scented corridor, I skipped the elevator and raced down the stairs, taking them two at a time.

Outside the hospital doors, I fought through a swarm of reporters.

A woman shoved her microphone in my face. "Are you Maya? You are, aren't you? You're the woman who saved Neon Bloom. How is he doing? Is he okay? They say he was shot in the leg. Will he be able to walk again? Maya, what can you tell us?"

She spoke in one continuous monologue.

I shoved the microphone away, fighting the impulse to slam my fist into her pretty face.

A second reporter replaced the first, a man this time. He shoved the microphone at me. "Do you know what the gunmen wanted? How many were there? Why did they kill the hostages?"

I dug my elbow into his stomach, shoving him back, and sprinted away.

In my car, I strapped in and exited the hospital parking lot way faster than I should have. I hit the speed bump at the end of the road so hard it was a wonder my Rav4 didn't snap in two.

Turning up my music, I blasted Jimmy Barnes from my radio as I hit the highway connecting Rosebud and Risky Shores. The moon was a beacon directly in front of me, and I aimed for it, trying to block out the turmoil crashing through my brain.

I did the right thing. Neon and I should not be together. *So why the hell does it hurt so much?*

I pulled into my carport just as the time ticked over to ten o'clock. My brain told me to have a hot shower and go to bed.

My body wasn't listening though. I poured myself a glass of American Honey on ice, opened my computer, and typed John Grayson into the search bar. My father had vanished when I was nineteen—the day after I'd confronted him over my sister's death.

He'd taken every cent from his and Mom's bank account, not that it was much, and one suitcase of clothes. He didn't even leave a note for Mom, his wife of twenty-four years.

A week after he'd vanished, the police told me they had proof my father had taken a flight to Indonesia. But from there, his trail had gone cold.

He was going to pay for my sister's death.

And he would know it was me who put a bullet through his brain.

It was the least I could do for my poor sister.

It was the *only* thing I could do for her.

And it was exactly the distraction I needed to keep my mind off Neon.

Chapter Twenty-Two

MAYA

Four Months Later

I put my Executive Rush adventure business A-frame sign outside the door of Firefly Café and strolled inside, inhaling delicious scents of muffins baking and freshly ground coffee.

Zena welcomed me with a steaming mug that she passed across the counter. "Morning, Maya. How are you doing?"

"I'm super. How about you?"

"It's a bit slow this morning. With all that sunshine out there, everyone probably went to the beach first."

"Maybe. It's a beautiful day."

"What are you doing today?" Zena wiped her hands on her apron embroidered with a little firefly at the top.

I cupped my hands around the coffee mug and inhaled the delicious aroma. Zena made the best coffee. "I've got a group from Brisbane for white water rafting. Hopefully they're as much fun as last week's group. What's the muffin special? It smells amazing."

"Raspberry and white chocolate."

"Stop it! You know I can't resist them."

"And the toasted sandwich special is honey roasted ham with Jarlsberg cheese with a touch of my homemade mango relish."

"Oh my god. How can I choose?"

"Have both." Zena grinned.

"Done."

We giggled. It was the same ritual we did nearly every time I came in before a tour. My cooking skills were negligible, and Zena's were amazing, so why fight it.

"I'll have the muffin to go though. I'll save it for later."

"Perfect." Zena disappeared out the kitchen doorway.

I pulled my phone from my pocket. As I sipped my coffee, I ran through dozens of messages Zena had forwarded to me from the Alpha Tactical Ops website. Reporters from all over the world had been hounding me non-stop since Neon's stupid manager announced my name.

As I set about deleting all the messages from reporters requesting interviews, my thoughts drifted to Neon. He was still under attack from the paparazzi, too.

Zena had made it her mission to show me every snippet of him she found on social media. He seemed to have fully recovered from the bullet wound that had nearly killed him and it had been good to see him jogging again.

Thank God. After what had happened to Kai on that mountain in Kyrgyzstan, I couldn't handle another man in his prime losing his life while on my watch.

A man in a baseball cap, sunnies, and a decent-looking beard stepped through the doorway of Firefly Café. Wondering if he was one of the men for today's white water rafting trip, I swiveled on my chair to face him.

He smiled, and removing his sunglasses, he angled toward me like he knew who I was.

I stood, ready to offer my hand. My jaw dropped. My damn heart skipped a beat too. *Neon!*

He strolled right up to me, gracing me with a waft of his incredible cologne and hot-blooded man.

"What are you doing here?" I peered out the windows, expecting to see a horde of reporters in his wake. But there were none.

"Is that any way to greet your customer?"

My jaw dropped even further. "You're my white-water rafting party for today?"

He swung a backpack off his shoulder and settled it at his feet. "Sure am."

"I thought you hated water."

"Being in it, yes. But the pictures on your website showed that we'd be on the water."

"Ha! Very funny. There's a good chance you'll fall in."

"That's why I signed up with you. I figured you'd save me."

I huffed. "Don't be so sure about that."

Zena appeared through the kitchen doorway and pushed a steaming toasted sandwich toward me. She grinned at Neon, but it wasn't a grin that confirmed she recognized him. As much as she'd kill me for not telling her, I had no intentions of blowing his cover.

"Zena, this is Cooper." I introduced him as the name he'd entered on my website waiver form.

Neon offered his hand over the counter. "Hi, Zena, I've heard all about you."

She cocked her head, frowning.

Damn it. It seemed Neon wasn't so concerned.

Fearing she would recognize him anyway, I put my finger to my lips, hoping she wouldn't squeal, and leaned over the counter to whisper, "It's Neon."

Her eyes bulged. Her jaw dropped. And her chest filled like she was setting to scream the café down.

I slapped my hand on the counter, drawing her attention. "So, Cooper. Did you want a toasted sandwich?"

"I'd love one." Grinning, he pulled out a barstool and sat beside me.

I sipped my coffee and tried to get my thumping heart to settle. I hated how he affected me like this.

"How have you been?" Neon asked.

I couldn't believe how casual he was. "Fine. And you?"

"Fine."

He flashed a spectacular grin. It was the smile that had captured me in so many ways on the island. It was the smile that made my heart sing and commanded me to smile back.

But I fought it by eating my toasted sandwich.

"What are you doing here, Neon?" I asked.

"I'm waiting for a toasted sandwich, then you're taking me rafting."

"Hmm. You booked for a group of four."

He palmed his chest. "Yeah, sorry about that. Just me." He winked. "I wanted you all to myself."

My heart skipped a beat. "You'll have to work damn hard on the river."

"I'll do everything you ask."

"Huh, you don't have a good track record in that area."

"That was extreme circumstances."

This is also extreme circumstances.

I had planned to never see Neon again. For four months, I'd been trying to squeeze my feelings for him out of my heart, and yet the second I recognized him, my body started zinging like crazy all over again. His gaze lingered on me, making my body hum.

Keep cool, Maya. He's just a customer. A damn sexy customer.

"So, um, can you drive?" I asked.

Neon curled his fingers through his thick hair. "Of course."

"It's a valid question. Knowing you, you'd have a permanent driver and limos at your fingertips."

"I do. But I can still drive. I had to learn for a movie I did a few years ago."

"Huh. How about a stick shift?"

"It's been a while, but I should be okay."

Zena returned with a steaming toasted sandwich and a massive grin on her lips that she'd added gloss to. She pushed the meal across the counter. "So, Cooper. Maya always gets a photo with her customers. And me. I'm always in the photo. Would you mind if—?"

"Of course. Where would you like me?"

"I'll come around." Zena whipped off her apron, fussed about with her hair, and raced around to our side of the counter like she was on her rollerblades.

"How about this?" Neon hugged both of us to his sides, and with all three of us grinning, Zena snapped a number of selfies.

"That's great, thank you." She leaned into Neon's ear and whispered something.

"Does she now?" Neon looked at me, all cocky.

I scowled at Zena. "What did you say?"

"Nothing." She winked at me like we had a secret code. We didn't.

Grumbling, I grabbed the second half of my toasted sandwich. "We'll have his sandwich to go, thanks. See you outside."

I nodded at Neon.

"Roger that."

"Wise ass." I turned to walk away.

"Maya, you forgot your muffin," Zena called after me.

I swiveled back to her. She handed over the paper bag but wouldn't let go. "Be nice."

"I'm always nice." I yanked the bag free and strolled out to the sunshine, trying to wrestle my thoughts into something that made sense.

Neon should not be here, disguise or not. Yet I couldn't help the butterflies in my stomach.

I'm in trouble.

Resisting the urge to pace back and forth, I devoured my toastie, waiting for the man who had my veins going all tingly to join me.

Neon had his sunglasses on as he stepped out the door with his thumb hooked through the shoulder strap on his backpack, carrying a paper bag and grinning like the superstar he was.

Hot damn, he couldn't get any sexier if he tried.

I threw him the keys to my Rav4 and pointed toward it. "You can follow me."

"Cool car."

"Thanks. Try and keep up." I couldn't help the smile inching across my face as I strode to my second car a little way up the street.

I jumped into the driver's seat and shoved a chunk of hot muffin into my mouth. Chewing the delicious treat, I put the old Jeep into gear and pulled out from the curb, dragging the trailer carrying my white-water raft behind me.

I drove through the center of town, heading toward the road that zigzagged up the mountain range. We couldn't have asked for a better day. The temperature was perfect: not too hot that we would get heat-stroke or too cold that we would need wetsuits.

Not that we'd be doing any rafting. The river was too much to handle with just two people in the raft, but I didn't need to tell Neon that just yet.

He had booked for a tour; I planned to act like he was getting one. He's bound to beg me to change my mind.

In my rearview mirror, I caught the handsome Hollywood star in the Rav4 behind me and my stupid heart danced pirouettes. "Calm down, Maya. Just get through today, and then send him on his way."

After I'd left Neon in the hospital, I had honestly thought I'd never see him again. Yet I still thought about him every damn day. It didn't help that Zena kept a constant vigil on social media and let me know every move Neon made.

Whenever she showed me his photo, my mind would swing back to the moments we'd shared together on the island. Neon's beaming smile in the photos masked the turmoil he'd had when he was in water. I was the only person other than his parents who knew what he'd lived through when he was a child.

That knowledge was both a burden and a treasure.

At the top of the rise, the river appeared ahead as a glistening streak of blue that reflected the clear skies above. It looked mighty serene in this section of river, giving zero indication of the treacherous rapids several miles upstream.

I turned into the parking area that I'd been using nearly every second day since I'd started my adventure business and did a U-turn, so my Jeep faced to head out again.

I pulled to a stop, jumped out, and directed Neon where to park my Rav4.

He cut the engine and climbed out. His jeans hugged him in all the right places.

I pointed at them. "I see you replaced your favorite jeans."

"Not really. These ones aren't half as good."

Could have fooled me.

"Did you bring a change of clothes?" I asked.

"Yeah, shorts and a T-shirt. Should I put them on now?"

"Yes, do that. And leave your gear in the Rav."

As Neon unzipped his backpack and tugged out his clothes, I returned to my Jeep. While I pretended to be busy moving the water bottles from my fridge in the rear of my car to the dry-bag we'd take downstream with us, my damn gaze kept drifting to the superstar.

His shirt was off, and his back was to me. His olive skin was flawless. His shoulders were broad, and he had muscles in all the right places. *Has he been working out?*

He stepped out of his jeans and the nasty red welt on his right thigh looked like a hideous bullseye. Four months ago, Neon had died twice: once in the helicopter taking him to hospital and once on the operating table. It was a miracle he survived.

Thinking of how close he had come to death made me want to show him the best time ever. And what better way to do it than showing him the mighty Thunder River and explaining how I'd attempted to tame it.

He turned toward me, dangling the keys. "Want me to lock it?"

"Yes, please."

The Rav's lights blinked as he locked it, and grinning, he strode my way.

Neon was everything I was looking for in a man: funny, confident, open, brutally honest, a touch crazy, an amazing kisser. Everything except his superstar status that put him in the center of attention every minute of the day. I could never live with that.

I returned his spectacular smile. "You ready to do this?"

"Sure am."

I shut the rear door and we climbed into the front.

"Why don't you have your bodyguards with you?" I asked.

"I have you."

"I'm serious, Neon."

"So am I. When I'm with you, I'm the safest I could ever be. Besides, they still think I'm on my yacht. I have it moored off Amber Island, but I gave them the slip."

"Great." I rolled my eyes. "How long before they realize you're gone?"

He pulled on his sunglasses. "Knowing them, it could be all day."

Crazy bastard.

Shaking my head, I was grateful I had my gun in the back of my car.

I crunched the Jeep into first gear and returned to the road that continued up the mountain range.

Gun laws in Australia were so strict that permits were only handed out under severe circumstances. Alpha Tactical Ops had a range of weapons that were registered for our protection and dignitary duties, but all of us also had our own unregistered weapons.

Ever since the mess at Arrow Dynamics, and Mr. Chui evading the law, Blade insisted that we all carried weapons. I had four: one beside my bed, one in my kitchen, one in my Rav, and one in the trunk of this car, slotted next to the tire jack.

Neon ran his hands down his thighs, drawing my attention to that bullet wound that nearly killed him.

"How are your wounds?"

He huffed. "I think my modeling days are over."

He raised his left leg, showing the red scars from crashing through the timber veranda. It looked like he'd wrestled with a tiger.

"Nasty. You should've let me stitch those wounds when we'd had the chance."

He shrugged. "I don't mind them. Kind of gives me an edge, don't you think?"

"I think you've got lots of jagged edges, Neon."

He chuckled. "So do you, Ghost."

I turned onto the road that led to the drop-off point at the river.

"So how long have you been doing this rafting thing?" he asked.

"A couple of years."

"From your website photos, it looks like you have fun."

"I do most days." I opened the paper bag with the hot muffin, peeled off a chunk, and ate it. "Want some?"

"Sure."

I gave the bag to him, and he repeated my move. "Oh, yum. Did Zena bake this?"

"Yep. She's an amazing chef."

"I agree."

I frowned at him. "Huh."

He cocked his head at me. "Huh, what?"

"It's just, I imagine you're always eating five-star meals."

He handed the bag back to me. "There's a lot you don't know about me, Maya."

"So, can you cook?"

"Nope. Can you?"

I scrunched my nose. "Does reheating count?"

He laughed. "See, there's another thing you and I have in common. I'm a master reheater."

We finished sharing the muffin, and Neon licked his fingers, which I found way sexier than I should have.

"So, I heard the movie you were working on has been scrapped."

Neon opened his palms. "Do you blame them? It would be impossible not to look like heartless bastards if we still made the movie after all those senseless murders."

I nodded. "I'm glad they made that decision."

"Me too."

"Are you working on something else then?"

He shook his head. "Taking some time out. Besides, I sacked my manager, so I'm looking for a new one."

"Oh, you weren't happy with Marc? You were with him for a while, weren't you?"

"Ten years. He turned out to be one of the heartless bastards I was talking about."

I winced. "Not cool."

"Definitely not cool."

At the top of the hill, the western side of the range was yet to be touched by the sun and the vast vegetation filled the entire mountainside, hiding Thunder River from us. It was why my drop-off site for the rubber raft was so special; hardly anybody knew it existed.

After navigating the winding path through the vegetation down toward the river, I turned onto a dirt track that was barely visible.

"Where are you taking me, Maya?"

"Patience." I grinned at him. "The magic is about to unfold."

I drove onto a patch of grass bordering the riverbank. Every time I arrived here, I contemplated why someone had cleared the trees in this section. It was like they'd planned to build a remote fishing hut but gave away the idea before they'd started. I drove in and parked at the edge of the clearing beneath a giant gum tree.

I slapped Neon's leg. "Get ready to get wet."

"Isn't the raft to stop us from getting wet?"

"You're a funny guy, Neon." I opened my door.

"No, really. That's what a raft is for, right?"

Giggling, I closed the door and strolled to the trailer. I unhooked the bungee straps to release the raft and they flipped over the top.

Neon appeared on the other side.

"Unhook the straps and toss them into the back of the Jeep," I said.

He clicked his fingers. "Hey, here's another idea. How about we scrap the rafting and just enjoy the scenery instead."

That was exactly what I'd planned to do, but I might as well make him work for it. "You paid me to take you rafting. So that's what we're—"

"But we can just pretend to raft."

"No such thing. Now undo those straps. Chop. Chop."

"Man, you're bossy."

With the straps removed, I came around to his side. "Okay, we have to lift this off here. It's going to be heavy. I'll take the front."

I shuffled ahead of him and grabbed the handle at the nose of the raft, ready to pull it off the trailer. "Ready?"

"Yep."

Working together, we lifted the raft over our heads and carried it toward the riverbank.

"Jesus, this thing weighs a ton." He moaned.

"Put it down here."

We wrestled it off our heads and onto the ground at the edge of the riverbank.

"Are you sure it floats?" His gaze was directed at the water. This stretch of the river was about fifty feet wide, so the flow was relatively calm.

"It floats. I normally only river raft with parties of four. You booked for four people."

"Well, I didn't think you'd accept my booking if I registered under my name and said it was just me."

"And here I was thinking that you were always brutally honest."

He strolled toward me, curled his hand around my back, and planted his lips on mine. His manly cologne tantalized my senses, and my damn heart skipped a few beats.

He released me, grinning like a jock at happy hour. "How's that for honesty?"

"I'll give you honesty, Neon Bloom." I shoved him in the chest. He toppled backward, bounced on the side of the rubber raft, and flopped into it.

As he wriggled like an upturned turtle, his laughter made our already perfect setting so much better.

Giggling with him, I offered my hand. "Come here, you big buffoon."

He clasped his hand around mine and pulled me forward. Squealing like a giddy teenager, I flopped on top of him.

Pushing up to straddle him, I pressed my hands to his chest. "What are you doing, Neon?"

"Admit it, Maya. We're already mated." His eyes twinkled.

"What?" I waggled my head.

"I peed on your leg. That means we're mated for life."

I giggled. "*That* was disgusting. You watch too many movies."

"I'm trying to swoon you."

"I don't need swooning. I need saving—from you."

He wriggled his perfect eyebrows. "Oh, so you do have feelings for me."

I curled my hand over his cheek. "That's why I need saving."

He removed his sunglasses and placed his palm over mine. "Then let's not fight it. Let's see where this takes us, Maya. We have something. We really do."

His words crumbled my resolve and my shoulders softened.

"We could christen your raft?" He grinned his sassy smile that probably had all his Hollywood fans drooling. "Unless you've already done that?"

"No, I haven't done that." I scowled.

"See, it's meant to be."

"You're impossible."

"And you're delightful."

There was so much longing in Neon's expression that my chest ached with a crushing desire that I'd never felt before.

Silent beats sizzled between us. Neither of us spoke. We just looked at each other and breathed.

And just like that, we'd crossed a line. A glorious, exciting, scary line that I could never nudge back, and yet I wanted to be there. I wanted to push that line as far as it could go. My gaze flicked from his eyes to his lips. The cologne he chose today triggered everything delicious inside me.

My senses begged for more.

My flesh demanded to be touched.

My insides curled and fluttered. I wanted to make love to him. *Right here. Right now.*

Neon curled his warm hand around my neck. "Come here, beautiful."

His voice was a breathless whisper.

I let him draw me down to him. Our lips molded together, firm, intentional, and brimming with lust. Our tongues danced and explored. Our breaths became one.

This was the kiss every woman dreamed about.

The setting was perfect. The timing was perfect.

He was perfect.

No. It was more than that.

We were perfect.

He caressed my breast through my shirt and bra, but I wanted his hands on me. On my skin. I released my lips from his, sat up, and whipped off my t-shirt. Reaching behind my back, I unclipped my bra, but the sports bra was a bitch to wrestle up over my shoulders.

Closing my eyes and performing the most unsexy move of my life, I wriggled the straitjacket over my head and flung it aside.

Neon grinned like a teenager caught peeking into the girl's locker room.

"What?" I smirked.

"That was the sexiest thing I've ever seen."

"You poor deprived man." I stood and kicked off my rubber booties. "What are you waiting for? Get your gear off."

"I love it when you talk sexy."

Giggling, we were like a pair of sex-deprived lovers as we tore off our clothes.

Standing naked in the boat, we paused, admiring each other's bodies.

His chest rose and fell with heady breaths as his gaze cruised up my body, devouring me with an intensity I'd never felt before.

Neon's body was stunning. His olive flesh was flawless. He was toned to perfection. His cock stood proud, aiming right at me.

My nipples grew hard, and my insides sizzled.

The sexual tension between us was like lightning.

Our eyes met, and something crossed between us that had my knees quivering. I rolled my lip through my teeth, anticipating his next move.

Neon closed the distance between us, pressed his body to mine, and kissed me. I wrapped my arms around his back, feeling the contours of his flesh as we swayed together.

Our tongues played in a hot desire to taste each other. I glided my hand over his back, exploring his divine flesh down to the curve of his magnificent ass. He did the same, and like we'd choreographed the move, we both squeezed each other's butt.

Our kiss deepened and our bodies molded together in perfection.

This was what a kiss should be like. Exquisite. Impassioned. Out of this world.

Neon curled his hand around my back, and as my insides throbbed, he lowered me down. His lips were incredible. His tongue was too, and with our warm bodies pressed together, I was officially in heaven.

He eased up on one hand and trailed kisses down my chest, then curled his palm beneath my breast and sucked my nipple into his mouth. Gasping at the delicious sensations dazzling through me, I arched my back, offering him more. He snapped my bud from his lips and with his eyes glistening, he curled his tongue around my nipple drawing out the exquisite sensations until it was rock hard.

"Oh, Neon." His name drifted over my lips like a lullaby as I drove my fingers through his thick hair.

"Hmm." His mumble vibrating over my breast added to everything perfect about this moment.

My insides pulsed a glorious beat, and my pussy demanded attention. I parted my legs, feeling the warm sun on my inner thighs. Neon was a master magician because as he continued sucking my breast, he cruised his hand down to probe my hot zone.

His finger worked its magic; his lips did too, rubbing and sucking me until I was a quivering mess.

"Please," I begged him to make me come.

"Hmm." He sucked harder on my nipple and as a deep rumble echoed in his throat, he drove his finger inside me over and over, drawing out a climax of mammoth proportions.

I cried out as an orgasm spilled from my body. I trapped his hand between my legs as every nerve in my body rode a delicious wave. Ragged gasps tore from my throat and the most exquisite orgasm of my life washed through me.

"Wow." My breath was a throaty whisper.

Neon filled my vision. His eyes were glazed yet radiated pure rapture.

"You like." He flashed his perfect smile.

"Uh-huh." Delicious pulses lit me in all the right places: my lips, my nipples, between my legs.

With the boat squeaking, Neon positioned himself between my legs. I parted my knees, letting him know I wanted him to make love to me. I wanted it so bad I would implode if he didn't.

He crawled forward, planting kisses on my belly and my breasts, and then finally hovered over me. "You are so beautiful. I could stay here all day."

My heart swelled to bursting, and I raised my hips and using my hand, I guided him into me.

Neon pushed himself inside me with measured control, showing me another side to this amazing man. I tilted my head back at the glorious sensation inching through me.

He kissed my neck, and I gasped as he sucked my earlobe.

We moved together as if we'd made love hundreds of times before.

He started slowly, and I savored every delicious glide of his manhood inside me. I wanted to watch him, to see his arousal, but my eyes closed so I could truly enjoy every sensation.

I pressed my hands to his chest and squeezed his nipples.

He sucked air through his teeth and his thrusts became a fraction faster.

A moan tumbled from his throat. "Oh, Maya."

"Yes."

He thrust into me, and an animalistic groan tumbled from his lips as he did it again and again, each time faster.

I gasped as his thrusts were equal parts glorious pleasure and just a hint of pain. I clutched onto his biceps as a second orgasm swept through me, taking my body and heart to new heights.

Neon drove into me once, twice, three times. He cried out. I did too and we shuddered together, riding out our climaxes as one.

He fell forward, and as I wrapped my arms around him, I listened to his ragged breaths that drifted across my neck.

He smelled incredible: sexy, sensual, and oh so manly.

I trailed my fingers up his back, and he shivered and rolled to his side.

The boat squeaked as I wriggled to face him. "Well, that was a first."

He grinned. "First time with a movie star?"

"No. First time with an annoying bastard." I slapped his chest.

"You didn't seem annoyed a minute ago."

I wriggled out from beside him and when he adjusted his position in the boat, I bounced off the side. In my attempt to get my balance, I unintentionally gave Neon a peek at everything I had.

"Wow, that's a first for me." His eyes bulged.

As I climbed out of the raft, I burst out laughing and it felt so good. Leaning over the inflated side, I slapped his chest again. "Get up and stop procrastinating. We have a river to tackle."

Neon sat up, grinning like a silly drunk. "If that's what you call procrastinating, I'd happily do that all day long."

"Ha, ha." I pulled on my sports bra, along with my shorts and t-shirt and tugged my scuba booties onto my feet. "Stay here. I'll grab my pack."

The raft squeaked as Neon wrestled to get out.

The sound of an engine caught my attention. *Someone's coming.*

I'd never seen another person here.

The nose of a black F100 truck edged into the clearing, but it stopped.

My neck hairs raised to attention.

My heart thundered in my chest. I shot my gaze at Neon.

He was pulling on his shoes.

"Neon. Get to the car. Quick. Run!"

Chapter Twenty-Three

NEON

"Neon, run!" Maya's distraught expression hit me like a bolt of lightning.

I snapped my gaze from her to a black truck fifty feet away. The passenger door popped open. A man jumped out.

Sloan!

He lifted his arm over the top of the truck door, aiming a gun at me.

My heart launched up my throat as I charged toward Maya's Jeep.

Maya yanked open her rear door and dove inside as I skidded to the side of the car.

"Stay down," she yelled.

A bullet shattered her front windshield and an explosion of glass glistened in the sunshine.

I ducked behind the front tire.

Maya yanked down the rear seat and crawled into the back of her Jeep.

"Neon, you bastard. Get out here!" The booming voice had fear scraping up my spine.

Bullets punched through the car door, missed my ear by three inches, and slammed into a tree behind me, shattering a branch to pieces.

"Neon! Come out, you bastard!" Sloan's voice was feral, unhinged.

"Stay here, Neon," Maya hissed as she wriggled out of the Jeep with a gun in her hand. She clicked out the magazine, checked the bullets, then snapped it back into place.

"Stay down." Crouching behind the rear tire, she pulled a band from her wrist and tugged her thick hair into a ponytail.

"What're you going to do?"

"Kill that bastard." Her jaw was clamped so hard it quivered.

My heart invaded my throat. "Be careful."

"Neon!" Sloan yelled. "If you cooperate, I'll let that bitch live."

"He's lying, Neon, and you know it."

I nodded. "I know."

Bullets shattered the window above us, showering us in glass. Shards glistened on Maya's shoulders as she rose to peer through her car toward Sloan.

She aimed and pulled the trigger.

"Shit." She ducked down, shaking her head. "He moved."

Bullets punctured her car. One. Two. Ten. A blast boomed from the hood. Black smoke spewed from the engine.

"Christ." She rose to her haunches, and a tiny breath left her lips as she fired again. One. Two.

A cry of agony roared from across the field.

"Got him."

Bullets pinged off the car doors, hood, and roof.

An explosion of pain ripped through my left ankle. I screamed and toppled backward.

"Neon!" Maya shrieked.

Gasping at the agony, I clutched my ankle. Blood oozed through my fingers. Pain speared up my leg.

Sucking air through my teeth, I dragged myself back behind the cover of the tire, sat on rubble, and prayed for the new nightmare to end.

Maya crawled to me. "Shit, Neon."

"I'm okay. Just kill that bastard."

Maya whipped her t-shirt over her head. "Press this onto the wound and don't let go."

Fighting agony, I held her shirt to the bloody wound two inches above my ankle bone.

Black smoke spewed from the hood of her Jeep.

"Damn it. My car is going to blow. Run." She grabbed my wrist, yanked me upright, and with her arm around my waist, we raced into the bushes.

Hiding behind a gum tree, I peered around the massive trunk in time to see Sloan get to his feet.

"Maya, Sloan's getting up!"

Maya dove to the ground and fired beneath her car.

Sloan fell backward like a sack of potatoes.

"That's it—die, you bastard," Maya said through clenched teeth.

The black truck slinked backward. "The car's moving."

"Who else is in there?" Maya asked.

"I don't know."

Black smoke spewing from Maya's car grew thicker, smothering my view. Flames curled out from the hood.

Shit, it's going to explode.

Maya shot out from our cover, raced around her trailer, and ran right at the F100. She pumped bullets into the engine. The front windshield disintegrated.

Son of a bitch!

The driver was Marc. My fucking manager.

Marc slammed the F100 into reverse and drove backward like a demon. Maya chased after him and picked up a gun near Sloan's unmoving body. Using both hands, she pumped bullets into the retreating truck.

The car was fast.

Maya kept firing, punching holes all over the black paint.

Marc screamed, but the truck still roared away.

"Fuck!" Maya hollered as she fired twice more at the disappearing truck.

I couldn't stand anymore. Gritting my teeth against the pain clawing up my leg, I slumped down and pressed her shirt to my ankle.

Peering around the tree trunk, I searched for Maya. *Please be okay.* I couldn't see her through the black smoke.

A massive explosion shot the hood off Maya's Jeep. All the remaining windows shattered. Chunks of metal and glass rained down on me.

A flock of birds took to the air as flames covered the engine and front.

Pounding feet drifted to me.

Maya sprinted to my side and fell to her knees. "Are you okay?"

I clutched her to my body. "Yes, and you?"

"I'm fine. The fucker got away though."

"That was Marc."

"Yeah, I saw him."

I shook my head. "I can't believe it. He's worked for me for a decade. Why would he do that? Why?"

Maya rolled her eyes. "Because he's an asshole."

"I told you, Maya, this shit is never going to stop. I'm over it. I can't do this anymore."

"Do what?"

"This. Be Neon Bloom. People will always try to kidnap me. I want out."

"Out? How?"

"I want you to kill me."

Gasping, she pulled away. "Jesus, Neon. What are you talking—?"

"Maya, I want you to fake my death. We have the perfect situation. You killed that bastard. And we have all those hostages who can confirm it was Sloan who tried to kidnap me before. Now that he's dead—"

"He's still alive."

I blinked at her, then glanced beneath her car toward his body. He wasn't moving. "Are you sure?"

"Well, he was a minute ago. I was letting him suffer."

"Take me to him."

"You need to stay—"

"Maya!" I didn't mean to yell. I softened my voice. "Maya, please take me to him. I need to know who he is."

She offered her hand, helping me to stand, and with her arm around my back, I hopped toward the body. Pain pounded my ankle bone like it was being pummeled with a sledgehammer.

We stopped at Sloan's body. Three bullet wounds dotted his blood-stained shirt.

Maya nudged him with her foot. "You still alive, asshole?"

His eyes rolled open. His mouth parted and blood oozed from his lips. "Fucking bitch."

Maya squatted next to him. "Who are you?"

His gaze drifted to me. "You still haven't pieced it together, have you?"

I lowered next to Maya. "Pieced what together?"

"You ruined my life, Stanley Walton."

Maya frowned at me.

"That's my real name."

She nodded like she understood why I changed from that dreary name.

"How do you know who I am?" I asked Sloan.

"I've known you since the day I was born."

Frowning, I shook my head.

Sloan coughed and a bloody bubble formed on his bottom lip. "Because of you, my father went to jail."

I searched my mind for answers. "Frankie-Lee?"

"Why didn't your parents just hand over the fucking ransom money? It could have been so simple." Sloan coughed blood onto his chin.

I blinked at him. "They did hand over the money."

My parents had handed over three million dollars cash.

"No, you stupid fuck. They didn't."

Did my parents lie to me?

I glared at him. "Your father held me captive in a stinking well for two days. Did you know that?"

"You were fine. Your fucking parents should have paid, and it would have been over in hours. Instead, my dad got nothing. He died in jail because of you."

"Because of me! Are you delusional? He kidnapped me."

Frankie-Lee closed his eyes. And as I searched for signs of life, I also searched for signs of the little boy who I'd played with nearly every single day as a child.

His eyes dragged open, and he coughed more blood. "I hate you. I always hated you."

My jaw dropped. "We were friends, Frankie. You should've looked out for me."

"We weren't friends, you idiot. I was nothing to you."

I jerked back. "Are you serious? We were best friends."

Sloan's eyes rolled back, and I thought they'd stay there this time. But then he locked his gaze on me again. "You really believe that, don't you? I only liked you for the things you had. You were too busy being rich to be fun."

My brain nearly split in two. "Bullshit! We had loads of fun. You've spent twenty years twisting those memories around and now you believe your own fucking lies. You killed people, Frankie. Innocent people."

Frankie-Lee moaned, and a thick blob of blood oozed down his chin. "I should have killed you when I had a chance."

A breath escaped his lips and his head slumped to the side. His eyes stared off to the distance.

Maya sighed. "He's gone."

Shaking my head, I flopped back on the dirt. "Jesus."

Maya shuffled next to me. "You okay?"

"No. He's wrong. We were best friends. I can't believe he remembers it so differently."

"What happened to him after his father was arrested for your kidnapping?"

I blinked at the bloody bullet hole in my ankle, searching for the answer. "I . . . I don't know. I can't remember seeing him again."

"Then that would be what he remembers. One minute he's playing in a mansion with the richest kid on the planet, next minute his father is in jail, and he's probably in a slum with a mother who's scrambling to pick up the pieces. Memories get warped with that kind of childhood trauma."

I jerked back. "Are you justifying his actions?"

"Fuck no! I'm trying to prove that you did nothing wrong."

I thumped my palm to my forehead. "I hate this shit."

"Hey, it's over now." She grabbed my hand.

I groaned. "It's never over, Maya. There's always someone after me for my money."

"Not this guy." She swept her hand to Frankie-Lee. His open eyes were riddled with red spider veins.

"I can't believe it was him behind this mess. I haven't thought about him in decades. And Marc? He's been my manager for ten years. What made *him* do this?"

"Money." She shrugged.

"See! That's exactly my point."

Maya stood and nudged her rubber boot against Frankie-Lee's thigh. His body wobbled. "I told you I was going to kill this bastard. After what he did to those women though, I wanted him to suffer more. But don't worry about Marc. He won't get away with this."

"I hope not." I reached for her hand and squeezed. "I can't live like this anymore."

"Like what?"

"Always watching over my shoulder. Having full-time bodyguards. Putting people around me in danger."

"It's not you doing that."

"It's because of me and my stupid wealth. I want to kill Neon Bloom. Can you do that for me? You and your team. Could they help?"

She cocked her head. "Neon, you don't know what you're saying."

"I do. I've wanted to end this crap for a while. This is the perfect opportunity. We can make it look like he killed me. We even have my blood." I raised my throbbing ankle to show the blood dripping onto the dirt.

"That's a radical decision."

"And one I've been thinking about for years, but I didn't know how to do it. This is perfect. You can say Sloan killed me, and you killed Sloan."

"But what happened to your body?"

A groan left my throat as my shoulders slumped. "Shit."

"It's hard to die without a body."

I glanced toward the water. "What about if I tumbled into the river? Could a body disappear forever in there?"

Maya turned her gaze toward the water, then looked at me again. "Come on. Enough of this crazy talk. We have to get this mess sorted."

Maya offered her hand, pulling me upright. With her arm around me, we hobbled toward her car that was now completely engulfed in flames.

"Damn it. I liked that car."

"Was it insured?"

"Of course, but they don't make Jeeps like they used to. And Jeeps that old, and in decent condition, are hard to come by."

"I'll buy you a new car."

She tutted. "No, you won't."

"Why not? It's the least I can do after saving my ass again."

"Yeah, well, don't make me regret it." She released her grip around my waist, and we stood back from the flames.

She pointed at the blazing wreck. "My phone was in there. Have you got yours?"

I shook my head. "I left it in my pack, and I left that in your other car."

"Damn."

I shuffled away from the heat and flopped to the ground to study my throbbing leg. Spears of pain shot up my shin, but I didn't give a shit about the bullet wound. If I didn't do something, I was always going to worry about being shot.

I looked at Maya. She was studying her car, shaking her head.

"Maya. I'm serious about faking my death. I want Neon Bloom out of my life, and the only way is to kill him."

Her frown deepened. "I'm sure that's not the only way. There are plenty of actors who have vanished from the limelight."

"It's not just because I'm an actor. It's my wealth, Maya. It will always put me in jeopardy."

"There are lots of rich people, Neon."

"Yes, and they need armed security guards around them twenty-four seven. And they live in fortresses. I don't want that. I . . . I want this." I swept my arms to the scenery surrounding us.

"You want bushes?"

"I want freedom. I want to be able to walk on the beach, and stroll to the shops, and buy a coffee without being flanked by two body-guards. And even them I can't trust anymore. But most of all, Maya . . . I want you. I haven't been able to stop thinking of you since you walked out of the hospital. I'll do anything to be with you."

She jerked back. "Don't make me the reason, Neon."

"I'm not." I banged my fist onto my knee. "I have dozens of reasons. Six of them are those poor women who Sloan shot because of me."

"Hey, that's not your fault."

"It is. I've made up my mind. If you and your team can't help me, I'll find someone who can. But . . ." I met her gaze. "But right here, right now, this is the perfect set up for my death."

"Jesus." She clutched her ponytail and flicked it over her shoulder. "But you could never go back to your current life."

"I don't care."

"You couldn't see any friends or family."

"I know. I can accept that. What I can't accept is not being with you."

"Neon . . ."

I loved the way she said my name.

"I've made up my mind, and we have the perfect opportunity."

"What about your money and assets?"

"I don't care about money."

"You say that now, but dead men can't access their bank accounts."

I rolled my eyes. "You're not understanding, Maya. I don't care about money. Or my assets. Or Neon Bloom. The only thing I care about is you."

I reached for her.

She lowered to her knees, and I pulled her to my chest. She wrapped her arms around me, and I had never felt so whole in my life.

"Maya, you mean the world to me, and I need to change my world to be with you."

"Oh, jeez, Neon. I don't know if I can live with that decision."

"It's not your decision. It's mine. But I need your help."

She eased back. "Neon, I don't—"

I pressed my lips to hers. She opened her mouth, and as I curled my hand around her neck, our tongues met in a heated kiss that smothered all my swirling emotions.

We parted, and she met my gaze.

"There's no turning back from something like that," she said.

"I know. And I'm ready."

Her chest rose and fell with a massive breath. She shifted her attention from me to her car to the raft. Then she stood and turned to Frankie-Lee's body.

Finally, she frowned. "What about your parents? You'll never be able to see them again. Or even speak to them."

I nodded. "I know."

"You'll have to change your appearance."

"Fine. I've gone in disguise many times." I tugged at the section of my beard near my ear to peel it off.

Her jaw dropped. "Your beard is fake?"

"Yeah."

"No. Leave it. We need you in disguise." She curled her hand over my beard. "It's very good."

"Thanks, I did it myself."

"Impressive." Shaking her head, she folded her arms. "You'd need a new identity."

"I've done that once before. I can do it again."

"Yeah, thanks for telling me Neon wasn't your real name."

"Sorry. I've been Neon for so long, I forget about my real name."

"Why did you change it?"

"Stanley Walton isn't a stuntman kind of name."

"I guess not. What about all your family money? You'll lose that."

"Actually, I have money set up in offshore accounts that I'm sure I can get access to."

"See! You're already thinking about how you can access your money."

I clicked my fingers. "Maybe it could look like we withdrew the money for a ransom, and then it vanished."

A frown drilled across her forehead.

"What?"

She shook her head. "Nothing."

"It wasn't nothing. You thought of something. What was it?"

"Cobra is brilliant with computer hacking. He'd have no trouble giving you a new identity, but maybe he could also get—" She stepped back, clenching her fists. "Christ! What am I thinking? This is stupid."

"Maya. Please, can you work with me on this?"

"Jesus!" She threw out her hands. "We can't make snap decisions like this. This is crazy."

"This isn't a snap decision, believe me. In the last five years, I've had three kidnap attempts on my life. In this last one, I nearly died, and I wish I had because six hostages were killed because of me. I can't do this anymore." I shook my head. "What if it was you who died? I couldn't live with that. I can't—"

A knot wedged in my throat that was so big I could barely breathe.

"I have to kill Neon Bloom. He's toxic."

She melted to the ground at my side and placed her hand on my bare knee. "Let me look at your leg."

Just the slightest touch from her had my heart skipping. "No. It's fine."

"It's not fine. You were shot. You need treatment."

"Maya, don't. I don't give a shit about my leg. I can handle it. What I can't handle is being shot at all the time. Finally, I have an opportunity to do something about it, and I'm not going to miss it." I leveled my gaze at her. "But I need your help."

She stood, flaring her blues at me. Then she stomped away. Her fists swung at her sides as she marched to the tree we'd hid behind. She snatched her shirt from the ground and stormed back to me.

She squatted at my ankle, and working in silence, she wrapped her t-shirt around my wound and tucked the edges in to secure it.

She stood back and folded her arms. "Here's what we will do. We'll take the raft to my other car and ring Blade. I need his help."

I shook my head. "We need to set the scene here first before someone stumbles on it."

She spun her back to me and her shoulders rose and fell as she inhaled a deep breath.

"Help me up." I offered my hand, and she yanked me upright.

231

Her face was twisted with a horrible mess of emotions, and I hated that I was the reason behind her turmoil.

"Maya, look at this scene. It all works in our favor. Just hear me out. Here's what happened. We put the boat over there. Those assholes drove in and started shooting. I raced behind your car with you. You got your gun, and you started shooting back. Sloan shot my ankle. You shot Sloan. I saw smoke coming out of the hood of the car and shuffled away. So far everything is exactly as it happened, right?"

She nodded, chewing on the inside of her cheek.

"Sloan was down, but Marc kept firing at us. The car was going to explode, so I ran toward the raft. I got a bullet in the back and went into the water. You saw it out the corner of your eye. You shot at Marc a few more times, but by the time you raced to the river, I was gone. And that's how Neon Bloom died."

Her eyes darkened. The turmoil twisting her expression matched the turmoil coursing through my veins. Except mine was also mingled with excitement. Finally, something made sense.

I reached for her hand. "This will work. I just know it."

"This isn't a scene from a movie, Neon. You can't just erase it in ten years' time. It will be there forever."

"Exactly." I reached for her other hand and angled her to face me. "Maya, I haven't been able to stop thinking of you. You've changed me. I want to live a normal life. I've wanted it for ages, but now I want it so badly I can barely think of anything else. But more than anything, Maya, I want you."

I cupped her cheek, and she leaned into my palm.

I pressed my forehead to hers and when she closed her eyes, I did too.

"We have something special, and I know you feel the same."

Shaking her head, she eased back and met my gaze. "We barely know each other."

I squeezed her hands. "And I can't wait to get to know everything about you. You're the most extraordinary woman I've ever met. You make my heart do crazy things. Tell me you feel that too."

A soft breath fluttered across her lips. "I do feel it, Neon. And it scares the crap out of me."

"So don't fight it."

"I have to, Neon. There's stuff about me you don't know. There's stuff that you will not—"

"Stop. Stop. I don't care about any of that. I care about you. It will be amazing getting to know each other."

She released her hands and stepped back. "I can't do it like this, Neon. I can't be the catalyst that changes your life forever."

"You already are."

"There you go with the brutal honesty."

"Exactly." I clenched my fists. "Maya, I'm begging you. I want to kill Neon Bloom, and this is my opportunity. Please. Please help me?"

She glanced down at the blood splatters in the dirt. "Here's what I'm prepared to do, Neon. We raft down the river to my other car. From there we use your phone to ring my team. If they agree that this is possible without any of us being arrested, then we'll do it."

"Thank you."

She raised her hand, halting me. "Don't thank me yet. We're still not out of danger. I wasn't really going to make you raft down the river, but now we have no choice."

"Really? Why not?"

Her eyes darkened. "I don't know if it's possible with just two people."

"Shit."

"Exactly. Damn it!" She spun to the flaming Jeep. "The life jackets just burned to a crisp in my car."

She kicked a rock, and it disappeared beneath the Jeep.

"We could wait here, and when someone comes, I'll hide in the bushes until it's safe for me to come out."

"No. The second someone sees this mess, this place will be crawling with cops. You could be stuck in the bushes for days."

She stormed away to the trailer behind the Jeep. I stayed where I was; it was too painful for me to walk anyway.

Clutching two paddles, she marched back to me. "Now stop fucking around and help me get this into the water."

She tossed the paddles into the bottom of the raft.

We each grabbed a side handle on the raft and dragged it to the water.

"Get in," she said.

The rubber wobbled as I fought excruciating pain and climbed over the inflated side into the raft. "Do you think we can do this?"

She simultaneously pushed off the shore and jumped in. "I don't know. It's going to be damn hard work. And knowing my luck, you won't make the trip."

"What a perfect way for Neon Bloom to punch out. Very dramatic, don't you think?"

She glared at me. "Yeah, the tabloids will have a field day."

"Which is exactly why I love this plan."

"Yeah, provided we don't die for real in this river."

The terror in her gaze added to the mess of emotions darting through me.

Chapter Twenty-Four

NEON

After pushing away from the safety of the shore, Maya instructed me to sit in the middle of the raft on the inflated side and she sat opposite.

"See this, Neon?" She pointed at her foot which she had wedged between the expanded side of the raft and the base. "Jam your foot right in there, nice and tight. That will help keep you in the raft."

"Oh, don't worry, I have no intentions of getting out."

She huffed. "You may not have a choice on some of the rapids."

"Trust me. It was why I excelled as a stuntman. If the stunt was over water, there was no way I was falling in."

She chuckled. "Fear is a great motivator."

"Isn't that the truth?"

She handed me an oar. Then using her own, she paddled us further from the riverbank. Behind us, the car was still ablaze, and black smoke drifted over the trees and dispersed into the sky.

"Sorry about your car."

She glanced over her shoulder at the flaming wreck. "Me too. That smoke is a problem, though. If anyone sees it, the fire brigade will come up here thinking it's a bush fire."

"That's what we want, isn't it? For the scene to be found."

"As long as I can get to my team before that happens, so we can work through a plan. Lucky for you, Viper will be one of the firemen."

"Would he help us?"

She squinted at the sunshine. "There's no telling with Viper. He's a cranky bastard."

"I noticed that. Why?"

Maya shook her head. "I wish I knew."

Her expression showed me how much she cared for Viper. And I'd already seen that with the rest of her team. They were tight. They had each other's backs, even if that meant taking a bullet. Just like Maya had said she'd do for me.

Before I'd met Maya and her team, I didn't have a single person who was like that with me. Even Marc and Derek, who I thought were there for me, turned out to be assholes.

"What's wrong? You changing your mind?" she asked.

"No. I was just thinking about Marc. I can't believe he was in on this."

"I can. It adds some sense to what happened on the island."

I still couldn't process it. "But how did Frankie-Lee convince Marc to do this? To commit murder?"

"Money. It's nearly always money. And in Frankie-Lee's case, it was both money and revenge, a toxic combination."

"He's been plotting this for twenty years." I stared into the water, picturing my childhood friend Frankie-Lee. We'd been inseparable. It was weird how I couldn't remember seeing him after his dad kidnapped me. Then again, I'd been messed up for a long time after I was rescued.

She clicked her fingers in front of my face. "Okay, dreamboat, you need to focus. I won't gloss this over. This is going to be damn hard work. I've only rafted down these rapids with four to six people, so believe me, it's deadly. You could die."

"Ha, ha."

She scooped the water with her paddle. "I'm serious. It looks peaceful now, but in a little while, you'll be wishing you were back in your fancy home in Beverly Hills."

"No, I won't."

She studied me, and I hoped she saw absolute conviction in my expression.

The river was peaceful, and the silence was incredible. I inhaled scents of eucalyptus and fresh air. With the plan we had already in motion, I felt a massive weight shift from my shoulders.

"What are you grinning at?" Maya frowned.

"It's beautiful out here. I can see why you love it."

"It sure is. I have the best office in the world."

She scooped the water again, gently maneuvering the raft toward the middle of the river. The burning car was no longer visible, but the black smoke still pinpointed the location.

"Okay, let's see how you go with these lessons," she said.

As we drifted toward a bend in the river, Maya gave me different paddling instructions. Her strong arms bulged and flexed as she demonstrated the moves. I copied, but damn, she made it look easy. It was surprisingly physical, which explained how she had such a magnificent physique.

As she was only wearing her sports bra and tight little shorts, with each stroke she made in the water, I relished the movement of her gloriously toned stomach.

Holy hell, she's sexy.

Around the bend, the river changed from as smooth as glass, to small bumps of rocks that created white waves as the water crashed into them.

Maya guided the raft down the middle, and we hit the first bump beneath the rubber. It slammed into the bottom of my foot, shooting pain up my leg like I'd been hit with a sledgehammer.

Crying out, I reached down my leg and squeezed below my knee, trying to cut off the blinding agony.

"Jesus, Neon."

Sucking air through my teeth, I fought the torture.

"That was barely anything. We have much worse coming up." Maya's concern was stamped all over her face.

"I'm fine," I said through clenched teeth.

Maya squeezed her thumb to her temple like her brain hurt. It probably did. We'd experienced a world of emotions in the space of a couple of hours, and I hated that our amazing sex was ruined by all that bullshit.

The river returned to glass and Maya kept us cruising down the middle.

"You need a hospital, Neon."

Fighting the pain, I released my clamp on my leg, grabbed my paddle, and attempted a smile. "I have you. You'll fix me."

"Ah, *now* you want me to stitch you up."

"I want you to do everything. Especially if it's as much fun as we had in the raft a little while ago."

She squinted at me and looked to be fighting the grin curling across her lips.

"You can't deny that was fun," I said.

"It was nice."

My jaw dropped. "Nice. Is that all?"

She shrugged. "Nice."

"Come here, you." I lowered my paddle to the raft and reached forward. She squealed as I dragged her toward me.

She bounced across the raft and kneeled between my legs. I curled my hands over her shoulders. "It was more than nice."

The cutest smile crossed her lips. "Let's say it was the perfect benchmark."

"Benchmark? So that means you want more."

She playfully slapped my chest. "I didn't say that."

I cupped her cheeks and lowered to kiss her. My intention was for a quick kiss, but Maya pressed her lips to mine. We moaned together, savoring the feel of our tongues as we tasted each other.

Maya pulled back, and her eyes darkened. "That's enough of that. We have important business to attend to, don't you think?"

"I think I'm in love."

Her hand went to her mouth, but her eyes dazzled. She seemed to have a mental battle before she bounced to the opposite side of the raft with a clamped jaw, picked up her paddle, and rowed us to the riverbank.

She wrapped her hand around a low-lying branch. "I told you, Neon, we barely know each other."

I spread my arms wide. "Okay, so here we are, just the two of us. Ask me anything, or if you like, you never did tell me about Lily?"

Her expression shifted to one I couldn't read as she slid her hand around the back of her neck, to her angel wing tattoo. "I can't believe you remembered my sister's name."

"I told you, since you walked out of the hospital, I've done nothing but think of you. I've replayed every minute we were together on that island over and over."

"Not all of it was good." She gave me a death stare.

"Our time together was."

She waggled her head. "Brutal honesty, huh?"

"Always."

She pushed us away from the shore with more aggression than was needed and paddled to return us to the middle.

Her expression grew serious. "Okay, fun is over. Time to focus. We have some more rapids coming up. Get ready."

"I will if you promise to tell me about Lily."

She pouted. "That's blackmail."

"Well, we've been here before, but you dodged out of it last time."

"If you don't get ready, you'll be the one dodging rocks in the water. Quick, paddle forward."

Adjusting my position, so my right foot was wedged into the gap in the side, I dug my paddle into the water and scooped.

"And again." Maya did the same on the other side. "We're aiming for that rock on the left. If we go too far right, we'll hit more bumps than you want."

Working together, we aimed for the left side of the river. Water tumbled over rocks and the sound was therapeutic.

Maya's reluctance to share her sister's story ate at me. But it also added to her intrigue. Every other woman I knew couldn't wait to unburden their painful past. Maya had hers under lock and key. I just hoped she'd find it in her heart to open that lock and share her pain with me.

There wasn't much I could do for Maya. She was a truly independent woman. But I'd do anything to help her with the pain I saw in her eyes every time she mentioned Lily.

Up ahead, a giant rock loomed from the middle of the river.

Maya pointed at it. "When I say go, we need to paddle as hard as we can to get across the river, so we go around the other side of that rock. Get ready."

"I'm ready." I strangled the paddle. My heart thundered in my chest.

The tiny rapids that crashed over rocks dotting the river became bigger.

Another noise drifted to me. It sounded like a roaring lion. "What's that?"

"Devil's Dive. The waterfall."

I glared at her. "Waterfall! You never said anything about waterfalls."

"Go! Neon. Paddle!" Maya stood and plunged her oar into the water.

I dug in, scooping the water, driving everything I had into each stroke.

"Go. Go. Go!" Maya was a machine.

Clenching my jaw, I matched her strokes.

We crossed the river in seconds. The roaring grew louder. I stared ahead.

The big rock seemed to divide in two, revealing another rock equally as big to its right. Water fed between them like a giant spout.

"Get that foot in there, Neon. When I say, you need to put the paddle handle to your ankles, the blade in the air, and hang on."

"Okay."

"Just like we practiced."

"Okay." My heart was in my goddammed throat as we were drawn to the gap between the two rocks like we were in a giant vacuum.

We were sucked into the gap.

"Now!" Maya screamed.

I did what she'd said with the paddle. I couldn't help the scream tearing up my throat as we shot between the rocks.

The front of the raft fell away, dropping us like a lead weight. I strangled the handle, drove my foot into the gap, and squeezed my eyes shut.

The raft bucked beneath me. My ass bounced into the air.

I shot my eyes open. The raft slammed into the bottom. A wave poured over the front, drenching me to my core.

The raft bounced once, then leveled out.

It was all over in seconds.

"You missed it." Maya grinned at me.

I bulged my eyes at her. "I didn't miss it."

"You closed your eyes."

I burst out laughing. "Do you blame me? You gave me no time to prepare for a waterfall."

"Of course. If I told you, you would've cried like a baby and wanted to get off."

"No, I wouldn't."

She drove her paddle into the water. "I think you would have."

"You still could have warned me."

She giggled and the delightful sound added to the perfect setting.

Peace replaced the roaring waterfall, and the river returned to its mirror image, reflecting the scattering of clouds above and the trees lining the riverbank. Birds chirped somewhere amongst the lush green backdrop.

"You need to stop making assumptions about me, Maya."

"Not assumptions. Just observations."

"Hmm," I mumbled.

"Hmmm, what?" She flashed her stunning eyes at me.

"My observation is that you're scared to share your sister's story with me."

The smile fell from her face. "I'm not scared."

"Yes, you are. You're scared to open your heart any further to me."

She plucked wet hair from her cheek. A sadness washed over her that was so dark, a chunk of my heart fell away.

"Maya, please, I want to help you, but I don't know how."

"You can't help me. No one can."

"Try me."

I felt like this was a test. If Maya didn't open up to me now, she never would.

But as much as my feelings for her took my breath away, I couldn't be with her if she didn't trust me.

Chapter Twenty-Five

MAYA

The pleading lilt in Neon's request clamped a vice around my chest. I scooped the water with my paddle, keeping the raft in the middle of the river. The serenity was a complete contrast to my pounding heart.

His request had confusion reigning in my brain. I wanted to tell him about my sister. I wanted him to know everything about me. Neon did crazy things to me that I'd never felt before, and as much as I fought my attraction to him, I simply couldn't.

I wanted to be with him.

I wanted to do everything in my power to make his wish a success.

I wanted him to be happy.

Energy sizzled between us that was as raw as the sunshine beaming down on us.

I scooped my paddle through the water, cleared my throat, and prepared to tell Neon the story from my past that had been aching in my soul forever.

I met Neon's gaze and sighed. "I told you I came home from school to find my sister covered in blood and vomit."

"Yes, you did. And that she was conscious, but no ambulance was called."

Pierced by a surge of sadness, I said, "The blood was between her legs."

"Oh, no. Did she lose a baby?"

I nodded. "Lily had been having an affair with our priest."

Neon whistled. "Shit. I wasn't expecting that."

"It was a surprise to me too when I found out. Before she died, my family went to church three times a week: Friday night and twice on Sunday. My parents were devout Christians. That's why they chose praying to God rather than calling an ambulance."

"Jeez, Maya." Neon shook his head and the concern in his expression was genuine, adding another layer to this truly incredible man.

I turned my attention to the lily flower tattooed on my finger. "But my parents' devotion to their faith meant they refused to believe Lily was pregnant to our priest."

"Asshole."

"Yeah. That's an understatement. Father Bastion was thirty-seven and married with five kids. His oldest son was seventeen."

"Fucking asshole."

"Yes, but my parents took Father Bastion's side, rather than Lily's."

"Oh no. Your poor sister."

I stared at a puddle in the raft that reflected the sun's golden orb. "I should have known something was wrong. Lily was always vibrant and happy. The life of the party. She was four years older than me, and I couldn't wait to be like her."

"She sounds just like you."

"Everyone said they could tell Lily and I were sisters. I missed her so badly. I still do."

I tilted my head at Neon, and my heart skipped a beat. The cocky Hollywood playboy was gone, replaced with a man who was calm, welcoming, and caring. He seemed genuinely interested in watching out for me. I had a team of burly special ops men who did exactly that, but Neon was different.

He's looking out for my heart.

"What happened when Lily told you this?" he asked.

"She didn't." Emotions twisted inside me. Disappointment. Rage. Confusion.

Neon frowned. "So how did you find out who the father of the child was?"

"Four years after Lily passed away. I was planning my outfit for my high school graduation, and I went to her room. I wanted to wear her formal dress, to honor her in a way."

"She would have liked that."

"Yeah, I thought so too. Anyway, I found the dress and as I was looking for the necklace she'd worn, I found her diary. I had no idea she'd kept one."

Neon whistled. "Here we go."

"That's how I found out she lost her virginity to Father Bastion. She'd been having an affair with him for four months. But when she fell pregnant, Bastion demanded that she have an abortion. She refused. Then he tried to make Lily say it was his own son who was the father of the baby."

"What? That's despicable."

"I know. Sleazy asshole. But Lily wouldn't name the priest's son as the father either."

"Good on her. So, what happened?"

"Lily went to Mom and Dad, but they didn't believe her. First, they didn't believe she was pregnant. So, she showed Mom the pregnancy test. Mom was furious because she should have saved herself for marriage. But Mom and Dad still refused to believe it was their priest's child."

"What did you do when you read this?"

I dug the paddle into the water for a couple of strokes, aiming the raft toward the slower water on the left. "I confronted Mom about it and told her I was going to expose Bastion. I was furious. Mom broke down and told me Dad made Lily drink something to get rid of the baby."

Neon gasped.

I squeezed my eyes shut. "Whatever it was, it killed her baby and her, too."

"Jesus, Maya. What did you do?"

"I went to the police to report Father Bastion and told them Dad poisoned Lily."

Neon's eyes widened. "Good on you. And . . .?"

"It turned out my sister wasn't Bastion's only victim. He was already serving twenty years for a string of offenses including sex with minors and child pornography."

"Shit! And your dad . . .?"

"Dad took off."

Neon's jaw dropped. "He didn't."

"He did. I've been searching for him ever since because . . ." I met Neon's stunning eyes. "Because when I find him. I'm going to kill him."

"Good." He raked his fingers through his hair.

I blinked at him. "You're okay with that?"

"With you killing the man who killed your sister?"

"Yes." I frowned at him.

"Of course."

"You'd be happy with your girlfriend being a murderer?"

His mouth fell open. "So, you do want to be my girlfriend?"

"No. I'm just saying—"

"You want to be my girlfriend. That's what you said. Everyone heard it." He spread his arms wide.

"Oh, everyone. Did they?" Despite myself, I giggled.

"Seriously, Maya. I would support whatever you did to that bastard."

My heart swelled to bursting as I nodded. "Thank you."

"What about your mom?"

"I made Mom's life hell. I went to her church and made it well known what she did to my sister. I haven't spoken to her since I left for the army."

He nodded like he fully understood that move. "So that's why you joined the army . . . to get away from her."

"No. I joined the army to be a sniper so I could kill my father and get away with it."

Neon's expression was unreadable.

"Still want me as your girlfriend?" I cocked my head.

Neon slipped off his side of the raft, and it wobbled as he limped to me. He fell to his knees between my legs and graced me with his spectacular eyes. "Maya, will you marry me?"

I burst out laughing and slapped his shoulder. "Stop that, you silly bastard."

His grin was truly spectacular. "I mean it. You are the most incredible woman I've ever met."

"Incredibly psycho, you mean."

"That, too."

Giggling, I slapped him again. "So, my plan to kill my father doesn't creep you out?"

"Not at all. Except his death should be slow and excruciating, not a sniper bullet. He deserves to be punished."

I glided my hand through his thick hair. "How did you get so insightful?"

He shrugged and eased up on his knees to kiss me.

Our lips met, and as I closed my eyes and fell into his embrace, I knew Neon had entered my heart.

Whatever happened from this moment on could ruin me forever.

A siren pierced the stillness. We jerked apart. Neon's eyes were wide with fear.

"Sounds like the fire brigade," I said. "They must've seen the smoke."

"Shit. What does that mean to our plan?"

"It means we need to stop mucking around and paddle. Get over there and get ready."

"Yes, my love."

"Hey." I pointed at him. "This is serious."

"So was I."

Scowling, I scanned the river, assessing what section we were in. "Okay, Neon, beyond the next bend in the river, we'll have more white water to tackle. We have one more obstacle to pass through and this one is deadlier than the last."

The blood seemed to drain from his face.

"Now remember, if you fall out, float on your back, aiming your feet downstream, and I'll come and get you."

"I told you, I won't fall out."

"Yeah, well, just in case. Now paddle. Come on, put your back into it. One. Two. One. Two."

Neon's strong strokes matched mine and we reached the bend in record time.

"Okay, Neon. See that giant rock in the water?"

He squinted ahead. "Yes."

"The river will try to pull us toward it. But if we go too close to that rock, we'll get sucked into a whirlpool."

"I'm guessing we don't want that?" A weird smirk crawled across his lips, but it didn't mask the fear in his eyes.

"No. It will be like an underwater tornado, and you won't know which way is up."

Neon groaned.

"So, this is our plan." I pointed to a tree that had fallen into the water so long ago, that all the branches had been stripped, leaving just the moss-covered trunk. "Once we get past that tree, we need to paddle hard to get to the other side of the river. The water is powerful and with just the two of us, we'll need to work fucking hard to get there and stay hugging that side as we cruise past the rock."

His eyes darkened. "What's the contingency plan?"

His attention was on a small boulder ahead that had water frothing at its base. My mind lobbed back to that situation at the swampy lagoon pool on the island. He'd been terrified. He was terrified now too.

"Neon, look at me."

He dragged his gaze from the river, and his Adam's apple bobbed.

"Just paddle as hard as you can, and I'll do the rest."

"And if we get sucked under?"

"Hold your breath for as long as you can, and you'll float to the surface, then just do as I told you."

He nodded, but his bulging eyes made it look like his head was about to explode.

"You'll be okay. If we go into the water, swim to the left-hand riverbank and I'll save you."

"You have already saved me, Maya." A sense of calmness seemed to wash over him.

His trust in me was extraordinary.

"Okay, here we go. The second we're around that tree, put everything you have into it."

"Okay." Neon twisted his body, ready to drive his paddle into the water.

I did the same. "Ready. Go!"

We dug the paddles and scooped the water.

"Go. Go. Go."

The water was too strong for just the two of us. For each stroke we tried to aim left, it dragged us right.

"Dig! Go. Come on!" I drove my paddle and scooped harder than I ever had in my life.

It was no use. The ass end of the raft was sucked into the whirlpool.

"Hang on!" I yelled.

The back of the raft dipped down like an almighty monster was pulling us under. The front rose up. The raft twisted.

"We're going in. Take a breath."

Neon's eyes were huge. A silent scream blazed across his face.

Water poured into the back of the boat, clawing us into the vortex.

The raft bucked and buckled at the torrential onslaught. The front aimed for the sky.

Neon screamed as the boat tipped over.

Chapter Twenty-Six

NEON

Fighting blinding fear, I gripped the raft handle. The boat flipped over the top of me. Water slammed into my chest, punching what little air I had left out of me. But I didn't let go.

The water roared like it was furious I was still with the raft.

"Maya!"

My heart exploded as I searched for her, but all I saw was swirling water.

I clutched the handle, desperate to keep hold. My legs were sucked into the raging torrent, but the boat's buoyancy kept me in an air pocket above the water.

Using my other hand, I searched the frothing mess. "Maya!"

My ankle smashed against something, and I screamed at the torture to my bullet wound.

"Maya!"

I scraped through the water, desperate to find her.

The torrent roared louder. The raft pulled against my stranglehold, spearing into the vortex, sucking my feet in with it.

Fucking hell!

I had to get out of here before the raft popped or sucked me under.

My heart thundered as loud as the river.

I darted my eyes about the mayhem. With every second, my little air pocket got smaller. The rubber shuddered like a wild animal trapped in a snare.

Water tore at my legs, dragging me deeper.

A panic attack took hold. *If I don't let go, I will die.*

I sucked in a huge breath, gushed it out, and sucked again.

Squeezing my eyes shut, I forced my fingers to release. The raging torrent yanked me under.

Invisible fists slammed my legs, back, ass, and shoulders.

My hip crashed into a rock, and I howled. Precious air burst from my lungs.

My chest burned. Stars dazzled across my eyes.

Every movement of my left foot had pain blazing through my veins.

I kicked with my good leg, aiming for the dazzling lights on the surface.

Popping through to daylight, I gulped in fresh air. "Maya! Maya!"

I spun around searching for her, and my leg smashed into something. Howling at the pain, I forced myself to do what she'd said. I sucked in air, rolled onto my back, and aimed my feet downstream. My ass bumped over hidden rocks and my head hit two before I raised my head from the water to look at what I was being speared into. Trees whizzed by at a million miles an hour.

"Maya!"

My hip bounced off a rock.

"Maya!"

Please be okay, Maya.

"Neon! Neon!"

I spun to the voice. She was on the riverbank, waving at me but I shot right past.

"Shit." I rolled onto my side and kicked toward the riverbank. "Maya!"

Maya jumped into the water and with strong strokes, she swam toward me like an Olympic swimmer.

She gripped my bicep. "Are you okay?"

"I am now. We made it."

We clutched hands, linking us together.

Behind us, white water crashed into the giant rock in an explosion of white foam. But I couldn't see the raft. "Did the boat make it?"

"Nope." She shook her head. "What happened to you?"

"I couldn't let go and the raft kept me above the water."

"Jeez. I can't believe you hung on so long. I thought I'd fucking lost —" The words broke in her throat, and tears pooled in her eyes.

"I told you I wouldn't let go."

"You crazy idiot." She flicked away tears.

"Sorry."

High on her cheekbone, a bloody cut had just missed her eye. "You're bleeding."

She touched her cheek, smudging the blood. "It's just a scratch."

"What do we do now?"

"Let's get over there." She pointed to the left-hand side of the river-bank. I rolled onto my side, and trying not to move my left ankle, I did a weird sideways crawl, dragging my battered body to safety.

I was exhausted by the time I reached the riverbank.

Maya clutched a branch and pulled herself onto the knee-high grass lining the shore. I crawled in beside her, and we both flopped onto our backs panting.

I rolled toward her and swept wet hair off her cheek. Blood dripped from the cut. "Are you okay?"

She nodded. "Just."

I collapsed back to the ground and the trees spun in lazy loops above me. "I'm thinking of asking for a refund. That was the worst adventure trip ever."

Maya chuckled. "And that's another opposite for us. I thought it was the best."

I propped on my elbow to look at her. "You can't be serious."

She rolled her head toward me, and my breath caught at how stunning she was . . . even after everything we'd been through. "Trust me, Neon, when you look danger in the face and come out smiling, that's a great day."

I glided my finger along her jaw. "I bet you've seen some scary stuff?"

"You could say that."

Continuing my exploration, I trailed my finger down her neck, heading toward her chest.

She snapped her hand around mine. "Hold your horses there, Randy. We have things to do."

"Randy?"

She sat. "Yeah, Randy. It suits you."

She stood and dusted her hands on her dripping shorts. With her in only her bra, and with the wet fabric of her shorts hugging her curves, it was like I had a front row seat to a glamor photography shoot for a racy sports magazine.

I rolled to sit and bit back the agony gnawing through my ankle.

Maya shielded her eyes from the sun with her hand to look upstream. "I can still see the smoke from my car."

I dragged my aching body upright and followed her gaze. "The smoke is blacker though, so they must be putting it out."

She scrunched her nose at me. "Why do you assume that?"

"I used to be a stuntman, remember? We did a lot of scenes with fire."

"Huh." She turned her attention downstream. "In that case, the firemen would have also found the dead guy, so we can assume the police are on their way too."

"Shit." I slumped back to the ground.

Maya squatted at my side, gracing me with a spectacular view of her cleavage. "The police were always going to be involved."

"I know. I just hope this doesn't mess up our plan."

She rested her hand on my knee. "You really are serious about ending Neon Bloom, aren't you?"

I looked right into her eyes. "I am a thousand percent serious. If I don't kill Neon Bloom now, I may never get another chance. Unless someone kills me for real."

"I was afraid you were going to say that." She tapped my knee and stood.

"What will it take to convince you? Another attempt to kidnap me? More people killed because of me?"

She spun to me with a scowl. "Shush. I'm thinking."

I picked up a twig, tossed it into the bushes, and flopped onto my back again. The trees had stopped swirling, and I squinted at the brilliant white clouds that drifted overhead.

Maya shuffled a few feet closer to the river. "The good news is from here to where we parked my other car, the river behaves itself."

"I'm sensing there's a bad news."

"Yes. We need to swim."

I shook my head. "Why can't we walk?"

"Because the car is on the other side."

A wail of sirens blared from the bushes across the river.

"That's the police," she said.

I groaned and Maya's face came into my view above me. "Are you changing your mind?"

"No."

She sat beside me, crossing her legs over, and huffed out a breath. "Okay."

I forced my groaning body upright, wondering how she could be so energetic. "Okay? As in yes, we're doing this?"

She rolled her eyes. "Yes. But if you ever regret it, I'll kill you for real myself."

"Fantastic." I clutched her cheeks and squished my lips to hers.

She pushed me away. "Randy, stop."

I clicked my fingers. "I need a new name."

"Listen, Randy," she said, rolling the name off her tongue. "You need more than a new name. You need a whole new life and backstory. And a new appearance."

She tugged on my fake beard, and it must've been half dangling off because I barely felt it come free.

"Do you think your friends can help me?" I asked.

She squeezed the water out of my fake beard and draped it over a bush. "I bloody hope so because we've run out of time to ask them."

"What do you mean?"

Clutching her ponytail, she wrung out water. "At this time of the day, there is a good chance people would be near my Rav4, anyway, so that was always going to be an issue if we rowed into shore on the raft together. Losing the raft can be part of our story. But the second I tell someone that you're shot and missing in the river, the ball is rolling. There's no turning back."

"Good." I forced conviction into my voice.

She searched the bushes behind me. "You have to stay here."

"Okay." In front of me, the river rushed right to left. A variety of shrubs were all around me and beneath my ass was thick-bladed grass. Behind me was a kaleidoscope of green vegetation.

"I'll swim across river to the car." She flicked her wet hair over her shoulder.

I caressed her arm, feeling her warmth. "Thank you for doing this."

Her eyebrows nudged upward. "I still think it's crazy."

"It's not crazy. It's perfect, just like you."

She squinted at me. "I hope you know what you're doing because you can't undo killing Neon Bloom."

"I know exactly what I'm doing."

She released a sigh like she'd finally reached the same space as me.

"Once I say you're missing, they'll start scouring the river. You'll have to shift away from here and hide."

I scanned the tiny landing area we'd crawled into. The bushes were so thick I could barely see three feet into them, and enormous trees hovered overhead, making an aerial sighting of me impossible. "How long?"

"I imagine they'll call off the search at nightfall. That's when I'll come and get you."

I nodded. "Okay, that's easy."

"Whatever you do, don't come out until you know it's me. I'm telling a lot of lies for you, Neon, and I—"

"I know, and I'll be forever grateful. I promise, I'll make it up to you."

"I don't need you to make it up to me. I need you to make it work."

"It will. It's perfect."

"Okay, let's do this." She pointed at my ankle. "I need my shirt back."

"Oh, right." I undid the knot and peeling her shirt away from my bloody bullet wound, I winced as the last section of fabric came away.

Maya knelt at my side, placed her warm hands on either side of my leg, and assessed the wound. "The bullet went straight through which is good, but hopefully it didn't nick any bones on the way through."

"Why?"

"You don't want to know."

I nodded. She was right about that. I didn't want to know.

Standing again, she pulled her t-shirt over her torso.

I pointed at the blood stain on the front. "That will add weight to your story."

She pulled the shirt out to examine the blood. "Yeah. As long as they don't charge me with your murder."

My jaw dropped. "Why would they do that?"

She gave me a you've-got-to-be-joking look. "I'm a skilled sniper."

I squinted at her. "So you have the means to kill me—"

"And the opportunity," she added.

"Okay, but what's the motive?"

"Oh jeez, don't get me started. You never follow instructions, you ruined a perfect sunny day, you crashed back into my life when I—"

"There you go again, fighting it." I grabbed her hand, attempting to tug her down to me, but she was too strong.

"Fighting what?" She pulled her hand free.

"Us." I wriggled my brows.

Maya giggled and it took my sexy magazine shoot idea to another level.

"Stop distracting me," she said. "I need to concentrate."

"Sorry." I flopped back again.

She turned to look upriver. "Do you remember my teammate Viper?"

"The cranky one?"

She huffed. "That's him. He's a fireman. And if he's at my car, he's going to be mighty stressed about me. But if I get a call to him, I can get him to help us with our plan."

I nodded. "That's good, right?"

"Maybe . . . you never know with Viper." She clicked her fingers. "What's the code on your phone?"

"My phone?"

"Yeah, you said you had one in your pack. I need to use it."

257

"Huh, you're good at this."

She scowled at me. "Code?"

"6969."

"Really. What are you, eighteen?"

I shrugged. "It's easy to remember." I grabbed her hand, pulling her down to my height. "We're doing the right thing, trust me."

She inhaled, inflating her sexy breasts toward me. "I truly hope so. I'll be back as soon as I can. Shuffle back from the edge and watch out for ants. You don't want them near your wound."

I winced. "Hell no. I sure don't."

She eased forward and our lips met. As our kiss deepened, I was taken to another world. A world where everything was safe, and kind. A world where Maya and I could be free.

She pulled back.

I gripped her hand. "Be careful."

"I will. You too. See you soon." Maya stepped to the river's edge, glanced once at me over her shoulder, then stepped into the water. With strong strokes, she crossed the water, and the river swept her away until I couldn't see her anymore.

Dragging my body upright, I hobbled deeper into the bushes and found a small section beneath a giant gum tree. After flicking away loose rocks, I sat with my back against the trunk. From my new vantage point, I couldn't see the river, just a field of vegetation.

As the leaves rustled around me, my heart thundered and for the second time in my life, I prayed. But this time I wasn't praying for my life to end.

This time I wanted to live.

As long as our plans to kill off Neon Bloom worked, that was.

Chapter Twenty-Seven

MAYA

After letting the river take me several miles downstream, I swam toward the other side. The last thing I wanted was to miss the tiny beach where I usually pulled my raft ashore.

I spotted it easily enough as there was a family of four on the sand. Two children were fishing and both adults were in folding chairs, reading.

Time to put on the act of my life. I just hoped Neon knew what the hell he was doing.

I swam to the beach and dragged myself onto the sand. "Help."

"Oh, Jesus, are you okay?" The woman threw down her book and ran toward me.

"Help. Please!" I huffed out ragged breaths.

I crawled forward a few feet and rolled over to sit.

She rested her hand on my back. "Oh my god, is that blood?"

Her eyes bulged at my shirt.

"Yes, I need a phone. Do you have one?"

"Yes, of course. Mike, grab our phone," she called to the man who remained near the kids.

The man sprinted toward the parking lot, and both the children came rushing toward us.

"Stay back, boys," the mother yelled.

The children skidded to a halt, kicking up the sand.

She turned back to me. "Are you injured?"

"No, but the man I was with, he was shot."

"Shot!"

"Yes, I'm a river rafting guide, and my customer, Neon Bloom—"

"Neon Bloom, the actor?" She raised her sunglasses.

"Yes, he was shot, and he went overboard."

"Jesus! Is he okay?"

"I don't know. I couldn't control the raft by myself, and it got stuck in a whirlpool. I haven't seen Neon since he went into the river. He was shot in the back."

"Who shot him?"

"His manager, Marc."

"What? Why?"

The man came back. I stood, dusting sand off my hands.

The woman turned to her partner. "Oh my god, babe. Neon Bloom was shot!"

"The actor?"

"Can I make a call?" I asked.

"Yes. Yes," the woman said, and the man offered me his phone.

As I dialed Zena's number, the couple turned toward the river, talking about Neon.

The ball is rolling now, Neon.

Zena answered on the third ring. "Hello, this is Zena."

"Zena, it's Maya."

"Jesus, are you okay? Viper is at your car. It's full of bullet holes. We've been going out of our minds."

"It's a long story. I'm fine, but Neon isn't. Can you get everyone together and meet me at the parking lot at the base of the Mackinnon Pass walking trail? Do you know it?"

"Yes. What do you need?"

"Just you guys. But Zena, is Brooke still dating that reporter?" Zena's sister had hooked up with the reporter a few months ago.

"Tiffany? Yes. Why?"

"Tell her that Neon was shot by his manager, Marc, and is missing in Thunder River, and—"

"Shit! Is Neon okay?"

"I don't know." I hated lying to her, but I couldn't say everything I needed to with the couple hovering nearby.

"Jesus! Okay, we'll be right there."

"And don't forget to tell Tiffany. We need people checking the river."

"Oh my god. The guys will be so glad you're okay. We'll be there ASAP."

I handed the phone back to the man. "Thank you."

"Are you hurt?" He nodded at the blood stain on the front of my shirt.

"I'm fine. That's Neon's blood."

"Shit, huh. And you say it was his manager who shot him?"

I nodded.

So, they were listening.

"Wasn't he involved in that hostage situation on Kangaroo Island?" the man asked.

"Are the police coming?" the woman added.

"They're already up where my car is." I pointed at the faint stream of black smoke drifting up from the other side of the mountain.

"Oh, we saw that smoke. Was that your car?" The lady palmed her chest and squinted at the smoke.

"Yes, they blew it up."

"But how did you get away?" The man cocked his head, suspicious.

The answer to that was going to come out anyway, so I said, "I shot one man, but Marc got away."

The pair gasped and stepped back.

I raised my hands in a peace gesture. "Look, I'm ex-army and a bodyguard, and I'm licensed to carry a weapon. They were shooting at us, and we hid behind my car. But Neon was shot in the ankle. Then my car caught fire and we had to get away from it. When it exploded, I fired at them and ran for the raft. I know I shot one man and thought I had shot the other. We were in the river when Marc chased us and that's when he shot Neon in the back."

The woman's eyes just about popped out of her head. "In the back. Oh, my lord."

"Yes." I forced tears into my eyes. "He went into the water."

I sniffed. "There was so much blood."

"But how did you get that blood on your stomach?"

Shit. Think, Maya.

"From his ankle. When he flipped out of the raft, I was holding onto his leg." Releasing a fake sob, I demonstrated holding Neon's ankle to my chest. "I tried so hard to get him back into the raft, but . . . but—"

"Hey, it's okay." The woman strode to me and ran her hand over my shoulder. "You tried very hard."

"I did, but I couldn't hold him. I can't believe he's gone." I drove my hand through my hair and peered at the water like I was searching for Neon.

"Come on, you must be freezing."

I let the woman guide me toward her car.

"Keep looking for him, Mike," she yelled to her partner over her shoulder.

I allowed her to mother me with offers of water and an egg sandwich, and she fired endless questions. Every second one was a version of, do you think Neon is okay?

Relief washed through me when my team came tearing into the parking lot in Billie's car. She was the only one of us who had a car big enough to carry five people.

The Camry screeched to a halt and Zena, Blade, Levi, and Cobra jumped out. I raced to them and was wrapped in massive hugs.

"Man, am I pleased to see you. When Viper called us about your car —" Blade's eyes darkened.

"I'm sorry. Those assholes just started firing at us."

"Who?" Levi grunted.

"Sloan, the guy who killed the hostages on the island and Marc, Neon's manager."

"His manager. What the hell?" Blade's eyes bulged.

"Where's Neon?" Cobra asked.

I turned to see where the woman was, but she was right there, hovering.

"He was shot and went into the river." At least that was the truth.

"Jesus. Okay, what do we need to do?" Blade asked.

I turned to Zena. "How did you go with getting people searching the river?"

"The water police should be on their way by now."

"And Tiffany?" I asked

"I told Brooke. She'll tell Tiffany."

"Okay, good. I need to talk to the police where my car is." I pointed to the drifting smoke.

"Let's roll." Blade swirled his finger in the air.

"Thank you," I yelled to the woman. "Keep looking for him."

"We will," she said, then turned and ran toward her husband.

We jumped into Billie's Camry with me in the front and Blade driving like we were in the race for our lives. We were, but only one life: Neon's.

At a stretch of deserted road, I made Blade pull over to the shoulder and cut the engine. I huffed out a breath and shifted my position so I could see Zena, Cobra, and Levi in the back.

Here we go.

"Okay, guys. Here's the deal. Neon is okay."

"What the fuck?" Levi blurted.

"Let me get this out, okay?"

"What's going on, Ghost?" Blade glared at me, and I hated the mistrust in his eyes.

I told them about Neon hiding in the bushes on the river and the bullet wound to his ankle.

"Oh, thank God he's okay." Zena sighed.

"Why's he still hiding? Didn't you shoot Sloan?" Cobra asked.

I explained what happened with Sloan, and Frankie-Lee being Sloan's real name and how it started when they were nine-year-old kids together and his vendetta that spanned decades.

"Jesus. He's been after Neon for years," Zena said.

"Yes, and it's not just him. Marc, his manager, was in on it, as well. I shot him too, but he got away." I clenched my fists, furious that I'd missed that bastard.

"Poor Neon." Zena shook her head.

"Neon has had enough." I cleared my throat. "He wants to fake his death."

Blade squinted at me. "Are you serious?"

"Yes." I told them everything Neon had said, and our plan to fake his death. "So, the wheels are already in motion."

"Do you realize what you're asking us to do?" Blade clamped his jaw.

"I do. And believe me, I tried to talk him out of it. But Neon feels so guilty after what happened to those hostages that he's petrified it will happen again."

"This is extreme," Cobra said.

"I know. Neon is adamant it's the only way. It's not just Sloan and Marc who'd tried to kill him. There was also Derek, his bodyguard. And in addition to his childhood one, he's had two other kidnap attempts that you guys don't know about. It never stops."

"He'd need a new ID. A new life." Blade shook his head.

I turned to Cobra. "That's where you come in. I'm hoping you can give him a new identity."

Cobra rubbed his hands together. "Now you're speaking my language. But is he sure?"

"He's a thousand percent sure."

"But why has Neon been so heavily targeted? There are plenty of famous people out there," Blade asked.

I told them about his family's wealth.

Levi whistled. "Lucky bastard."

"Neon doesn't feel that way. The money makes him feel trapped."

"But changing his identity means giving up all that wealth," Blade said.

I met Cobra's gaze. "Neon has his own wealth. He has money set up in offshore accounts. Do you think you could access them?"

Cobra cocked his head. "You know I love a challenge. But no guarantees."

I explained the perfect scenario we had to fake his death. I looked at Blade. "I'm sorry to get you involved in this, but—"

He raised his hands. "No need to apologize. I just hope he knows what he's doing because there's no turning back from this."

"I grilled him over this decision, and he's determined to go through with it. He's already had four kidnapping attempts on his life. One was successful. He can't live like that anymore."

Zena moaned. "Does this mean he won't be acting anymore?"

"That's exactly what it means."

Blade shifted so he could see the guys in the back. "What do you think, guys? Do we do this?"

"Yes, we do this. We have to save Neon," Zena said.

Blade rolled his eyes at her, and then peered at Levi and Cobra. "Guys?"

"I'm in." Levi nodded.

"I love a challenge," Cobra said.

"Right. That's it then. Let's kill off a movie star." Blade spun forward and started the car.

My heart swelled.

"Thank you." I turned to each of them. "Thank you."

Billie's old car was not cut out for Blade's aggressive driving up the steep incline. I was glad Billie wasn't here with us.

"Did you get hold of Viper?" I asked Zena.

"Yes, I told him you were okay. He was relieved, but he still said you were fucked."

"Probably because of the dead guy," Blade said.

Zena scowled. "But that was justified. He started shooting first. Right?"

I nodded. "Yep."

As we drove up the mountain, with every mile we covered, if the others weren't asking me questions or making plans, my mind crashed between wondering if Neon was okay and wondering if my acting skills would get us through this.

Once I was in front of the police, that was exactly what I'd have to do.

We were over the ridge and halfway down the other side when we hit traffic at a standstill.

"Looks like the word has gotten out," Blade said.

"Good. The more chaos there is, the better," I said.

"Should we walk?" Zena suggested.

"Nope." Blade pulled the Camry into the opposite lane, and as we passed the cars at a standstill, they beeped at us. We'd passed six cars before others joined us in the illegal maneuver.

Levi chuckled. "Man, I love you guys. Always an adventure."

I chuckled with him. I just hoped we were all still laughing come this time tomorrow.

We made it all the way to the entrance of the track before a lanky police officer came charging at us. "What the hell do you think you're doing?"

I jumped out of the car. "Hello, officer. My name is Maya, and it's my car that's on fire down there."

He blinked at me, and then his gaze fell to my shirt. "Is that blood?"

"Yes, but it's not mine. It's Neon Bloom's, and he's in trouble." I gasped a few times like I was on the verge of sobbing.

"Christ! Okay, come on through." The police officer urged me forward.

"Thank you, but I need my team with me. We're the team that saved Neon on Kangaroo Island a few months ago. We have information."

"Did you say Neon Bloom!" the woman in the car beside us called out.

I nodded at her. "Yes."

"Is he okay?"

I shook my head and pretended to wipe tears from my eyes. "He was shot in the back and fell into the river."

I projected my voice louder than I needed to.

"Neon Bloom. Oh no, is he alive?" The man with his elbow out the window of the second car looked as distraught as the young woman in the first car.

This was good. The more people who knew it was Neon the better. Come nightfall, the story should spread like wildfire through Risky Shores and would probably headline the six o'clock news tonight.

The police officer pulled the microphone on his lapel to his mouth, and as he relayed my request, he scanned the dirt trail leading toward my car. Flanked with massive gum trees, the bend halfway along the track concealed the clearing at the end.

"Okay, drive through and find Captain Baker," the officer said to me.

"Thank you." I jumped into the car.

"Nicely done, Ghost." Blade nodded at me.

"Thanks." Maybe my acting skills were okay after all.

Blade saluted the cop as we drove past. At a field of flashing lights, Blade parked the Camry behind a police car, and we all climbed out. With Blade leading the way, we marched toward a man with a crop of wild gray hair.

The police chief spun to us as we approached, rolled his eyes, and put his hands on his hips. "What the hell are you lot doing here?"

"Captain Baker, nice to see you again." Blade offered his hand, and thankfully Baker shook it.

"No, it's not." Captain Baker had grilled us for days after we'd rescued Neon and the hostages off Kangaroo Island. He hadn't been happy about the mess we'd landed in his lap. Thankfully, Hawk had pulled some strings at ASIO and helped us through the field of charges Baker had threatened to throw at us.

I stepped forward. "Hi, Captain Baker, I'm Maya."

"I know who you are." His glare could carve bricks.

"Okay, that's good. Well, that's my car." I pointed to the burned-out wreck.

"Oh, that's just great. I might have known it would have something to do with you lot."

"Not them, sir. Just me. All I was doing was taking my customer, Neon Bloom, on a river rafting tour when a couple of assholes started shooting at us."

"Neon Bloom?" He growled like a hungry dingo. "Not again."

"Yes, sir. They shot him in the back, and he went into the river." I raised my voice, pushing it to hysterics. "I lost him in the water, and we need everyone to look for him."

"Right, come with me." He hooked his arm around my bicep, then he aimed a fat finger at Blade. "You guys stay out of the way."

Captain Baker led me ten feet away from my team and stopped. "From the beginning, tell me what happened."

Viper stepped out from behind the charred wreck and strode to me. "Ghost. Thank Christ you're okay."

He wrapped me in a bear hug.

"Only just, Viper. It was scary."

"You get shot?" He nodded at the blood.

"No, but Neon did. Twice. In his ankle and in his back." For the benefit of Captain Baker who was watching me, I pressed my face to Viper's fireman uniform and released a cry, acting my grief like I'd never acted before.

"Shit! Is he okay?" Viper ran his hand down my back in a show of compassion that I'd never seen from Viper.

I sucked in shaky breaths, hating myself for lying to him. "I don't know. He went into the river."

I looked up at Viper, hoping he'd forgive me when he learned the truth.

"Christ." Viper's expression twisted to a scowl. "Poor bastard."

Viper actually looked like he meant it. It was rare for Viper to show any emotion other than rage.

He was going to kill me.

Forcing tears into my eyes, I angled my face to Captain Baker. "Please, can you get people searching the river?"

He spoke into his lapel mic. "Dispatch, this is Baker. We need the water police on Thunder—"

"I already had my friend call the water police," I interrupted.

"Never mind," he said into his mic. He glared at me.

I threw my arms out in frustration. "I had to do something. The longer they take to find him, the less likelihood of finding him alive."

I sniffed a little louder.

He scowled at me. "Oh, and did your friend also call the media?"

"Um, I don't know. It could have been the couple who rescued me from the water."

"Right." His voice was loaded with sarcasm. He glared at Viper. "Isn't one of you a chopper pilot?"

Levi stepped forward. "That would be me."

Captain Baker turned to the field of personnel in the clearing. "Flanagan," he yelled across the bedlam.

A young officer spun our way. "Yes, sir?"

"Get that man to his chopper ASAP. And then stick with him in case he finds something."

Levi rubbed his hands together like he was conjuring up a genie. As he and Flanagan ran toward the nearest cop car, Levi said, "Can we do lights and sirens?"

I stifled a chuckle as the pair jumped into the squad car. The car revved, spun around, and shot along the track with the sirens blaring.

Baker returned his attention to me. "From the beginning."

As I told the story, intermingling facts and fiction, pouring on the tears and sucking huge breaths like I was fighting a knot in my throat, organized chaos continued around us.

Police photographers took photos. Samples were taken of Neon's blood by my car and the drips that trailed to Sloan's body which was still on the ground with a tarp over it. Sloan's weapon and a pile of bullets that they dug out of my car and several trees were slotted into plastic bags. On the sections of my car that weren't reduced to cinder they dusted for fingerprints. They did the same on my trailer.

I recounted what happened in order of events and Baker asked all the right questions, like how I got a weapon, and did Sloan have any last words, and how did I get blood on my shirt.

His eyes drilled into me. "And why shouldn't I arrest you for murder?"

Chapter Twenty-Eight

MAYA

It took all my might to stop my legs from buckling beneath me at Captain Baker's question. "It was self-defense. They shot at us first. I'm lucky to be alive."

"Do you have a weapons permit?"

"Yes." I looked right into his eyes. "You know I do."

He glanced toward the body on the ground and back at me. "You're a good shot, Maya."

"Thanks. I served in the army for nine years, remember?" I didn't need to elaborate any further, yet I couldn't tell if he genuinely had forgotten our statements after the Kangaroo Island massacre, where I'd told him my military profession, or if he was trying to trip me up.

"Ah."

"Ah, what?"

He clicked his tongue. "Let's just say you don't look like the killing type."

If only he knew.

"You're a medic, right?" he asked.

He already knew that, too. "Yes, sir. In the army."

"What's the chances of Neon surviving that bullet wound?"

I sucked my lips into my mouth and shook my head. "Not good."

Captain Baker lowered his eyes. "Shot him in the back. Gutless bastard."

"We already knew that when he shot those poor women."

"And you're one hundred percent certain that body over there is the man who killed those hostages on the island?"

"I am."

Captain Baker cracked his neck side to side. "Between you and me, I hope you made him suffer."

I nodded. "Not long enough."

"Pity. Okay. I've heard enough to call it self-defense. But don't leave town, just in case I have reason to change my mind."

I melted under his words. "Thank you. I appreciate that, sir. I know at least one of my bullets hit Marc, so he may seek medical attention."

"Good to know. I'll put a call out to the hospital and local clinics. And do a broadcast for a black F100. Did you get a read on the number plate?"

I frowned, searching my recall for that information. Finally, I shook my head. "Sorry, no."

He rested his hand on my shoulder like we were old pals. "We'll find him. Stick around. I'll get some feedback from my men, and I'll find you when I'm done."

He waddled away, and I strode back to my team.

Zena placed her hand on my arm. "All good?"

"I think so. He's called it self-defense."

"See." She patted my arm. "I told you."

"That's one obstacle down. Only about a hundred more to go."

"Exaggerator." She winked at me and held Blade's hand.

A young police officer strolled toward us. "I, um, just want to say thank you to you guys for saving those hostages on the island. My wife was one of the ones you saved."

"Thank you, Officer Evans." Blade read the name on his badge as he offered his hand.

Officer Evans shook all our hands and when it came to my turn, he said, "Neon is lucky you were his bodyguard."

I lowered my gaze. "I wish I'd done better today."

The lie carved through me.

"I'm sure they'll find him." He nodded with conviction.

"I hope so. How is your wife?"

He kicked at the dirt and shrugged. "She's alive, thank God. But she has trouble sleeping and suffers guilt over how many were murdered. She'll never be the same again. Thanks to that asshole."

He glared at the tarp covering the body.

"I'm really sorry to hear that." No words were enough to compensate for the ongoing trauma to all those people. All because a selfish bastard wanted to get his hands on some money.

In that moment, I truly understood Neon's reasoning. He was doing the right thing. That made me so proud of him, my heart swelled to bursting.

"Anyway." Officer Evans did a fake tilt of his hat. "I hope we find Neon soon."

"Thanks."

Evans drifted away.

As the sun sank into the western skyline, the investigation continued. Levi's chopper circled overhead dozens of times, and constant reports came in from the water police relaying their negative results.

Once darkness settled over us, and the forensics people set up massive flood lights, the cicadas started their nightly chorus. Mosquitos made themselves known too, and I couldn't drag my thoughts off Neon.

Was he okay?

Did he keep the ants away?

How much longer before I could return to him?

The ambulance officer finally took Frankie-Lee's body away and the forensics guys were scouring the dirt beneath where he'd lay when Captain Baker returned to us.

"We're nearly done here. Is there anything you want to add to your statement, Maya?" he asked.

"No, sir. I think I covered everything."

"Well, everything checks out for me. I'll need you to come down to the station to make an official statement."

"Can I do that tomorrow? I'd like to take a shower." I pulled out my bloodied shirt, with a look of disgust on my face.

"Don't throw that out. We need it for evidence."

"I'll bring it with me."

"I'll see you at the station at nine in the morning." It was an order.

"Yes, sir. Thank you."

Captain Baker shook his head. "It's a damn mess, this. Sloan's victims would have liked to see that bastard rot in jail."

"I think just as many would be happy he's dead," I said.

"Probably. Try and sleep. I'll see you tomorrow." He glared at Blade. "Stay out of trouble."

"I'll do my best, sir." Blade stepped his feet apart and saluted the captain.

Captain Baker strode to his squad car and his timing had him following the ambulance onto the narrow track.

Viper and his two fellow firemen stacked their gear back into the firetruck.

Once that was done, Viper marched toward us. "Any word on Bloom?"

His voice was a deep baritone.

They all looked at me, and I shook my head.

Viper is going to kill me once he knows the truth.

"Well, we're finished here." Viper wiped soot from his hands onto his uniform pants. "Want me to hang around?"

"Yes, please." My insides clamped. The sooner I told him what was going on, the better.

"Okay, give me a sec." He strode away.

"Hey, Viper," Zena called out to him. "Would your guys give me a lift to Firefly? I need to get back to the café."

"Sure." He waved her forward.

"And me, I have a few things to sort out." Cobra winked at me, and I hoped those things were to do with Neon.

"No probs. They're leaving now." Viper strode toward the firetruck.

Zena wrapped her arms over my shoulders. "It's all going to work out. I just know it is."

I squeezed her to my chest. "I hope so."

We parted.

"Keep me posted, okay? And ring me if you need anything," she said.

"Thanks, Zena."

As Zena gave Blade a kiss goodbye, Cobra pulled me into his rock-hard chest. "I'll get cracking on those things we talked about."

"Thanks, Cobra, you're a lifesaver."

He eased away and winked. "Not a lifesaver. A life creator. This is going to be fun."

"I hope so."

He cupped my shoulder and squeezed.

"Chill out, Ghost. We've got this." He spun around and bounded away on his prosthetic leg, waving at the firemen. "Hey, wait for me."

Blade and I were left to watch the action.

"Viper's going to be pissed at you," Blade said.

I groaned. "I know. But he likes being pissed."

Blade slapped a mosquito away. "That's true."

I flicked a mozzie from my ear, and my chest clamped as I thought of Neon being all alone in the absolute darkness. The bright lights with moths swarming around the powerful beams made it impossible to see the night sky. Hopefully Neon was getting some light from the moon and stars.

The firetruck roared past, and Cobra and Zena waved at us from the back seat.

Viper strode our way wearing black jeans and a black t-shirt with his Tornado Motorcycle club insignia in bold letters across the front.

"How'd you go with Captain Baker?" Viper swept his hand over his cropped hair.

"He's okay. Viper, there's something I need to tell you." My heart thundered.

"Oh yeah, what's that?" He squinted at me.

"I haven't had a chance to tell you until now, so don't be mad at me, okay?"

"Don't tell me not to be mad at you. Spit it out."

After scanning the area behind Viper where the remaining police were packing up their gear, I leaned into Viper's ear. "Neon is alive."

He pierced me with his gaze. "And . . .?"

As Viper remained rigid with his hands folded over his chest, and I kept watching to make sure nobody was listening, I told him everything.

Viper glared at Blade. "And you agreed to this bullshit?"

"I did." Blade didn't elaborate.

"Fucking hell!" Viper scraped his hand over his beard stubble.

"I'm sorry," I said. "I wanted to tell you earlier but couldn't."

"He's going to regret it. Fucking idiot."

"Hey." I punched Viper's bicep. "Watch it. You don't even know him."

He glared at me. "And you do?"

"Yes. Actually, I do."

"I hope you know what you're doing because you're putting us all in a fucking bind protecting him."

"I do. And so far, everything is going to plan."

"Where is he hiding?"

I detailed Neon's position. "As soon as they finish here, we're going to get him."

Viper eyeballed me. "We."

"Yes. Us three. I need your muscles to get us upriver to where Neon's hiding."

"Great."

I punched him again. "Stop being a grump. You know I wouldn't ask if I didn't need you."

The giant spotlights blinked out, plunging us into darkness. It was a couple of seconds before my eyes adjusted to the blackness around us. Stars dotted the sky above, and a light reflecting on Thunder River had to be the moon, but it wasn't visible from where we stood.

"Looks like everyone is finished here. What's the plan?" Blade asked.

"We have to go to my place and get the canoe."

"Canoe? Fucking hell." Viper grunted.

Chuckling, I hooked my arm into Viper's and walked him to Billie's car.

We exited the dirt track and hit the road. The earlier traffic jam was gone and had been replaced with a police barricade. We dodged around it, and as we headed up the mountain, I used Blade's phone to call Zena and give her an update. The noise in the background confirmed she was still at Firefly Café and Bar.

"Are you taking him back to your place?" Zena asked.

I frowned. We hadn't thought that part through. "No, the paparazzi will be all over me once this gets out."

"Oh, speaking of that, Brooke said Tiffany would like an exclusive interview with you. I told her you'd do it. I hope you don't mind?"

"Shit, Zena." After how much they'd hounded me following the massacre on Kangaroo Island, I did not want to talk to reporters ever again.

"Sorry. Please, can you do it for Brooke? She's pretty keen on Tiffany."

"Great," I said with as much sarcasm I could muster.

"Thanks, babe. I'll make it up to you with cupcakes."

"Wine. I want wine."

Zena giggled. "Done."

When we reached the top of the mountain, the full moon hovered over the black ocean in the distance. At least we had a beautiful clear night for the next aspect of our plan.

"So, where are you taking Neon?" Zena's voice was muffled, and I imagined her cupping the phone so nobody could hear.

"Cobra's place. Can you ring him and let him know? Tell him to set up a bed and clean the kitchen counter. We'll need to do some surgery first."

"Ew. Okay. Good luck. Let me know when you have him and you're on your way to Cobra's."

"Will do." I ended the call.

"She all good?" Blade asked.

"She's fine. Busy as usual."

I turned to Viper in the back seat. The glow from the car's front console made his scowl seem even darker. I smiled at him.

He grunted at me.

Things were looking up.

I turned to Blade. "We need to get my car from that parking lot first. Tell me you can hotwire a Rav4."

"I can hotwire anything."

"I was hoping you'd say that. My keys were blown up with my other car." I directed Blade back to the parking bay at the base of Mackinnon Pass where he'd picked me up.

Cars and people were everywhere. My heart sank.

"What the fuck's going on here?" Blade groaned.

He drove in as far as he could before he stopped, and we all climbed out.

Along the beach were about a hundred people, all holding candles.

"What's going on?" I asked the first person I came across. The young girl had a hand-drawn heart on her cheek with *Neon4Eva* written inside the heart.

"Didn't you hear? Neon Bloom was shot, and he fell into the river. We're holding a vigil for him."

"Fucking great," Viper grumbled, and I elbowed his ribs.

The girl frowned at Viper and ran her gaze up his body, scowling.

"That's so cool," I said to the girl, drawing her attention back to me. "How long will you be here?"

She shrugged a delicate shoulder. "I don't know. Till midnight, I guess."

Shit.

"Anyway, got to run. Have fun." The girl skipped away.

Blade clapped Viper's shoulder. "Lighten up, princess."

"What's the grand plan now?" Viper snarled at me.

"We'll have to put the canoe in further upstream, that's all. We have to get my car out of here first."

"I'll hotwire it," Blade said. "You two find out who owns those cars blocking us in."

The moon was high in the sky by the time we found the owners of the three vehicles who'd trapped my Rav4.

I took the Rav, leaving Blade to contend with Grumpy Pants, and with them following, I led them through town to my house and parked beneath my carport. I jumped out and pointed at the canoe hanging from the carport roof. "You guys get that down and onto my roof racks. I'll get changed and grab some equipment."

"Get me a beer," Viper said.

"Please . . ."

"Don't test me, Ghost."

"Don't be an ass, Viper."

His death stare was so nasty it was a wonder his eyes didn't explode.

278

I raced up my stairs. Thankfully, I still had a key hidden in a fake green frog beside my door from when Billie had lived with me.

I sprinted along my hallway, removing the bloody t-shirt over my head. In my bedroom, I tugged on a black t-shirt and running around like a soldier ant on speed, I grabbed my first aid kit, flashlights, food, water, and anything else I could think of. Deciding I had everything, I locked my house and ran back out to my carport.

The men were finishing off the knots securing the canoe to the roof racks on my Rav. "Good work. Got your beer. Let's go."

Blade reversed Billie's car onto the curb, and the three of us jumped into my Rav with me driving.

"Beer is in the bag," I said.

Viper unzipped the bag and took a swig of Corona before we'd even left my street.

The trek back toward the river seemed to take forever and when the clock on the dash ticked over to eleven o'clock, I wanted to scream.

I'd been away from Neon for fourteen hours.

He would be starving, thirsty, and exhausted.

The insects would have made a meal out of him.

And worse than all of that, his bullet wound could be deadly.

Please. Please, be okay, Neon. We're coming.

Paddling upstream in the canoe was going to be damn hard. As was getting it through the bush to the river.

We'd be lucky if we reached him before sunrise.

Rescuing Neon in the dark was hard enough.

Rescuing him in broad daylight would be impossible.

Chapter Twenty-Nine

NEON

The helicopter had stopped flying overhead about the same time darkness swallowed all the light. That was when the mosquitos arrived. My mouth was bone dry, and my cramping stomach rivaled the pain threading up and down my leg.

A sting pierced my ankle and thinking it was another ant, I slapped it away. But I hit my bullet wound and cried out. That was the fifth time I'd done that.

I rolled my foot side to side, hoping it would stop the bugs and keep circulation to my toes which had started tingling well before darkness settled in around me.

My ankle throbbed like a crippled engine, demanding attention, but at least it kept me awake. Most of the time. I'd dozed off three times already, and each time I woke with a jolt and struggled to remember where I was.

When the moon finally appeared, I'd never been so happy to see it. As the minutes and hours ticked on, I found myself talking to the glowing white orb. Mostly I asked it questions. Most of them were about Maya, and how she was going with the police.

I'd never watched the moon so much as I did now. It was my only way to judge time. With each glance, it seemed to have risen another foot in the sky. Did that represent five minutes? Ten? An hour?

I'd had the same questions when I was trapped in that well, but the moon glow had only penetrated that narrow tube for a short amount of time. Once it slithered away, blackness crept in like an evil ghost.

I glanced at the moon again. It had risen about three feet.

Huh? Did I nod off again?

Rubbing my eyes, I stood and hobbled back and forward.

It wasn't silent out here in the bush like I'd expected it to be. Noises were constant.

A hooting owl had kept me company for ages, but it had either moved on, or fallen asleep. The river bubbled and gurgled with monotonous repetition. The mosquitos buzzed in my ears nonstop like erratic white noise. Each time I flicked them away, they seemed to multiply. One became two. Two became ten.

I pulled my shirt over my head, but the reprieve was only brief before the mosquitos stung my back and stomach, forcing me to pull the shirt down again.

When I couldn't stop the images of insects attacking my bullet wound, I stripped out of my shorts and undies and sitting my bare ass on the dirt, I wrapped my jocks around my ankle, tucking the edges in to keep it in position.

Exhaustion washed through me. I could barely focus, let alone move.

A mosquito stung my butt. "Fucker."

Slapping it away, I forced myself upright. I bent over to tug my shorts on again, but a wave of dizziness wobbled through me. I stumbled sideways and crashed into a shrub covered in spikes.

I cried out in agony and fury, and my holler echoed off the water.

Fighting the new onslaught to my body, I dragged myself off the bush. Thorns scraped across my bare flesh.

Shit. Shit. Shit!

Stunned, I paused on my hands and knees, sucking in breaths, waiting for my brain to catch up. A dense fog consumed me, and I tried to work out what was going on. My whole body ached. The pain from my bullet wound, though, was king.

A mosquito buzzed in my ear, and I flicked at the annoying bastard.

"Keep moving, Neon." My tongue was like a slab of jerky, and I smacked my lips together, trying to produce moisture.

Crawling on my hands and knees with mosquitoes buzzing around my ears and attacking my body, I searched the darkness for my shorts.

Rocks jabbed my palms and scraped my knees with every movement

My stomach cramps twisted into angry knots. Dozens of tiny nicks from the thorns added to my hell.

Slapping at the relentless insects, I begged for the nightmare to be over. Just like when I was a kid trapped in the well. That had taken two days.

I couldn't handle twenty-four hours of this hell.

"Come on, Maya, where are you?"

Thoughts crashed into my brain like a wrecking ball.

Was she arrested for Frankie-Lee's death?

Has she abandoned me?

Something scurried through the bushes behind me. "What the hell was that?"

Darting my gaze left and right, I strained to hear where it was. The creature rustled again, getting closer. Was it a kangaroo? A dingo? A shudder ripped up my bare back.

I ran my hands over the gravel, searching for a rock to throw at it.

Where the hell are my shorts?

Squinting at the darkness, I could just make out shadows. I glanced toward where I thought the moon would be and frowned. It wasn't there.

On my knees, I searched the sky. The moon was over my right shoulder. I'd turned around. I was crawling away from the river. "Shit."

My heart thundered in my ears.

I turned back toward the river, and keeping the moon over my left shoulder, I swept the gravel.

Come on. Come on. Where are they?

My left arm buckled, and my face crashed into the dirt. Gravel grazed up my cheek as I slumped to the ground.

I rolled onto my side, pulled my knees to my chest and groaning, I closed my eyes.

A mosquito buzzed in my ear. "Fuck off!"

Something touched my foot, and I tucked my leg higher.

My hand grazed over my bare legs.

Why am I naked?

Blinking into the darkness, I rolled onto my back and a million stars dotted the sky above me.

Where am I?

I squeezed my eyes shut, trying to piece things together. Smacking my lips, I tried to swallow but my tongue was so dry, swallowing was impossible.

Maya's beautiful face came into view.

I'm telling a lot of lies for you, Neon.

What lies? I rolled my head side to side and a pair of eyes emerged from the darkness.

I froze. *What the hell is that?*

The creature nudged closer, clambering on all fours.

A fierce sting attacked the instep of my foot.

"Shit!" I dragged myself off the ground and sat.

I blinked at where the eyes had been, but they were gone.

"Neon." A voice drifted to me like an angel's song.

"Neon! Shit. Where is he?" said another voice.

A light carved through the bushes. What was that? I ducked down, trying to make myself as small as possible.

"Neon. Neon, where are you?"

A mosquito buzzed in my ear, and I slapped it away.

"Neon." A man's voice thundered to me.

"I found his shorts."

My shorts. I pushed myself up. "Hey, they're mine."

"Neon, there you are."

A light pierced my brain.

"My shorts," I said.

"Oh, babe." Soft arms draped around me.

I inhaled a delicious scent. "Maya?"

"Yes. It's Maya. We're here to take you home."

"What about the lies?"

"He's delirious. Blade, hold him up and I'll get his shorts on."

"Why's he fucking naked?" A man growled like a tiger.

I was lifted up and my shorts were wrestled onto my legs.

With one person on either side, I floated through the air.

Their voices wobbled in and out, and I couldn't work out a single word.

"Hold the canoe, Viper." Maya spoke in angry whispers.

"Viper," I said. "He's the cranky one."

"Shh, Neon. Close your eyes."

"Maya? Is that you?" I reached out.

A soft palm gripped my hand. "Yes, now close your eyes and keep quiet."

"You came for me."

"I told you I would, babe. Now go to sleep."

Babe. She called me babe.

Or maybe I'm dreaming.

* * *

I tried to open my eyes, but it was so bright, I groaned.

"He's awake." A woman's voice tumbled to me.

A hand gripped mine.

"Neon, it's Maya."

"Maya?" I wanted to see her, but the glare hurt my eyes. A tear spilled down my cheek, and she wiped it away.

I tried to sit up, but she eased me down. "Hey, take it easy."

When I forced my eyes open, Maya came into my vision. "Maya."

"You gave us quite a scare."

I cleared my throat. "What?"

"I'm getting mighty sick of saving your ass." Despite her words, her grin lit up her face.

"Where am I?"

"You're at my place, buddy." A man slotted in next to Maya. "I'm Cole, or Cobra. Remember me?"

"Yeah." I tried to sit up again. This time, Maya hooked her hand around my elbow and eased me toward her. Cobra shoved extra pillows behind my back.

"Man, am I glad you're awake." Cobra bounced around to the other side of the bed. "We've got work to do."

"Hey, let him rest. He's only just woken up. Now shoo." Maya flicked her hand at Cobra.

"I hope you know what you're in for, buddy. She's a bossy one." Cobra winked at me.

"Go make yourself useful." Maya tried to slap him, but he shot away.

She turned to me, gracing me with her stunning blue eyes. "How are you feeling?"

Trying to blink the fog from my mind, I reached for her hand. "Are you okay?"

A chuckle left her lips as she squeezed her hand to mine. "I'm fine. Now."

I cleared my throat. "What happened?"

"Tell me what you remember." She pierced me with her eyes like she was searching my brain.

I felt like this was a test.

As I scoured my memory, images came crashing back to me like a runaway freight train. "Sloan, no Frankie-Lee—you killed him. Did they charge you?"

"No. No. I'm fine. What else do you remember?"

"I got shot in the ankle?" I peered down my leg and moaned.

"What else do you remember?"

It would be easy to get lost in her eyes, but her expression told me she was digging for something. *Did I do something wrong?* "Your car blew up."

"Ah huh." Her eyes intensified. There was something I was missing.

I blinked at her, trying to go back there in my mind. The explosion. Sloan dead. Maya naked. That was it! "We had sex."

She waggled her head. "Of course, you remember that."

I frowned. "Absolutely. It was unforgettable."

She clenched her jaw and worry crept into her eyes.

Jeez, what else could—

"Oh, do you mean faking my death?"

Her breath hitched.

I sat taller. "Did it work? Is Neon Bloom dead?"

She chewed on the inside of her lip. "Do you want him to be?"

"Yes. Tell me that worked."

She huffed out a breath. "Yes. It worked. The entire world is mourning the death of Neon Bloom."

"Oh, Maya." I pulled her to my chest. "Thank you."

Cobra returned with a tray. "Did he change his mind?"

"No." Maya pulled back, grinning at Cobra. "I told you he wouldn't."

"Good." He placed the tray down on a side table. "Because I've put a ton of work into your new identity, buddy. You're going to love it."

I gasped. "You have a new name for me already?"

Cobra rubbed his hands together. "Well, it wasn't easy. I had to find the name of a deceased person who was born around the same time as you, and had the same ethnic background, and make sure they didn't have a dubious history. But . . . ready for your new name?"

My heart thundered in my chest. I flicked my gaze from Maya to Cobra. "Yes, don't keep me in suspense."

"Cecil Inchbottom." Cobra announced the name like he was introducing a WWE wrestler.

My jaw dropped.

Maya nodded at me like she was about to burst.

Horror crawled through me. "What . . . but . . . no."

"Ha!" Cobra burst out laughing. "You should see your face."

"You bastard." Chuckling, I pointed at Cobra. "Now that was funny."

"We needed to test if your sense of humor was still intact," Maya said.

I gasped at her. "You were in on that?"

Maya giggled and it was so genuine and delightful, my heart swelled. She winked at me, then nodded at Cobra. "It was his idea."

Cobra handed a plate toward me. "Cheese sandwich?"

I reached for the fresh bread. "Thank you, I'm starving."

"That's a good sign." Maya cruised her hand up my arm. "Get some food into you, then we have things to do."

I devoured the sandwich and gulped a glass of water with it. "Help me up."

"Go steady." She pressed my shoulder, trying to hold me back.

"Are you kidding? I've been reborn, literally."

"Funny, but you've also had another operation, so go steady."

I put my feet down and winced at the pain in my ankle.

"See." She thumped my shoulder.

"It's nothing." I forced through the pain to smile. Nothing was going to ruin today.

"When you two lovebirds have finished messing around, meet me in the computer lab." Cobra took the tray and bounded away.

She wrapped her arms around my waist. "I thought I'd lost you again."

I hugged her to my chest. "Thank you, Maya. For everything."

She pulled back from me, scrunching her nose. "Before we do anything, you need a shower."

"Sounds great. Show me where?"

With her arm around my waist, she led me from the tiny bedroom and along a wide corridor. The ceilings were high, and we passed several closed doors.

"What is this place?" I asked.

"It's an old schoolhouse. Cobra bought it for next to nothing, but he's been renovating it for about a year. For a nerd, he's bloody good with his hands."

We stepped into a large bathroom with black and white checkered tiles.

"He hasn't renovated this section yet."

"As long as there's hot water, that's all I need."

The large bathroom was like an old-fashioned locker room. Six sinks lined one wall with frosted mirrors above them. Two urinals were on the wall with yellow stains covering the bottom half of them. Along the back wall were four toilet stalls.

"Take your pick." Maya swept her hand toward the four shower cubicles. "I used the end one. The spray goes everywhere, but I've had worse. Towels are over there."

She pointed to a series of gray lockers, all with the doors popped open.

I peeled out of my t-shirt and wriggled my eyebrows at her. "Want to wash my back?"

"You don't give up, do you, Randy?" Her smile cruised up to her eyes, making her even more stunning. But her smile morphed to a frown as she glided her finger along a small cut on my chest.

I blinked at the gash. Next to it was another. I glared down at my chest and stomach. "What's all that from?"

"You don't remember?"

"Did you give me a whipping?"

"I *should* give you a bloody whipping. No, the best we could work out was that when you undressed to put your undies over your ankle wound, you fell over while trying to get your shorts back on. Looks like you fell into a shrub covered in thorns."

"Shit. I'm glad I don't remember that."

"When we found you, you only had your t-shirt on, and you were barely conscious."

I groaned. "I'm glad I don't remember that either."

"I bet Viper and Blade wished they didn't remember."

"No. Damn it." I cringed at the thought of them seeing me like that. Or Maya.

"Yes. I was lucky I had them with me. Once we got you into the canoe, we couldn't go to the place where I would normally get out of the river because a hoard of your fans were holding a vigil on the river."

"Really?"

"Yep." She rolled her eyes like the vigil was the most ridiculous thing. "Viper had to carry you over his shoulder through the bush."

"Tell me you put my shorts on first."

Giggling, she swept her ponytail over her shoulder. "Of course. Viper wouldn't have gone near you otherwise. You'll have to buy him a carton of beer for that one."

I chuckled. "I'm going to buy all of you more than a carton of beer."

"Yeah, well, hold your horses on that. Remember you don't have any money. You don't even have a name."

"I'm glad it's not Cecil Inchbottom."

"Ha. Me too. Now don't get that ankle wet. Do you need a hand in the shower?"

"You just want to see me naked again." I curled my arm around her shoulders and kissed her forehead.

She wriggled away. "I do, but not until you're fully recovered."

"I bet you say that to all your patients."

She placed a hand on my chest. "Only you, Randy. Only you."

She kissed my nipple, then strode out the door.

"Take all the time you need," she yelled from the corridor.

Grinning like a giddy teenager, I peeled out of my shorts. As I turned on the faucet and waited for the water to run hot, I studied my body. I had cuts and insect bites all over me.

Jesus! My ass alone had about thirty mosquito bites.

How long was I naked before Maya found me?

I stepped into the shower, careful to keep my left ankle out of the water run-off. As the hot needles pummeled my body, I closed my eyes and enjoyed the cleansing therapy. I felt like I was in a hot air balloon and all the dread that had been plaguing me for years was being thrown out with the sandbags, drifting higher, elevating me to a safer place.

I felt free. Alive. And so fucking incredible.

Now I just had to pull all the other aspects of my life together and everything would be perfect.

I also hoped Marc wouldn't turn up and ruin our plans.

If he's caught, and tells a different story than us, then Maya could be in real trouble.

And that would truly crush us both.

Chapter Thirty

MAYA

Sitting on a chair beside Cobra, I cupped my coffee mug to my chest, watching his fingers glide over the keyboard. In front of him were eight large monitors and he seemed to be populating every one of them with data at the same time.

Three television monitors were on the side wall, and Cobra had somehow made them into split screens so we could watch six channels at once. While Neon had been recovering from his surgery, our eyes had been glued to those screens, watching dozens of news reports on the disappearance of Neon Bloom.

Neon hobbled into the room, rubbing a towel over his hair.

I swiveled to him. "Feel better?"

"Like a new man." He breathed in like he was sucking the air from the room.

"That's good. Because you are," Cobra said.

Neon grabbed another chair, rolled it toward us, and sat.

"You're just in time." Cobra pointed toward the television screens and aimed a remote. The camera panned over about fifty reporters all holding microphones and then zoomed in on Captain Baker who stood behind a podium looking equal parts pissed off with the attention and thrilled by it. Everyone seemed to be speaking at once.

Captain Baker raised his hands to silence the crowd. "Good evening."

The crowd hushed.

"As you all know, Neon Bloom has been missing since approximately ten o'clock yesterday morning. We have been searching for him in Thunder River, however we have now scaled down our search."

The crowd groaned.

"Based on the information we have, we presume Mr. Bloom didn't survive and we are now looking for his body."

A woman in the crowd released an ear-piercing wail, and about a dozen reporters asked questions at the same time.

Captain Baker pointed at the woman in the front row with the perfectly coiffed blonde bob, and she stood. "Kimberly Adams, NBC news. Sir, has anyone been arrested for his murder?"

He cleared his throat. "We are still piecing together the information, however two men are believed to be responsible for shooting Mr. Bloom. One man passed away at the scene of the crime, Mr. Frankie-Lee Dickens who was also wanted in connection with six murders on Kangaroo Island."

The crowd gasped and a murmur rolled through them like a tsunami.

"A second man, Mr. Marc Harkness, was involved in this latest shooting incident. He is currently missing and is wanted for questioning."

"Wasn't he Neon Bloom's manager?" someone called out from the crowd.

"Was he shot too?" another person yelled.

"Is he dangerous?" a woman asked.

A police officer strode to Captain Baker and whispered in the captain's ear.

Baker raised his hands. "I'm sorry. I have to go."

Captain Baker made a dramatic exit with the field of reporters shouting questions at his back.

"What the hell?" Neon frowned.

"Did they find Neon's body?" Cobra chuckled.

"Try another channel," I said.

Cobra flicked through the screens, but nothing additional came up.

"That was weird." Cobra shook his head.

"I hope Marc hasn't been found." A wedge of dread slotted into my chest.

"Why?" Cobra asked.

"Because his story is going to be different to ours?"

"But nobody would believe him. Surely?" Neon scowled.

I placed my empty mug down. "He's the shadow of doubt that we don't want."

Cobra tossed the TV remote onto the table. "So, are we moving forward with the rebirth?"

"Of course." Neon's expression was more serious than I'd ever seen on him, even when we were being shot at.

"Fantastic." Cobra turned his attention back to the computer monitors.

I picked up my mug and Cobra's empty one.

"You want a coffee?" I asked Neon.

"Yes, please. I'll get it. Where is it?"

"No, I'll get it. You stay here." I stood. "Cobra has a pile of questions for you."

I walked out of the room and along the corridor. Cobra had concentrated his renovation work to the living and kitchen areas of the old schoolhouse. The vaulted roof and whitewashed exposed beams made the main section of the building look much bigger than it was.

The kitchen was made entirely from secondhand kitchens that Cobra had scored from people who were looking to update their existing ones. It was eclectic styling that came together perfectly. One thing he did have brand new, though, was a quality coffee machine. I ground the fresh beans and pressed the button to percolate. While I waited for the pot to fill, I paced the room.

Finding Marc would be a spanner in our plans that could ruin everything. I couldn't believe I'd missed him. I was an excellent shot, yet I'd panicked and missed. And I knew why. I'd been too worried about Neon.

We were lucky to get away.

We were going to need more luck now.

Neon had entered my heart. I wanted him so much, I ached when we weren't together. I had never felt like that before. Before he came along, it was anger that had been driving me. Anger over my fucking father getting away with what he did to Lily.

Now, it was love driving me.

And it was so real, frightening, and exciting, that I was going crazy trying to figure out how to deal with it.

I filled our mugs with fresh coffee and put three sugars into Cobra's mug. I hadn't thought to ask Neon how he liked his coffee. It was just another thing I had to learn about him.

I carried in the mugs, entering the computer lab in the middle of their conversation about name choices.

"I didn't know how you liked your coffee." I handed a mug to Neon.

"That's fine. Have you seen this?"

He pointed to the screen on the bottom left with a spreadsheet. In the left-hand column were sixteen names. The columns to the right listed dates of birth and death, how the people had died, parents' names, and any other pertinent information.

"Yes. Cobra showed me."

As he studied the names, Neon sipped his coffee but showed no emotion to the taste. He turned to me. "Which one do you like?"

I jerked back. "It's not up to me."

"Yes, it is. You'll probably say it more than me."

"I am not choosing the name you'll have for the rest of your life. So, forget it." I went to walk from the room, but he grabbed my arm.

"Okay." He half scowled; half smiled. "Is there any you hate?"

"Cecil Inchbottom."

"Come on, you two. We don't have all day." Cobra put his mug down and caressed his computer mouse.

"Okay, let's do this by elimination." Neon pointed at the screen. "I can't have Mark or Derek for obvious reasons. And I'm not having Cecil."

Cobra deleted those lines from the spreadsheet.

Neon sipped his coffee, studying the names as I studied him. Finally, he leaned back. "There's only one name for me."

"Which one?" I asked.

"Guess?"

"Which one?" I growled at him.

"All right, bossy boots. What do you think of Zac Carrera?"

I nodded. That was the one I'd hoped he would choose. "Perfect."

"Yes." His eyes darkened like he was running the name through his mind. "That's me. Zac Carrera."

"Great. Zac Carrera it is." Cobra deleted all the other names from the spreadsheet.

"What happens now?" Neon asked.

"I need to create your new identity. You need background stuff, like where you lived and what schools you went to. You need a driver's license." Cobra's fingers moved faster than his lips as he populated the monitors with a field of websites. "You need some bank accounts."

Neon clicked his fingers. "Speaking of that. Can you access my money?"

Cobra clasped his hands together and turned to Neon. "That depends on where it is, and how secure it is."

"Most of my money is at the Fidelity Bank in the Cayman Islands."

Cobra swiveled back to the keyboard. "Did anyone else have access to your account?"

"Yes. Marc."

Cobra spun back around to eyeball Neon, blinking several times like he was piecing things together.

"What?" I asked.

"We could make it look like Marc stole your money?"

Neon nodded. "Works for me."

"It would be amazing if you knew his password." Cobra raised his eyebrows.

"I know a few he used."

Cobra slapped his hands together and spun back to the keyboard.

As Cobra fired questions at Neon, I sipped my coffee and turned my attention back to the television. The screens were all still headlining with Neon's disappearance. There were dozens of images of young girls with tears streaming down their faces. And scenes from Neon's movies: him jumping through flaming doorways, smashing through a plate-glass window, kissing his co-star and riding a horse while shooting a gun at the same time.

A middle-aged couple, both dressed in black, came onto the screen. My breath hitched.

"Mom and Dad," Neon said, deadpan.

"Oh, Neon."

"Zac," he said with little emotion.

"They look so sad." I shuffled to his side and squeezed our hands together.

"They always look like that. There's not much fun in their life."

"They still look sad."

His lips drew to a straight line, and I had the impression he was fighting tears.

"You look just like your dad."

"So I've been told. The reporter must've done some serious digging to link me to them." He shook his head. "I told you they never give up."

"No regrets then?" Cobra asked.

"Not one."

Neon's coldness toward his parents surprised me. I made a mental note to ask him about it later.

Another middle-aged woman came onto the screen, dabbing tears from her cheeks with a tissue. "Mrs. Callahan. She homeschooled me after my kidnapping."

"Wow, they really are digging deep."

"Maybe. Either that, or people are coming out of the woodwork to say they knew me. Get their fifteen minutes of fame and all that. I'm surprised about Mrs. Callahan though."

I frowned at him. "Why?"

"I didn't think she'd be like that."

"She looks distraught to me," I said.

He nodded. "Yes, she does, doesn't she? More than my parents."

"I got it." Cobra cheered. "I'm in. Holy shit, man, you're loaded."

I peered at the screen where Cobra pointed at the numbers after the dollar sign. My heart skipped a beat.

Neon shrugged. "I told you I didn't need my parents' money."

"How much do you want to take out?" Cobra rubbed his hands.

Neon looked at me.

I shrugged. "Don't ask me."

"The whole lot. Marc would've taken every penny if he'd had the chance."

Cobra whistled. "Okey dokey. Four hundred and thirty-six million coming your way, Zac Carrera."

Neon draped his arm over my shoulder, and I nestled into his side. We both turned to the television as a woman came onto the screen wiping tears away with a tissue.

"That's Christina. She was one of the co-stars on the island. She must've been one of the hostages."

Tears spilled down her cheeks from her bloodshot eyes.

As Cobra made weird noises and attacked the keyboard like he was possessed, Neon and I silently watched the screen. It seemed neither of us wanted to turn up the volume.

"I want to help them." Neon sounded absolutely exhausted.

I looked up at him. "Who?"

"All the hostages. Everyone who was hurt because of me. I want to give them money."

"Neon—I mean, Zac—we talked about this. You can't."

A frown corrugated his forehead. "Cobra, can you make anonymous donations to those people?"

Cobra turned to us, nodding, but also scrunching his nose. "I could do that. But—"

"No, Zac." I cut Cobra off. "If you do that, they will know it came from you. It's too risky."

I stepped back from him, folding my arms.

He lowered his eyes and clamped his jaw.

Cobra swiveled back to the monitors.

Neon raised his head. His eyes glimmered as he clicked his fingers. "Did Alpha Tactical Ops invoice Marc for your services?"

I frowned. "Zena did, but it was never paid."

"Yes!" Neon stomped his foot and winced. "Shit. Shit. My ankle."

He sucked air through his teeth.

"Are you okay?" I pulled over a chair. "Here. Sit."

"What were you going to say?" Cobra asked.

Neon sat, and I grabbed another chair and raised his left leg onto it. "We'll make it look like Marc paid Alpha Tactical Ops ten million dollars for their extraordinary services on that island."

"Ten million," Cobra and I said in unison.

"Not enough? How about twenty?"

"Jeez, no. It's more than enough." I blinked at Neon.

Is he serious?

"I want it to be twenty million. And once that's sorted, Alpha Tactical Ops can donate two hundred thousand dollars to every surviving hostage and four hundred thousand to the estates of those who died. Then you'll look like the good guys that you really are."

I cupped my mouth and spoke through my fingers. "Are you sure?"

Zac stood and clutched me to his chest. "Yes. This is perfect."

Cobra burst out laughing. "Levi is going to piss his pants when he sees that money in the bank account."

"And Zena," I added.

Neon released me, and I cupped his cheek. "That's a very nice thing to do."

"You can thank me later." He wiggled his eyebrows.

"Oh please." Cobra plugged his ears, and we laughed together.

Neon's gaze drifted over my shoulder, and I swiveled to the television screens behind me. The image on the middle screen showed a small child being carried by a police officer.

My heart thundered in my chest as I pointed at the screen. "Cobra, turn that up, please?"

"Do you know that boy?" Cobra asked.

Neon nodded. "That's me. After they rescued me from that well."

Chapter Thirty-One

NEON

The image on the television changed from the police officer holding the pale boy, to a female reporter standing in a paddock. In the background were the aboveground bricks of a well. The woman flipped her hand in a nonchalant way like she was presenting a new lipstick range, rather than the site where my life changed forever.

"Before Neon Bloom adopted his stage name, he was Stanley Walton."

"Great." I moaned. My childhood name and my kidnapping had been one secret I'd been able to contain. Not anymore.

"Our research has discovered that he was kidnapped when he was nine years old by Joseph Dickens, who is the father of Frankie-Lee Dickens, the man accused of murdering Neon Bloom."

The reporter shifted her stance so the camera could zoom toward the well. "Neon was held captive in that well until the three-million-dollar ransom money was paid."

I huffed. "Frankie-Lee said it was never paid."

The screen changed again to two photos of Joseph Dickens. The picture on the left was the man I remembered, my butler before he ruined my life. The second photo was his arrest mugshot. It barely looked like the same man.

"Why would Frankie-Lee say his father never got the money?" Maya asked.

I shrugged. "Because he's a liar."

"Or, maybe he didn't." Cobra swiveled around and seemed embarrassed by his comment.

I cleared my throat. "You think my parents didn't pay that ransom."

"Or a crooked cop kept it for himself."

I blinked at him. "Shit. I never thought of that. Can you access police records?"

Cobra rubbed his hands together. "I don't know . . . I'd need much more caffeine for that challenge."

He raised his mug.

Chuckling, Maya snatched it off him, and carrying the two other mugs, she disappeared out the door.

"Okay, tell me about that kidnapping, Zac," Cobra said.

It was weird being called my new name. And yet, it also sounded perfect.

I told him everything I'd tried to forget about those two days: a white cloth being shoved over my mouth, waking up in that well, days and nights with barely any contact, being starving and scared, and how the police pulled me from that well forty-six hours later.

"My parents told me they handed over the ransom money at a location dictated by the kidnapper."

"Okay, that's good." Cobra keyed something into the computer. "So, how did they find you?"

"Joseph, my butler, let them know where he'd held me captive by leaving a note in the letterbox. But that note is what led them to him in the end."

"The butler did it, huh. They should have checked him out first."

"Maybe they did."

"Okay, let's see what we can find." Cobra's fingers danced over the keyboard, and he mumbled to himself as the eight monitors on the wall filled with different websites. He was so fast it was impossible to take it all in.

"What are you searching?" I asked.

"The police database. News reports. Transcripts of the kidnapper's court hearing."

"Huh. You're good."

"Thank you."

Maya returned. "Coffee and three sugars for the computer nerd."

"Ta." Cobra paused, typing with one hand to reach for the mug.

As Maya and I watched Cobra work his magic, my gaze was divided between the computer monitors, the television screens, and Maya.

Maybe she felt me watching because she turned to me with a mixed expression. "Are you close to your parents?"

"Close? Hmmm. I wouldn't say close. I ring them occasionally."

"Did you see them in the last four months?"

"Not physically. I rang Mom though, to let her know I was okay. But she hadn't heard about the Kangaroo Island bullshit, so I had to tell her."

Maya jerked back. "She hadn't heard? Does she have her head in the sand?"

"I told you . . . she's like a hermit. She doesn't watch television and Dad's only interested in the financial news."

Maya scowled. "Wow. Your face was on the TV for months after that mess. It was pretty hard to miss."

"It still is." Cobra pointed at the television screen with a remote and dialed up the volume.

The footage showed the scene where I was reunited with my parents after being rescued from the well.

My father spoke into a large microphone. "We are very grateful to everyone for finding our son alive. Now please, respect our privacy."

Dad turned and walked between two double doors that were closed behind him.

"There's a man of few words," Cobra said.

I nodded.

"Were you close to him during your childhood?"

I shook my head. "My parents were never around. I was raised by nannies. Driven around by my butler. Schooled at home by teachers. Fed by chefs. We very rarely sat together as a family. Usually just birthdays and Christmas. I saw them even less after that kidnapping. I spent more time with my bodyguards than my parents."

Maya swayed toward me, gracing me with her incredible scent. "That's terrible."

"I guess. But I didn't know any different. It was normal to me."

"I get that. I grew up going to church three times each weekend. That was normal to me."

Cobra swiveled to Maya with his jaw dropped. "You did what?"

She shrugged. "Yeah. Unfortunately."

"Wow. How does someone go from that to the best sniper in the world?"

I cocked my head at her. "You haven't told Cobra?"

"No." Maya lowered her eyes.

I rested my hand on her shoulder. "Does this mean you haven't asked Cobra to help search for your dad?"

Maya curled her hands together, running her finger over the lily flower tattoo on her middle finger. Sighing, she shook her head.

"Hey, I'll do anything for you. You know that." Cobra touched her wrist, and it was such a familiar gesture it reminded me just how close they were.

Before I'd met her, I didn't have any friends like that. Being famous and extremely wealthy meant finding friends was a minefield. Knowing who to trust often came at a price. I couldn't wait to get to know Maya and her friends better. And I'd do anything to be their friend. I just hoped they were willing to let me try.

Cobra patted her arm. "I can keep secrets. If you want something, just ask."

She nodded. "Thanks, Cobra. It's a long story."

"And I always have time for you and your stories." He swiveled back to his keyboard.

I met her gaze, frowning.

She looked completely gutted. Like she'd let Cobra down.

I pulled her to my chest and kissed her forehead. No words could help her from that guilt, but I hoped she didn't beat herself up too much. I knew what it meant to keep secrets and sometimes they were buried so deep, they could eat up your insides and make it nearly impossible to let them free.

Maya pushed back from me, but the sorrow in her eyes had my chest squeezing.

Deciding to give her some time alone with Cobra, I patted my stomach. "Hey, Cobra, do you have any more of that yummy bread you gave me earlier?"

"Sure do. I'll have a cheese sandwich with you."

I nodded at Maya and a tiny smile swept across her lips. "Me too. Thank you."

After grabbing the three empty coffee mugs, I hobbled away as Maya said, "I'm sorry, Cobra, I should have told you this . . ."

A wave of relief washed through me. I just hope Maya felt the same way. I'd put her on the spot and there was a chance she'd be pissed at me for doing that.

But I had to do it. Maya and I both had childhood nightmares that shaped our adult lives. She helped me with mine. I hoped I helped her with hers.

It took me way too long to figure out the coffee machine, but once it ground the coffee beans and started dripping into the glass pot, I turned my attention to making sandwiches for the three of us.

As I pulled cheese and butter from the fridge, my thoughts drifted to my parents. My dad had always been an enigma in my life. A burly voice that boomed about the sparse rooms of our sprawling mansion from time to time. Wafts of a cigar as he traipsed from the upstairs bedrooms down to his den that was the size of a basketball court. I couldn't recall him ever smiling unless it was when he was trying to impress some fellow oil magnates.

Mom also had a permanent frown.

I'd had more hugs with Maya than with my own mother.

I'd never thought about that before.

After I was rescued from that well, my contact with Mom became even less. Almost like she was embarrassed by me.

As the coffee dripped into the pot, I tried to compare Mom before the kidnapping to after. She was definitely much more distant after I was rescued.

Was that because of guilt?

"Hey, are you okay?"

I jumped at Maya's voice. "Oh, you snuck up on me."

"You were deep in thought. Are you okay?"

"Yes. Are you?"

She inhaled deeply and let her breath out in a huff. "I am. Thank you."

"Really? You're not going to kick me in the balls?"

She burst out laughing and my heart swelled at her delight. "Not today, but I'm not ruling it out."

I raised a finger. "Noted. Remind me to buy a groin protector."

She giggled some more. "You're a funny guy, Zac Carrera."

I smiled. She said my name like she'd been calling me that forever.

"You like my new name?"

She draped her arms around my waist and looked up to me. "I love it. Suits you perfectly."

"Hey, Zac, I've got something for you." Cobra's voice boomed down the hallway to us.

Maya helped me carry the coffee and sandwiches, and we returned to the computer lab.

"I don't think you're going to like this." Cobra pointed to the top row of monitors.

The screens were filled with a report that had dates, times, and notes.

Maya handed out the coffees. "What is it?"

"It's the police report with the timeline of your kidnapping, Zac."

"And . . .?" Maya asked.

Cobra swiveled toward me. "Your parents refused to pay a ransom."

I slumped onto a chair. "Shit."

"Your father actually said, and I quote, 'my country doesn't negotiate with terrorists, and neither do I'."

"What the hell?" Maya gasped. "It's very different when it's your own child."

"Especially when they had bucket loads of money," Cobra added.

"What did they hand over at the ransom drop then?" I asked.

"Fake bills," Cobra said.

"Son of a bitch!" I thumped the bench and my plate jumped. "I thought they were the only people I could trust."

Maya strode to me, and our hands slipped together like we'd been doing it forever. "I thought the same about my parents."

"You know what. I'm glad I know this. I was feeling guilty for faking my death. But fuck them. I hope they rot in their own selfishness."

Maya kissed the top of my head and as I squeezed her hand, an image on the TV screen caught my attention. "Cobra, turn that up."

Maya spun to the television as Cobra dialed up the volume. The camera image zoomed in on a field of giant gum trees. Wrapped around a massive tree trunk was the tail end of a black truck.

My blood drained. "Oh shit. That's the F100. Marc's truck."

Chapter Thirty-Two

MAYA

The vision on the TV showed four men in Hi-Vis uniforms carrying a stretcher up the steep incline through the trees.

"Is he dead?" I asked.

"I hope so," Cobra and Neon said simultaneously.

A blonde reporter stepped in front of the camera. "We believe the body that was discovered in the vehicle is Marc Harkness. He was the man who was wanted for the suspected murder of Neon Bloom."

"She said body," Cobra said.

We watched in silence as the men carrying the stretcher reached the top. As they walked over skid marks in the dirt shoulder, the camera zoomed onto the body.

A blue tarp covered his face.

We all breathed a sigh of relief.

I clutched Neon's hand. "Maybe I did kill him after all?"

He clutched me to his side. "Woohoo, this is fantastic. Now we don't have any loose ends."

Cobra shook his head. "I never met a bloke who was happy that his girlfriend was a killer."

Neon released me, grinning. "Well, you've met one now."

I curled my arm around his waist, nudging us together. "That's what makes him so special . . .. He gets me."

"And she gets me."

We smiled at each other, and my heart swelled to bursting.

"Okay, well, I'm just gonna . . ." Grinning, Cobra swiveled around to the computer monitors.

"So, what do we do now?" Neon asked.

Cobra clicked his fingers at me. "You need to get his new look sorted because I need a photo of Zac Carrera for new ID docs."

I rubbed my hands together. "Yay. I was looking forward to this part."

Cobra turned to Neon. "Good luck, Zac. You're a braver man than me."

"What? Why?"

"Come on." I clutched Neon's hand and dragged him down the corridor.

"While you were recovering from surgery, Zena and I did a little shopping in Rosebud."

"Shopping. What for?"

"Not what for . . . who for . . . Zac Carrera."

"Oh."

Back in Cobra's large bathroom, I made him sit with the leg I'd operated on elevated on a stool.

I removed two grocery bags out of the lockers and spilled the contents onto one of the sinks.

"We have hair dyes, colored contact lenses, makeup, clothes, and a tattoo gun."

"A tattoo gun! What the hell? Have you done tattoos before?"

"Nope. How hard can it be?"

"Oh, shit."

"Shut up, you big sook. Now, what color would you like your hair?" I placed a few hair dye choices onto the bench, and he picked them up.

"I've never been blond."

"Blond it is then. Take your shirt off."

"Yes, boss."

As I dyed and cut his hair and gave him a spray tan, our conversation flowed. We talked about everything from our favorite music to our favorite ice cream. We compared our first cars, a Toyota hatchback for me and a Bentley for him. He told me about his first acting role, and I told him about Mahmoud Shah Al Aziz, who, thanks to me, would never hurt another woman or child again.

He was so easy to talk to, it was like we'd known each other forever.

It took a few attempts to get the colored contacts in, but by changing his eyes from hazel to blue, with the blond hair and darker skin, he could pass as any one of the guys I surfed with at Diamond Beach. The transformation was dramatic.

Zac leaned toward the mirror. "I don't look too bad."

"It will get us through until you can do something more permanent."

He blinked at me. "More permanent? Like what?"

"I don't know, cheek implants or change the shape of your eyes. You should know. You're from Hollywood. Don't they do that stuff all the time?"

He released a breath. "I never thought about that."

"Your face is very well known, and with your body never turning up, people will probably be searching for you for years. So, I don't think you have a choice."

Frowning, he stared at his reflection. "You're right. But I guess the first thing would be finding someone to do the surgery secretly."

"Agreed. Until then, we have to do this." I held up a stainless steel surgical-looking weapon. "Now hold still. I need to tattoo a mole on your cheek."

"Whoa." He jerked back and shot his gaze between me and the tattoo gun. "Shit. You're serious."

"Where do you want it?"

"Hang on. Hang on." He raised his hands and his eyes bulged. "How about you draw one first until we make any permanent decisions?"

I giggled.

He cocked his head.

I burst out laughing.

"Oh, my god. You're messing with me again."

"Sorry, couldn't resist. That one was Zena's idea."

"I think you're enjoying this way too much."

I pulled a dark pencil from a makeup case.

"Where do you want it?" I pointed at a spot high on his cheek near his right eye. "How about here?"

"Sure."

"Good choice. Now hold still."

As I inhaled his glorious scent, I drew a spot on his cheek. "Done. Don't touch it."

He inspected my artwork in a mirror, and then nodded.

"Hey, Ghost, have you got a minute?" Cobra called me.

Neon winced as he put down his feet. His bullet wound was giving him grief. As he hobbled down the hallway, he sucked air through his teeth. The anesthetic from his operation was wearing off, and he'd barely rested his leg since he'd woken up. If he wasn't careful, his leg would swell up like a balloon.

We stepped into the computer lab together, and I said, "Cobra, meet Zac Carrera."

Cobra whistled. "Hey, that's bloody good. I wouldn't recognize you." He leaned forward. "Is that a mole on your cheek?"

"Yep. She wanted to tattoo me. I managed to stop her from doing that." Neon rolled his eyes at me.

Cobra jerked back. "Jesus, mate! You're game. I'd never say no to Ghost."

He did a weird shudder like he was possessed.

Chuckling, I stood next to Cobra. "What have you got for me?"

"Brace yourself," he said.

"Shit, what now?"

He pressed a button, and a facial image of a man appeared on the middle monitor. "Is that your father?"

Gasping, I slapped my hand over my mouth. "Oh my god. You found him?"

"Yep."

"Where? How?"

"He's in Bali. He changed his name, but the stupid bastard named his son John Grayson."

"He has a son?"

"And two daughters. He married a Balinese woman eight years ago."

"Fucking bastard. I can't believe how quickly you found him. I've been searching for years."

"It's always the little things that get them caught. His son needs life-saving surgery and they've set up a Go Fund Me page. Here's the family photo."

Cobra clicked a button and a family of five appeared on the screen. My dad had his arm around a young Balinese woman who was holding a baby. On Dad's left was a little boy in shorts and a t-shirt with a dinosaur on the front, and beside the woman was a little girl in a bright yellow dress.

"One big happy family," Cobra said.

"Yeah. Just like my family had been until Dad killed my sister." A wave of anger washed through me.

"The police have him listed as a missing person, and the file is currently a cold case. They probably take a look at the file once a year. If that." Cobra shook his head.

Neon slipped his hand into mine. "Now that you found him, what are you going to do?"

I blinked at him. I'd told him I was going to kill my father when I found him. He'd suggested I make my father suffer.

I shook my head and sighed. "I have no idea."

My phone and Cobra's phone pinged at the same time and we both frowned.

It was our messenger app from Alpha Tactical Ops.

I pulled my phone from my pocket. "Blade wants to see us."

Cobra nodded at his phone too.

I slipped my phone away and looked at Neon. "You need to get some rest. I'll take you to my house while I go to Blade's place."

"I can't come with you?"

"No. You need to rest that leg before you do any more damage. That's not negotiable."

"Let me get your photo before you go," Cobra said to Neon, "and I'll get your paperwork organized."

As Cobra snapped several photos of Neon's new appearance, I grabbed my gear.

"You ready to go?" I asked Neon.

He said goodbye to Cobra, shaking his hand and thanking him for everything.

Cobra slapped Neon's back. "See you soon, Zac."

During the drive to my place, Neon continued his request to come with me to Blade's place, but I was unyielding. So much had happened in the last twenty-four hours that I hadn't had a chance to debrief with my team. I needed to make sure they really were okay with how we'd handled Neon's fake death.

I'd put my team in an awkward position, and I'd be gutted if I'd made them do something they were not comfortable with.

After checking that no reporters were lurking around my place, I pulled into my carport. Once inside my home, I gave Neon a quick tour.

"Make yourself at home. Help yourself to anything in the fridge." I scrunched my nose. "Not that there's much."

I pointed to a bowl on the coffee table. "The TV remotes are in there. What else do I need to tell you?"

He swooped his arm around my waist and pulled me to him. "Just how long you'll be."

I rested my hands on his arms. "I won't be long. Please get some rest."

"But I'll miss you." He curled a slip of hair behind my ear.

No man had ever done that to me before. It was such a simple gesture and yet it was so absolutely perfect, it stole my breath away.

I glided my hands over his arms, feeling his warm flesh as his gaze consumed me.

My heart ached with a desire that was so deep it was a wonder it was still beating.

All at once, I knew I was in love.

This gorgeous, generous, funny, kind man had captured my heart. I'd never thought I would want a man permanently in my life. Now I didn't just want it; I needed it.

I needed Neon. Zac Carrera.

Did he feel the same?

I wanted to tell him, but was it too soon? We'd been through a lot together, yet we still barely knew each other.

What if, once we got to know each other, he didn't feel the same way?

Or worse, he wished he'd never killed off Neon Bloom.

Chapter Thirty-Three

MAYA

I pressed on Neon's chest and stepped back from his embrace. "I'll be back as soon as I can. Make sure you rest."

"What will you do to me if I don't?" His sassy smile was enough to make me want to tear off my clothes.

"You don't want to know." Just looking at him had my heart doing all sorts of crazy things.

"Does it involve spanking?" He smacked his sexy butt.

Giggling, I shook my head. "Rest. And that's an order."

I forced my legs to walk away, and in a daze, I grabbed the spare car keys I've been using and returned to my Rav4. Somehow, I made it to Blade's place without incident and parked out the front of his warehouse alongside Billie's Camry and Viper's Harley.

I pressed the intercom and Zena let me in.

Charlie raced across the concrete to greet me, and I scooped her into my arms.

"Hey, there's my beautiful girl."

She licked my hand as I carried her toward the counter where everyone had gathered around.

I was the last to arrive, and there was a weird vibe amongst them.

Normally, whenever I came to Blade's warehouse apartment, the men would be playing pool and the women would be chatting in the kitchen area. Today, there was no chatter. They all looked like someone had declared war.

"Hey, guys, what's going on?" I slipped onto my usual barstool next to Billie and settled Charlie onto my lap.

"Hey," Levi said, then he and Blade sipped their beers.

Zena pushed a full wine glass across the kitchen counter toward me. "Cobra was just showing us pictures of Zac Carrera. You did a great new disguise."

"Oh, thanks. He looks very different."

"Great choice in name too," Zena added.

She seemed guarded. It wasn't the usually jovial Zena. A vice squeezed around my chest as I prepared for bad news.

"Where is he?" Viper grunted.

"At my place."

Viper clamped his jaw like he was holding back something that was burning up his insides.

"Is everything okay?" I swept my gaze from Levi to Zena to Blade.

Blade plonked down his beer. "Okay, now that everyone is here, do you want the good news or bad news first?"

"The bad news," I said before anyone else.

"The good news," Viper disagreed. He always disagreed.

"I'll go with the bad news first," Cobra said.

"Me too," Levi added.

"Right," Blade said. "Bad news it is."

Viper groaned.

Blade leveled his gaze at Billie. "I took a call from Hawk earlier."

"Hawk?" Billie frowned.

Levi reached for Billie's hand. "The other member of our team. She's in ASIO, remember?"

"That's right. And . . .?" Billie asked Blade.

"Hawk admitted they found a flash drive in Aaron's jacket. It shows footage of your drill hole in the ice."

Zena flinched at the mention of her father. Although she hadn't been close to him, his death had still come as a shock.

"Oh my god." Billie clutched her chest. "That's fantastic news. The footage on that flash drive proves the submarine was in my glacier. Now everyone will believe me."

Blade raised his hands, calming Billie down. "Hawk says the information is classified."

Billie's shoulders slumped as she groaned.

I rested my hand over hers and squeezed.

"It's okay." Levi curled his arm over Billie's shoulders and tugged her to his side. "We'll make your boss pay for sacking you."

"Not if we have to keep hiding the proof." Shaking her head, Billie twirled the stem of her wine glass that was still full.

Everyone went silent and unlike Billie, I took a big sip of wine.

I felt for Billie. Hawk has concrete proof that would expose the false accusations against her. But once again, the evidence couldn't be used. Levi kept telling her that her boss would pay, but I wasn't so sure. Not when the details of what went down in Antarctica were being fiercely guarded by the Australian Security Intelligence Organisation.

"What else did Hawk say?" Viper cracked his knuckles.

Blade cleared his throat. "She confirmed it was a sub in the glacier, and she let it slip that it was a German sub."

"A German sub," Cobra said. "How did she know?"

"She didn't say, and I think she was pissed that she'd mentioned that." Blade shook his head.

"Well, that's new info for us," I said, turning to Billie. "That's a bit strange, don't you think? It had that Russian writing on it."

Billie frowned. "I agree. But it may explain why I was having so much trouble finding details about a missing Russian sub. Did Hawk have any other information?" Billie asked.

"Yes, Hawk had something very interesting . . ." Blade paused and when his eyes flared, I sat up. "Hawk told me that the gold bar that Aaron had with him in that ice cave in Antarctica has identical markings to one gold bar that was found in a mountain range in . . . guess where?"

"Kyrgyzstan," I said at the same time as Cobra and Viper.

"Holy shit!" Levi smacked his hand onto the counter. "Is Hawk positive?"

Blade nodded. "The one found in the mountain and the one Aaron had, both have the same lion embossing."

I gasped. "Oh, my god. What can she tell us about the one in Kyrgyzstan?"

Blade pressed his hands on the counter and leaned forward. "In 1958, a goat herder found it on a mountain he was taking his goats over. He claimed it was wedged between two rocks like it had fallen from the sky. A week later, he returned home and showed the gold bar around. Photos were taken and his village celebrated. That night someone killed him and his family and stole the gold. But the goat herder never told anyone exactly where he found the gold bar. The photos are the only proof, and nobody has ever been convicted of those murders."

I clicked my fingers. "The gold is cursed! Remember, Levi, that's what the guy said in Antarctica before he died."

Levi nodded. "That's right. Is this what he was referring to?"

"Dad died holding onto a gold bar too." A wave of sadness washed over Zena's expression, and she shrugged.

Billie gasped and turned to me. "And all those Russians that you, um—"

"Killed." I finished Billie's sentence for her. "But that was self-defense. They were shooting at us. What happened to the goat herder and Zena's dad, that was different."

Billie nodded like she was relieved.

"Can I get another look at the gold bar?" Cobra asked. "I'll do some more searches on that lion embossing."

"Sure." Blade strode around the corner to where he had a hidden safe.

"This is crazy." I shook my head, trying to piece our massive puzzle together. These gold bars had left a trail of murders in their wake.

Yet I was certain the killing spree was far from over.

Blade returned carrying two gold bars and handed one to Cobra.

Levi snatched the other one off the counter.

Billie slipped off her chair and strode to the giant crime scene wall in Blade's apartment. She returned with a pen and paper and drew a picture of the gold bar and the lion embossing.

"Looks like we need another section on the wall," I said.

Once Billie finished the drawing, I lowered Charlie to the floor. "Mind if I add to this?"

"Sure."

Beneath Billie's drawing, I summarized Hawk's intel regarding the gold bar found in Kyrgyzstan.

I grabbed the drawing, and everyone followed me to the wall.

At the next section of blank bricks, I taped the gold bar drawing to the top. "At least we can now link the gold to three places: Kyrgyzstan, Arrow Dynamics, and Antarctica."

We all stood back, studying the field of clues.

"Does anyone else feel like the answer is right in front of us?" I asked.

"Nope." Viper grunted.

"Nah, me neither," Levi said.

Sighing, I turned to Blade. "So, was this the good news?"

"No." Blade grinned at Zena, and she spun her back to us.

She spun around holding her hand toward me, showing off an elegant diamond ring. "We're engaged."

My jaw dropped. "Oh my god."

I squealed. She squealed.

I wrapped my arms around her, squeezing her as we jumped up and down. "Congratulations."

The men all clapped Blade's back and shook his hand. Billie and I alternated hugging Zena and admiring her beautiful engagement ring.

I gave Blade a hug. "I'm so happy for you."

"Thanks, Ghost." Blade didn't smile often, but this one lit up his face and his eyes.

"Damn, I wish Zac was here to celebrate with us," I said.

"Who?" Viper glared at me.

"Neon. His new name is Zac Carrera, remember?"

"Fucking hell!" Viper clenched his jaw so hard it was a wonder he didn't crack his teeth.

"What?" I glared at him.

"Don't tell me he's also going to get in on this investigation, too." Viper waved his hand toward our wall of clues.

I put my fists on my hips. "Why can't he?"

"We don't need anyone else knowing about the gold." The veins in Viper's neck bulged blue.

"Jesus, Viper. He's not interested in cashing in on the gold."

His gaze pierced me like heat-seeking missiles. "You don't know that. You barely know him."

I stormed to Viper and shoved his chest. His back slammed against the wall.

"This afternoon, Neon donated twenty million dollars to Alpha Tactical Ops. Believe me, he doesn't need the money."

Viper blinked at me like he was lost for words.

"So, I do know him, and he's a better man than you. You need to sort your shit out, you cranky bastard." I shoved him again and stepped back, shaking my head.

"For fuck's sake." Viper threw his hands up in frustration. "I'm outta here."

"Viper. Don't go," Levi called out to him.

"You lot have no fucking idea." Viper's stomping boots tracked his departure.

"About what?" I yelled to him as he disappeared out the door.

Viper's Harley roared to life and faded into the distance.

Heaving a sigh of frustration, I turned to Zena. "I'm so sorry."

"It's okay." She shook her head.

"No, it's not. I ruined your celebration."

"No, you didn't." She scooped her arm over my shoulder and led me back to the kitchen counter. "Don't worry about him."

Everyone else joined us, and as Blade topped up our drinks, Zena pulled food from the fridge and oven that she must've prepared earlier.

"Are you serious about the twenty million?" Levi drove his hand through his wavy hair.

"Yes. Ask Cobra."

Damn it. I hadn't intended to tell everyone about the donation that way. I hadn't intended to tell them at all. Neon should have been the one to share that news.

Too late now.

"It's true." Cobra rubbed his hands together, grinning like a mad scientist. "Did the transfer myself. Tell them what he wants us to do."

Groaning on the inside, and wishing Neon was here to share this moment, I explained his generous offer to the hostages.

"That's a really lovely thing to do for those poor people," Zena said.

"Yes, it's a pity he won't get any accolades for it though," Billie added.

I nodded at her. Billie and Zac both had secrets that could change lives, but there was nothing they could do about it.

"Zac doesn't mind. He's a good man." I swept my gaze toward the front exit. "Unlike some people. Viper can be such an ass sometimes. I wish he'd lighten up."

I looked to Blade for an answer.

Blade shook his head and shrugged.

"And me," Cobra said.

"Yeah. Well, I'm getting sick of his grumpy attitude." I sipped my wine.

Cobra cleared his throat. "Well . . . I've been thinking that maybe with the money from Zac, we could buy Alpha Tactical Ops a new headquarters."

I shot my gaze from Cobra to Blade. "That's a great idea. What do you think, Blade?"

Blade shrugged. "I don't know. I have—"

Zena slapped his chest. "It's a great idea. Then this place can be for our fun times, and the new building can be for work."

"As long as we have a fully stocked bar in the new place, I'm in." Levi raised his beer.

"And I could have a dedicated room with a whole bank of computers," Cobra added.

Blade nodded. "It seems like a valid idea. Let's have a meeting on it next week once the money comes in and Zena has distributed the funds as per Neon's—I mean, Zac's—wishes. Then we'll know how much we have to spend."

"This is so exciting. We must thank Zac," Zena said.

A wave of pride rolled through me, and my heart fluttered.

Zena raised her glass. "Here's to Zac."

We all raised our glasses and cheered.

"I can't believe he gave us that much money. It's so generous." Zena twirled her new ring on her finger, and the princess-cut diamond glistened in the kitchen lights.

As Levi made suggestions on what he would like to add to the new office—a dart board, a dedicated weapons room, ramped-up security—I glanced at my hands and ran my finger over my lily tattoo.

Cobra glided his hand over the counter toward me, and when I looked at him, he nodded like he was trying to convey something.

I frowned at him, and he tilted his head toward Zena and Blade.

Oh jeez. He wants me to tell them about my father.

Maybe it was a secret he didn't want to be burdened with.

He was right.

My life was on the cusp of a new phase. A glorious new phase.

I was in love with a man, and I looked forward to seeing where our journey took us.

I had the best job in the world.

And I had a group of friends who meant the world to me. Friends who should know the secret that had been shackling me for years.

I drained my wine glass.

"Hey, guys, there's something else that happened today that I need to tell you about." I slid my empty glass across the counter to Zena.

She grabbed a bottle from the fridge and filled my glass to the brim.

As we shared the finger food Zena had prepared, and drank more wine, I told them about my sister: her death, my father, and how Cobra miraculously found him.

A tear spilled from my eye, and I flicked it away. I had no idea why I was crying. It felt good to unveil the heartache that had driven me to become an army sniper.

Zena came around the counter and wrapped her arms around me. "I'm so sorry about your sister. Thank you for sharing with us."

As I squeezed her to my chest, I nodded at Blade. He nodded back. I wouldn't be in this team if it wasn't for him. I would be forever grateful to him for believing in me.

He'd changed my life.

So had Zac.

And Cobra; without him, I may have carried that secret forever.

Zena eased back from me. "What are you going to do now?"

I turned to Blade, and he raised his eyebrows. I'd told him many years ago that I'd joined the army so I could kill my dad. Now he knew why.

"What do you think I should do?" I asked Blade.

He tilted his head like he was cracking his neck. "A bullet is too good for him. He should be punished."

Huh. That's exactly what Zac said.

And they were right. That bastard needed to hate every day of the rest of his life.

I nodded. "Agreed. I'm going to make sure he rots in jail."

Billie squeezed my arm. "Good on you."

A sadness washed over her. The poor woman was genuinely suffering over what had happened with her asshole boss. Maybe we could get Cobra to dig up some dirt on him and make him wish he'd never messed with Billie.

But first, I had to visit the police station. Now that I'd made up my mind, I wanted to tell them about what my father did ASAP.

I stood, and Charlie curled around my legs. I scooped her up and brushed my hand over her back. "Thanks for a good night. Congratulations, guys. I'm so happy for you."

"Thanks, babe," Zena said. "We're happy for you too. Tell Zac I want to see him with you next time."

"Oh, trust me, he wanted to come here." I put Charlie down and grabbed my car keys off the counter.

"Good, and don't let that grumpy bastard Viper tell you any different," Cobra said.

"I won't." As I strode out of Blade's apartment, I felt like I could walk on air. A huge brick had been lifted from my shoulders and it was time to put that brick to bed.

Night had fallen and the streetlights had come on while I'd been with my team. I drove onto Oak Avenue, and a half moon hovered over the ocean in the distance.

I wound down my window and breathed in the fresh ocean air.

Just like Zac, I too felt like I'd been reborn.

After the hostage situation at Kangaroo Island, I'd been interrogated many times at the police station, so I knew the place well. I parked out the front, climbed the stairs, and the bell over the door tinkled as I crossed the threshold.

Officer Bailey manned the front counter, and I grinned at her as I approached.

She blinked at me, and her eyes lit up. "Maya, have you found Neon?"

Shit. I wiped the smile from my face and shook my head. "No. I was hoping you'd have some good news for me."

"Unfortunately, no." A sadness washed over Officer Bailey that was so dark, you'd think she'd lost a kidney.

I heaved a dramatic sigh. "Is Officer Evans on tonight?"

"He sure is, take a seat, and I'll let him know you're here." Officer Bailey scooted away like she was on rollerblades.

I turned to the corkboard that stretched the length of the side wall. A large missing person poster of Neon took up prime position in the middle. I was halfway through reading the summary of his disappearance when my name was called.

I spun toward the counter, but Officer Evans was at an open side door. "Come on in, Maya."

"Thank you."

He indicated that I lead the way and directed me to the small interview cubical where I had already spent way too many hours.

We sat on opposite sides of the metal table.

He spread his hands. "Do you have some more information about Neon Bloom?"

I shook my head. "Sadly, no. But I have some information regarding a different case. Would you have time to listen? It's a bit of a long story."

"I always have time for you."

"Thank you. How is your wife?"

"Some days are good. Some are bad. Today was a good one."

"I hope she has many more."

Hopefully, too, the money Zac sent their way would provide them some joy.

"So, what's this different case?" He removed a small notebook and pen from his pocket and flipped to a blank page.

As I told him everything about Lily's death, the sorrow inside me swelled up and curled around my heart. I would never get over losing my sister, but hopefully the capture of my father would give me some closure.

Just like Neon had closure with his new identity.

"I'm sorry for your loss." Officer Evans met my gaze, and I felt the sincerity in his words.

"Thank you." I swept my hand over the metal tabletop. "I was told many years ago that Father Bastion went to jail for having sex with minors and a string of other disgusting offenses. As much as I'd like to add to his sentence with proof he was also the father of my sister's unborn child, it's likely pointless as he's already serving two life sentences in jail."

"Okay." Officer Evans scraped his hand through his hair. "What would you like me to do?"

I told him about Lily's death being recorded as a suicide and about my father being listed as a missing person, and his file being a cold case. Then I detailed what I found in Lily's diary, and my mother's confession to me.

From my pocket I removed the printouts with the photo of my father and his new family, and the Go Fund Me post, and pushed them across the table. "I finally found my father. He's living in Bali, and I want him arrested for the murder of my sister."

"But I thought you said your sister's death was recorded as a suicide."

"That's why I'm going to give you Lily's diary. And I believe my mother will confirm what I have told you. If necessary, I give permission for Lily's body to be exhumed."

"Woah. Okay." He put his pen down and reached for the note.

I gave him time to read the details of my father's new life in Bali.

"Let me do some digging," he said, "and I'll get back to you."

"Thank you. I look forward to your call." I offered my hand across the table.

As I drove home, my thoughts were consumed by Zac. I couldn't wait to wrap my arms around him. And kiss him. And get naked.

I drove into my carport and as I stepped from my car, a wailing siren blasted my ears. I ran up my front steps and threw open my front door. My heart was in my throat as I ran along a smoke-filled hallway.

Zac was on a chair, madly fanning at the smoke alarm on the ceiling.

"What are you doing?"

His wide eyes darted to me. "Oh, thank God you're here. How do you turn this damn thing off?"

I pointed to the smoke detector. "See that little button on the side? Press it."

He did, plunging us into silence. Coughing at the smoke, I raced around, opening all the windows and doors.

Zac eased down from the counter and huffed. "Well, that was fun. Not."

He opened the oven door, groaned, then shut it again.

"Are you cooking?" I frowned at him.

"More like cremating."

Giggling, I opened the oven and black smoke poured out the door.

"What were you making?" I shut the door and fanned away the smoke.

"Cheesy pasta bake. I got the recipe from there." He pointed at a magazine on the counter. Zena was constantly giving me recipe magazines in the hope I'd catch on to her love of cooking.

So far, no good.

"Wow." I smiled. "I can't believe you were cooking. Call me impressed."

"It was Zac's idea."

I burst out laughing.

"I love watching you laugh." He clutched my hips and lifted me onto the counter. I opened my legs, and he slotted his hips between my knees.

He smelled incredible: soap and shampoo and hot-blooded man.

"I'm still impressed that you attempted to cook. You're braver than me."

"First, nobody is braver than you, and second, it would be impressive if we could actually eat that black mess."

I shrugged. "I've probably had worse."

"It's always a competition with you, isn't it?" He pressed his lips to mine; it was just a brief kiss and yet it spoke volumes.

We were so comfortable together. It was like we'd been a couple for years.

That was how a relationship should be: easy.

He glided his hand up my thigh. "How did your meeting go?"

I didn't want to go through all the crap that went down at Blade's place, so rather than attempt to explain the saga over the gold, or Viper's issue, I said, "Zena and Blade got engaged."

His eyes lit up. "Wow, that's so good."

"It's great. They are perfect together."

He placed his hands on my hips. "Just like us."

My heart skipped a beat at how open he was.

I nodded. "Yes, just like us. So, no regrets over killing Neon Bloom?"

"Hell no. Honestly, Maya, I truly feel like I've been reborn. It's amazing."

Sighing with relief. Those were the words I wanted to hear.

"You know what?" His eyes dazzled me.

"What?" I matched his sassy grin.

"Zac Carrera is still a virgin."

I burst out laughing. "Well, we need to do something about that."

"I was hoping you'd say that." He scooped me into his arms and carried me to my bedroom.

I nestled into his chest and with my hand on his cheek, I said, "I love you."

A breath left his throat, and he captured me with his gaze. "Oh, Maya, you have made me the happiest man in the world. I love you too."

THE END . . . for now

Continue the action and sizzling romance with Viper's story in STEALTH MISSION, book 4 in the Alpha Tactical Ops series.

Turn the pages for more action-packed books by Kendall Talbot.

Stealth Mission

He's a grumpy explosives expert. She's trapped in a living hell.
When he's assigned to protect her, the sparks that fly are both real and deadly.

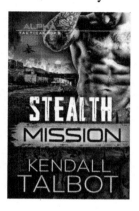

Hippie at heart, Harper MacBride has been controlled by her powerful parents since her teenage recklessness ruined her life. That's bad enough. But when her father is elected as Australia's Prime Minister, she's forced into her parents' political spotlight and hates her life even more.

Guilt over a disastrous decision Drake St Claire, (Codename: Viper) made in his twenties, had anger fueling his veins when he joined the army. But when that too implodes, his reckless thirst for danger and his unique detonation skills forges his fireman career *and* his role in the Alpha Tactical Ops team.

Bad-tempered Viper is assigned to protect rebellious Harper, who is a complete pain in his ass, yet damn irresistible. When an explosive attack on the prime minister has them in a deadly race for their lives, they witness something that puts them square in the killers' crosshairs.

As the body count rises, Harper and Viper must learn to trust each other, or they'll become victims in the biggest conspiracy Australia has ever seen.

STEALTH MISSION, book four in the Alpha Tactical Ops series, is an action-packed, opposites attract, quest for answers, steamy romance, featuring a grumpy alpha hero who is battling his guilt and a stifled heroine who doesn't trust anyone.

Alpha Tactical Ops is a series of standalone books with inter-connecting characters, featuring ex-military men and women and the partners trying to tame them.

Lost In Kakadu

WINNER: Romantic book of the year.

Two complete strangers survived the plane crash. Now the real danger begins.

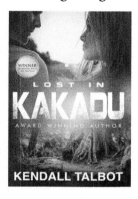

Socialite, Abigail Mulholland, has spent a lifetime surrounded in luxury... until her scenic flight plummets into the remote Australian wilderness. When rescue doesn't come, she finds herself thrust into a world of deadly snakes and primitive conditions in a landscape that is both brutal and beautiful. But trekking the wilds of Kakadu means fighting two wars—one against the elements, and the other against the magnetic pull she feels toward fellow survivor Mackenzie, a much younger man.

Mackenzie Steel had finally achieved his dreams of becoming a five-star chef when his much-anticipated joy flight turned each day into a waking nightmare. But years of pain and grief have left Mackenzie no stranger to a harsh life. As he battles his demons in the wild, he finds he has a new struggle on his hands: his growing feelings for Abigail, a woman who is as frustratingly naïve as she is funny.

Fate brought them together. Nature may tear them apart. But one thing is certain—love is as unpredictable as Kakadu, and survival is just the beginning...

Lost in Kakadu is a gripping action-adventure romance set deep in Australia's rugged Kakadu National Park. Winner of the Romantic Book of the Year, this full-length, stand-alone novel is about a woman who needs to find herself, and the unlikely hero who captures her heart. Lost in Kakadu is an extraordinary story of endurance, grief, survival and undying love.

Extreme Limit

Natures deadly beauty isn't the only danger on Whiskey Mountain.

There's also a killer who'll risk everything to stop Holly and Oliver.

Holly Parmenter doesn't remember the helicopter crash that claimed the life of her fiancé and left her in a coma. The only details she does remember from that fateful day haunt her—two mysterious bodies sealed within the ice, dressed for dinner rather than a dangerous hike up the Canadian Rockies.

No one believes Holly's story about the couple encased deep in the icy crevasse. Desperate to uncover the truth about the bodies and to prove her innocence, Holly resolves to climb the treacherous mountain and return to the crash site. But to do that she'll need the help of Oliver, a handsome rock-climbing specialist who has his own questions about Holly's motives.

When a documentary about an unsolved kidnapping offers clues as to the identity of the frozen bodies, it's no longer just Oliver and Holly heading to the dangerous mountaintop . . . there's also a killer, who'll do anything to keep the case cold.

Will a harrowing trip to the icy crevasse bring Holly and Oliver the answers they seek? Or will disaster strike twice, claiming all Holly has left?

Extreme Limit is action-packed romantic suspense full of action, danger, passion and a few tears featuring a broken woman who

needs to find herself, and the sexy mountain guide who'd do anything to save her.

Head to the Canadian Rockies and get ready for the adventure of a lifetime, with a happily ever after guaranteed

First Fate

No power. No comms. And nobody coming to save them.
Prepare for the cruise from hell.

When an electromagnetic pulse (EMP) strikes Rose of the Sea, the pleasure cruise becomes a drifting nightmare. Powerless and desperate, the eleven hundred passengers and crew must face their new reality: No one is coming to save them.

The First Mate. The EMP destroys the captain's pacemaker and when he dies, Gunner McCrae is thrust into the top position. But no amount of training could prepare him for the savagery of desperate humans and an unforgiving ocean.

The Anchor-woman. Gabrielle Kinsella is known for bringing shocking stories to the world. She should be reporting on the headline of the century. Instead she's fighting for her children's lives.

The Acrobat. Held captive by a predator as a child, Madeline Jewel found freedom as the ship's acrobatic dancer. But being trapped in an elevator brings her worst fears back to life.

The Gambler. Zon Woodrow, notorious gator hunter, won his ticket in a poker match. But that isn't the only pot he's looking to score. With the ships security system obliterated, Zon turns his attention to the casino's vault. And this time, the house won't win.

As resources dwindle aboard Rose of the Sea, the body count continues to rise. Will ordinary people survive an extraordinary disaster? Or will human nature drown them in darkness?

Find out in this gripping survival thriller. FIRST FATE is book one in the Waves of Fate series.

Treasured Secrets

A clue to an ancient lost treasure reveals a deadly mystery spanning centuries.
But will Rosalina and her ex-fiancé, Archer, live to salvage it?

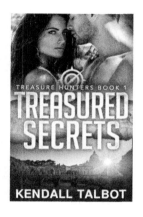

The last place Rosalina expected a clue to a vast treasure to lead her was back into the arms of Archer, the bastard who broke her heart.

Archer desperately wants to salvage the relationship with Rosalina that he shattered, but his talent for finding lost treasure is almost as good as his talent for finding trouble.

Some secrets are better left buried.

Rosalina and Archer are thrust into a treasure hunt that scrapes the underbelly of Italian history, and into the crosshairs of a ruthless enemy. As they dodge bullets, and wrestle fiery emotions, protecting Rosalina becomes the deadliest quest of Archer's life.

Treasured Secrets is a steamy, second chance romance, featuring a protective alpha hero who doesn't know he's broken and a kick-ass heroine with secrets of her own, and their deadly quest to unravel ancient riddles.

Treasured Secrets is book one in the complete six-book Treasure Hunters series, spanning exotic locations in Egypt, the Greek Islands, Brazil, the Caribbean, and Archer's luxury multi-million-dollar yacht.

Jagged Edge

A grieving detective with nothing to lose.
A dying town with everything to hide.

After the shocking death of his daughter, suspended detective Edge Malone who seeks oblivion in a bottle and plans to photograph a rare blood moon in isolated Whispering Hills, California. But his night takes a deadly turn when a high-tech drone is shot from the sky—and a ruthless gunman murders an innocent bystander who dares to visit the crash site. Driven by instinct, Edge seizes the drone and escapes into the woods.

Now being hunted, Edge unwittingly thrusts Nina Hamilton into the chase—a street-smart beauty who is no stranger to men with dangerous motives. But when the drone data leads them to a shocking discovery, they quickly learn that no one in Whispering Hills can be trusted. The truth of the small town is anything but quiet, and the price of secrets runs six-feet deep...

Get ready for the adventure of a lifetime with Jagged Edge, a full-length, stand-alone thriller featuring a kick-ass woman and a jilted man who needs to find himself again.

Printed in Great Britain
by Amazon

22172705R00199